TRUE NORTH

BAD IDEA: VOLUME III

NICOLE FRENCH

Raglan
Publishing
books that love hard

Copyright 2018 Raglan Publishing.

ISBN: 978-1-7292-1611-8

Published by Raglan Publishing.

I

THE BITTER AND THE SWEET

CHAPTER ONE

AUGUST 2004

Nico

LONGING. DESIRE. EXCITEMENT. ABSOLUTE FUCKIN' JOY.

Finally, fuckin' *finally*, Layla Barros is in my arms again, right in the middle of John F. Kennedy airport, having launched herself at me with the force of an NFL football player.

"Hey!" I shout as I swing her around and around.

Layla's legs come around my waist with a strength I didn't know she had, forcing me to drop my hands and get two handfuls of my favorite body part in order to hold her up. Jesus fuckin' Christ. I'm already hard and she's the only thing hiding that fact from the dozens of other people milling around the baggage claim.

But before I can say anything—a smart-ass comment that's about to roll off my tongue—she's kissing me. And it's not a tentative kiss either. Gone is the fear she had when she left over three months ago. This isn't a gentle kiss. It's hungry, forceful, full-throated. Her thin arms are vises around my neck. My girl is fuckin' devouring me, and I'm consuming her right back. Three months—no, scratch that, over a fuckin' *year* of pent-up longing is released in this kiss. I'll kiss her forever if that's what she wants. God knows I'll never get tired of it.

Around us, there's even a smattering of applause—our joy is infectious. And that's the thing about New Yorkers—they might be grouchy as fuck sometimes, but when it comes down to it, they're also real. And when they see joy that's honest, authentic, as deep as what Layla and I feel for each other, no one in my city would be anything but happy for us.

Fuck me, we really can't stop kissing each other. We need to find a room, an empty closet, fuck, even a bathroom somewhere. But I know I can wait. Right now, in this moment, I might be happier than I've ever been in my life, and if the look on Layla's face is any indication, she feels the same way.

"All right," I tell her as I take her hand. "Where's your bag? We need to get out of here. I need to get you home."

Layla lays her head on my shoulder. Even just that simple touch sends tremors of happiness through my chest.

"What do you mean?" she asks with another bright smile. "I am home. I'm with you."

Her tongue dips around mine again as her legs. I groan as I squeeze her ass, which I've been dreaming about all summer. I've While I waited for her to heal after the year from fuckin' hell she had last year. While we talked on the phone so long I thought I was going to burn my ear off. While we breathed, hot and heavy, late at night, listening to each other lose control from three thousand miles away. Just the memories of that make me feel like I'm about to lose control now. I need to get my girl alone, like *yesterday*.

"Layla?"

Her lips break from mine, and I growl. I actually growl, like I'm a dog, and someone is trying to take away my bone. Or, you know, boner. Same difference right about now.

"Who the fuck is that?" I ask, seeking her mouth all over again.

But she's done for now. Layla sighs, rolls her big blue eyes, and drops her feet to the ground. She tries to step away, but I'm not having it. So she tugs on a handful of her dark hair, which, if I'm not mistaken, looks even shinier than it was before. Her pale skin is just a little sun kissed. Damn. Three months of enjoying the California sun has done my baby *good*.

"Surprise," she says weakly. "Nico, this is my mother, Cheryl."

Her...mother?

My hands fly off Layla's ass like I'm touching a hot plate. Shit. *Shit*. This wasn't the impression I was looking to make when I met her parents for the first time. I already know I'm not really the type of guy they probably want to see her with. Older, tatted up, and with a record to boot. I'm a long shot from the kind of guy they want in family pictures. Her father's a doctor, for fuck's sake, and I've seen her grandparents' mansion in Pasadena. Not exactly the one-bedroom apartment I grew up in, shared between me, my mom, and three other kids.

But Layla doesn't see any of that. She doesn't care about where I come from; she never did. And she's the only one whose opinion I give a shit about anyway.

So I straighten up and turn to her mother, glad that my skin color hides my flush.

"Hi, Mrs. Barros, how you doin'? It's nice to finally meet you."

"Cheryl, please."

I tip the brim of my Yankees hat. I feel like an idiot when I do it. Who the fuck am I, an old timey cowboy? John fuckin' Wayne? Should I just go all out and say "Howdy, ma'am?" Have a little hoedown in the middle of JFK arrivals?

Layla giggles, like she can sense what I'm thinking. And she probably can, too. She knows me better than anybody. I roll my eyes, but I have to grin. Whatever. It's polite, right?

But then my smile falls when I catch the look on Cheryl's face. A dark-blonde brow arches over one of her bright blue eyes—the same eyes she shares with her daughter. She's imperious. And currently very suspicious.

You wouldn't know that Cheryl and Layla are related unless they told you. I've never met her dad, but Layla probably has the coloring of her Brazilian father: dark-brown, almost black hair, deep-set eyes that get circles when she's tired, full pink lips that I would like to go back to sucking on, thank you very fuckin' much. But Cheryl Barros definitely gave her daughter those eyes the color of a bluebird sky, sharp as a kitchen knife. And right now, I've got two pairs of them zeroed in on me.

Bam. Gutted. Just like that.

"You must be Nico," she says evenly.

She says it like she knows me. And to be fair, she probably does. Cheryl and I have only spoken once, but it was one of the most intense conversations I've ever had. Imagine calling your girl's mom for the first time, and you tell her that her daughter is basically in pieces—not because you did anything, but because you found her that way. After I moved to LA for a year and her dad left her and Cheryl for Brazil, Layla spiraled all last year. In her vulnerability, she was taken advantage of by the worst possible person. Giancarlo —*fuck*, I don't even like thinking that piece of shit's name, let alone saying it—was a monster if I ever met one, the kind of dude who cuts a woman down to make himself feel stronger. The kind of guy who takes his anger out on her face in the end.

A pang of guilt shoots through me. I'll never forgive myself for what happened, knowing that if I had just stayed in New York, Layla wouldn't have gotten wrapped up with that abusive motherfucker. It's a memory I'll never shake: Layla crushed under a much larger man, with blood all over both of them while he used her beautiful face like a punching bag. If I hadn't gotten there when I did...

I shudder, same way I do whenever the memory reappears. No. I'm not going to go there. Returning to that day is the quickest way to bring me to The Dark Place, as I've come to know it. The place where harder Nico lives, a Nico who knows himself for the asshole he can really be, the Nico I've been working really fuckin' hard to keep buried for the last several years.

Layla gives a hopeful smile. Her face shines with that light that only my girl has. It lightens me too.

Not today, asshole, I tell myself. Maybe not ever again.

Cheryl holds out her hand, palm down, like she's expecting me to kiss it or something. Should I? I start to lean down, but end up standing up straight. Going from John Wayne to Prince Charming is a little much, don't you think? Instead, I shake it a little, accepting her light squeeze before she pulls away, looking like she wants hands sanitizer.

Okay, yeah. My hands aren't exactly clean. Thirty minutes ago, I was doing pushups on concrete with a hundred other FDNY cadets, and there are still smudges of dirt on my palms. Well, sorry, lady. I wasn't planning on touching anyone else but your daughter, and I'm pretty sure *she* doesn't mind if I came straight for her instead of washing up first.

"Mom's here to help me find an apartment," Layla says as she takes my hand. See? I knew she wouldn't care about the dirt.

I turn to her. "You're not living at the dorms this year?"

For whatever reason, Layla and I haven't spoken much about her living situation. We talked every day this summer, when we could get the spare moments to do it. But we've both been crazy busy. I'm at the academy five days a week, usually from sunup to sundown, and then I've been doing security again at AJ's, the nightclub where I used to work. The extra cash helps supplement the shitty probationary salary I get as a new recruit with the FDNY. Layla took a couple more language classes to keep up her Spanish and Portuguese requirements for her degree, and I know she's been working a lot at a local women's services center too. So when we did talk, it wasn't about monotonous shit like apartment hunting or bills. It was usually what we did that day for a few brief moments before we both fell asleep. Just enough time to reassure her that I was still here, waiting for the day she was coming back.

I didn't really think about what would happen when she did.

Layla shakes her head. "Jamie and Quinn are still rooming together, so Shama and I decided to find a place off campus..."

She drifts off, but I know where she's going. Up until the end of last year, Quinn was Layla's best friend, her roommate through the first three years of college. But their friendship was tested when Layla's life fell apart, and Quinn couldn't handle it. Bitch. Layla's better off without her.

"Okay," I say. "So we need to find you an apartment. You know, you could just stay with me—"

I can't quite cut myself off in time before I realize what I'm saying. While I'd like nothing more than to wake up and fall asleep with Layla right next to me every day—I probably like that idea *too* much, if we're being honest—all I have to offer is a pullout couch in the living room of a crowded apartment uptown. My old place is currently occupied by me, my brother Gabe, my sister Maggie, and her daughter. I'm on the couch until the academy's done and I can even start to think about finding a new place of my own. What kind of offer is that?

I frown to myself. It's just another reminder of how little I actually have to offer someone like Layla. She says she doesn't care, but I do wonder every now and then if she really knows what that means.

"Do you have a car?" Cheryl interrupts my brooding before Layla can respond. "Or do we need a taxi? We have an appointment with a realtor at six, and we need to drop Layla's bags at the hotel."

Her toe taps on the linoleum floor so loudly I can hear it over the crowd.

"Ah, no," I admit, feeling suddenly weird about it even though most people in New York don't have cars. "We'll have to get a cab."

"All right." Cheryl looks me up and down. She's dressed casually in short white pants and a striped shirt, but the woman has a presence that would intimidate my sergeant. I don't know why Layla ever described her mother as meek. This lady is anything but. "I suppose we can drop you in the city on your way home."

"Mom," Layla starts, but I cut in anyway.

"That's all right, Mrs. Barros," I say. "I'm happy to help out. You'll need a local anyway to make sure you don't get scammed by the brokers."

I wink, even though I don't really know what the fuck I'm talking about. I've only had one apartment here in New York, and it was a rent-controlled lease passed to me from K.C.'s cousin. I don't know the first thing about hunting for an apartment in the city, even though I'm about to learn myself. But right now, there isn't a thing that could stop me from being by Layla's side. Definitely not a little white lie.

Cheryl opens her mouth, surprised, then closes it again. If I'm not mistaken, there's a little quirk of lips before she looks away.

"Well, let's go," she says and turns abruptly toward baggage claim.

I pick up Layla's carry-on and heave it over my shoulder, then sling my other arm around her waist so I can sneak another kiss. She stops walking and returns it, with a lot more tongue than I was initially planning, but hey, I'm not going to argue. Fuck me, she tastes good. Like vanilla and some kind of fruit and maybe some kind of soda she was drinking on the plane. But mostly she just tastes like Layla. She tastes like home.

"Damn," I whisper when we break again. We have *got* to find a room.

"Yeah," Layla whispers, keeping her nose to mine.

It's still there: that magnetic pull that always made us feel like we couldn't get close enough. Fuck the fact that we're in the middle of an airport. Fuck the fact that her mother is ten feet away, watching me carefully. I'd take Layla right here if she said the word. I'd take her for the rest of my life.

"Come on," Layla says, finally stepping away and tugging me forward. "She's right. We do need to get going."

I just nod and follow her through the crowd. But I don't let go of her hand. Not now. Not ever.

CHAPTER TWO

Layla

Nico waits in the hotel lobby while Mom and I check into our room and change. He looked like it was physically painful to stay behind, and I get it. Those brief kisses in the airport were *not* enough. Not even close. I'd been waiting for that moment all summer, and the complete and utter rightness of being in his arms again was enough to banish the shadows I've been fighting for the last year. It was enough to make me feel unafraid for the first time in so, so long.

At least for a moment.

I run a brush through my hair, checking my face still for bruises. It's a habit, considering it took nearly a month for all of the damage Giancarlo inflicted to disappear. Three months ago, Nico yanked my ex-boyfriend off me, but only after I'd been kidnapped and viciously assaulted. It took me weeks to walk without a limp from my sprained ankle. I had stitches in my eyebrow for two, and a thin white line still runs through my brow line. Mom wanted to have a surgeon clean it up, but I told her no. I'm not sure I ever want to forget what happened completely. I want to keep it as a reminder. Of what, I'm not sure. But I'll figure it out at some point.

I blink in the mirror, and for a second, I see his face. Not Nico's. Giancarlo's. Long, lean, with deep shadows under his dark eyes and a mop of thick black hair. The Wayfarer glasses that were cracked by Nico's fists before I was carried out of that room. The complete and utter hatred seething through his pain.

It's a face that still haunts me, that wakes me up at night. I grip the edge of the counter, wondering again why I chose to return to the city where my attacker still roams free. His trial isn't for a few more weeks, and though I won't have to stand as a witness, I know that my statement will be read aloud. Nico thinks they'll ask for a plea bargain, but he's hoping for maximum penalty. I just want it to be over. I just want to move on. But if he's acquitted, I'm not sure I can.

"Layla? Are you ready?"

Mom pokes her head into the bathroom and checks me over. It's a look I've been getting since she helped me off the plane, when it finally registered what kind of hell her daughter had been dealing with all year. She had gotten medical privileges to meet me at the gate, like I was an unaccompanied minor. They wheeled me off the plane in a wheelchair, even though I could actually walk, and when she saw me that first time, I genuinely thought my mother was going to pass out.

She's calm now, but flashes of fear and shock still cross her face every so often. She hasn't said anything because I was so adamant, but I think she's as nervous about me coming back here as I am. There were hints all summer, mild suggestions that I might want to stay in Pasadena, maybe even transfer to UCLA to finish my degree. It's why she insisted on coming with me to find an apartment this time. It's why, I suspect, she won't leave until she knows for sure when I'm returning to Pasadena.

But I had to come back. I don't want to be the kind of person who runs away when things are scary or hard. And, like my therapist says, facing your demons is as important as understanding them. New

York feels like a city full of demons to me right now, but it didn't always. For a short period of time, it felt like home, more than the house I grew up in. Maybe it can feel that way again.

Plus, there's him. Nico. If the events of last year forced me to confront the reasons why I would allow myself to be abused in the first place, they also forced me to realize the other truth in my life: that Nico is where I belong. It was his deep voice that spurred me on this summer, whispering sweet statements of faith and sex and longing and love. He believes in me when I'm not sure I can. He assures me, again and again, that I'm stronger than I feel.

If you had asked me two years ago if I believed in soul mates, I would have said no. But here is a person toward whom, from the start, every cell in my body seemed drawn. I just don't make sense without him. And I don't want to, either.

The thought reins in my fears. He's here. I'm here. Together, we can move forward.

"Yep," I call out. "I'm ready."

———

Nico's sitting in a chair in the lobby when we arrive, chatting up a little kid who spotted the big FDNY letters displayed across his broad chest. I used to think he looked hot in his FedEx uniform, but that thing had *nothing* on the FDNY gear. The plain navy t-shirt hugs his biceps in a way that should be illegal, and it was really hard not to stare at his ass pretty much the entire time he was leading us to the taxi line at JFK.

The thing is, he's completely unaware of the effect he has on people. He takes off his hat and sets in on the kid's head, making him giggle, and Nico laughs right along with him. His smile lights up the room, but he's oblivious to at least five women, including the kid's mother, and likely a few men who are outright ogling him. I don't even blame them. The man is impossibly gorgeous.

"See you, buddy," he says, clapping a hand on the kid's head as

Mom and I approach. He stands up, all smiles for me while he fixes his hat. "So, where are we headed?"

My mother looks him up and down. She isn't a talker—while my dad was full of lectures and opinions, Mom always sat next to him, watching. Her eyes are the quickest things about her. Her expression is veiled, but I can see hints of appreciation there. Great. My mom thinks Nico is hot too.

"The office is in..." She pulls a printed email out of her Coach bag. "Murray Hill." She looks up. "Where is that?"

Nico takes the paper and glances at the address. "Oh, that's only about ten blocks from here, Mrs. Barros. We could walk, unless..." He sneaks a look at her shoes, pristine white pumps that aren't exactly made for the grimy August humidity. New York in the summer is gross. "Come on," he says with a grin. "I'll get us another cab."

———

Nico

It's a little awkward walking around with Layla and her mom from apartment to apartment for the next two hours, but after the first, Cheryl seems to figure out that I'm here for good. I'll give her credit. She's not treating me like a piece of furniture or a derelict the way most women like her—rich and white, I mean—would usually treat someone who looks like me, to the point where I kind of feel bad for assuming she would. But she's also a little wary. I catch her giving me the eye up and down a few times, sometimes resting her gaze on the tattoos that snake around my right arm. I can't really help the way I look. I can't help my dark skin, the tattoos, or the fact that to women like her, I look dangerous.

But Cheryl and I share something more important than appearances: Layla. And again, I remind myself, her opinion is the only one that matters.

"Oh, Mom!" Layla murmurs as we walk into the final apartment of the night.

The places that we've looked at have varied. One was a crazy nice place in Murray Hill, complete with a doorman, which Cheryl clearly liked, but the price was way too high. Honestly, my jaw dropped when I heard it, and I've lived in this city my whole life. If this is what I'm up against when I look for a place in a few months, I'll be sleeping on a pullout for the rest of my life.

The others have all had different problems. One was above a nightclub, which Cheryl and I both vetoed before we even went upstairs. No fuckin' way am I having Layla live above a bunch of drunk assholes who would just as soon follow her as flirt with her, and Cheryl seemed to agree completely, even though Layla liked the neighborhood. Another was in a decent building, but was about the size of a drainpipe. My shoulders literally touched both sides of the hallway.

This one isn't perfect either, but it's easily the best we've seen. Down where Chinatown, the Lower East Side, and Little Italy all meet, it's in a newly renovated walk-up that looks over Delancey Park, which, as far as I can tell, isn't one of those parks you'd spend a lot of time in, but also doesn't seem to be a magnet for junkies either.

The apartment itself is on the top floor of the six-story building. The top two floors are the only ones that are available yet, and the owners are eager to get them rented to subsidize the construction going on below. Cheryl sniffs her nose at the term "construction," and Layla rolls her eyes and nudges her. I'm more interested in looking around the actual apartment.

It's nice. A lot nicer than any place I've ever lived, although that's not saying much. Two big bedrooms look over the rooftops of China-town. A kitchenette next to a pretty big living room, with new fixtures in the kitchen and the bathroom.

Layla wanders into one of the bedrooms, and I follow to find her at the window, looking over the rooftops of Chinatown. Maybe ten blocks away, I think I see the top of her old dorm, the one where she was living when I first met her. A final few rays of sun are setting through the buildings, lighting up her face. The room has great light. I could sketch Layla in here for hours. Laid across a big white bed. Preferably naked, and giving me that look she does when she's about to go down—

"How much?" Cheryl's voice echoes as she and the realtor follow us into the room.

I turn toward the windows to hide the, ah, *evidence* of my imagination. Shit, I really need to get my girl alone before I embarrass myself completely.

"They're asking nineteen hundred a month," says the realtor, a kid who looks like he should be in a punk band, not showing apartments. Everyone needs to make a living, right? "But I think we could negotiate down to eighteen, maybe even seventeen-fifty. They really need to rent the available units."

I raise an eyebrow, and so does Cheryl. We've seen enough today to know that's a damn good price for an apartment like this.

"Dude," I say. "Why didn't you just bring us here first?"

The realtor shrugs. "Honestly, I didn't know it would be available until about thirty minutes ago. They literally just posted it. You're the first ones to see it."

Cheryl examines the space appreciatively, checking things like the tile in the kitchen and the molding around the doors. The rooms are big, with ceilings that are about three feet taller than the average apartment in New York. Layla's not going to find better than this, not anywhere. I'm not going to lie. I'm a little jealous.

Cheryl turns to her daughter. "What about a roommate?"

"Shama's coming tomorrow."

Layla turns to me and smiles. Even if I sort of wish I was the one who got to stay with her, I'm glad she's still rooming with Shama, one of the few people who really stood by her last year. Out of all her friends, Shama's the one I like best.

"She didn't want to help find the place?" I wonder.

Layla shrugs. "She said it was fine if it was just my name on the lease. I'll send her some pictures before we sign anything. But..." She trails off, looking around the bedroom appreciatively. "I don't think we'll find anything better than this, do you?"

"Do you?" Cheryl's voice repeats, and she looks straight at me.

It's a direct look, one without any judgment. She just wants my opinion. She trusts me. It's scary, but it also feels kind of good.

I clear my throat. "I agree. This place is a steal for an apartment without rent control."

Cheryl nods. "Still, the building isn't secure. What do you know about the neighborhood?"

Again, she's asking *me* this question, not her daughter or the realtor. I straighten up a little and look her in the eye.

"Mom," Layla says. "I used to live maybe ten blocks from here. Remember my dorm sophomore year? That was in Chinatown too. I was fine."

Cheryl says nothing, just waits for my answer.

"I'm not going to lie," I say. "You walk about five or ten blocks east of here, you might end up in a place you wouldn't want to be at night alone. But honestly, that's everywhere in this city. And Layla's smart. This is a well-lit street, and Delancey Park is safe. She'll be all right."

I want to add that *I'll* keep her safe, but I feel like that might be overkill. Still, Cheryl seems to get the message.

"Okay," she says, turning back to her daughter. "This is where you want to be?"

Layla gazes at me, her blue eyes full of promise. *Shit*, I really need to get her alone.

"Let's get things started. We can sign the lease tomorrow, if you want," Cheryl tells the realtor, who immediately flips open his cell phone and starts tapping away. "Is there anywhere around here to eat that won't make us sick?"

Laya snorts. "Mom, this is New York, not New Delhi. There are a ton of good Chinese and Italian places within walking distance." She turns to me. "You're coming, right?"

I grin. "Wild horses couldn't stop me, baby."

———

We make it through dinner, an overpriced meal of pasta and salad at one of those places in Little Italy where the tourists like to go. Cheryl chose it because it seemed "authentic" to her, and I didn't have the heart to tell her that most of the servers are probably Latino, not Italian. She seemed to enjoy the fact that they were all dressed like penguins and served our dinners on white linen tablecloths.

Afterward, Cheryl decides that she wants to go have a nightcap somewhere with her daughter, and gives me a knowing look that says "get lost" in the nicest possible way. With some regret and a lot of guilty thanks after Cheryl pays the tab in full, I have to say goodbye. It's almost eleven o'clock, and I have to be at the academy early in the morning, which means an even earlier wake up to get the train on time.

"Thanks again for dinner, Cheryl," I say as I stand up from the table. I drop a quick kiss on Layla's cheek. "I'll call you tomorrow, sweetie."

It's late, but Mulberry Street is still crowded, full of tourists out and about during the last few weeks of summer. Green, white, and red lights are strung between the fire escapes, casting a romantic glow down the alleys, while occasionally you can hear a cheesy violin or accordion filter out from one of the restaurants. It's dumb, but as I walk by couples finishing up their meals on the sidewalk tables, I'm irritated I had to leave. This is just the kind of place I wouldn't mind walking around with Layla. Where I could kiss her on the corner under these lights, like I did on our first date. Sweep her into a dark alley and let her know how much I missed her.

I'm still fighting the disappointment when my name echoes off the old brick buildings.

"Nico!"

I turn to find Layla barreling through the crowded sidewalk toward me.

"Hey," I say. "Everything okay?"

"Yeah," she says, breathing hard. Her face is flushed. "You just forgot something."

I frown, patting my back pocket for my wallet. "What's that?"

Layla grins. "This."

Then she kisses me. It shouldn't surprise, the way she's willing to do that in the middle of a crowded street, where everyone can see her. Layla has never been shy about showing how she feels. It's one of my favorite things about her.

So of course, I kiss her right back, wrapping my hands around her waist and lifting her into my chest. I tease her mouth open to taste her, taste the remnants of coffee and tiramisu still lingering on her tongue. Fuck *me*, she's so sweet. Somehow, I have a feeling that waiting for her mom to fly back to Pasadena is going to be harder than waiting an entire summer. Things go from zero to sixty in about two fuckin' seconds with this girl. They always did.

"Fuck," I breathe as she breaks away. I steal another kiss, then another until she giggles, and I set her down. "I missed you so goddamn much, you know that?"

Her eyes flutter shut. "I missed you too."

She leans her head on my shoulder and hugs me tight. There's still desire there. I can feel it in the way she presses her entire body into mine, including the part that's missed her in an entirely different way this summer. Then she sighs, full and long. I know the feeling. I don't ever want to let her go.

"She leaves the day after tomorrow," Layla whispers in my ear. She leans back to look at me. "Do you have to work tomorrow night?"

"No." The answer is knee-jerk. And also wrong. "Wait. Yes. *Coño*, I have a shift at AJ's tomorrow night." I rub my nose to hers. "I'm sorry, baby. I thought we'd, you know, have tonight..."

"It's okay." She kisses me again, this time more softly, sweetly, sucking lightly on my bottom lip before releasing it. "Maybe I'll have to come pay you a visit at work." She bites her lip. "I mean, if you don't mind. Crap, I didn't mean to assume—"

I cover her mouth with one more kiss, shuttering her doubt. I want more, but I'll take whatever I can get. After all, now we have all the time in the world.

"Baby, you don't *ever* have to ask to hang out with me," I tell her. I'm rewarded with another sweet smile.

"Okay," she says. "Then I'll see you tomorrow night."

CHAPTER THREE

Layla

"Isn't that what they say?" I asked. "That we all fall in love with our parents?"

Through smudged glasses and under a hat that never seems to stay on straight, Dr. Parker, my therapist, watched me kindly.

"Well, it's a very Freudian way to think about relationships," she replied. "Or have you been reading too much Sophocles in your classes?"

I shrugged. Oedipus Rex was required reading for most college students at some point. I wasn't sure a parable about marrying your mother and killing your father applied here, but I knew the origins of Freud's theory.

"I don't think it's as simple as that," continued Dr. Parker. "Do you think you were trying to replace your father with Giancarlo, Layla?"

It got right to the heart of the issue. The idea was grotesque. Who tries to replace a family member with a lover? Ew. But when she said Giancarlo's name, it hurt. I saw his stern look, the one that was half-

terrifying, half-erotic. Sometimes, when he would pin me down to the bed, controlling every part of me so I couldn't move, I was shocked by how much I liked it. By how strangely...familiar it felt to be controlled that way.

Until the last time, when he did it to hurt.

Or maybe it hurt the whole time. I never could tell.

"No," I said too quickly. Suddenly it was hard to speak. My chest felt like it was bound in cement. I couldn't breathe.

"Close your eyes. Inhale deeply. Focus on where you are now. The room. My voice. The here and now, Layla. The here and now."

It wa a routine Dr. Parker came up with about two weeks after I started seeing her, when she diagnosed me not just as a trauma victim, but also with mild post-traumatic stress disorder. It was common, she said, for women coming out of abusive relationships to experience some measure of PTSD. Flashbacks. Shortness of breath. Dizziness. Those, she said, were my symptoms. We were working on learning my triggers.

"Say it out loud," she urged gently.

"The here and now," I whispered. I didn't shut my eyes. Instead, I opened them wider, trying to let the light of the room banish the darkness that threatened.

"He's gone, Layla," hummed Dr. Parker. "He can't hurt you anymore."

"But he's not gone." Those are the words I could finally muster when my breath started to return. "He's not."

———

"Layla?"

My name interrupts the memory, and I blink at my reflection in the mirror. The dark circles that have been stamped under my eyes since last fall are still there, but they are slowly starting to fade a bit more.

I run the water in the pristine new sink and splash a bit on my face. It's been a long day. After signing the lease this morning, Mom and I went to get my stuff out of storage, and then spent the rest of the day getting the other furniture I'll need. Shama and I can figure out the main room when she gets here, so we just bought a bed and a desk, along with the necessary sheets and basics that I'll need, along with a few things for the kitchen. I'm actually really thankful she came—my mom knows a hell of a lot more about setting up a new house than I do.

But now it's done. The living room is still completely empty, but I am the proud owner of an entire taxi cab full of linens and kitchenware from Bed, Bath, and Beyond, plus a brand-new double mattress set and a plain oak desk and chair.

"It's late. I'm going back to the hotel to pack," Mom says as I exit the bathroom. "Are you sure you wouldn't rather just stay at the suite with me? You'll have the rest of the year to sleep here."

I shake my head. "You have to leave at four a.m. to catch your flight home. I'm good."

Mom looks at her tasteful white-gold watch and tucks a nonexistent flyaway back into place. "Hmmm. Yes. I suppose."

Then she looks up, and her blue eyes, the same bright shade as mine, float over me, in that same way they always do. Checking to make sure everything is there. Nothing's broken. Nothing's out of place.

"Maybe I should stay until your roommate gets here." Mom taps a nail on the wall. "Maybe this is too soon. I don't like you being alone."

I sigh. I'm so tired of being looked at this way. It's been three months of this, of her and my grandparents treating me with kid gloves, walking around me on eggshells. It's almost like they thought I beat myself up last spring, like if they left me alone, they'd come back to find me bruised and bloodied all over again. Ever since Dr. Parker mentioned the letters PTSD, everyone has treated me like a basket case. Everyone except Nico, who doesn't know.

Things like that don't happen in her family. In Pasadena, abuse is done nice and neat, behind closed, carved-wood doors and the pretty white stucco walls. It's done with cutting words, neglect, and bank accounts, not knives and fists. But abuse is abuse. And I think my mother took her fair share for years.

"I'll be fine, Mom."

I cross the room and give her a hug. Her thin form is stiff in my arms. We've never been a touchy-feely family. But eventually her hands clasp my waist, and she squeezes tightly before letting go.

"What about your prescription? Do you have enough?"

I cringe. There's an orange bottle of pills sitting in a drawer of my new desk—a low dose of Valium that I'm supposed to take in the event of a trigger. I don't like them. They push away the shadows, but they veil the rest of the world too. Somehow, I don't think I'm going to find my way back to my old self when I'm on a bunch of mood stabilizers.

"There's plenty," I assure her. "I'll be *fine*."

"That boy..."

At that, I look up. Mom hasn't said much about Nico since we've been here. She watched us, carefully, when he accompanied us from apartment to apartment the night before. She listened and laughed at his jokes, but always focused sharply whenever he brushed my arm, held my waist, snuck a few kisses. I think she was relieved that he had to spend the day at the academy today before going straight to his weekend job.

"The way he looks at you...Layla, he's very in love with you."

I frown. She says it like it's a bad thing.

"Well...I'm in love with him," I say plainly. I don't know why it makes me so nervous to say it out loud. It's the truth.

She cocks her head and worries her lower lip. "Yes. I see that too."

I know what she's thinking. That the connection between Nico and me is too much, too soon after everything I went through. That if I was smart, I would take more time away from him or any relationship. That I wouldn't jump into anything too quickly.

Too bad that's not an option. Not with him. Not now, not ever.

"Mom, you don't have to worry about Nico." I clasp my arms around my waist. "He'll take care of me."

I wish that were true. On some level, I believe it. But another part of me, the scared, anxious part, can't contain its echo: *he sent you away.*

But that was after he saved you, I tell myself. Before he flew across the country to rescue you. He sent you back to your parents so you could be together again, the right way. So you could pull yourself back together.

Still...I'm not the same person I was when we met, or even when he put me back on that plane last May. He loved me then. Will he love me now?

I shake the question away. "I'll be fine."

Mom purses her lips, like she doesn't quite believe me.

"Mom?"

She blinks, like she thinks I've changed my mind. I haven't, but I do have one question that's been bothering me for a long time. It's taken me all summer long to ask the question my therapist and I bandied back and forth again and again. How did I learn to be loved this way?

"Did Dad...did he ever hurt you?" I ask.

Mom pauses and takes a long time to examine the grooves of one of the doorframes. When she looks up, her blue eyes, the ones that are so like mine, are serious and wide.

"Not like you're asking," she says. "But in small ways, yes."

I don't need to ask what she means by that. I know my father. I know what kind of a demanding, overbearing, unforgiving bear he can be.

"You never really forget," she says quietly. "And you shouldn't. Because if you forget, then it might happen again."

I narrow my eyes. I don't like what she's insinuating. The only person in my life who could "do it again" is the same man who saved me. That's not fair to him at all.

"Okay." Mom looks me over one more time and nods. "I'll call you when I land."

"Fly safe."

With one last lingering look, she leaves, and I'm alone in my new apartment, with no one here to pull me out of my daydreams. Memories. Nightmares.

I didn't want to tell her how scared I really am to be here again. How the corners of the city, painted gray with time and people, felt all day today like they were hiding the face that's been tormenting me all summer. He could be anywhere.

I wander back into my bedroom and sit down on the mattress. I pull out my phone, thumbing the keypad. Nico and I talked every day this summer. Mostly at night, when he was off from the academy. He didn't know why I had a tendency to call him at twelve at night or even later. How I'd wake up in the middle of the night shaking, and the only thing that could calm me down was the deep burr of Nico's baritone, even lower when he'd been sleeping. But it would hum me back to a calm place while he sleepily told me about his day, told me to be good. Told me he loved me.

He never cared that I would wake him up in the middle of the night. Never asked why. He was only ever happy to hear my voice and fall back asleep on the phone with me. He doesn't know yet that his voice is the only thing that really keeps those nightmares away.

Almost as if on cue, the screen lights up with his name. I smile. At least this time, I don't have to call him.

"Hey," I answer. "I was just thinking about you."

"Good things?"

I grin into the new mirror propped against the wall. "Of course."

"Naughty things?"

My face practically splits, but I can't quite answer. Nico laughs, like he knows my face is bright red. I don't know why. It's not like we haven't had *much* dirtier conversations this summer.

"I just wanted to make sure you were coming up to the club tonight," he says. "I need to see you."

I can't stop smiling. My cheeks are starting to hurt.

"Is your mom there?"

"No," I answer. "She went back to the hotel to pack."

"So...she's not staying at your place tonight?"

I glance around the empty room. "No..."

"So, does that mean I can?"

I freeze. For a split-second, there's a war within me, one I quickly quash. How could there even be doubt about that? This is what we've been waiting for since the spring.

"Of course," I say quickly. Maybe too quickly.

"And, baby?"

"Yeah?"

"I'm not saying you have to or anything...but if you *did* want to come up to AJ's tonight, I wouldn't mind seeing you in something short. And tight."

I bite my lip. Again with that weird freeze. I don't know what's wrong with me. I used to love it when Nico talked about me like this. I can easily imagine the look on his face when I walk up in one of the tiny dresses I used to wear at nightclubs. The way his full mouth will drop as his gaze sears over every curve I have. It's a look of pure, unadulterated desire. Like there is no one in the world he sees but me.

"I'll, um...I'll see what I can do."

There's a chuckle. "Okay. See you later, beautiful."

The phone hangs up before I can reply—before Nico can hear the doubt in my voice. I push away that cold feeling and focus on the night ahead as I unzip my suitcase and start pulling out clothes to change into. But one thing is bugging me. Outside, it's dark. The shadows are long beyond the telephone poles. And beyond the safety of this room, people lurk. A person, maybe, lurks.

I pick up my phone and dial the first safe person who comes to mind. Vinny, my old friend from freshman year, picks up the phone.

"Whaddya know?" he crows. "Barros is back from the dead! What the fuck is *up*, yo!"

I snort. We didn't really hang out much last year because we were in totally different dorms, but Vinny, a business student who was always determined to sound as bro-y as possible, seems like he's the same as ever.

"I'm back," I say. "Just finished moving into my new place over in Chinatown."

"No shit," Vinny says. "I'm at Lafayette again, if you can believe that. But I got one of the senior singles. Dude, it's *sweet*. I'm going to get so much ass this year."

I grin. Vinny talks like a douchebag, but he's totally harmless. I can't really see him using his single room as anything other than a gaming area. "Awesome, Vin. Let me know how it goes."

Lafayette was our dorm sophomore year, where I used to live with Jamie, Shama, and Quinn, my former best friend. The thought makes me ache a little. We had fun in that dorm. It was a good year.

"So I heard about what happened last year..." Vinny drifts off, waiting for an opening.

With one finger, I press a circle into my comforter. "Oh, yeah."

"Jamie mentioned it when I saw her at the student union yesterday."

My shoulders drop with relief. Jamie wouldn't tell much, and she wouldn't make me sound atrocious.

"Damn, Lay. I wish I was around. I coulda beat that dude's face in a long time before then. You guys always looked out for me."

I smirk. Chasing away the silly girls Vinny likes wasn't exactly a hardship. Those girls had voices like Disney characters and were ridiculous.

But what hurts more is the fact that I'm calling Vinny right now instead of Quinn or Jamie. Even though Jamie came with Shama and Nico to help me last May, she's barely said a word to me all summer. It was like she saw what was really happening to me and just couldn't handle it. Quinn and I totally parted ways when I left last spring. After the way she treated me, there's no love lost there. Best friends don't stand aside when their friend is in trouble. They don't scold and hate on them when they need to be held the most. I'm better off without her, as Nico frequently tells me.

But, I realize, it's going to be a little lonely without a posse. Starting over might be harder than I thought.

"So hey," I say, "I'm supposed to be meeting Nico—"

"Nico? FedEx guy? You back with him?"

I sigh. I'm going to be hearing that a lot, and I know Nico doesn't like it.

"Well, he's a firefighter now," I correct Vinny, enjoying the little thrill I feel when I say that out loud. I'm so proud of Nico for what he's doing. Not to mention he looks insanely hot in his uniform. "He graduates from the academy in a few more weeks. But yeah, we're back together. He's, um...he still works the door at AJ's on the weekends. Any chance you want to go up there tonight? I could be your wingman..."

"Are you kidding? I've been trying to get into AJ's for months! They *never* let dudes in!"

"Well, good," I say with a grin as I pull one of my shortest dresses out of my suitcase with renewed enthusiasm. "Then it's a date. Here, I'll give you my address."

CHAPTER FOUR

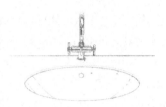

Nico

"Sorry, ladies. You'll have to go elsewhere tonight."

The three girls in front of me stick out their lips, looking even more like the children they are. I doubt they're even eighteen, let alone twenty-one. How their parents let them out of the house looking like two-bit prostitutes almost makes me feel sorry for them, but not sorry enough to let them into the club.

The taller one, who's wearing the tightest jeans I have ever seen and earrings so big they would give my sister Selena a run for her money, cocks her head and extends a finger to run up and down my shoulder. I glare at it. It's hot tonight. We're in the thick of late summer in New York, and the city smells like sweat, hot garbage, and alcohol.

"Come on, handsome," says Earrings. "I bet we could make it worth your while."

She leans in so I can smell the gallon of perfume she's wearing. I cough.

"We come as a package deal, you know," she purrs. "And my friend's parent' have an empty penthouse on Fifth."

Ah, so that's what's going on. Rich Mommy and Daddy are probably at the Hamptons for the weekend, just like all the other rich people in the city, leaving their very underage daughters to play house for the weekend. I stare at the hand on my shoulder until she removes it, looking slightly scared.

"Look...*Wanda*." I flip her shitty ID back at her. "We don't let kids in here. And word to the wise, asking strange men to your apartment is gonna get you into trouble. Go home before I call the cops, and they call your parents for you."

The girl's lip trembles, and her friends, both of them wearing so much makeup they look like sad, underage clowns, stare at the concrete. For a split-second, I almost let them in, thinking that maybe it's better if I keep them here. Then at least I could keep an eye on them. Make sure they don't go home with anyone they shouldn't.

Shit. I'm not these girls' dad. The last thing I want to be doing is babysitting, especially when my girl is going to be here any second. Then I have an idea.

"Tell you what, lemme see your IDs again, sweetheart," I say. "Maybe I was wrong."

I almost feel bad about the hopeful looks on their faces when I collect the plastic cards. Even if the pictures hadn't been grainy as fuck, their flimsy weights would have told me they were fakes. Wanda, Josephina, and Marilyn. Jesus, these are the worst fake names I've ever seen. They probably spent good money on these too. Poor kids.

I pretend to examine them closely while I fish a pair of scissors out of my pocket. And then, before they can stop me, I slice them in half, then hand them back the broken pieces.

"Hey!" "Wanda" cries out, holding the broken pieces while her friends look on in horror. "What the hell!"

"You'll thank me in about five years," I say. "Now go home, before I really do call the cops."

With a few more cries of protest, the girls finally leave, with nothing more to do. I know that most likely, they'll just buy new IDs. Maybe this week, maybe next month. But at least tonight they won't be going anywhere that sixteen-year-olds have no business going. I swear to God, the day I check my last ID will be the last time I ever set foot in a nightclub again. Ten years of my life I've spent working in these shitholes.

And now. Maybe a year. Maybe less. Once I'm off a probate's salary and making a regular income from the fire department, I won't have to do this shit. Any. More.

I settle back on my stool and run a hand through my hair. It's too long, the tight curls getting a little bushy on top, which means more shit I have to comb through it to get it to behave in this humidity. Normally I keep it short, but the memory of Layla's hum when I mentioned it to her last month stuck with me. I close my eyes, remember the way her fingers wove through it at the airport. My girl is a hair-puller. I'd like to make her pull on it *really* hard. Soon.

"That was kind of harsh."

I look up at the familiar sweet voice that brings an instant smile to my face, and immediately, every thought I have about protecting innocent girls' decency flies out the fuckin' window, because right here is an innocent girl I want nothing more than to corrupt.

I can't remember the last time I've seen her like this, all dressed up for a night out. Twelve months? Eighteen? Maybe more?

She's in a slinky black dress that's short enough to be underwear and leaves absolutely *none* of her curves to the imagination. Her hair curls over her shoulders, and she's got a pair of high-heeled shoes that make her legs look indecently good. Is it just me, or did her waist get even smaller this summer? If that dress clings the same way from the back, I'm not going to be able to focus for shit the rest of the night. Which, let's be honest, I wouldn't mind at all.

You asked for it, asshole.

"Hey, baby," I greet her as she leans in for a kiss. Fuck, she smells good. Like coconut and flowers. Familiar and exotic at the same time.

Her lips open to mine a little more than I was intending, but just when things are getting good, she breaks the kiss. I keep an arm around her waist, keeping her trapped between my legs. It's all I can do not to press my nose into her cleavage, street traffic be damned. What can I say? My girl is smokin'.

"I guess you're glad to see me, huh?" she whispers.

My hand hovers low on her back, just below where's really decent. "I'm always glad to see you, baby."

I tip my head up for another kiss, but she smiles coyly, and to my disappointment, steps away. She gestures behind her, and it's only then I realize she hasn't come alone.

"You remember my friend Vinny, right?"

For a second, I'm all glares at the well-dressed schmuck behind her. He looks just like all the Wall Street jokers, in a pair of perfectly distressed jeans and a button-up shirt, with his hair mussed with too much gel. But then I recognize him. He's a little more filled out now, but this is the kid who used to live in her dorm in Chinatown. The gawky, awkward kid who used to look out for her and her friends.

He extends a hand, looking uncertain. I shake it and smile. He immediately relaxes.

"How you doin', man? I'm Nico."

"I remember," says Vinny. "Nice to see you again, bro."

I nod. "You too. Thanks for keeping my girl company tonight."

Vinny nods. "Hey, this was my lucky night. I can never get in here."

I quirk an eyebrow. "You twenty-one?"

Vinny nods and hands me his ID. "Yeah. As of last week, anyway."

I check his New Jersey ID, which looks pretty damn legit, not that it would matter. He's Layla's friend, which is good enough for me.

I hand it back and nod. "Happy birthday, man. Go on in. Nah, you're good. Cover's on me, so have fun."

Gleefully, Vinny practically runs into the club. Layla gives me a grateful smile, then turns to follow. She pauses for a second at the doorway. It's brief, but I don't miss the way she bites her lip and examines the handle like it's about to bite her. Just when she's about to step inside, I reach out and snag her hand, making her jump.

"Hey," I say. "You okay, beautiful?"

She holds a hand to her chest, and it drifts up to the delicate skin around her neck—the skin that was a mosaic of bruises last May. I tug her back for another kiss, one that's deeper than before, since we don't have an audience other than the random passersby. She sinks into it, and slowly, that tension that was written all over her melts away. Good.

"Mmmm," she hums once I'm certain that her body is totally relaxed again. "That was nice."

I nod and close my eyes for a moment, enjoying the feel of her smile against mine. "Tell the bartender who you are, okay? He knows you're coming. I'll be inside as soon as I can."

She giggles as I bite her lip lightly, then absorbs me in another soul-searing kiss.

"Okay," she says, finally stepping away. "Don't make me wait too long."

With a grin, I watch her walk into the club. And Jesus *fuckin'* Christ, that dress is even more dangerous from the back than I thought. I groan and rub a hand over my face, then check to make sure there's no one watching before I adjust myself. Twice. It's going to be a long night.

———

About an hour later, I head inside for my thirty-minute break, in search of one thing: Layla. AJ's has a great band tonight—a local trip hop group that basically sounds like sex on a stage. They're in the middle of a synth set while the singer croons against the beat. The combination of the sultry keys and the bass line basically has the whole crowd writhing together like snakes, lost to the rhythm. It's hot. It's sticky. It's foreplay.

Like a magnet, I'm drawn to her. Layla stands on the edge of the crowd, a drink in one hand with her other arm wrapped around her middle as she sways a little from side to side. She's stunning, of course, but that's a posture I know well—one that says she's feeling a little uncertain. Immediately, I feel terrible I didn't just take the night off. It's her first night in New York by herself. I should be there for all of it.

I approach from behind and she jumps about three feet when I slide my hands around her waist.

"Ohmygod!" she shouts, then softens when she turns around and finds me there.

"You okay?" I ask her, chuckling when she smacks me on the shoulder.

She sighs. At first I think I see a tremble of her lips, but it disappears by the time I pull her close. The taste of whiskey and Diet Coke is strong on her breath—I'm guessing she's had at least two.

"You all right there, baby?" I ask again.

Layla smirks, her hazy expression sharpening when it lands on my mouth. "I am now."

Then she kisses me, and this one is different from any kiss we've had since she got back. It's a far cry from the downright Amish kisses when her mother was around, but it's not exactly the joy or love that I'm feeling right now. This is a kiss that's only about one thing: lust.

"Jesus," I breathe when we finally come up for air. "That was—"

But I can't continue before my girl fuckin' swallows me whole all over again. Jesus, she's voracious, and the effect is immediate. Suddenly my hands are everywhere, and the only thing I can think about is the fact that it has been a *very* long summer—no, fuck that, a very long year—and I need this body. I need to be *inside* this body. Right fuckin' *now*.

"Nico," she breathes as she presses every single one of her curves against me, especially one part that is aching to be let out.

"Ah." I literally lose my voice as she grinds into me again. *Coño*, I didn't know it was possible to want someone this bad. But I do. I always do with her.

"Where can we go?" she asks, somehow without removing her lips from mine. "I...I don't want to be here anymore. I need you now."

My throat constricts with need as my fingers dig into her hips. It's been a long time since we were like this, and I'm hit with flashes of when we first met. Layla has always had a voracious streak. I wouldn't call her an exhibitionist—it's not like we ever did it in front of people. But there were times, like in Central Park or in the back of a cab, where my girl just could not wait to get her hands on me.

"Seriously? You don't want to wait until—"

"*Nico*." Her hands drop to my ass and squeeze. Hard.

That's usually my move, but the fuck if it doesn't have an immediate effect on me too. I groan into her neck. "Ahhh. Okay. Yeah. Follow me."

I turn and guide her through the mass of gyrating bodies., including her friend, who's rubbing up on some blonde girl. This isn't where I'd do this if it were totally up to me. It's not that I don't want to fuck Layla. Fuck me, I've wanted to do the dirtiest things imaginable to this girl since I met her, things I'd never even say out loud because I'm pretty sure she'd slap me, things that make a fuck in a nightclub seem downright demure. But for our second first time, I'd have wanted it to be nicer. Special.

But apparently, that's not what my girl wants. And if she wants me to give it to her right here, then that's what she's going to get. I tow her down the employees' hallway in the back, checking for my manager before I knock on the door of the employees' bathroom. It's nothing much. A bunch of stored paper towels, some cleaning supplies, and a toilet and sink that haven't been used by two hundred people. But it's not exactly the most romantic spot in the world.

I lock the door, suddenly filled with uncertainty. You asshole. She deserves better than this.

I turn around. "Sweetie, you sure you want to—"

Again, my words are cut off by her kiss as she rams me against the door.

"Stop talking," she mumbles. "Just fuck me."

Her raw, brutal words undo the last bit of restraint I've got. In about a half a second, I've flipped us around so she's shoved against the bathroom wall while I devour that sweet, filthy mouth. Another half second and my pants are unzipped. My cock falls out, throbbing against her thigh. She moans while I hurry on a condom. Almost as quickly, I toss her legs around my waist, yank her strip of underwear to the side, and thrust inside her with all the fury that's been mounting since I left her for California over a year ago.

And she feels. So. Fucking. Good.

Tight. Wet. This body was fucking made for me to do this. Made to be taken in every possible way. Made for me to slip inside, made to undo me completely. Her body squeezes, and as she moans loudly into my mouth, I just about come right there. With two handfuls of the sweetest ass on the fuckin' planet, I'm the happiest man alive as I pound home again and again.

Any time. Any place. That's how it's always been with us. Once again, I'm taken back to memories of everywhere we gave into this need all over the city. Central Park. A restaurant downtown. The far corner of a subway station. Another in Chinatown. It doesn't matter that I've lived here my entire life. This city will always be marked by Layla and me—marked by us and the connection that can't be denied.

"Baby," I moan against her neck. Her legs are in a vise-grip around my waist—I'm not going to be able to hold it much longer. "Baby, are you close?"

"I..." She drifts off as her head bumps into the wall with one particularly hard thrust. The sound brings me even fucking closer. *Fuck.*

"Just do it," she whispers, her voice low and guttural. "I want to feel you come."

Fuck. That's all I need.

"Jesus *Christ!*" I shout, slamming my fist into the wall behind her head while my other arm holds her up.

She arches against me, her entire body quivering. We come together, our bodies clenching tight, and, at least for me, the world goes black. Gone is the thump of bass vibrating through the walls, the dingy walls of the bathroom, the stale scent of alcohol and cleaner. All I can hear, see, smell, touch, *feel* is her. Layla. Only Layla.

I shake out the rest of my orgasm, and she shakes too. Her feet fall back to the floor while we both collapse against the wall together to catch our breaths. But it's not until the world comes back into focus that I realize she's still shaking long after I'm done—but not from ecstasy. From tears.

"Oh, *shit.*"

I yank up my pants, not even bothering to zip everything up, and gather her into me. She curls into my chest and sobs. What the *fuck* is going on?

"Shhhh," I croon as I stroke her hair. "What's going on? Talk to me, baby. This wasn't the right place, was it? Shit, I'm so fuckin' sorry. The bathroom of a bar—what the fuck was I thinking, right?"

"N-no," she stutters as she stands up fully. She wipes the makeup bleeding under her eyes, but remnants of tears make her blue eyes glow. She's so beautiful, even when she's sad. "I'm sorry. I–I don't know what's wrong with me."

I run a finger over her cheek, then through her hair before I pull her back to my shoulder. She sighs as she lays her head there, and we just stand for a minute as her emotions settle. I don't press her with the questions swirling around in my head. Something about this was totally wrong. At some point, I'm going to need her to tell me. But not now. Right now, I just want her to feel better.

"I think I should probably go home," Layla says after another minute or two. She stands back up and gives me a sad smile, but doesn't maintain her gaze.

I toy with her fingers. I don't want her to go. Or actually, I do, but I can't leave work just yet. I have at least three more hours of tossing drunk assholes out on the street before I can climb into bed with her and hold her until she's herself again.

Damn.

"Okay, sure. Give me a minute and we'll get you a cab."

She nods and waits patiently while I put myself back together. She doesn't have much to do. That dress of hers is short enough that one tug puts it back into place. I give her forehead another quick kiss before we go back through the club.

"What about your friend?" I ask her as we step outside.

Paul, the other bouncer, gives me a nod as he gets off the stool. I gesture that I need a minute as I lead Layla to the curb.

"Vinny will be fine," she says. "He was cozied up with some girl. I'll send him a text that I went home."

I hail a cab, then turn to my girl and cup her face, urging her to look at me. Her blue eyes, usually so bright and full of attitude, right now are clouded with uncertainty.

"I love you, you know that, *mami?*" I've said it to her a million times all summer, but it occurs to me I haven't said it once since she got off that plane. Fuck, I really am an asshole.

She cracks a smile, and her small frame relaxes a little. Okay, we're on the right track.

"I love you too," she whispers. "So much."

I kiss her again, this time gently, even though I can already feel that yearning for her that never stops. Put it away, asshole. That is *not* what she needs right now. I don't know what exactly that is, but it's not a boner pressed against her leg in the middle of the street.

"Can I come over after my shift is up?" I ask. "Not for that, I promise. I just...goddammit, baby. I just want to fall asleep with you in my arms again. Would that be all right?"

Again, that sweet smile appears, and it just about lights up the street at damn near close to midnight.

"Sure," she says. "Just call when you're on your way. Don't worry about waking me up."

I give her another more innocent kiss before she gets in the cab. I have questions, so many questions. But for now, I'm content just to be with my girl. I'll take Layla any way I can get her. That will never change.

CHAPTER FIVE

Layla

It's not until past four thirty that my cell phone buzzes on the windowsill.

Nico: Still up? I'm downstairs.

Oh, I'm awake. I've been lying in this room for hours, staring up at the ceiling and listening to the hum of the city outside my window. Every sound makes me jump. Every creak of the fire escape. Every blare of a horn. Every drunken shout on a street corner. This is a decent neighborhood, but it's true what they say. New York really never sleeps.

I buzz Nico in and unlock the door before I pad back to bed, turning on my side toward the window. Beyond the fire escape, the city twinkles against a sky that never quite grows completely dark at night. At the edges, the glow of the sun is already starting to make itself apparent. I've been watching it for hours, staring at the lights, burrowed under my covers, and trying to make sense of what happened at the club.

I still don't have any good explanation. Just one that I don't want to say.

Trigger.

I listen to the door open and close, then the sound of Nico locking up before he enters the room. He pauses for a minute at the door and smiles when I turn to look at him.

"Hey," he says. "Sorry to wake you up."

I sit up. "I wasn't asleep."

"No?" He enters the room and sits on the bed to remove his shoes. "So, you gonna tell me what that was about back there?"

"What do you mean?" Wow, he's not wasting any time, is he?

Nico cocks his head. "NYU, come on. You can't hide things from me. Layla, you totally froze. One second we were going at it like rabbits; the next, it was like I was doing a dead girl." He leans over and slips a finger under my chin. "I'm not into necrophilia, baby. I like you alive"—kiss—"and kicking"—kiss.

His lips feel good. Soft. Full. Pliant. But my lips, damn them, don't move.

Nico sits back. "Okay, really. What is going on?"

I scoot farther into my pillows and lie down. "I—"

Nico kicks off his other shoe, then scoots up the bed so he's lying on the other pillow, facing me. A hand drapes over my waist, and gently, he turns me toward him. His eyes are wide and kind, full of concern.

No.

The word echoes through me, and I hate myself for it. I don't want to feel this way. And a big part of me doesn't. A big part of me just wants to lose myself in him again, like I wanted to do in the club. For a little while, it worked. The combination of whiskey, music, and Nico made me forget for a minute what a damaged person I am. Let him touch me the way only he can, the way that

makes me forget my name, where I am, everything but the name-
less notion of what we are together. I was close, so close, until his
hand hit the wall next to my head. Just like someone else used
to do.

My shadow threatens. My muscles tense. That ability to let go
isn't back yet. I stare at the wall behind him. I don't want to see the
disappointment I know is all over Nico's beautiful face.

A finger tips my chin up again.

"Hey," he says. "It's all right, *mami*. I got you."

My lower lip trembles before I can stop it. Nico's face clouds.

"Hey," he says again, pulling me to him just as the tears start all
over again. "What is it? Talk to me, Layla."

"Fuck," I whisper. "*Fuck*."

He chuckles. "That's usually my line."

I shake my head, rubbing my nose into his chest. He smells so
good—like detergent and sweat and soap and man. Nico. I want
nothing more than to get lost in him—get lost in this perfect, strong
body that's never done anything but protect me.

But I can't.

"I don't want to be this girl. I wanted tonight to be perfect. You've
been so patient, and I'm just..."

My voice warbles irritatingly as I trail off, but Nico just chuckles.

I frown. "What's so funny?"

"You."

He strokes the side of my face, and his grin is contagious. I smile
back, despite the fact that I have no idea what he's laughing about.

"What about me?" I demand.

"The fact that you think I'd be disappointed by literally anything
about you." He touches his forehead to mine. "I lived almost twenty-
seven years loving you, and I didn't even know you. I spent another
year and a half dreaming about you, day and night. Layla, I'll take
whatever you have to give and still be the happiest fuckin' bastard on
the planet. You want to fuck in the nightclub, I'm down, obviously.
But if you decide you want to wait until marriage or some shit like

that, I'll do that too. I'd do anything for you, baby. Don't you know that by now?"

I can't help it. I grin. His words are balm to my aching heart, my aching soul that's still not quite healed. He pulls me close, and so I do what comes naturally and kiss him. His mouth stills—he's surprised, since he was just moving in for a hug. But quickly, he adapts, and before long, we're right back against the brick wall, the back of the cab, the stairwell of my apartment. It's several more seconds—minutes?—before we break again, both of us heaving.

Nico gulps and smiles bashfully. "I mean, it's going to be a *little* harder if you keep kissing me like that."

I giggle, and he sighs contentedly.

"God, I love that sound. You mind if I make myself a little more comfortable, sweetie?"

I shake my head, then watch openly as he gets up and strips off the black pants and t-shirt he wears when he's checking IDs. It's been a long time since I've seen him like this, casual and at ease in his own body, uncaring that he's on display in front of me. He grins when he catches me ogling, but I don't care. He's mine to look at. Right?

And he's beautiful. His skin is smooth and golden, and practically glows in the moonlight, which casts shadows on his chest and stomach, playing over the ridged lines of hard-wrought muscle. His lips are full and open, and his eyes glitter, two black diamonds as they settle on me.

"Come here," I beckon, and he immediately obeys, sliding under the covers and tucking me comfortably into his warm body.

I don't have on anything but a thin camisole and my underwear. His warmth surrounds me, skin to skin. We lapse into silence, remembering the feel of each other again. This is good. This is right. My first night in this apartment, my first night back in the city, and he's here. With me.

We lie there a moment, letting the sounds of our breathing fill the empty space of the apartment, until Nico puts a few inches between us so we are looking at each other across the pillow.

"Tell me what happened," he says. "If you can."

I worry my lower lip between my teeth, thinking hard until Nico reaches a hand and plucks my lip free.

"And maybe don't do that," he suggests sweetly. He arches a sly brow. "It makes it hard to focus."

I open my mouth, then close it and exhale through my nose. "Okay. Um...I..."

How do I say this without giving it all away? Without making myself sound like a complete lunatic? A deranged girl? Nico doesn't need another burden to carry in his life on top of all the people he already supports. He doesn't need to know that the bathroom was just the start of it. That I rocked back and forth in the back seat of the cab, repeating "here and now" all the way back to my apartment while the Sudanese driver gave me strange looks. That I stared at the tiny pill in my palm for close to thirty minutes before I put it back in the bottle, choosing to feel crazy over feeling numb.

"I don't...I don't want to think about...him."

It takes him a second, but when he figures it out, Nico's eyes widen. "*Him*? I made you think about that motherfucker? How?"

"When you...on the wall...with your hand."

His brow crinkles. I don't blame him for not remembering—he was in the middle of an orgasm at that moment. I doubt he can remember his own name when he's coming like that, much less what he's doing with his hands.

"Is this...do you think about him a lot?"

Yes. "No, not really." I am such a liar.

Nico seems to think so too. "Baby, come on."

I sigh. "I'm still working through it, okay? I was doing really well this summer, actually. I thought I was ready to come back here. But last week, the police called to let us know that his trial date was scheduled, but that he was still out on bail..."

I trail off as a chill settles over me. Nico rubs my shoulder. His touch is a welcome warmth.

"He's still here," I whisper. "He didn't go back to Argentina. Nico, he's still here."

Nico's expression turns black, and a muscle in his jaw starts ticking. "When's his court date?"

I swallow. "In a few weeks. September seventeenth."

"That's a Friday," he says. "What time?"

"The police said one thirty."

My voice grows small. Nico looks like he wants to punch something. It takes me back to that day again, when he lost himself completely with Giancarlo. I don't want to tell him that some of my dreams involve him and the rage I witnessed that day. That sometimes, very, very rarely, I dream that he might turn it on me.

I shiver and resist the urge to rock myself.

"Baby, I know you don't want to hear this, but you gotta go."

My head jerks. "What? No!"

"Baby—"

"*Nico.* I don't want to see him!"

The words are more vehement than I intend, spitting out like bullets. Suddenly my voice is choked, and I can't breathe. *The here and now. The here and now.* I chant the words over and over again to myself. But it doesn't work. Everything feels tighter. My breath draws shallow, and everything starts to spin. I gasp for breath, but none of it seems like enough.

"Layla."

It's Nico's arms folding around me that open up my lungs again. It's his lips on my neck, the soft vibration of his voice on my skin. He hushes me, holds me until I calm. Until I'm ready to push away the memories of Giancarlo's looming face and terrible touch instead of this man, a man who truly loves me.

The here and now.

"Okay," I say. "I'm okay now. Um...sorry."

"You don't have to be sorry about anything," Nico murmurs. "But, Layla..."

I sigh. "What?"

"I have demons too," he says. "Which is why I know they'll stay with you until you face them. You don't want that shit chasing you forever. Don't let those memories hold you hostage."

I blink into his chest. There are times from his life that Nico hates to discuss. The years when Gabe's father lived with them and used to beat their mother, and probably the kids too. The two years he spent at a detention facility in upstate New York, which is all but a mystery to me, mostly because Nico absolutely will not go there. Plus, I've seen the tiny, terrible apartment where he grew up. Poverty is its own kind of trauma, and his lasted a lot longer than the six or so months I was with Giancarlo.

"You won't be alone," he says. "I'll be with you."

I look up. "You will?"

He snorts lightly and gives me a surprised half smile. "Of *course* I will, baby. What kind of man do you think I am?"

I blink. "I...I guess I don't really know, do I?"

We stare at each other as the reality of the words sinks in. For as much time as we've spent this summer flirting and talking, we haven't really *been* together in well over a year, and even then, it was tenuous, with his departure to LA hanging over us the whole time.

"Yours," he says softly. "I'm *your* man, Layla. No matter what, I'm here for you. You can believe that."

Just as quickly, the shadows fade away. His warmth envelops me.

"I'm yours too," I whisper back.

Nico smiles, almost a little sadly. Slowly, he takes one hand to his lips, then the other.

"Not yet," he whispers. "But I have faith."

He's honest, but without judgment. There's no doubt in his words, just the knowledge that things *will* be all right if we just give it time. It's a knowledge I didn't know I needed until now. A knowledge that scoots me across the pillow and back into his arms.

I kiss him again, and just as quickly as before, what starts sweet almost immediately turns into something more potent. Nico gasps into my mouth and tries to pull away, but I don't let him. I want more.

I want to be *us* again, whatever that means. His hands drift down my back, and he groans lightly as he finds my ass and squeezes that favorite body part of his, pressing me into the hard length that's suddenly tenting the front of his shorts.

"Okay!" he shouts suddenly, rolling away and forcing some space between us.

I scowl. "What are you doing?"

"You're not ready, baby. I...gah. That's not why I came here tonight." Nico folds inward, like he's protecting himself. Almost like he's in pain.

The blanket has fallen down, and I can see the obvious bulge in his shorts. It turns me on, but just when I go to move his hand away, I stop, stricken again with fear. And immediately, shame.

Why do I have to be like this? My body wants nothing but him. All day. Every day. But some other part of me is screaming to put on the brakes. It's ruining everything.

"Let's just go to sleep," Nico's saying, but I can barely hear him over the fighting thoughts in my head.

"I..."

I can't stop staring at the bulge in the front of his shorts. Almost unconsciously, like he's not even aware of it, Nico's hand drifts down to adjust himself, then rests there.

I look up. "I can't."

"What do you mean, you can't? Just turn over."

"What if...I don't want to?"

Nico sighs. "Layla..."

"I could watch you," I blurt out and immediately flush. Holy shit. I am some kind of pervert. I could *watch* him?

A black brow rises playfully. "What?"

I gulp, and the flush gets worse as my gaze drifts back down to the, ah, package he's now casually stroking. On purpose. Yep, I'm still going to ask.

"If...if you'd let me," I say, mesmerized by his gentle strokes. "I wouldn't mind watching you...do that."

Nico follows my gaze to his cock, and, as if he just now registers what he's been doing, his eyes brighten considerably. With a bit more purpose now, his hand cups the bulge, straining against the thin black fabric. It's perfect—not too big, not too small. Slightly curved. I remember exactly how it feels when it presses into that one, perfect spot inside me. How it completely undid me only a few hours before.

Well, almost.

Nico licks his full lips. Then, without a word, he tugs down the waistband, revealing himself completely. When I meet his eyes again, they sparkle with knowing, and he leans in for a kiss.

"This okay?" he asks as his hand starts to move. "Can I kiss you again?"

I nod. "You can always kiss me."

So he does, moving slowly, softly, until our tongues are wrapped up in that delicate dance together that sets both our bodies alight. It's a light that can't be banished, even when the darkness threatens.

"What about you?" he murmurs a bit later. "This ain't just the Nico show, baby. I have another hand I can use here."

I glance down to where he works. There's an ache between my legs now, one I wouldn't mind taking care of either. But there's something about watching...I'm not quite ready to give it up.

"I...I think I can do it."

"Then can I watch too?" That sly brow is back up.

I bite my lip and nod. His eyes dilate as I slide my fingers down and under the band of my underwear. He's as transfixed by the movements as I am by the way his hand works his solid length. His breathing grows harsher as I find my sweet spot, that small bundle of nerves that makes me come undone. It's a good interim, a touch I know, a feeling I know. We've listened to each other do this countless times over the summer, but this is the first time either of us has watched.

The idea turns me on even more.

"Oh, *God*," I groan as my fingers pick up their pace.

Nico grunts, and his hand also moves faster. "Can you see this?"

he asks, his deep voice somehow even deeper. "Do you see what you do to me? This isn't me, Layla. This is you. All you."

I can't answer. I'm too busy, too mesmerized by the tension in his body. Nico's not a big man, but he has the presence of one. This close, seeing the way each well-defined muscle ripples with every flick of his wrist. The way his bricked abdominals squeeze with the effort to keep his cool. The way the compass tattoo over his heart seems to tick ferociously every time his breath picks up a notch.

"Layla," he croaks, and his other hand snakes around my head and pulls me into him for another fierce kiss.

I return it with as much vigor, finally lost in this moment, lost in him as my fingers work to join him.

"Layla!" Nico cries as his body seizes up suddenly. Every muscle is cast suddenly in high relief, caught in the shadows of the night and the city.

The knowledge of his undoing spurs my own. I shout my release as suddenly as his, but he swallows my cries with yet another kiss as we come together, side by side as the world falls apart, but we come closer to being one.

"Fuck," he breathes slowly as he comes down. "You wanted to watch..." He chuckles. "I love you so goddamn much, you know that? You're bananas, but I love you like crazy."

I can't do anything but giggle, but his wide, lazy smile tells me he sees everything I'm feeling on my face.

Nico looks down sheepishly to the mess in his hand. "Got a towel? I don't want to mess up your sheets."

"Bathroom," I tell him.

I enjoy the view while he walks away in nothing but his birthday suit, admiring the prize-winning ass that literally stopped me on the street once. I wait patiently while he cleans up and returns to bed. For the first time all night, I feel a sense of peace, which is only heightened the second he slips back into the bed next to me.

"I love you," he says again as he gathers me close.

I smile behind closed eyes. "I love you too. Good night." Then I turn over and scoot to the other pillow.

"What are you doing?"

I turn back. "Giving you space."

He looks at me like I'm crazy. "Baby, why the fuck would you think I need space? When the fuck did I *ever* want space from you?"

I open my mouth to answer, but just as soon, realize the answer. Never, of course. That was Giancarlo who always insisted on a full three feet between us at night. Who pushed me to the edge of the bed so he could splay his long limbs while he slept.

As if he sees the answer on my face, Nico tugs me back toward him immediately. His arm slips under my neck, and the other one drapes over my stomach, pulling my back firmly into his chest. The man is a furnace, and I crave his warmth.

"I just want to fall asleep with you in my arms again," he murmurs into my ear, his low voice vibrating over the sensitive skin as he repeats his earlier request. "Is that okay?"

I sigh and nod. I want to tell him that this would be okay every night for the rest of my life. That when I'm with him, I have this feeling like nothing out there could hurt me. Instead I let him gather me close, hold me the way we've both wanted for so, so long until his breaths grow deep and regular.

But as the room grows cold again, and the darkness outside fades, that sliver of fear still lingering at the edges of my heart remains. I shut my eyes and focus on the sound of Nico's breath. The fear will be back tomorrow, and probably the next day too. But for now, I'm safe. For now, I'm where I belong.

CHAPTER SIX

Layla

"Happy birthday, baby."

There's a bright light shining in my face, visible even through closed eyelids. When I open them, I see the source: a flash glinting off bright gold. The whole bedroom seems cast in light. Bouncing off the east-facing windows on the other side of me, the early morning sun casts everything with a warm glow.

It's the first solid night of sleep I've had in months. The first night where I didn't wake up in the middle seized with terror. The first where I didn't have to spend an hour or more chanting myself back to sleep for another few pitiful hours.

I turn back to the trinket next to me and the eager man holding it. "It's not my birthday. That was way back in June."

"I know," Nico says, holding out the jewelry. "But I wanted to give this to you in person."

Gingerly, I take it from him, and it's only when my vision comes fully into focus that I realize what it is.

A gold watch. More specifically, it's *my* gold watch. The watch my dad gave me for Christmas last year, which I had to pawn when Giancarlo sent me, unwittingly, to pay off a drug-related debt of his in the South Bronx. Nico helped me sell it in order to avoid much, *much* worse happening if we didn't. I turn it over and find the engraved inscription: *a minha filha.* "To my daughter" in Portuguese, my father's native language. It's a little bittersweet to see, since he refused to teach me Portuguese while I was growing up, insisting that I needed to be as Americanized as possible to succeed. It was one of the reasons why his absence last year hurt so badly. Not only did he shield me from a half of myself I had always wanted to know, but then he abandoned both my mother and me to run back to it just the same.

————

"What did he say when you told him what happened?" Dr. Parker's face was kind and patient. Everything my father is not.

I stared at my hands, braced in my lap. "I didn't tell him."

There was a long pause. Then: "Would you like to tell me why not?"

I sighed. No, I wouldn't. But I knew I should. Dr. Parker didn't ask questions she didn't think I needed to figure out. And unfortunately, the hard ones usually ended up helping the most.

"I...I don't really want to hear what he would have to say," I whispered.

She said nothing, just waited for me to gather my thoughts. I wove and unwove my fingers, suddenly remembering the old nursery rhyme I used to play with my dad. The one he would do to get me to go to church. Here is the church. Here is the steeple. Open the door, and look, all the people.

It was a rhyme that always made me laugh, until he launched into his lecture on piety. That I needed to be one of the people inside, or else I'd burn with everyone else. My father, so concerned with my mortal soul, seemed to have given up on his own in the end.

"He will tell me I earned it," I said. "That I brought it on myself."

One word about last year would deliver endless lectures over the crackling line from Brazil. It would be questions about what I did to provoke it, just like the police asked me. What did I wear, what did I drink, when did I skip church, who was I hanging out with? But most of all, the conversation would spell out his disappointment. That his daughter would never let this happen to her. That we get what we earn.

The worst part is, I asked myself those questions too, all the time. No matter how many times Dr. Parker told me it wasn't my fault what Giancarlo did, I still wondered what I should have done to stop it.

It was the same reason I never said that I had lost the watch he had given me. The last thing he had given me, one that, after months of silence, explicitly recognized me as his daughter. His blood.

———

I shake my head, then clasp the watch around my wrist. Nico blinks, trying to gauge my response.

"How..." I shake my head, overwhelmed. "When did you do this?"

A dimple appears with a shy smile. "About a day after I put you on the plane."

"But this must have cost you...Nico, it's too much."

The watch was taken in exchange for a debt of a thousand dollars. I sincerely doubt the pawnbroker would have taken anything less than that plus interest.

"I...I don't know." He rubs the back of his neck, like he's nervous. "I needed to do something, you know? To make things right again. This was a start."

The memories from last spring darken the morning light before either of us can stop them—I see them playing clearly across Nico's face, and feel them just as clearly on mine. The dingy apartment.

The stained floors. The slam of bodies on wood and plaster. Blood dripping down my face.

My chest squeezes again. My breath recedes.

No. Not this morning.

So I do the only thing I can think of that will banish the shadows and protect this light. I tackle Nico.

"Thank you," I say as I cover his face with kisses. "Thank you *so* much. This is crazy. *You're* crazy."

He laughs, the bright sound bouncing around the high ceilings, and I nuzzle into his neck, eager for the light he exudes to permeate through me.

"It's done, all right? I had some cash from selling my truck. It's fine."

"I'll repay you, I promise. Every cent."

He shakes his head. "No way. It's a birthday gift."

"It's too much. I have to do something to show you how grateful I am."

That sly smile reappears. "I'm sure I can think of some ways."

I set my chin on his chest, enjoying the solid feel of him. "So what's your plan today? Saturdays are laundry day, right?"

Nico lies back on the pillow and nods. "Laundry. Cleaning. Pay my bills. Shit like that since I'm usually ready to drop by the time I get home during the week. You want to meet up later for dinner?"

Reluctantly, I shake my head. "I can't. Shama should be here by tonight, and I promised her we'd hang out. Chicks before dicks, you know."

Nico pouts. "I'd ask if I could come over later, but I doubt it would be the best impression to jump off with, having your boyfriend stay over on day one, huh?"

Sadly, I nod. Shama's my friend, and we've shared an apartment before. But things are different now. She's seen me spiral away with a man, and I doubt she'd be comfortable with me jumping straight into something intense all over again, even if it is with Nico. But the thing is, I don't want him to leave. I want to sleep like this every night, wound up around each other, and I want to wake up in the morning to his bright smile. Still, that's a little too much to say to him on literally our first day back together. It's a little much for anyone.

Nico appears to have the same reluctance as he stretches out his limbs across the bed. It's not a huge mattress—just a double bed—but it's certainly better than the saggy pullout he's been sleeping on since May or the twin mattresses the college gave us in the dorms.

"*Coooooñoooo,*" he yawns, almost looking like a cat. "I'm already gonna miss this bed tonight. Shit. I need to start looking for an apartment too. I can't deal with my siblings anymore." He rubs his face. "Maggie is driving me crazy. It's the oatmeal, man. She decided last month that oatmeal is the best thing for Allie to be eating in the morning because, I don't know, it's high in iron or some shit like that. But Allie's five, so she hates it, right? And every damn morning I have to listen to the two of them squawk like chickadees about fuckin' cereal. With no damn door to shut."

I chuckle. "The apartment's feeling small, huh?"

Nico groans. "You have no idea. I got spoiled over the years with my own place. My own room."

"It doesn't seem quite fair that you get stuck with the couch," I remark. "You're the one who pays for it, right?"

Nico sighs. "Gabe's been putting in some, actually, and so has Maggie. We basically split it three ways now. I can't afford to pay for everyone anymore. Wanna know something, baby? The FDNY doesn't pay shit the first year and a half."

"Well, then there's no way you're paying for dinner every time we go out," I reply as I stroke a hand over his smooth skin.

"Nah, it's fine. I got it—"

"No." I say it gently, but firmly. "That's not what I need from you anyway."

Nico opens his mouth, then closes it. "I just want to get off the couch. Oatmeal. Too much Marc Anthony. Listening to Gabe beat it every night before he falls asleep."

"Wait, *what?*" I turn bright red. "You listen to him *what?*"

Nico grins. "I swear to God. I love my little brother, but that's all he does: study and jerk off in *my* bedroom. Do you know he talks to himself when he's doing it? He's like a cheerleader. I can hear him muttering, 'get it, *papi*, get it.'"

I'm laughing hard now. "You don't know he's doing that to get off. Maybe he's revving himself up for a test or something."

Nico gives me a look like I'm crazy. "You think I don't know when my baby brother is jacking it? Trust, I wish I didn't know what that particular groan sounds like. But we grew up sleeping next to each other, NYU. That shit is ingrained."

He contorts his features into a fake-orgasm face, and I dissolve into giggles all over again. Nico grins, clearly pleased by the response.

"You're one to talk," I tell him once I've recovered. "You look pretty tortured when you do that too."

In response, one side of his face quirks with an impish half smile. "What's the saying? 'Hurts so good'?"

He rolls over and cages me against the pillow with his arms. The sunlight makes his tan skin look awash in gold; the twisting lines of his tattoos shimmer.

"You can hurt me like that anytime you want, *mami*," he rumbles, low and suggestive before pressing his lips to mine.

We sink into the kiss together, and it's not long before I feel another part of him ready and willing between my thighs. Half of me is dying to surrender to it, open my legs and take him inside where he fits so perfectly, feels good in a way that really does border on torture. But at the same time, the word "hurt" causes me to stiffen, and Nico senses it.

"Ah," he mutters as he pushes off me. "Another time, then."

I grimace and bite my upper lip. "I'm sorry. You shouldn't have to deal with this."

"Hush. You're fine, baby." He kisses me one more time, then rolls back to his side of the bed. "Besides, I'm a patient man. Most of the time, anyway." He sits up, then pauses, looking over his shoulder. "It's not me, is it? I don't gross you out all of a sudden, do I?"

"*No,*" I insist, sitting up myself and tugging his arm until he faces me again. His handsome features are drawn with sudden doubt and vulnerability that makes my stomach drop. This is exactly what I was afraid of. "Nico, I swear to God. It's hard to explain. I want you like crazy, you know? I just...it's like when we get started, something just..."

I trail off, unable to finish the sentence as sudden tears rise. I feel defective. Like I broke something last spring, and now I'm starting to wonder if it will ever be fixed. I thought for sure that when I came back, when he touched me, it would. And truthfully, I *do* feel better when we are together—better than I've felt in so long. But there's a wall I can't quite climb yet. And I don't know how to start.

"Hey." Nico strokes my shoulder, and then his fingers float around to clasp my chin. His lips touch mine, and tenderly, he opens up another long, lingering kiss that seems to last for hours. "However I can get you, remember? That ain't ever gonna change, Layla."

His words, his patience soothes. I bury my nose into his chest, the divot between his strong pectoral muscles. The tattooed compass under my cheek thumps with his heartbeat, and I close my eyes while his hands play up and down my back. He wants to do more, I know. But for now, he seems content to just be together. Finally, we have the time to do that. It will take some time to trust. To get used to the fact that maybe, just maybe, I'm not going to lose him all over again.

I'm just about to say as much when the angry cry of the buzzer cuts through the apartment. I look up, confused, while Nico glares in the direction of the door.

"Who the fuck is that?" he growls, clearly as annoyed as I am to have the moment ruined.

I swallow and get out of bed, pulling on a pair of shorts before going out to the entry to answer.

"Who is it?"

"Layla?"

I frown and press the button again. "Yes?"

"Dude! It's Shama! Let me up!"

"Oh my God! Of course!"

I buzz her in, then scurry back to the bedroom to get dressed. Nico is already pulling on his clothes from last night, staring at his wrinkled shirt and pants with disgust. They are covered with dust left over from setting up the furniture yesterday.

"Jesus," he mutters, brushing off the black material. "I look like I spent the night in a sawmill." He looks up. "Is it too soon to ask if I can keep a change of clothes here, baby?"

The shy hope on his face makes me want to tackle him back to the bed all over, but instead, I just step up on my tiptoes and give him a quick kiss. "Of course. I'll free up a drawer for you."

He grunts, kisses me again, then goes back to fixing his clothes while I pull on a sundress. Nico looks me over with appreciation and shakes his head ruefully.

"All right," he says. "I'm gonna go, let you guys have your time. Are you free for dinner at Alba's tomorrow night? I know everyone wants to welcome you back."

Again, the thought warms. A year ago, I would have found spending the evening with Nico's family terrifying. To them, I was *la blanquita*, the rich white girl slumming it with their brother, to whom they were *very* loyal. And with good reason, since Nico has basically carried all of them on his broad shoulders his entire life.

But in the spring, something changed when Nico carried me into their apartment and put me into the care of his sister and mother, both of whom had their own stories of abuse. What Nico's family lacks in money, they more than make up for with love and community. They had taken care of me when no one else would. Shared their stories. Given me a safe space. In their own ways, his mother, brother, and sister rescued me last spring just as much as he did.

I grin. "Absolutely."

Nico grins right back. "Perfect. You wanna come to Mass too? You'd probably make my mother the happiest person on the planet. If you can deal with her and Alba planning our wedding, that is."

Immediately, a flush blooms over my face. Wedding? That

sounds like a great way to send most twenty-eight-year-olds running for the hills. But to my surprise, Nico's dark-brown eyes don't waver as he waits for my answer.

I nod. "Of course. Just let me know what time to show up."

His wide smile makes the warmth in my chest bloom throughout the rest of my body. A knock sounds at the front door, and with a kiss to Nico's cheek, I skirt through the empty living room to answer with Nico at my heels. I open it to let Shama in.

"Hey!" she cries out, practically tackling me with a hug the second I open the door.

We twist around and around while Nico pulls in her two suitcases. When she finally lets go, Shama looks at Nico curiously. "I was wondering if you two had reconnected yet. Not wasting any time, huh, FedEx?"

Nico returns from her room looking less than pleased by the nickname, giving Shama a tight smile before he kisses her on the cheek.

"How you doin', Shama?" he says, his voice low and rumbling. "You have a good summer?"

Shama nods, her dark eyes twinkling. "I did, yeah! I had an internship at this advertising company in Philadelphia, and after that, I went to Florence with my folks for a few weeks. Oh my *God*, Italian men are crazy hot. Actually, a lot of them look kinda like you, FedEx."

Shama looks Nico up and down, assessing him openly. For a second, I see what she must see: a disheveled, obviously muscled man dressed completely in black, with his arm tattoo snaking over his elbow from one sleeve. That, combined with the black stubble dusting his absurdly strong jaw and eyes that are so dark they're almost black, makes him look anything but harmless.

Nico rolls his eyes. "I think that's my cue." He lands a brief kiss on my cheek. "See you tomorrow, beautiful."

When the door closes behind him, I turn to Shama. I already know this afternoon is going to be spent recounting the last strange twenty-four hours, and I'm not quite ready to have my mental state of mind pulled apart.

"Well," I say with a shrug. "I guess I should show you around."

"That's right," Shama says as she follows me inside. "And then... it's time to dish!"

CHAPTER SEVEN

Nico

WHEN THE THICK GREEN DOOR CLOSES BEHIND ME, I immediately want to pound my way back inside. Is that fucked up? I feel like a Neanderthal, for real. She's been back for three days, and it's a little scary how much I just want to stay with her. She's doing her best to make a new home for herself. I don't care how pathetic it makes me: I just want to be a part of it. I don't want to leave.

But it's not only that. The fear on her face last night just about killed me. It's not that she doesn't want to be close—we spent the entire night wrapped around each other like vines. But anytime things got to that point where a little bit of fury, a little bit of crazy entered into our touch, she'd pull away.

Maybe other guys would be running for the hills, but that's not an option here. Layla is my heart, my soul. My other half. I know it, and I'm pretty sure she knows it too. So really, it's taking everything I have not to go back in there and face whatever crap is going on in her head together.

I want to spend the rest of the weekend making her remember

what we are together. I want to lie there straight through the next two days until I have to be back at the academy. Call off from AJ's tonight just to hold her and touch her until I can chase that terror away whenever things get just a little too much.

She's scared. To an outsider, it might be nothing. We're just getting used to each other again, right? It's only been a few days. So, it shouldn't feel as terrible as it does that she froze the way she did, refused me the way she did.

But I know her. We've been laughing, joking, flirting all damn summer. It's been three months of foreplay, and last night, I was about ready to explode. I thought she was too. There is nothing —*nothing*—more I wanted to do last night than give it to my girl. I mean really give it to her, not just with my body, but with my whole fucking heart and soul. Here we are, finally with our chance to be together, and there's this hulking ghost between us, taunting with his shadows.

I shake my head. She's not hiding anything, is she? No, we're past that. After everything we've been through together, I know Layla just wants to move forward.

And so every thought I have keeps spiraling back to one:

Fuck that guy.

Seriously. *Fuck* that guy. Fuck that nineteen-fifties-glasses-wearing, Lurch-looking, drug-dealing, Don't-Cry-For-Me-Argentina mother*fucker* who beat up Layla last spring and turned her into a scared mouse. It's his ghost she sees. On the street. In the club. In our fuckin' bed. Yeah, that's right. *Our* bed. Because the fuck if anyone else but me is gonna end up there ever again.

I clench my fists, resisting the urge to shove one through the new plaster in the hallway. Because the thought of that guy interfering with what used to be magic every damn time makes me feel like committing murder. I take a deep breath and start jogging down the stairs. I'll run out this frustration for as long as I have to. And then, tomorrow, the next day, however long it takes, Layla and I will face it. Together.

Two hours later, I'm walking out of my boxing gym in Hell's Kitchen. It used to belong to Frank, a gristly old dude who took me in when I got out of juvie. I started fighting in detention, but it wasn't until Frank took me under his wing, gave me a job and a room to sleep in so I could stop being a burden to my mother and start helping her, and started training me to boot, that I really grew up. He died a few years ago, and I miss him like crazy. He was the closest thing to a father I ever had.

After he died, Nate, one of the fighters Frank used to train, bought the place. I was his sparring partner when he got a title match and won back in the day. You could say he's grateful. I have free access to the gym for as long as Nate owns it.

I'm out just in time to meet my mom and sister for lunch, but the workout has done nothing for my mood. After beating the shit out of a heavy bag for two hours, my fists are still balled up at my sides. Every few minutes I'm taken back to that terrible day last May, when I tore into that shitty apartment uptown and let loose the rage I've managed to beat into submission at the gym since I was eighteen. It's still simmering now, and every time I see Layla's face, I want to break out some vigilante justice on this city. Track down that asshole and do the job the police are taking their sweet fuckin' time with.

Whoa. I can practically hear K.C. sitting on my shoulder, saying *slow down, papi.* I shake my head and pull out my phone. I could use some sense talked into me right now. If anyone can calm me down, it's K.C.

"*Acho,* what the fuck? It's before noon, asshole. You know what time I got in last night? It was light outside, that's what time. *This morning,* that's what time."

Shit. Of course. I knew K.C. was spinning last night, like he does just about every Friday and Saturday. He wouldn't have gotten home until close to four or maybe even five. And if he brought home company like he usually does...

Right on cue, there's a very female voice purring in the background.

"Nah, honey, it's all good. I'll be right back. Go back to sleep. Or, you know, *don't*." Then, to me: "Hold on, man." The sounds of movement filter through the speaker as he switches rooms. "All right, *cabrón*. What the fuck is up that got you pullin' me out of my beauty sleep?"

I sigh. "I'm sorry, man. We can talk later. I'm about to get some lunch with Gabe and *las gatitas* anyway."

"Well, fuck that. I'm up now, so you better tell me why you're walkin' around Hell's Kitchen instead of holin' up with your girl this weekend. Everything okay with NYU?"

I swallow. That's the thing about best friends. They always know.

"She's..." I sigh, staring down the busy street.

K.C. just keeps talking. "I'm surprised you're even walkin' around right now. If I went as long as you without gettin' that cookie, *mano*, I'da gone full Cookie *Monster*, y'know? I'da torn that up—"

"That's enough," I bite through his words. I open my mouth to tell my friend what happened last night, but then pause. I'm not sure I want to share Layla's secrets when I'm not actually sure she has any. Right now, this is just a gut feeling. So I tell him the other truth instead: "Her roommate just arrived. They needed some space, so I went to the gym."

"Is she hot? The roommate?"

I roll my eyes. And just like that, he's distracted from the fact that I am definitely not where I should be right now. "Don't you have a girl in the other room?"

K.C. clicks his tongue suggestively a few times. "Eh. She can wait. Answer the question."

"It's just her friend Shama," I say. "Indian girl from New Jersey. I don't think you ever met her, did you?"

"Don't think so...she sounds worth meeting, though. Hot girls always run together, am I right? Maybe I need to come with you to pay NYU a visit. Make sure the apartment is safe and all."

I chuckle. "We'll see, man. I don't need you getting me in trouble with Layla's friends." Something else occurs to me. "Hey, you gonna be at your mom's tomorrow?"

I can hear K.C.'s brain churning on the other side of the phone. "Yeah, I was planning on it. You gonna bring NYU?" He doesn't ask about Shama, but that's no surprise. K.C. doesn't like to mix his, ah, personal exploits with his family.

Leaving Layla here was the worst mistake of my life. The consequences almost cost Layla her life, and she's still paying for it psychologically in some ways. I just want her back. I want *us* back. I don't have much to give a girl like her, someone who comes from money, but I do have family and friends in spades, and all of them are ready to welcome her with open arms.

For the first time this morning, I feel like I have a plan to help.

"Yeah," I say. "She's coming. I'll mention something to Alba too for Sunday. Let's make it a thing, all right? Welcome her back the right way."

I come to a stop in front of my family's old apartment building on Forty-Ninth Street, the one where my mother lived up until last year. The one where K.C. and I grew up together. The vigilante thoughts disappear as I look at the crumbling bricks that now have a demolition notice in front of them. Looks like Mr. Pineo finally sold out to a developer. It's a shithole, but for a long time, this place, the people in it, they were home. Until I met Layla. I may not be able to give her much, but I can at least give her that. Family. Home.

"All right, man," I say. "Go back to your, ah, morning. I'll see you tomorrow."

I keep walking until I get to the pizza joint where I'm meeting my siblings for lunch. Ma is taking my niece, Allie, for the afternoon, giving us some time to get together without her knowing. According to Gabe, there is some stuff to go over.

"Hey," I say as I slide into the booth my sisters and brother have staked at the end of the restaurant. "I'm starving. Did you order a pie, or do I need to get a couple slices?"

"I'm on a diet," Selena says, twirling her curly hair, which she's letting grow natural now. "I'm doing a cleanse. I can't eat anything but fruit for a week."

"So basically, you're planning to gain ten more pounds at the end, right?" Maggie retorts.

"Maggie, be nice," I say. "Sel's an adult. She can eat fruit all day if she wants to. It's just more pizza for us."

"I'm only telling the truth," Maggie says. "It happens every time she does one of those crazy diets. Lose five, gain ten. Maybe if you just ate normal, you'd lose your spare tire instead of adding to it."

"*Gata*, don't be sayin' shit like that," I cut in just as Selena starts spouting a round of expletives.

Gabe just rolls his eyes at them and purses his lips like he's whistling. His expression is bright through his smudged glasses. For a second, I smirk. My little brother has turned out to be such a damn brain—he finally had to get some specs this year. I won't tease him though. He's killing it in school, and I couldn't be prouder.

"We ordered a pie," he says, finally answering my question. "And in the meantime, maybe we can stop talking about Selena's dumb diet. This came in the mail yesterday."

Gabe drops a thin white envelope in the center of the table, and his hand shakes a little. I glance suspiciously at him, but then I see the words "U.S. Department of Treasury" printed in the return address.

"*Coño*," Selena mutters to herself while Maggie looks at me expectantly.

"Well, open it," she says. "We've been waiting since yesterday, and it's addressed to you, big brother."

A little over two months ago, the four of us were crowded with Ma in the office of Ileana Perkins, the immigration worker helping with Ma's case. Up until last spring, none of us thought there was any hope for our mom, who was born in Cuba, but immigrated illegally to Puerto Rico as a toddler. Her father drowned during the voyage, taking her documentation with him (or so she thinks). After being taken in by K.C.'s grandparents and flying with them into the country, she spent the rest of her life dodging authorities, mistakenly operating under the assumption that as a Cuban citizen without a birth certificate, she was not ever going to qualify for amnesty.

Shows what we knew. It nearly cost her life to tell us, but as Layla learned in one of her Latin American history classes last year, there were ways for us to return to Cuba to get our mother's birth certificate. Maybe it was even possible to get relief without it, but Ma was always too scared to try. And as a Cuban citizen who has been in the U.S. for a *lot* longer than two years, she would automatically qualify for permanent residency.

That said, the textbook chapter that Layla read us was a little misleading. Cuba doesn't require documentation to enter, but the U.S. government sure as fuck does, and weirdly, it's the U.S. Treasury that processes the licenses to go. That's right. It all comes back to the money. According to Ileana, money is the real reason family visitations to Cuba were cut off at the knees this past June.

"They decided that U.S. visitors were spending too much," she told us when we met her in June, literally a few weeks after a new law was passed making it even harder to go unless you had an immediate family member still living there. "Freakin' Bush and his cronies. They just want all the money to stack in their coffers, don't they, the vultures?" she spat as she helped us fill out the application for a general license for me to travel to Santiago.

I didn't know what to say. Ileana is nice, but she's definitely a type: about as liberal as you get, ready to denounce any politician she sees, and certainly no fan of the president. I'm fine with that, even though I don't really know anything about politics. Her taste for vengeance is going to help my mother get her freedom.

The pizza arrives, stacked on an elevated plate. But we don't touch it, staring at the letter in the middle of the table. I pray to God it contains what we need. I'd like to wipe that scared look off my mother's face too.

"Well, what does it say?" Maggie asks as I tear open the letter.

I scan the short paragraphs, and my shoulders drop.

"What does it say?" Gabe asks.

"Fuck," I say as I drop the letter into the middle of the table. "We're fucked."

Maggie snatches up the letter and reads it out loud:

Dear Nicolas Soltero,

This is in response to your application dated May 24, 2004, requesting authorization to engage in travel-related transactions involving Cuba for the purpose of a family visit.

The Cuban Assets Control Regulation 31 C.F.R. Part 515 (The Regulations) prohibits all persons subject to U.S. jurisdiction from dealing in property in Cuba unless the Cuban National has an interest, including all Cuba travel-related transactions for the purpose of visiting a member of a person's immediate family who is a national of Cuba.

We have reviewed your application and determined that the issuance of a specific license is inconsistent with current U.S. policy because there is no record of the family member you have listed as a Cuban national. Accordingly, your request is hereby denied.

We note that, consistent with §515.561 (a), it would be inappropriate for you to make an application with the Office of Foreign Assets Control for a specific license to visit a member of your immediate family without documentation of the relation.

Sincerely,

Ethan Farrow

Sanctions Coordinator (New York)

Office of Foreign Assets Control

———————————————————————

"What?" Selena glances around at us. "What does that mean?"

Gabe reads the letter, mouthing the words softly to himself. "Inappropriate?" he scoffs. "Who the hell are they, your homeroom teacher? Are they gonna send you to the principal's office?"

I snort. "No. They're gonna stop me from going to school in the first place." I drop my head into my hands and groan. "Fuck. *Fuck.* What are we gonna do?"

But when I look up, my sisters and brother have no answers. The pizza sits on the table, growing cold while they look to me for the next steps.

I got nothing. No ideas. *Nada.*

It's a feeling I'm really getting sick of.

CHAPTER EIGHT

Layla

"WHAT ABOUT THIS ONE?"

I turn around to look at the futon Shama's pointing at and shrug. "It's all right." I sit down and immediately scowl. "Okay, I wouldn't want to have a movie marathon on it, though. You try that."

Shama flops down on the mattress with me and shakes her head. "Don't people sell discounted furniture that's actually comfortable?"

"Maybe we should try that craigslist site instead."

"Yeah, but I don't want to get ax-murdered."

I giggle, but she has a point. We get up and start looking around the other selection of couches. We have a small allowance, supplemented by Shama's parents and my mom, that's supposed to help us furnish our living room. But I can't help but notice that my friend hasn't been that interested in picking out couches. Or unpacking her bags. Or really looking for anything.

"So...I saw Quinn and Jamie last week. We went to lunch."

I pretend to be interested in a really ugly pink sofa. "Oh, yeah?"

"Yeah. Jamie says hi."

I narrow my eyes. It doesn't escape me that Quinn didn't say anything at all. Jamie, on the other hand, has disappeared from my life, like a distant relative you keep forgetting to call back.

"For what it's worth, I do think Quinn feels bad about everything," Shama remarks as we both flop down onto a very brown couch. "This one is comfortable."

"This one looks like a cow pie," I reply, making Shama laugh. "And that's great that she feels bad. But I still think it's better if we're not friends. I miss J. I miss our group, actually. But the more I think about it, the more I realize that maybe it wasn't good for me to be around Quinn."

Last spring wasn't just about extracting myself from one toxic relationship—it was about getting out of all of them. With her constant belittling and negativity, Quinn definitely qualified as toxic. I need people in my life who can be supportive and constructive. People who don't have to cut down others to feel good about themselves.

"I just hate that it puts you in a weird position," I say. "Jamie sort of peaced out over the summer and ended up taking Quinn's side. I think when she really saw how bad things were, it freaked her out."

Shama nods. "Well, it was pretty crazy to walk in on you like that. But it's not like it was your fault. I think Jamie at least knows that." She sighs. "I remember when I was going through everything with Jason..."

"I'm sorry I wasn't there for you more," I say. I squeeze her wrist, and Shama gives me a sad smile.

"Yeah, well. You had your own stuff going on."

"Quinn and Jamie were there?"

She shrugs. "Jamie was. Mostly. Quinn, you know how she is. She had a lot to say about it. Mostly criticizing why I let him come back so many times."

I nod. "Yeah, I do know how she gets like that."

"Yeah. Well. One day they are going to have hard shit to deal with too. They think they're above it, but they're not. You and I are just early bloomers."

We collapse together, giggling, even though the casual mention of her heartbreak cuts me through again. I really wasn't there for her the way I should have been. I've been a pretty awful friend.

"What about Romeo?" Shama asks. "He's been around a lot? You guys pretty much back to normal?"

I shift uncomfortably, and Shama raises a black brow.

"Dish," she says. "What's going on?"

"Nothing," I say lamely. "I just got back. Everything is fine."

"You're such a terrible liar, Lay. What is it?"

I give a heavy sigh. "It's not him. It's me. I'm...I'm still so messed up, Shams."

"What do you mean?"

I pull absently at my hair. "It's weird. We started hooking up. And it's like it always was, you know? That crazy chemistry."

Shama smiles dreamily. "Yeah, you guys always had that going for you. Damn, if I could get a guy to look at me the way he looks at you, I don't think I'd ever be walking."

I giggle. "That's how I usually feel. I met up with him last night at AJ's, and dude, we couldn't stop. I practically chased him into an employees' bathroom."

"Sounds good so far," Shama says.

I nod. "It was. In the beginning." That familiar chill hits. "But then...we almost got to the end, and he lost it, slammed his hand into the wall. And it...it freaked me out a little, that's all."

"Just the one time?"

I sigh. "I...no. The rest of the night, it was like, we'd get to a certain point, and he'd start to get, you know, really, um, passionate."

"Like, toss you against a wall and screw your brains out?"

Sometimes I really think my friend is psychic. I sigh. "Well, yeah."

"Good. You gotta put those muscles to good use, right?"

I smile to myself. "He's good at...letting go."

Shama leers. "Oh, I know. I shared an apartment with you before, remember? Lafayette had reeeeeally thin walls, my friend."

I blush. "Are you serious?"

She nudges me in the shoulder. "Please. You never cared. We had headphones."

I'm surprised by how un-embarrassed I actually am. But that really was how Nico and I were with each other. Anytime. Anyplace.

"So, what's the problem?"

"I freeze." I stare at my hands, now clasped in my lap. "One second he's making me lose my mind, like he always does. And the next, I'm a scared rabbit, in full-on flight mode. I just want to stop."

"And *does he?*" Shama's tone sharpens significantly.

"Oh, of course. It's not like this has happened a ton, Shams. I just got here a few days ago. But it's...I wasn't expecting it to be like this. And I don't know what to do."

Shama sighs, then slings a thin arm around my shoulder and pulls me close. I lay my head on her shoulder and sigh.

"I hate it," I admit. "I thought we would be good. All summer, it was hot phone sex and sweet conversations. He loves me so much, Shams, and I just want to make him happy. He doesn't deserve this, having a freaking basket case for a girlfriend."

Shama rubs my back for a minute, letting me get past my thoughts. "Layla, you went through hell last year. And then you had to go to Pasadena for three months, which is basically the seventh circle, right?"

I snort. Pasadena, boring and suburban, isn't my cup of tea, but it wasn't that bad. I filled my time with therapy, volunteering at the YWCA, and taking Spanish and Portuguese classes. It could have been a lot worse.

"You just need time, dude. And if he loves you like you say, he'll give you that."

I nod. "He will. He's the best. I just want to make sure he gets what he needs too."

"Correct me if I'm wrong, Lay, but I'm pretty sure Special Delivery just needs you. He never really seemed to care how."

I cringe. "Let's *not* keep that terrible name going, shall we? Quinn made that up, and he really, really hates it. Not to mention she's not his favorite person either."

Shama chuckles. "Fair enough." Then she sighs. "I have to tell you something, Lay."

I twist my body to look at her. I had a feeling something was coming. Time to be a good friend back. "What's up?"

"I feel really freaking bad about this. But...okay. I applied to do this study abroad thing through Oxford last spring."

"What? Shams, that's so cool! What a great thing to do!"

"Yeah, I thought so." She brightens a little, considering it. "My dad went there, you know. When he left India, he originally went through Oxford to do his degree, and then he came to the U.S. to do his Ph.D. stuff."

I listen curiously. I've met Shama's parents a few times, but they are pretty private people. I know they emigrated from India before Shama and her older brother were born and then settled in New Jersey after her dad finished his graduate work at MIT. He works for some kind of engineering firm in New Jersey, and her mom stays home.

"Anyway," she continues. "I never heard back, so I didn't think I was accepted. But last week, I got a call. A spot opened up in the program, and..." She trailed off, looking at me with her big eyes. "Look, I don't want to leave you in the lurch. I know you need a roommate, so I'll pay the rent for as long as you need. But, Lay...I just really need to do this. I feel like I need to get out of the city. Away from Jersey, New York. All of it. See what else is out there."

I'm quiet for a second, processing the news. Shama watches me nervously.

"Are you mad?" she finally asks. "I know it wasn't supposed to be this way. Are we done? Am I written out?"

"Shama..." I shake my head and turn to her with a smile. It's hard. I had expected to get through this year with my friend, and I can already feel the loneliness threatening again. But I manage it, because I know this is what she wants, and when I think about it, I'm actually really happy for her.

"Shams, of course I'm not mad," I tell her. "This is so great for you. You must be psyched."

Relief floods her face. For the first time, I can really see her fatigue. Last year wasn't an easy year for her either, what with her boyfriend cheating on her. Shama dealt with her heartbreak much more quietly than I did, and managed to help me with mine too. She spent most of her summer working, not really dealing with the stuff that happened. She deserves, more than anyone, the change of pace she so obviously craves.

I give her a giant hug, ignoring the fear at the idea of being alone in that apartment. "I'm super freaking happy for you."

She grins, a bright smile that lights up the room. "Thanks, dude. I'm actually crazy excited. I have to leave on Monday to get there in time for classes to start. But, you know, holy shit! I'm moving to England!"

We hug again. But another question pops into my head. "Why are you looking for a couch with me if you aren't going to stay?"

Shama snorts. "I like shopping. Plus, I couldn't let you do it by yourself."

We sit there for a moment, a lull falling between us. We're both thinking the same thing. I'll be in an apartment alone, at least for the time it takes to find a new roommate. Alone, and with a tendency toward breakdowns.

But Shama sees me as alone in this city without her. I realize it's not quite true.

"Hold on," I say as I pull out my phone. "I have an idea." A few rings later, and Nico's deep voice echoes down the line. "Hey. Do you think Alba would be okay with another at dinner tomorrow? I was thinking maybe Shama could come too."

There's a pause. And for a minute, I think he's going to say no.

But after another beat, his deep voice rumbles, speaking to a place deep inside me, like a match that's lit to start a fire.

"Sure, baby," he says. "Anything you want."

I grin. "That's not necessary. Just tell us what to bring."

CHAPTER NINE

Nico

At six o'clock the next day, I find myself escorting not one, but two girls up to Alba's apartment. Ever since she moved into the classy west-side high-rise courtesy of the dough K.C. started raking in a few years back, K.C.'s mom loves to host just about anything. Parties, dinners, backgammon nights, whatever. It's from her that K.C. gets his party skills. He's just as social as she is.

She also knows exactly what Layla did to help my family, and once she heard that Ma wanted to get everyone together to welcome her back, she insisted on hosting there instead of at our railroad apartment uptown.

"So, your friend," Shama says as we enter the lobby. "He, um, does all right, huh?"

The doorman gives me a quick nod. He sees me enough that I don't get any suspicious looks. Shama looks around, her eyes growing big. I smirk. After she saw my place up by City College, I bet this is the last place she expected me or mine to be.

Layla elbows Shama in the side, and she immediately grimaces. "Sorry. I sound like a total bitch, don't I?"

I shrug, staring at the elevator buttons. "Hey, no worries."

When we get to Alba's floor, the sounds of my family laughing filters all the way down the hall. When we enter the apartment, Layla and Shama take in the decent-sized living room, the picture windows, and the simple furniture. It's a nice apartment, but it's nothing crazy. Alba has a knack for making it feel homey.

Layla looks around curiously. "It looks different when there isn't a giant party in here."

I nod. "Alba always moves all the furniture into the back room when she does her holiday stuff."

As soon as everyone sees us, they're up from the table to greet Layla. I watch happily as my sisters, my brother, and even my mom all take turns giving her bear hugs and kisses to the cheek. Layla's blue eyes shine and her cheeks flush as she returns every one of them. Having met her mom, I get how different this is from what she grew up with. Cheryl is nice, but stiff, and even with her daughter she keeps her distance. Mine, on the other hand, has absolutely no concept of space.

"Dang," Shama murmurs beside me. "Your family really loves her, huh?"

I grin. I didn't realize how much this meant to me until right now. "Yeah. They really do."

"What's up, *mano*? Who's your friend?"

K.C. pops up after he's done giving Layla kisses like everyone else does, even though they've only met a few times. It's just what you do. She's already being dragging into the living room to play dolls with Allie and chat with my sisters. I open my mouth to introduce Shama, but she takes care of that for me.

"His *friend* is right here. And her name is Shama."

K.C. darts a suspicious look at me, but I just shove my hands in my pockets and pretend the pigeon on the balcony is the most interesting thing I've ever seen. I purse my lips, sucking back a laugh, but behind K.C., Gabe doesn't bother hiding his.

"She told you!" he crows, through several bouts of laughter. "Damn." He extends a hand to Shama around K.C.'s glowering form. "How you doin', Shama?"

"Hey, good to see you." Shama accepts Gabe's awkward kiss to her cheek. His hand lingers a little too long on her waist. When Shama's eyes bug at me a little bit, I choke on another laugh, though she continues to look suspicious.

"*I'm* KC." My friend recovers his shock and gives his trademark smile. It's funny, with his thin frame and ghost-like skin, K.C. isn't what you would call a stereotypically handsome man, but somehow he makes up for it with swagger.

When Shama takes his hand with a snort, he kisses her cheek, dodging a little with her first. "You'll want to remember that name, pretty."

"Man, shut up." I elbow him in the ribs. "She's not here to get picked up."

"I can handle myself, thanks," Shama says. "If you'll excuse me... I'm sorry, what's your name again? Kaylen?"

Gabe breaks into another round of hyena-like laughter, and I can't help but join him as K.C. steps back, glowering. Shama skips neatly around him to join the girls on the couches.

"Don't feel too bad, man," I say as I rub K.C.'s shoulder. "It's broad daylight. We know the real K.C. magic happens at night."

"Damn right," he mutters. "Whatever. I'm ready to eat. We've been waiting for you for*ever*."

———

Layla

Dinner is good. And when I say good, I mean amazing. Alba, K.C.'s mom, really likes to pull out all the stops, and she and

Carmen filled the table with about ten different kinds of Puerto Rican food, including a mashed plantain dish called *mofongo*, which I discover is Nico's favorite after he eats close to half of it. Carmen's wink and nod tells me she'll pass on the recipe at some point. I don't know, though. I'm not much of a cook, and I'd be kind of upset it he didn't devour my version the same way he does his mom's.

But the best part of the evening, other than being surrounded by this family that, for all of their difficult history, is incredibly close, is seeing Nico in his element, including with his best friend.

For most of the time I've known Nico, K.C. has lived in LA, pursuing his growing career in music. I knew he had done well for himself. Just the fact that he can afford this place for his mother, not to mention the beautiful brownstone he has in Hoboken, tells me that. He's not a billionaire or anything, but his job pays well, and considering the way he shares his fortune with the people around him, I like K.C. already. Generosity is something he and Nico have in common. Honestly, it's something both of their families share, through and through.

It's so different from my family, people who have everything but who, for most of my life, maintained their wealth with iron fists.

After dinner, which is loud, boisterous, and consists mostly of Allie doing imitations of Elmo, K.C. flirting with Shama while his mother smacks his wrist, and Selena and Maggie bickering, everyone helps clean up, and then the boys collapse on the couch to watch the last of the Yankees game while the girls sit back at the table to enjoy coffee and gossip. Alba and Carmen speak in rapid Spanish that I can't understand very well, but Selena and Maggie have stopped translating, piping up every now and then in English or Spanglish here and there.

"Hey, you okay?"

I look up from washing dishes in the kitchen. At some point, I drifted away from the table when Selena and Maggie started debating whether or not Selena could *really* be confused for a young

J.Lo. Maggie's position on the matter was firmly in the negative, and it was not being received very well.

Shama hands me a plate. I glance behind her to where Alba and Carmen are chattering as they stow the leftovers, then back to Shama. I turn back to the sink and shrug.

"I'm fine," I tell her. "This is great."

I should feel happier than I do. I'm in Alba's beautiful apartment with its view of Midtown. I'm surrounded by people who care about me, people who took me in last spring when I needed it the most. Nico's family and I still don't know each other very well, but we all have a connection. I'm a part of that now, both because of what they did for me, and what I did for them too.

But I don't miss their concerned glances every so often. I don't miss the way Maggie, Nico's sister, floated her gaze over my neck and cheeks, where, three months ago, she applied makeup thick enough to hide the nasty bruises. I don't miss Gabe's featherlight touch on my shoulders, or the way Selena scooted away from me at the table now and then, reacting to my every movement like I was about to break.

But then again...aren't I? Sometimes I still feel it. It's why I'm in here instead of the living room with the rest of the younger people. Through the kitchen door, we can hear them all playing some kind of game.

"You should go back in there," I tell Shama. "I'm almost done."

She shakes her head in faux horror. "It...was getting a little awkward. K.C. and Gabe kept taking each other's seats next to me. K.C. wouldn't stop calling me pretty, and Gabe kept trying to slide his arm around my shoulders while he yawned, Grease-style. Then they brought out Twister, so I was done."

Another round of laughter and a few unintelligible Spanish phrases bounce through the room. I smirk. "Awww, who's the prettiest girl at the party, Shams?"

I'm rewarded with a giant eye roll. "Shut up. Gabe is about fourteen, and K.C., well..." She looks behind her to see if Alba's within earshot. She and Carmen have gone out to the living room. Shama turns back to me. "Let's just say that I've been there, done that, you know?"

I set a casserole pan in the dish rack and start on a handful of forks. "Gabe's only a year younger than us, Shams. And come on, K.C. is nothing like Jason."

"They're both DJs. It's a solid start."

"That's like comparing a Big Mac and a steak. K.C. gets to travel the world to do what he does. He bought his mom this apartment, and his place in Hoboken is super nice too. Jason plays shitty college bars."

Shama pulls a hand through her long black hair and gives me a grim smile. "Can you really tell me he's not the womanizing type? I feel like I have to walk out of a room backward if I don't want him to wolf-whistle me."

I open my mouth to argue on K.C.'s behalf, even though I don't really know him that well. He's a person I know more from Nico—the surrogate brother he grew up with, one who features heavily in his stories. The guy I know has given Nico places to stay, helped him find jobs when he needed them, basically just given him the best support he's had in his life. For that reason alone, I like him.

But then I'm taken back to the first night Nico and I were together. Nico was housesitting and took me to K.C.'s apartment. During a tour of the place, we ended up in the master bedroom, with its cheesy, all-white decor except for a giant splattered painting of a man biting a woman's nipple. It was the opposite of subtle. For a room that screamed sex like that, there wasn't a drop of intimacy in it. As badly as I wanted to be intimate with Nico at the time, I had absolutely no desire to do it in that room or anywhere near the white canopy bed. I wasn't about to become another notch on that particular bedpost.

"Fair enough," I say, even though the memory of what happened later that night does cause a tingle between my thighs. Nico's hungry lips. His hands, urgent and slightly rough. His slap on my thigh, the flip of my body. From the living room, I hear Nico's deep voice joking with his brother and his friend. The tingle heightens.

I scrub a little harder than necessary at a couple of knives. Other than our moment in the club, it really has been a long time, and even longer since I had the kind of sex that used to make me ache for someone like this. The thought makes me swallow, hard, just before another cloud of dread settles over me.

Will I ever be able to get there again?

"Anyway, I have to get going," Shama says.

I look up. "What? Why? I'm pretty sure Alba still has flan or something like that."

Shama gives me a tight smile. "I, um, said I'd meet up with some people."

I frown at first at her oblique references. Then it hits me. "You're meeting up with Quinn and Jamie."

Shama sighs. "Well..."

I turn back to the dishes. "It's fine. Tell Jamie I said hi."

"Lay..."

I stop washing. "It's okay, really. Have fun. I'll see you later. Or, depending on how good your night is, tomorrow." I plaster on the widest grin I can manage until finally, Shama starts laughing.

"You're a terrible liar," she says. "And you look like a zombie when you smile like that. But I love you anyway. Have fun tonight. And give your man some. He's starting to look like he's going to shrivel up from blue balls."

I nod, but turn back to the sink, ignoring the clench in my stomach at her words. She doesn't need to know just how much it hurts that I can't give someone I love what he wants. What he probably needs.

———

Nico

"She seems sad," Maggie remarks after Shama says her goodbyes.

K.C. tries to escort her to the elevators, but I have to laugh when Shama practically shoves him back into the apartment. I haven't seen my boy work that hard for a girl's attention in a very long time.

"Who, Shama?" I ask. "Why?"

"No, you fool. Your girl. The one playing Cinderella in the kitchen."

I follow her gaze to where Layla's doggedly scrubbing a pan. She's cleaned almost the entire damn kitchen. Since she started, Ma and Alba have disappeared into the bedroom to look at some hand-me-downs, and we just switched the Yankees game back on after Allie cleaned the floor with her uncles and aunties at Twister. Seriously, who knew a five-year-old could be that flexible?

I twist my lips guiltily. "I think she just wanted a second alone, Mags. We can be a little much, don't you think?"

I nod to where Gabe and K.C. are busy punching each other in the shoulders, like they're actual brothers instead of surrogate ones. Selena is lying facedown on the floor while Allie braids her hair. No one has even started putting away the mess of games that are out.

Maggie doesn't say anything. She knows what I mean.

"She's not quite herself yet," I admit quietly, folding my hands together.

"I can see that," Maggie replies. "She was really different at Thanksgiving last year. Sad then too, but in a different way."

K.C. and Gabe shout something at the screen, but I'm not even watching anymore. It was right here in this room, filled at the time with family and friends celebrating the holiday, that Layla let me teach her salsa in front of all of those people. Then she cried in my arms on the balcony. Then let me hold her for hours. Back then she was mourning the loss of her family, but not the loss of her innocence. She wasn't completely broken. Not yet.

I have to close my eyes while anger punches its way up and then recedes. I hate that she's like this—one minute sunshine, the next a rain cloud. I hate that there's nothing I can do to help. I want to make her happy, connect with the one person on this planet I'm supposed to be with. She needs time, more time to heal, but it's so fucking hard when she has to hold me at arm's length to do it, and all I want to do is come close.

"You know what helped me the most?"

I look at my sister, whose face has been marred like Layla's, also by a man who was supposed to love her. Maggie was pretty once. When she was younger, she was one of those girls who would laugh louder than everyone else. Her moods were always a little crazy, but when she smiled, so would everyone else. Now she's as stoic and hardened as ever. It's a look I understand. Everyone from my neighborhood looks like that sometimes. It's a look of self-defense, one that knows better than to be vulnerable, because that's how you get hurt.

But it's also a look I never, ever wanted to see on Layla. At some point, the numbness she has is going to turn into that hardness. And it's going to kill me.

"What's that?" I ask.

"Do you remember showing me how to throw a punch after... what happened with Jimmy?"

I squint. I remember showing Jimmy what *I* could do with my fists, but not much more than that. I was too angry to think about what I was doing. "Sort of. I took you to Frank's."

Maggie nods. "Yeah. You showed me how to use my legs and make a fist that wouldn't break my thumb when I hit someone. We did it for maybe an hour? I don't know."

"Yeah, yeah. I remember that now."

"Well, it helped," Maggie continues. "The next time I saw Jimmy, I clocked him in his stupid face. He never saw it coming. And I think *that's* why he never did it again neither. Not just because he knew you would fuck him up. But because he knew maybe I could too."

I almost choke on my water, imagining Maggie, who's maybe five foot three with heels, coming at her ex, a guy at least as tall as me, with a balled-up fist. "*Mana*, you never told me that."

She shrugs. "Broke his nose too. We got into some fights after that, but Jimmy always knew he would get as good as he gave. He never hit me again."

I look at her for a long time, but she keeps her gaze on Allie. My siblings are a lot stronger than they seem. It's easy to look at Maggie and see someone who kept going back to a man who mistreated her, just like our mom did. It's easy to think that she was weak, even though she was also doing it to keep a family for her daughter. In the end, she got them both out when they came to live with me for good. That alone took more strength than I give her credit for.

I forget sometimes that I'm not the only one who grew up fast in our house. That they don't need me to take care of them the way they used to.

"My two cents: give her something to hit," Maggie says. "See the way she's scrubbing that pan in there? She's not just sad, Nico. She's angry. And right now, she has nowhere to put it."

We both watch Layla in the kitchen, the way her small shoulders tense as she goes to fucking town on the pan. Maggie's right. Layla"s wielding the sponge like a weapon, and her rose-petal mouth is twisted together, her forehead bunched.

It's a look I know well. Really, really well. Anger and me, we got a long history together. And for once, that history makes me happy. Because as I watch my girl take out her frustrations on the dirty dishes, I finally feel like I might have a way to help her.

CHAPTER TEN

Nico

"Where are we going?" Layla wonders when I steer her across Tenth Avenue instead of back toward the train.

It's dark outside now, and a few blocks away, the bars around the heart of Hell's Kitchen echo through the streets, even though it's a Sunday. I sling an arm around Layla's shoulder, trying to ignore the way she tenses slightly before melting into my side. I bury my nose in her hair and inhale her flowery scent. I don't know what goes into her shampoo, but it's addictive.

"I want to try something with you, baby," I say. "Do you trust me?"

Her blue eyes dart up at me suspiciously, but she nods. "Yes. I do."

I guide her toward the unlit end of the street, then up Eleventh, past some new nightclubs that have taken the place of the old, empty warehouses that used to be here when I was a kid. But the next corner is the same as it used to be. Still darkened, without the benefit of a streetlight. An old concrete building with crumbling sides. It's the first place I ever lived without my family, other than juvie. The first place anyone ever gave me a chance to be something more.

"Come on," I say as I push on the scratched glass door. "I want to show you something."

I hold her hand tightly as we walk into the gym. Even though Frank died a few years back, Nate's kept it pretty much the same. Still three rings, one after another. Still a row of heavy bags hanging from creaky chains on the back wall. Still a bunch of training equipment on the right side, bathrooms to the back. And beyond that, the storage room where I used to sleep. I wonder if it still has the cot, ready for some other poor kid to get his chance.

"What the fuck. Nico motherfuckin' Soltero. How did we get so blessed to see you twice in one weekend?"

I turn around as Nate jogs over from the front ring. At this time of night, barely anyone is here. Only the hardcore boxers, the ones who aren't pro yet, but want to get there. Nate still competes, but it looks like he's on his own tonight. Even his trainer is gone.

"Hey, man," I say after we slap hands. "This is my girl, Layla."

"Oh! NYU, huh? I've heard a lot about you." Nate extends a quick, sweaty handshake, and Layla, still a little shy, accepts and murmurs a quiet greeting back.

"Can we get on the back ring for a bit?" I ask. "I want to show Layla some stuff."

Nate nods. "All yours, man."

He flickers a kind smile over Layla. I do my best to ignore the way it skims over her curves, which are fully on display in a pair of leggings and her t-shirt. I know I can't help the way men look at her. And Nate's good people. I've known him for almost ten years, back when Frank was training me and let me be Nate's sparring partner. I might as well ask him to poke out his eyes than not notice my girl. But it doesn't mean I like it.

I lead Layla to the back of the gym, past the last few fighters still here. We take off our shoes, and then I hold up a rope to let her in. She steps onto the padded blue surface. I jog to the storage room and return with some equipment: a spare set of wraps, gloves, and some punch mitts. I approach Layla and turn her to face me.

"Hold your fingers out, sweetie."

I turn her palm up so I can weave the long strips of fabric around her knuckles, through her slim fingers, around her wrist, and back up. The repetitive movements are kind of hypnotic. When it's done on one side, I switch to the other. She watches silently as I do the same to my own hands, then put the gloves on. She still hasn't asked me what we're doing here, a fact that kind of kills me. The Layla I know would be questioning every damn thing. Not in a critical way. She was curious. Naive, maybe. But never afraid to ask.

"These are a little big," I say quietly as I pull the Velcro tight around her wrists. "They'll work for today, but we should get you some in your size."

When I'm done, I look her over. With the massive boxing gloves hanging off her thin arms and her eyes all big and wary, she looks like a cartoon bunny. A scared, beautiful cartoon bunny.

So what does that make me? The big bad wolf?

"All right," I say as I grab the mitts and slide them over my hands. "First up, let's fix your stance. You want to be on the balls of your feet, and hold your body at an angle, with one foot just ahead of the other. Good, good."

I adjust her a little bit, then mimic the stance back. I bounce back and forth between my feet, and she automatically starts to do the same.

"Okay, so, rule number one is: protect your face. Frank—that was my old trainer—used to tape my left hand to my neck so I wouldn't let it down. That's how important it is. Here's where you want to put your hands."

I hold the mitts up around my face, and Layla mimics me awkwardly, clenching her lower lip with her teeth as she practices. She's so damn adorable, I almost bat the gloves out of the way so I can kiss her, but hold off. There will be time for that, and maybe more if this works the way I hope.

"All right, baby. Let's start with a jab. Turn your wrist like this. Then, real fast, just tap the mitt with your knuckles, and pull them back to your original position. Try it."

I hold up the mitts, ready to take her punch. Looking uncertain, Layla looks at the pieces of foam. Then, she offers a weak punch with her right glove. It's...pathetic.

"NYU, come on now. I know you can give better than that."

Layla's not a boxer, but she's no slouch after playing soccer for as long as she did. I've had her legs wrapped around me enough times to know exactly what kind of muscle she's got going on down there. It's firm, but just soft enough so that when you get a really good handful...

I shake my head. Stop it, you asshole. This is not the time to be thinking about that.

She frowns. "I don't like it when you call me that, you know."

"What? NYU?"

She nods. "It makes me sound like a spoiled princess."

I cock my head. "Well, then, maybe you should stop acting like you're afraid to break a nail."

She scowls harder. "I don't want to hurt you."

I stifle a laugh and drop the mitts. "Baby, you're not going to hurt me. You wouldn't be able to do it even if I didn't have these things on, I promise."

She still looks doubtful. I sigh, then take a chance. Maybe another strategy will work.

"Yo, Nate!" I call out. "You got a second, man?"

From one of the heavy bags, Nate lopes over to the ring. "What's up?"

"You mind showing my girl a quick combo? I want her to see what it looks like when it's done right."

Nate shrugs, then steps into the ring. He's covered with sweat, and I try not to notice the way Layla's eyes bug out a little while he starts throwing punches at the mitts. We run through a few basic combinations, ones we've been doing to warm up with each other for years. He's a lot better than me now, of course, but until I left for LA, we'd still get in the ring here and there.

Layla watches, transfixed, and she mimics the movements slightly with her gloves. It's adorable, even though I don't love the way her eyes catch on Nate's muscles. It's distracting enough that at one point, he pushes past the mitt and lands a soft cross on my chin, waking me from my daze.

"You're getting soft, Soltero." He chuckles with a wink at Layla. "You getting love handles too?"

Without another thought, I tear off my shirt and toss it in the corner. Nate's cut, sure, but I'm not exactly a doughboy over here. That's what a summer at the academy, heaving fuckin' tractor tires and running incessant laps around Randall's Island, will do for you.

"My turn," I say, tugging off the mitts and hurling them at him.

Nate laughs while he puts them on. He knows exactly how to push my buttons. I turn to Layla for her gloves, and enjoy the way her tongue slips out of the side of her mouth a little while she watches me put them on. That's right, baby. Now who's got drool-worthy abs, huh? I remind myself to keep my sit-up regimen going no matter what. If it'll make her look at me like that, I'll do planks until I'm eighty.

"No wraps?" Nate asks when I turn around. "You're looking to break a knuckle."

"Fuck you," I shoot back. "Okay, baby, this is what you want to do. Ignore this joker's shitty form. That's why he got knocked out in his last fight."

"Oh, you just *had* to go there, didn't you?" Nate shakes his head. "All right, pretty boy. This ain't the heavy bag like yesterday. Let's see if you remember how to do this for real, huh?"

I whip through a bunch of punches and combination moves, much more complex than the ones Nate was doing. He blocks them like the pro he is, but I can see his muscles straining with the effort to keep up.

It feels good. I'm out of practice, having done barely anything in the gym since starting the academy. My muscles strain, even though they've been working hard in other ways all summer. After just a few minutes, I'm drenched in sweat and breathing hard.

"Last three, two, *one*," Nate calls before I smack the mitts one last time with a loud pop that tosses Nate back a few steps.

I step away, breathing hard and wiping sweat off my forehead.

"Fuckin' waste," Nate says, shaking his head as he pulls the mitts off and tosses them into the corner. "Why you never went pro, I'll never know." He mops his head with the towel he brought in, then steps out of the ring. "Don't let him push you around, beautiful. Just clock him in the kidney, and you'll bring him to his knees."

And before I can toss him another for calling my girl beautiful, Nate skips back to the other side of the gym to continue his regimen, laughing all the way. I turn back to Layla, unsure of what I'm going to find as I take off my gloves. I just wanted to show her the moves, show her she could do it, but I ended up showing off a little instead. I just wanted her to stop looking at me like she's scared.

Well, mission fuckin' accomplished. Except now the way that Layla's staring at me with her mouth open, a wrapped hand at her heart, does absolutely nothing to stop a whole bunch of energy straight to my dick.

"Holy shit," she breathes. "Nico, that was...incredible. I didn't know you could move like that."

I bite back a grin as I towel off my face. "It was just a little warm-up."

She shakes her head, her blue eyes dark and heavy as they drift over my body. "I, um...I don't think I could ever do that."

I finish mopping off my chest and arms, then toss the towel on the mat and grab the mitts. "Sure you can. I just wanted you to see that you can give it whatever you got, baby. I can take it, okay? Let it go."

It takes her a bit, but soon she starts hitting the mitts with a satisfying pop every time. I guide her through some of the other basic punches—cross, hook, uppercut—until she can do them on command. Layla's a natural athlete. She picks up the moves quickly, and it's not until Nate comes back and slaps the mat that I realize just how long we've been going at it.

"Hey," he says before leaving. "I'm done for the night. Lock up when you're finished, all right? You still have your key?"

"Yeah. Thanks, man." I turn back to Layla, who's breathing hard.

Her t-shirt clings a little to her stomach, more than a simple white t-shirt should. She's red in the cheeks, and tiny tendrils of hair stick to her forehead and neck. She looks crazy fuckin' beautiful. And also tired.

"You want to go?" I ask.

She inhales heavily, but shakes her head. "No-no. I'm...can we keep going a little while longer?"

I'm tired. She's tired. We've been at this for over two hours, and my stomach has been growling at me for half that time, having already burned through the three servings of *mofongo* I had at Alba's. But the look on Layla's face—a look of pure determination—is worth every rumble.

I nod and hold up the mitts. "Let's go, baby."

———

Layla

It must be close to midnight when I finally can't throw another punch. I don't know why I wanted to keep going like I did. It was seriously addictive. Every time my fist hit the weird foam blocker, it was like I was punching through the haze of doubt, anxiety, worry, fear that always seems to hug me close. The heaviness of the last year starts to break down. Pop! There went last week. Pop! The week before.

"Oh, God," I groan as I flop backward onto the mat.

Nico collapses next to me. Allowing me to remain still, he gently removes my gloves, then the hand wraps. My knuckles are going to be black and blue in the morning. I couldn't care less. I haven't felt this exhausted, this sated, in, well, years.

No, since the last time Nico and I slept together. It was after Thanksgiving, when he'd made me feel more adored than I'd ever been in my life, and then taken me back to my apartment and demonstrated every bit of that devotion all over my body. I try and fail to ignore the lines of sweat dripping down Nico's naked torso. His muscles ripple as he sits up to toss the wraps and gloves into the corner, and when he twists back to me, he pauses.

"What?" he asks. "What are you looking at?"

I sit up, and then, on a naughty impulse, I do something I've been wanting to do for the last fifteen minutes. I lick him. On the shoulder. Around the dip of his triceps and up to where I nip at the curve of his deltoid.

"What the..." He looks at his shoulder, then back at me, his dark eyes dancing. "You nasty, NYU." This time, there's not a hint of resentment in the name. It's a tease, a taunt. Playful.

So I do it again, this time on his neck, then tracing my tongue around the other side of his jaw. The taste is salty, and his skin is warm. It's divine.

"Layla." His voice is low as I suck a little on that right-angled corner of his jaw.

"You taste good," I whisper against his cheek. "I want to..." I look down his body, the way it glistens from our workout, and I linger on the two, muscled ridges that disappear under the waistband of his pants

I bite my lip and look back up. Tiny lines have erupted over his forehead. He looks like he's almost in pain.

"I want to taste you," I say as I reach out and slide my hand across the zipper of his jeans. "Here."

His body lurches slightly as I unzip his pants and reach under his boxers to take him firmly in my hand. My breath hitches right along with his. He's so hard. So ready for me. And I've barely even touched him.

"Are you—" He gulps. "Are you serious?"

"Nico?"

"Yeah?"

"Take off your damn pants so I can give you a blow job you'll never forget, okay?"

If he'd been eating anything, he'd have choked on it right then. But then another wide grin spreads on his handsome face.

"Fair's fair," he says with a smirk. "Take yours off too, baby. Spread those beautiful legs for me."

I balk, even though I'm already shimmying out of my leggings. "You want to...do that...right here?"

Nico tips his head back and laughs, a booming, joyful sound that ricochets off the high metal pipes hanging from the ceiling.

"Baby," he says in between wheezes. "You just offered to suck my cock in the middle of the gym. What does it matter if I'm eating your pussy at the same time? *Now* you wanna be coy?"

My mouth drops. He's been so gentle, so cautious with me. All summer. When he got back. And now he's talking like a dirty magazine and I...love it. Should I love it? What does that say about me?

"Hey. *Mami.*" His deep, curt voice pulls me out of my spiral. He raises one black brow. "I didn't say no, did I?"

I open my mouth, then close it. Then I grin. "No. You didn't."

One side of Nico's full mouth pulls wide in that sly half smile I love. "Then lie back down, baby. And spread your legs. Don't make me ask again."

Slowly, I do as I'm told. I lie down on my side, curled inward with my knees together. Nico reclines on his side and kisses my ankles, up my legs, tracing his soft lips over my thighs until he reaches my underwear.

"We're not going to need these," he says as he tugs them off and tosses them across the ring.

He presses a hand between my thighs, nudging them apart again. His tongue slips out and licks the sensitive skin on either side, his tongue flickering between that slight gap. I shudder.

"I said"—Nico wrenches my legs apart—"spread 'em."

And before I can answer, he dives between my thighs, his warm, urgent mouth immediately finding my clit. With closed eyes, I lounge on the floor, opening more as I grind into his mouth—oh, that magical mouth. He hums a little while he licks, sucks, even bites lightly, both of his hands palming the backs of my legs and kneading every so often.

My eyes fly open as his teeth lightly close over my clit, and I'm confronted with his own *very* strong desire. Thick. Perfect. Pointing right at me.

I lick my lips. Would he be shocked if I did it? Maybe that's what I want. I don't want to be cautious. I want to taste him, all of him. I want to do it while he's tasting me.

So I don't say anything, just take him in my mouth, relax my jaw so he can slide in nearly all the way.

"*JESUS!*" Nico shouts.

And *oh*, he tastes so good—a salty essence mixed with his own unnamable flavor. I close my eyes, relishing in the feel, the utter control we have over each other's pleasure at exactly the same time. As his mouth works intensively at that most sensitive of places, and I savor every dimension of his, I forget that I'm in the middle of a freaking boxing ring, laid out on a mat, where anyone could see us if they just walked in the door. I forget about all of my worries, frustrations, anger. All of it fades away as we feast on each other's bodies and lose ourselves to the animalism of the moment.

"Mmmm," Nico groans, then slams a hand to the mat. But this time, I don't freeze. In my mouth, he grows just a bit bigger, and the knowledge makes me shake. Oh, *fuck*. He's going to come. He's going to come in my mouth, and I'm going to take it, and I'm going to come in his, and together we're going to—

Suddenly, every thought, the thrill of what we are doing is too much, and without warning, my entire body seizes up as my orgasm hits. It crashes through me, tossing me around, tightening every muscle I have. Nico grabs my thighs roughly, keeping them apart so he can finish me off, not letting up for a second as wave after wave of tension ripples through my limbs. I moan around his cock, my body quaking as his hips thrust forward lightly as he comes as well. We grasp, claw at each other, eager to get closer, yet somehow unable to take it all completely. I savor every bit until I'm completely sure he's finished. And then, just as my legs fall limp, forcing him to roll out from between my thighs, I release him too, and flop onto my back, completely out of breath.

"Holy. Shit." Nico's deep voice is raw, like he's been shouting. His chest rises and falls visibly. "Holy *shit*."

I loll to the side, curling against the mat. "Good?"

"Fuckin'..." He sorts through a few strings of unintelligible Spanish, then blows out a long breath. "No words, baby. No fuckin' words for what you do to me."

"Mmmm, good." I close my eyes. "Do you think..." The adrenaline starts to fall, and immediately, I miss it, along with the strange high that accompanied my earlier exhaustion. "Do you think we could do this again?"

When my eyes open, Nico's twisted around so we're lying face-to-face. His dark eyes sparkle, and his mouth is spread in a peaceful grin. I grin back.

"The boxing or the sixty-nine?" he asks cheekily, and his dimple on one side comes out to play. He strokes my face, and even through his joke, there is tenderness in his expression.

I blush, and immediately he laughs. It's infectious, simmering through me. I shove him playfully in the shoulder, which only makes him laugh louder.

"Why not both?" I tease.

Before he answers, Nico scoots in closer for a kiss. His tongue gently seeks entry, looking to mingle in a delicate dance that still carries the lust of the moment, but is mostly made of something deeper: contentment.

"Any time you want, sweetie," he says as he breaks away. "It's a date."

CHAPTER ELEVEN

Layla

Nico drops me at the train station with a kiss and a promise of more boxing later in the week. I'm disappointed—I had hoped we might continue things at my apartment. But aside from the fact that he has to be up early to get to Randall's Island on time for the academy, we both know we can't push it. I'm just not ready for what we both want to do.

Still, I feel lighter than I have in months. I never knew how much I wanted to hit something, maybe even some*one* like that, until the pop of glove on mitt cracked through the air. Nico has said before that learning to box saved him. It was the one good thing that came out of his time in a detention facility, and it kept him from going down some really bad paths. I feel like I get it now, just a little. If he'd been carrying this kind of pent-up anger and frustration for most of his childhood, an outlet like that must have changed his entire life.

But it's not just that. Wrapped up in each other like that on the mat, a sticky, sweaty, pheromone-soaked mess of desire, only made me want more. We were animals, diving into one another, wanting only to be closer, get closer. That wall, the familiar block on my senses didn't rise when things got too heated. A veil has lifted, and even though I'm not totally at the point where I feel open and free again, I feel like I can imagine it.

Dr. Parker would call that progress, I think.

Once I'm home, I sit at my desk, fingering the bottle of pills, which I've been taking at night, if only to calm my anxiety enough to sleep. Shama's still out with our—her?—friends. The apartment is empty, with the streetlights outside casting shadows through the fire escape outside of my window. For the first time in months, my heart beats at a regular pace at the thought of being alone. Maybe I can sleep by myself tonight.

And at that, my heart thumps loudly. My hands grow cold. A shiver passes through my body.

Okay, maybe not.

My phone buzzes in my pocket. I pull it out.

Nico: I forgot to say *te amo*, baby.

I smile at the text. When he's not smiling, he looks like he could mess up your face if you looked at him wrong, but underneath it all, Nico is really just a big softie.

Me: I love you too. Thanks for a great night. ALL of it.

The phone buzzes again almost immediately.

Nico: Anytime. Can't wait for more.

I stare at the words for a few minutes, ignoring the way my heart continues to beat a little too fast, and instead focusing on the warmth that grows through my belly when I think of him. I close my eyes and imagine the feel of his hands on my skin, his mouth between my legs, his skin pressed to mine. One of my hands creeps down and slides under the waistband of my pants, toying a little bit with the sensitive spot his tongue worried into a frenzy earlier.

A few moments later, I get up to take a shower, and finish what I've started. While the hot water runs over my body that aches for just one person, I'll think of Nico the entire time.

It doesn't take long to find my release, though my body wants more, wants the other part of me who is sleeping on a couch uptown. But when I come back, I slide into bed and fall asleep quickly and peacefully. I leave my pills where they are.

———

I tap my watch. The hands don't move. I'm sure Nico's late, but the watch has been stuck at ten o'clock for what seems like forever. It's lonely on this street corner, this part of the city so desolate it doesn't even have street signs. Over the tops of grimy brick buildings, I can see the glow of Manhattan, a halo over the jagged lines of skyscrapers and high-rises, the dips where the apartment buildings only reach five or six stories. Even from this far away, the city hums. But I'm here, waiting in one of the pockets that never make it into movies or the news.

"Come on, Nico," I mutter to myself. A shiver passes through my body. I hug myself, but stop when bruises appear on both shoulders. "Dammit. I'm out of makeup."

Heavy footsteps echo down the empty street. I look up, eager when I see the outline of a dark male form striding toward me.

"You're late!" I call out, though I'm already running toward him. My anchor. My everything.

"I would have been here earlier if you hadn't called the cops."

The voice, low and heavily accented, stops me in my tracks. The man's deep voice curves around me like a snail's shell. You can practically hear his lips curl as he speaks. He steps under a streetlight, revealing a long body dressed entirely in black, a mop of thick black curls that have been tamed with wax, and a thin, brooding face with eyes like obsidian, framed with Wayfarer glasses.

Giancarlo.

"Mi joya," he whispers, extending a hand while he pronounces that name he loves to use for me. Joya. Jewel. "I have been waiting for you."

I take a step back, then another. "Where's Nico?"

"Nico? Who? He left you. He went back to California. But it's you and me, joya. It always was, no? No one else matters."

I scramble back another few steps. Giancarlo looms in the dark, like he just grew another few inches. Only a few steps bring him close.

"Say it," he demands as he grabs for my hand. "Say you're mine."

I shake my head. "No."

His face, always long and gaunt, grows longer, gaunter. He stretches taller, nearly as tall as one of the buildings, until he blocks out all the lights—the stars, the moon, the lights of New York. The world is black, except his pale, hollow face.

I take a step back into an unknown street, yet another darkness in this city.

"No," I whisper, even as I turn to run.

"Say it!" Giancarlo shouts.

From an impossible distance away, he grabs me by the neck and yanks me into his chest, his long arms seeming to wrap multiple times around my body. He grows, one, two more feet, picking me up off the ground,

"Stop it!" I flail. "I don't love you! I never did!"

A hand claps over my face to shut me up. I can't breathe, struggling to move until I manage to stick my nose through a crack in the giant's hands.

"Let her go!"

I look up, barely able to see. But I do catch a glimpse of white: the stitching on a Yankees hat glows as a man charges through an alley. Nico.

"All right, cabrón, *I tried to warn you," he says before spilling into Spanish I seem to know, but can't totally understand.*

Giancarlo jerks at the sound. Nico pulls his fist back, ready to throw the punches, the blows he's been practicing all of his adult life. I brace myself.

But Giancarlo grows again, seemingly unaffected as Nico rains down fury onto his legs, his calves, now his ankles, a tiny David to this giant Goliath.

"Nico!" I scream again and again, voice muted by the slippery, cigarette-stained palm.

Giancarlo picks up one long, black-soled shoe and takes aim at the Yankees hat. Then he brings it down.

"NO!"

I wake up, my heart pounding wildly. My sheets are half-soaked with sweat, twisted around me like I just traveled through a tornado.

"Lay?"

Shama's voice calls from the other side of my door. I glance at it, but remain curled into a ball while I rock.

"You okay?" she asks.

"I...I'm fine," I manage to call back, cursing myself as my voice quivers. "I was tossing around in my sleep, that's all."

There's a pause. "Um, okay. Do you need anything?"

I shake my head, even though she can't see me. "N-no. I'm good. Go back to sleep, Shams."

There's another pause before finally I hear her shuffle back to her room and shut the door. I grab my pillow, flipping it over so it's no longer damp with sweat.

On my nightstand, my phone sits innocuously. I could call him, let his deep, soothing voice lull me back to sleep, a lullaby for my soul. He'll never know the way he does that, the way his whole presence brings me peace the way no one else can.

But it's three in the morning. He needs his sleep, and so do I. And he doesn't need to know that I'm going a little crazy. I don't need to be yet another burden on his life.

So instead, I reach for the pills on the other side of the nightstand. I clap one to my mouth, and swallow tightly without any water. I'm going to spend the next twenty-four hours feeling like a zombie, but that's better than feeling like a crazy person.

"The here and now," I whisper to myself as I burrow back under my sheets, waiting for the numbing effect of the drug to work its way into my system. "The here and now."

But the mantra doesn't work. Because right here, in this small, cold, white room, I am scared. Right now, I am alone.

CHAPTER TWELVE

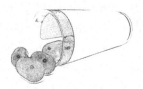

Nico

"Time's up."

I set my pencil down onto the table next to this week's exam. It's Friday, and I'm ready to get the fuck out of here for the weekend. All week I've been cooped up on "The Rock," as a lot of people call the academy, trapped half the day in this cinder block of a room with fifty other dudes who smell like feet and Old Spice, and spending the other half of the day puzzling my way in and out of smoke-filled buildings. Don't get me wrong: I love it. I love everything I'm doing, but it's fuckin' intense. I'm looking forward to getting to work in a real station. With real hours. And real people.

I flex my fingers and shake out the cramp in my hand. I swear to God, if I never take another test in my life, it will be too soon. I've got one more month until I'm assigned a station—one more month before we take our final exams and graduate. I can't fuckin' wait.

The sergeant collects our exams, raising his brow a little at me as he passes back the last ones.

"Nice job, Soltero," he mutters, then keeps moving.

I flip over the packet and see the perfect score I got on the last test. I might hate doing them, but having Layla in my ear all summer, coaching me on study methods, has helped me more than she knows. I might even graduate top of my class if I'm lucky. Who would have thought?

I thought, you goon. I can see Layla looking at me, her bright eyes smiling with pride while she chases away my doubts. She hates it when I think badly about myself, and while I used to brush it away as naivety, the truth is, I'm starting to believe her faith in me. I'm starting to expect myself to succeed rather than fail. It's a weird feeling. But a really good one.

"You doing anything fun this weekend, Soltero?"

I turn to Mike, one of the probies in my class, as we're filing out of the classroom. He's a nice enough kid from Staten Island who just barely managed to squeak into this class. He looks at my test score and breathes a "damn" under his breath. I roll up the paper and shove it into my backpack.

"Probably hang with my girl tonight," I say, feeling a little excitement in my stomach even as I say it. God, I love calling her that again out loud, not just in my head. My girl. "Then I gotta work tomorrow, family stuff on Sunday. Do some studying. Nothing too crazy. You?"

Mike nods his head. "Nah. I'll probably sit at home and watch *Fear Factor* or something. By this time at the end of the week, I usually just want to sleep all weekend. Who's your girl?"

I can't even hide the smile this time. "Layla. She's a student at NYU." I pull out my phone and flip it open to the picture. She doesn't know I even have the stupidly blurry snapshot from my phone that I took from across the room when she was laughing.

Mike nods approvingly. "Aww, that's nice, man. She's cute. You're a lucky man."

I nod. "Sure as fuck am."

"So, what kind of stuff you doing with your family?"

"The usual. Church. Family dinner. That sort of thing." I don't mention the fact that on Sunday we have a meeting with our social worker to talk about my mother's status and our travel license to Cuba.

We file out of the building, most of us making our way toward the bus stop.

"You need a ride?" Mike asks as he sees me turning that way. "What direction are you going?"

I chew on my lip. I should go home and change out of my uniform, but I remember Layla's face when I picked her up at the airport in my regulation gear. I wouldn't mind seeing her look at me like that again.

"If it's not too out of your way, you could drop me in Williamsburg," I say.

———

"So seems like you're doing good on the tests," Mike says once we're on our way.

I look out the window at the mostly boring buildings of Queens. "Um, yeah. I'm doing all right, I guess."

"Top recruit in your class means something," Mike says as he turns on to the freeway. "Friend of my brother's was top recruit. I heard he made lieutenant in less than a year."

I roll my eyes. It's not out of the realm of possibility, but you hear stories like that all the time. Would I like to make lieutenant? Sure. But honestly, I'll just be happy to graduate and be a legit firefighter, same as I've wanted since I was just a little kid. That alone is enough for me.

"You have a degree?"

I frown. "Nah. I started community college way back, but it wasn't for me." I don't want to get into the real reasons I didn't stay in school. Truthfully, my head wasn't in it, but I needed to work. I needed to support my family when my mom couldn't.

"Too bad," Mike said. "The guys like you. They listen to you. I heard the sergeants are always looking for people to groom, you know? You could probably be a battalion chief at some point. But you need a degree."

I blink in surprise. "What? Why?"

Mike nods. "Yeah, some bullshit requirement about leadership. Ain't that some garbage? Like, what the fuck is a bunch of college courses gonna do to teach you about being a firefighter? What is writing a bunch of crappy papers going to teach you about leading other guys? Nothin', that's what."

He switches gears, talking about the last Yankees game, but I only give a couple of nods and yeahs here and there. My mind is still lingering on that bombshell. I started this job because I wanted to do something real with my life, not just push boxes around all day. Even though I didn't have any major goals of jumping up the ranks immediately, it feels fuckin' shitty to realize that even from the start, I'm doomed to stay at the bottom.

———

Mike drops me off at a J stop in Williamsburg with a shout that we should get a beer next Friday. I give him a maybe. Mike's a nice guy, but I'll be real. By Friday, after five days of not seeing Layla, I'm not really interested in anything else but tackling her.

Too bad she's not freakin' here.

"Hey," Shama says as she lets me into the apartment. "She's on her way back from the gym, I think."

"Oh yeah? She been working out?" She hasn't said anything about that to me, not since our little session at Frank's last weekend.

Shama nods with a funny look on her face. "Every day. She hasn't told you?"

I frown. "No. But I'm glad she is again. She seemed to have a good time on Sunday when we did some boxing."

"Yeah, I saw her knuckles. They were bruised all week."

Immediately, a pang of guilt shoots through me at the thought of Layla bruised again. And *I* did that.

"She seemed happy," Shama continues as she moves a bunch of books around a cardboard box. She gives me a look that tells me my instinct to keep on my uniform was a good one. I give her a knowing look back, and she snorts.

"Don't get too excited, Special Delivery," she says, using the nickname that Quinn, their old roommate, started when I first met Layla and was working at FedEx.

Immediately, my shoulders tense. I fuckin' *hate* that name. It's a name that reminds me that to some people, I'm always going to be some rat from the street. A blue-collar schmuck not worth their time.

"Ah," Shama says as she catches my face. "Sorry. Force of habit, but I didn't mean anything by it."

I relax, a bit surprised. "Maybe don't call me that anymore. I haven't worked at FedEx in more than a year, you know?"

"Well, maybe don't look so damn pleased with yourself that you look good in your uniform. That's what uniforms do. They would make Shrek look hot."

I chuckle, and Shama goes into the kitchen, where she grabs a beer from the fridge and tosses it to me. I sit down on the couch, the only furniture still in the mostly empty living room. They bought it last weekend, but other than that, there's not much else in here yet.

"I forget you guys are twenty-one now," I say as I crack open the can. "No more fake IDs, huh?"

Shama snorts. "Now who's stuck in the past?" she asks as she goes back to the boxes.

"How'd the week go, with your classes starting and everything?"

Shama shrugs. "Mine don't start until next week."

I frown. And then it registers that Shama's putting stuff in the boxes, not taking shit out. Through her bedroom door, everything is packed up tight. "Didn't you just move in here?"

"Ah, not really. I got a late acceptance to a study abroad program in London. I'm leaving next week."

For a second, I'm not sure if I heard that right. "You're *what?*"

Shama sets the tape down on the box and comes to sit next to me on the couch. "She didn't tell you?"

I shake my head. "Layla didn't tell me anything about that."

Shama shrugs. "I just found out last week. I'm guessing she didn't want you to worry about her."

I'm about to say there's nothing to worry about, except, of course, there is. It's not that Layla's not old enough to be living on her own—obviously that's fine. But I know my girl well enough to know that she doesn't actually want to be alone. That she's felt alone most of her life. I honestly think she liked living in the dorms, sharing a tiny apartment with three other girls, because it made that feeling go away.

But last year she lost most of those friends, and now Shama's taking off too? Shit. Now I know why she was so sad last weekend. One more thing this week she didn't tell me during our brief conversations at night. I try not to let it bug me, but it does.

"So, hey," Shama says. "I think maybe you should know something."

I look up. Shit, what else?

Shama glances nervously toward the front door, but obviously no one is there. She gets up and scurries into Layla's room, then comes out carrying a small orange prescription container. She tosses it to me with a light rattle, then comes to sit on the couch next to me.

"What's this?" I examine the bottle, reading the label. "Diazepam? This says Layla's name on it."

"Valium," Shama clarifies. "It's for her panic attacks."

I look up. "Panic attacks? What the hell?"

Shama sighs. "I knew she hadn't told you. But I'm leaving on Monday, and someone here needs to know. She was diagnosed this summer with PTSD after everything that happened with Giancarlo."

I stare at the bottle, unsure of what I'm hearing. "Did she tell you this?"

Shama shakes her head. "I called her mom after I heard one of the attacks. Cheryl told me a lot more than Layla probably would want."

"PTSD? Isn't that what like, combat soldiers get?" I've heard of war vets having PTSD, but not normal people.

"I looked it up, but honestly, I don't know that much about it," Shama says. "But I think anyone who's endured significant trauma can experience it. And I would consider what happened with...*him* to be a trauma, don't you think?"

In a second, I'm back in that room. I'm looking at that guy, who sliced his wrist just to fuck with Layla's mind, dripping blood all over her while he slams his fist into her face again and again. Forcing himself between her legs.

I rub my hand violently across my face. "I mean, sure. Yeah. The guy abducted her, abused her, pummeled her, and tried to rape her." I close my eyes, shoving away the image before that wave of rage overtakes me again. Fuck. Instead I focus on where I am. This conversation. Right now. "Why are you telling me this?"

Shama takes another long drink of her beer. "I'm telling you because I'm worried about her. You know Lay. She won't say anything because she won't want to burden you. She loves you like crazy—I hope you know that."

I nod. "I know. And, just so you know, the feeling is mutual. She —she's *everything* to me, Shama. I love her so fuckin' much."

She nods . "I know you do. She's lucky to have you."

For some reason, her endorsement feels really, really good. I don't know why it means so much to me that this rich, twenty-one-year-old chick from New Jersey gives me her approval, but it does.

"Thanks," is all I say. "So...these attacks. What do they look like?"

Shama presses her lips together. "She's pretty good at keeping them secret. But honestly, I think that's why she doesn't go out much. I think she's afraid of being psycho around people. The city freaks her out." She passes her beer from hand to hand a few times. "I'm kind of worried about what she'll do without someone here with her. That's the real reason I'm telling you."

I weigh the words. Suddenly, a lot of Layla's behavior becomes clearer. Her skittish looks. Sudden withdrawals. The way she freezes up, shies from my touch. I don't say anything to Shama about our challenges in the bedroom, but I bet she knows. Girls tell each other everything.

"I hear them," Shama says sadly. "Sometimes she'll wake up at night, and I'll hear her shouting about it. A few times I've gotten home when she's in the shower, and she sounds like a wild animal."

My chest constricts. Fuck. What has Layla been dealing with? And why the fuck hasn't she told me?

"She's supposed to have weekly sessions with a therapist, but she hasn't gone since she got to New York," Shama says as she stands up. She puts her empty can into the trash in the kitchen. "If you can help her see someone again, I think it would be good."

Dumbfounded, I stay on the couch, processing. Shama stops on her way back to her room, standing behind the couch.

"Hey, Nico?"

I look up. "Huh?"

Her expression is sympathetic. "I know it's a lot. But for what it's worth, she doesn't have those episodes when you're around. I think you make her feel safe."

She holds out her hand for the pills, then leaves me to brood while she returns the bottle to Layla's room and goes back to packing boxes. I just sit on the couch, lost in thought. Because as glad as I am that I'm something good in Layla's life, there's the other reality to contend with: I can't always be with her. At some point, she needs to feel safe on her own.

The front door opens with a bang, and my girl herself strides in, red-faced and bright-eyed when she spots me on the couch. She drops her bags on the floor, and before I can even get up, she's flying at me, covering my face with enough kisses to make me laugh and forget about the bomb her roommate just dropped.

"Ah! I missed you this week," she exclaims as she nuzzles her nose to mine.

I open my lips and pull her close for another hungry kiss. She has no fuckin' clue. All day long, I have to think about things like escape routes and oxygen levels. But then I come back to my apartment, hungry for her voice more than I want my Dominican takeout. I fall asleep thinking about her, and I wake up dreaming about her face.

It's only been five days since we saw each other last, but it feels like five weeks. Which is why suddenly we're zero to sixty in about ten seconds flat, I'm hard as a rock, and Layla's got her hands up my shirt while we're devouring each other.

"Dudes, get a room," Shama says loudly as she pulls a loud piece of tape across her box.

Layla breaks away with a flush. I can't do anything but grin.

"You really shouldn't wear that uniform unless we're alone," she murmurs, pulling down my shirt.

My grin just about splits my face. Oh, I'm *definitely* going to wear the uniform again. I may not ever take it off.

Layla bites her lip, then turns. "Sorry, Shams. We'll be good."

"Nah, don't worry about it," Shama says as she closes the last box. "But I'm sorry I can't give you the house tonight. I have to finish packing before the movers come in the morning."

"It's okay." Layla turns back to me and delivers another kiss that's sweeter, but could easily turn feral if she just gave it a few more seconds. "I'm glad to see you," she says, blue eyes glowing. "Pizza and a movie? Or do you want to go out?"

I shake my head. I'm dead tired. Vegging out on the couch with a pie and my girl sounds like a winning lottery ticket. Shit, *she's* my winning lottery ticket.

I turn my baseball hat backward so I can kiss her again, more thoroughly. God, I really can't stop. "You order the pizza. I'll pick through your DVDs and see if I can find something that won't cost me my man card."

Layla giggles, but seriously. She and her friends have *way* too many chick flicks in their movie collection.

Within an hour, we're on the couch like we've been there all night, lounging lengthwise over the cushions, Layla's back spoons against my front with my arm draped over her middle as we fit together, two pieces of a puzzle. Every now and then, she turns over, nuzzles into my chest, and sighs. Every so often, I get a whiff of her scent—coconut. Midway through the movie, Layla's asleep on my chest, and I'm almost out myself, but I keep waking myself up because I don't want to miss it. Not the movie—I've seen Top Gun about a million times. Her.

Sometimes I can't believe that we're finally here again. That finally we have something like normal together. Layla sighs and burrows into me a little more. I drop a kiss on her forehead, and she murmurs something sweet and unintelligible against my shirt. My heart hurts, but in a good way. Like it can't totally understand this level of happiness.

Still, even as I watch Tom Cruise whizzing his jet all over the Indian Ocean, I can't help if any minute, Layla's going to wake up with that look of terror in her eyes. I wonder if she took one of those pills today or not. And mostly I wonder what else she's not telling me.

CHAPTER THIRTEEN

Layla

At some point, Nico moves us both to my bed for the rest of the night, and we spend the majority of Saturday morning there too, including a solid forty-five minutes he spent mostly under my sheets while I shouted at the ceiling. He wanted to do more. I wanted to do more. But every time he crept over me and I felt *him* there, right between the slipperiest parts of me, I would freeze. I wanted it. *So. Bad.* But the rest of my body would stiffen and close up. And Nico would move to the side, turn me in his arms, and hold me until the feeling passed.

I hate it. I hate it so much. I just want to be normal again.

We sleep in and study together for another several hours while Nico reads his assignments for the weekend, I start my first assignments for a class I'm taking on Brazilian political history, and the movers come for Shama's stuff. The normal comes back, little by little. So in the middle of the afternoon, when I return from taking a shower to find Nico sitting at my desk, passing the prescription bottle of Valium back and forth between his big hands, the realization of the farce slams into my gut like a freight train.

"Where did you get that?" I ask as I enter, shaking out my hair.

Nico looks up. He's dressed again in his uniform, which is now creased, but still makes him look indecently handsome. "I was looking for a pen and found them in your desk. But actually, Shama showed them to me last night." He sets the bottle on the table like it might explode and looks at the instructions that come with them. "Those have some serious side effects, baby."

I sit down on the bed, pulling my robe tight over my body. "I only take them at night. When I—when I can't get back to sleep." I shake my head. "I don't like them. They make me feel woozy."

He frowns. "Why can't you sleep?"

I sigh and wrap my arms around my waist. Nico watches the motion, and his frown deepens.

"I just...I worry."

That's all I can say. How can I tell him about the psychotic dreams I have when I don't take them? Dreams about giant Giancarlo stepping on a tiny Nico. Dreams about long, skeletal hands encircling my neck and never letting go. Dreams about losing my breath. Losing my life.

Nico drums his fingers on the desk top for a moment and sets down the instructions. "They used to drug us with this kind of shit at Tryon, you know. Way worse than this, actually. But this is bad enough."

I cringe. He barely ever talks about the two years he spent at the detention facility, mostly because I know it hurts. They aren't memories he likes to relive, but here he is, bringing them up for me.

When Nico looks up, his big eyes have softened. "I hated it too."

I sit down across from him on the bed. "Why did they give it to you?"

"They overmedicated us. A lot of kids had real problems. Kids who came from homes where they'd had seriously bad shit happen to them all their lives, way, *way* worse than mine ever was. Their minds couldn't deal with it, and they really didn't have many ways to learn how." He fingers the bottle again, then pushes it away before looking back up at me. "But this doesn't fix things, baby."

"You make me sound like a crazy person," I whisper, staring at the floor.

I don't blame him. Sometimes I do feel crazy. Everywhere I look, that same shadow follows me. At school. In my sleep. When I close my eyes. And sometimes when they're open too. Only two things seem to make him go away: these pills and Nico. And Nico can't be around me all the time.

A finger tips up my chin, and I find Nico looking at me with sympathy. Understanding.

"No, baby," he says. "I've just been there. And what that fucker did to you last spring, I don't want it to poison you for the rest of your life. Take these pills if you need 'em, but they won't make it go away. You gotta find a way to deal with what's going on inside you, not numb it."

I take a deep breath, suddenly unable to prevent a tear from sliding down my cheek. Silently, I get off the bed and crawl into his lap, where he pulls me close and strokes my back, humming softly. He really is the best therapy I could ever ask for.

"I'm sorry," I whisper. "God, I'm so fucked up, aren't I? You can't even have sex with your own girlfriend because she's too freaked out."

"Stop. I'm not here for that. I'm here for you. All of you. However you come."

He looks down and catches a glimpse of my cleavage, then exhales like he's in pain. His full lips purse, and I kiss them, because I can. Reflexively, my hips roll into the length suddenly pressing between them.

"Mm," Nico groans. "You don't make it easy on a guy, though, NYU. And fuck. I gotta go. I'm supposed to be at AJ's by eight, and I still have to go back uptown to get my fuckin' monkey suit."

"You need to just bring a bunch of clothes here, not just a change," I say as I get up and go look for some clothes of my own.

"That way when you come on Fridays, you can just stay until you absolutely have to go on Saturdays."

I stop, realizing what I'm saying here, and flush. "I mean...if you want to. No pressure."

Immediately, I want to smack myself in the head. Stupid, stupid! You only just got back together all of five minutes ago. You've had sex one terrible time in a nightclub, and now you're offering him closet space?

But before I can turn around, Nico encircles me from behind, his strong arms wrapped around my waist.

"You really want me here all weekend?" he asks, his low voice rumbling against my neck. One hand slips under the fabric of my robe, playing over my bare stomach.

The effect is immediate. I sigh, melting into his touch as the rest of me wakes up fully. "I do."

There's another low rumble of contentment. "Good. I want to be here too. Probably too much."

He trails a few delicious kisses up and down my neck, running his teeth over my earlobe and catching it between them for a split-second.

I press back into him and moan. "Do you...do you have to go right away?"

Slowly, my head is tipped back, and with an open, warm mouth, Nico delivers a kiss that erases all doubts. Our tongues twist together delicately, a dance we never forget. I press back more against his tented pants—he's ready now. He wants this as badly as I do.

"Are you? Are you sure?" he murmurs.

Am I sure? I'm sure I want to feel good. I want to feel normal, and this—*this* insane, magnetic connection we've always had—is our normal.

I nod and then suck on his full lower lip. Nico groans. The hands at my waist slowly undo my robe so that it hangs open over my still-damp, naked body.

Nico sucks in a breath as he looks down my front. He cups my breasts with both hands, brushing his thumbs over my aching nipples.

"Can I make you come, baby?" he asks as he sucks on my earlobe again.

I hum. "Mmmmmm."

In the mirror hung over my closet door, we both watch, transfixed, as he slides a hand down my front and places two fingers over my clit.

"Look at you," he says as he runs his teeth up and down my neck. "So fucking beautiful. You drive me crazy, baby, you know that?"

I can feel his rigid length pressed against the cleft of my ass. In the back of my mind, I see us clearly: me pressed against this mirror, bent over so he can thrust his cock into my depths. I want it so badly... and at the same time, I'm content to fall against him and let him continue the insistent caresses he's started. His fingers continue their work while his other hand drifts from my breasts, over my stomach, and around my back. It palms my ass and squeezes lightly, playing with the curves of Nico's favorite body part.

"So fucking luscious," he growls as he squeezes again. He slides his tongue over my neck. I can't stop watching.

"Wrap your arms around my head," he says as he continues to knead my backside. I obey, and the motion causes my robe to spread further, leaving nothing he's doing to the imagination.

The fingers in front press a little harder and move a little faster. The ones behind slip further south, between my legs, nudging them apart. I suck in a breath as a finger enters my dark, slick entrance. One at first, then two.

"Do you need to come, baby?" Nico asks, his low voice vibrating lightly over my skin.

I lean back into him as both hands work my body from the front and back, the fingers inside me thrust lightly in time with the ones at my clit.

"Fuck!" I hiss as he slips a third inside. He curves them slightly, pressing them against the sensitive bundle of nerves there, the ones on the other side of my clit. That same spot inside my body is getting this delicious treatment from both sides.

"Come on, baby," Nico says. "Let it go. I got you."

His teeth close down on my ear, and the slight tinge of pain is my undoing.

"Oh, *fuck!*" I cry out as the orgasm shoots through me. The fingers inside thrust harder, deeper, causing pleasure to ricochet through my limbs with a force that makes me shake.

"I got you," Nico murmurs again and again through his teeth. "Take it, baby. I got you."

And he does. I shake in his arms for what seems like minutes until slowly, slowly, I fall from the high where only he can take me. I collapse backward against his strong form, feeling a different kind of wooziness—one where my body feels alive and contented all at once.

"What about you?" I murmur, still slouched into his shoulder. He's still long and hard, pressed against my backside. I nuzzle backward, noting with a little satisfaction the shudder that passes over his face at the motion.

"Later," he replies with a sharkish grin at me through the mirror. "I'll bring clothes tomorrow. That reminds me: what are you doing tomorrow? What do you think about going to Mass?"

I turn around and grin. "Are you going to save me with Jesus?" I ask, poking him in the stomach. I don't bother to close my robe, enjoying the way his gaze plays over me.

Nico tips his head back and laughs. "What the fuck kind of hypocrite would I be to do that?" But then he sobers. "No, I'm going to save you with family. Mine's a little crazy, but they love you. Come with us."

I don't have to think twice. I used to hate going to church as a kid, and even now, I only ever go out of guilt or maybe nostalgia. But the idea of going to Mass with Nico's family, a roomful of people who love, pester, annoy, and care for each other, seems really nice.

"I'll be there," I say just before he delivers another kiss. "Just tell me where and when."

CHAPTER FOURTEEN

Layla

WHEN TURNS OUT TO BE FIVE THIRTY IN THE AFTERNOON, AND the where turns out to be a familiar church on Forty-Ninth Street. I find myself standing, looking up at the red brick exterior, my palms sweating while the priest stands at the door, greeting all of the parishioners in Spanish.

"Hey, baby."

I turn around to find Nico approaching with Gabe and Carmen trailing behind. He gives me a lingering kiss on the cheek, and it's only then that I take in his blue button-down shirt and black pants. His dense, curly hair has been tamed a bit, and the blue of his shirt makes his skin glow. He looks way too delicious for church.

"Hi," I greet him with a tame kiss, then accept kisses on the cheek from both Carmen and Gabe. "Where are Maggie and Selena?"

"The *gatitas* went to the zoo for the day," Gabe says. "Allie was driving everyone crazy this morning, so no church. Thank God—er, I mean, thank goodness."

"Why do you call your sisters little cats?" I ask.

Next to us, Carmen rolls her eyes and shakes her head.

Nico gives me a lopsided smile. "*Gata* is a common phrase for girls. We called them that when they were little because Selena and Maggie used to fight like cats. Now Allie sometimes acts like one too."

"Ah," I say with understanding.

Their apartment is a packed place at the moment—one small bedroom for Gabe, one for Maggie and her daughter, while Nico sleeps on the couch. I wouldn't be surprised if a five-year-old was acting out here and there.

"I'm glad you're here," Nico says as he takes my hand. "You look way too beautiful for church, but I'll just have to deal with that."

I look down at my clothing, a green sweater dress that fits the slight nip marking the beginning of fall. It makes my eyes pop and sets off the olive tones in my pale skin.

"Thanks," I murmur. "But you're one to talk. You'd corrupt a priest any day."

Nico gives me a lopsided smile that brings out the dimple in his left cheek. But just before I can tell him to stop doing that lest I combust completely, Carmen calls for us to greet the priest and file inside.

"What did you do this morning?" I ask as I follow them into one of the pews near the front.

Nico shrugs. "Gabe and I had to patch a hole. A mouse got in last weekend and chewed up half the food in the kitchen. And then we had an appointment with the social worker."

He says the last sentence in a hushed voice and glances around while we sit, and I know he would prefer not to talk about that particular meeting right here. Places like this would actually be a perfect place for an immigrations officer to eavesdrop.

"Did it...did it go well?" I ask, careful not to give anything away.

Nico looks around again sharply, but his eyes soften when they land on me. "It is what it is. The last license was rejected, you know. But Ileana says we can apply for an informational one, since Gabe's in school. Maybe he can apply to travel as a student on a research project. We'll see."

I understand by his clipped tone that there isn't anymore he wants to say about it, so I drop it. But I can't help but feel like there has to be something more that I could do.

I look around the church, and before I can stop it, memories of the last time I was here come floating back just as the altar boys walk down the aisle carrying the incense. Last Christmas, for another Spanish-language Mass with...

Suddenly, that familiar freeze is back, along with a deep fear that hits me in the belly.

"I see him here sometimes," Gabe says on my other side in a low voice, clearly checking to make sure his brother doesn't hear him.

I jerk my head around. "What?"

Nico immediately turns from a conversation with his mom. "What's going on?"

Gabe looks uneasy. "I, um, was just telling NYU that I've seen her, ah...you know. Evita. Here sometimes." He shrugs. "Maybe once or twice."

Nico's eyes practically bug out of his head. "And you didn't think to fuc—you didn't think to tell me?"

Gabe frowns. "So you could get yourself into trouble while you're in the academy? Yeah, no. I thought that would be a bad idea."

Nico practically growls, earning a light slap on his shoulder from his mother, urging him to calm down before the Mass begins.

"See, that's what I'm talking about," Gabe whispers harshly. "Your temper gets you in trouble. He has a court date, doesn't he?" He looks at me for confirmation.

I nod. "Next week," I murmur. Is it really that close?

Gabe looks back at his brother. "Nobody needs you playing superhero anymore, *mano*. That's how you got yourself into trouble in the first place."

I wince, and I don't have to look next to me to know that Nico's hurt. Gabe's talking about the stint at Tryon after Nico helped rob a bodega to feed his brother and sisters. It's correct, yes. But it's also incredibly unfair.

But the church quiets before I can say it, so instead, I edge closer to Nico.

"Hey," I say.

I nudge him in the shoulder. His muscles barely move, but I can still see the shape of them, evident in the way they test the confines of his dress shirt. He looks at me sadly, but doesn't say anything.

"You're *my* hero," I whisper. "And I'll never be more grateful than I was when you busted through that door and saved me."

Nico stares at me for a moment with an expression that's a cross between pained and relieved. Then briskly, he stamps a hard, close-mouthed kiss on my lips, completely ignoring Carmen's smack on his shoulder as he does it.

"I love you," he whispers fiercely, and squeezes my hand so hard I wonder if he'll ever let it go.

The priest begins the service, and we both straighten up. But I know that neither of us are really listening to what he's saying. Even if I could understand the entire Mass in Spanish, like Nico can, I would be just as busy scanning the crowd. Watching for the face I pray I'll never see again.

———

By the end of the Mass, I couldn't have told you a single thing the priest said. Seriously, you try focusing on Holy Scripture when you've got a hundred and eighty pounds of muscled man next to you who smells like heaven and licks his lips every time he looks at you. Church is doing *nothing* to temper all the illicit thoughts going through my head as I file down the aisle with a prime view of Nico's ass in those pants.

"*Gracias, Padre. Próxima semana.*"

The sound of the voice stops me in the middle of the center aisle.

Gabe and Carmen have already left the church, but Nico, still holding my hand, looks up when I jerk to a violent stop.

"What's..."

He doesn't even finish his sentence when he sees my face. I'm still staring ahead at the tall, pale man, chatting comfortably with the priest. Giancarlo adjusts his glasses and runs a big hand through his full head of wavy black hair. And then, like he knows he's being watched, straightens and turns his head. His eyes land on me, and his mouth drops slightly.

"Layla?" he asks.

The priest steps out of the church to speak to other parishioners who are leaving. Giancarlo blocks the exit, whether on purpose or not.

"You ruined me," he says, just loud enough that I can hear him across the three or so pews.

Nico takes a step forward, shielding me with his body. Still frozen, I'm happy to let him.

"Move on, man," he says. "Let's not do this here."

"This is my last week here," Giancarlo continues, staring a hole through me over Nico's big shoulder. "My lawyers, they say I will go to jail or to Argentina." He gulps, and for a second, I can see genuine fear in the eyes I never remember as anything but stern and threatening. "All because of *you*."

He holds me captive with his glare for what seems like several minutes. Move, Layla. Don't give him the satisfaction of watching you crumble.

By some miracle, I manage to turn to Nico. "Let's go," I murmur, tugging on his hand. "Please."

After pausing for a second like he's genuinely trying to decide whether committing murder—in the middle of a church no less—is really a mortal sin, Nico finally nods. With eyes as dark as night, Nico leads me down the aisle, making big movements that force Giancarlo down one of the pews. Nico's doing his best not to lose it. Every muscle in his neck looks like it's about to snap, and his teeth grind together as we walk.

But just as we reach the door, my other hand is snatched, and when I look up, Giancarlo is glaring at me with eyes like death.

"Say something!" he hisses. "You cannot just walk away. *You* did this to me. God will not forgive you for it!"

"W-what are you talking about?" I finally sputter. "You did this to yourself. N-no one made you do the things you did to me."

"Let her go," Nico orders as the vein in his temple throbs visibly.

"You'll never get away from me," Giancarlo replies in a low, gruesome voice. "You haven't yet, have you?"

I see his face again, but in the back of my mind. All the times it flashed before me at school. On the street. Around every dark corner.

Was it ever him for real? I honestly don't know. It doesn't really matter.

Before I can ask, Giancarlo pulls on my hand, like he wants to yank me out of the church. My heart is beating out of my chest, but before I can even think about fighting, Nico drops his arm down and breaks Giancarlo's grip like he's snapping a pencil in half.

"Just try it," Nico growls, so low that only the three of us can hear him. "You do, and ain't no church gonna protect you, motherfucker. You think God's above vengeance? I guaran-fuckin-tee he'd be on *my* side of this fight."

"Don't," I murmur as I start to shake. "D-don't. Nico, just leave it."

"Layla." Nico's gaze flashes down at me, and I grip his shoulder, desperate for the warmth I need to calm my thrashing heart. When we both look up, Giancarlo is gone, having fled the church without a sound. A muscle in the side of Nico's neck still ticks. He looks like a feral cat dying to set out on the chase. But I squeeze his hand again, willing him to calm down even though my heart is beating wildly.

Then he looks back down at me. "How many times have you seen him?"

I take a step back, ignoring the people leaving the church who are watching us with interest.

"I—none."

"Goddammit, Layla," Nico hisses, earning a shocked look from one of the parishioners, an old lady who mutters "*Vergüenza!*" under her breath before automatically crossing herself. Nico grabs my arm and tows me toward one of the small apses, where an array of candles burns. "How many times?"

I bite my lip. "I...I don't think it was him. He was surprised to see me too."

Nico frowns, staring at the open door again, like he thinks Giancarlo might reappear. "Then what the fuck did he mean, you haven't gotten away from him yet?"

I shudder. "I...honestly, I don't know. Maybe he just knows that he's inside my head. I was never sure it was him. Honestly, I've just been imagining him."

"What do you mean, *imagining* him?" Nico's voice cuts, still sharp.

"I–I see him sometimes," I admit. "And then I shake my head, and he's not there. The doctor—my therapist in Pasadena—told me they were flashbacks. That they're c-common for victims of trauma."

I hang my head, grateful that no one else appears to be hearing this conversation.

Nico exhales, long and heavy. "But maybe he really was there?"

I shrug, and even the possibility causes a pit of dread to spread throughout my stomach. "I...I don't know. Could be."

Nico shoves his hands up and down his face. "We gotta tell the police."

I frown. "Tell them what? That we ran into him at a church he attended long before I ever did? That I think I've seen him around, but we've never made contact, and that I'm not really sure which of those times were hallucinations or which were real, if any of them were? What do you think they're going to do?"

Nico groans through his fingers. "Fuck!"

"You really shouldn't say that in a church," I whisper.

"*Fuck*," he says again, more vehemently, though he still glances back toward the altar guiltily. Like the crucifix hanging on the wall can hear him. "Come on. We're getting out of here."

Outside, he looks around for Gabe and Carmen, shouting across the street in a rapid Spanish that I can barely translate, roughly meaning we're going somewhere else. Gabe, knowing better than to question his brother when he looks like this, just nods and starts shepherding Carmen back to Alba's apartment. Nico grabs my hand and tows me toward the Hudson.

His head is on a swivel as he practically jogs me through Hell's Kitchen. He's keeping an eye out for Giancarlo, I know, but that tall, slouching form is nowhere to be seen. It's not until we're a block from Frank's gym that I realize his intention. Nico pushes through the door, startling a group of people working out together on the open floor in the front.

Nate appears from the office at the top of the stairs.

"You got a free ring?" Nico asks.

Nate checks his watch. "In about an hour, yeah. Can you wait?"

Nico growls, but nods his head. "It's fine. We'll do some bag work first."

I'm towed toward the lockers at the far side of the gym, where Nico stops and unlocks one. Out of it he pulls some workout clothes for me, and a bag of his own stuff.

"How—what is this stuff doing here? Hey, I was looking for this sports bra!"

"Shama gave it to me before she left," Nico says, his voice still abrupt and curt. "I thought you should have some stuff to keep here for when we came back." He jerks his head toward the changing rooms in the back. "Get dressed and meet me by the heavy bags."

"But, wait, shouldn't we talk about what just happened? You're obviously mad, and I'm kind of freaked out." Now that I'm finding my voice again, I can't stop talking. "We need to figure out what to do—"

"Layla." His deep baritone stops my babbling.

I blink. "What?"

"We'll take care of all of that. Right now, I *really* need to do this, okay? This is what I do when I'm about to lose it."

I open my mouth to say something, but my words escape me. "Okay."

CHAPTER FIFTEEN

Nico

After we change, we take some time to warm up, and then spend about a half hour on the heavy bag practicing combinations until we're both breathing heavily. Layla clearly likes throwing punches, but I barely notice, going harder than I've gone in months. With every punch I throw, it's that motherfucker's face I see. It's his glasses I'm breaking. It's his teeth I'm knocking out.

Fuck. *Fuck.* Why didn't she tell me? From what he said, it sounds like this guy has either been stalking her since she got here, or else she's literally *seeing* the asshole everywhere she goes. No wonder she's been acting like a scared rabbit. She's terrified, and for good reason.

Eventually, the gym clears out after the evening classes are over. Nate comes over to tap me on the shoulder. It's past eight, and he's about ready to lock up early.

I look up. Layla is sitting on the bench, taking a drink of water.

"It's all yours," Nate says, jerking his head at the empty gym. "Lock up, okay?"

"Thanks, man." I nod and watch until the door swings shut behind him. Then I turn to Layla.

"Come on, baby," I say. "In the ring. And take off your shoes."

I toss my sneakers and gloves toward the lockers and hop into the ring. Confused, Layla follows, and then we're standing, facing each other.

"You can take off your hand wraps," I tell her. I'm not wearing any, and my knuckles are going to fuckin' throb tomorrow. But I don't really care. The pain actually feels kind of good.

Layla does as I say and drapes the reams of black fabric over one of the ropes. Then she faces me. "What are we doing?"

"I wish I could be with you all the time," I say quietly. "It's crazy, but I do. I just want to protect you from fuckin' everything."

I look at her straight on, and her blue eyes are wide, scared. The expression guts me every time. I walk around this city feeling like I have a hole in my stomach. I just want that look to disappear. I want her to look at the world, at *me* with confidence again. With openness, love, excitement, optimism. Just like she used to.

"I know," she whispers, clenching her hands together. She looks down.

I sigh. "But I can't, baby. It's not...that's not reality. So...I want to show you how to protect yourself."

"Isn't that what we started doing this last month?"

I smirk. She's learning to throw a decent punch, but she's still only a hundred and twenty pounds soaking wet. Things like height and weight matter in boxing. But there are other things she could learn to do better.

"If a guy like *Giancarlo*"—fuck, that name really does put a bad taste in my mouth—"forced you down again, do you think you'd be able to fight him off?"

Layla bites her lip and shuts her eyes. I'm taking her somewhere she doesn't want to go. But I have to. *She* has to.

I shut mine and say a quick prayer, asking God, whoever that is, to forgive me for what I'm about to do.

Then, I attack.

"What the—WHAT ARE YOU DOING?" she screams.

It doesn't take much. A quick twist of her wrist and a knock on her knee to push her to the ground, pinning her under my weight. I'm sprawled on top of her, and to my surprise, she barely fights, lost more in the confusion.

"Nico," she cries as her voice wavers. Tears start to fall down her face, and it just about breaks me. "Nico, please. W-what are you doing to me?"

"Listen to what I tell you to do," I say low. I'm going for soothing even as my heart breaks. I don't want to do this. I don't want to hurt her ever again. But she needs this. Maybe just a little more pain to fight through.

"You have strong legs," I tell her. "Maybe even stronger than mine. Push up on your heels, and twist your body as hard as you can. Throw me off, baby. You can do it."

She opens her mouth like she's going to argue, but then she tries, lifting her pelvis into me, and then twisting around. I move a little— it's actually hard to stay on top of her like this when she does that— but I don't fall completely off.

"Keep going," I tell her as I brace her wrists with mine. "Come on. I'm not a good guy right now, NYU. I'm a fuckin' asshole. I'm taking advantage of you. Get me the fuck off!"

"I can't," she whimpers, and beneath me, I feel her body deflate. It wrecks me, inside and out. My girl, my *strong*, beautiful, incredible fucking *woman*, withers like a blade of grass without water.

But she can do this. I know she can. She has to.

"As hard as you can," I growl into her ear.

"Stop," she mewls. "Please stop."

"Make me."

And then I release one hand and draw it down her face, closing it around her neck. I take a deep breath and close my eyes, repeating a prayer again. God, forgive me. Lord, give her strength.

And then I squeeze.

"NO!"

Layla howls like a wolf, her body suddenly coming to life. She pushes with her hips, once, twice, gaining momentum for a third, final push, combined with a twist that's more awkward than anything else. But, as if she just stuck her finger in a light socket, a shock of power courses through her body. She throws me off, forcing me a solid two feet away, giving her enough space to roll over, wheezing while she clutches her neck. I lie on my back, rubbing my sore ribs where she kicked me on the way out. I couldn't have stopped her if I'd tried. But I'm so fuckin' glad of that fact.

I turn to her, unsure of what I'm going to see. Layla's scrambling up, her hand still at her neck. She glares, her eyes lit up like blue fire.

"*What* the fuck was that?" she spits. "What were you *doing?*"

"Teaching you to protect yourself." I clamber up, a silly, stupid grin on my face despite the fact that my head is fuckin' throbbing. Knuckles *and* headache in the morning. I couldn't care less.

"Fuck!" Layla shouts, kicking at the ground. "Why-why are you fucking *smiling*, you asshole?!"

"Because you did it!" I crow. "You fuckin' did it, woman! And if you can do that to me, a trained fuckin' fighter, you can protect yourself against anyone, baby. Don't you see that?"

But when I look at her, ready to see victory all over her face, she's crying. Her beautiful face is marred with tears, her blue eyes shining and red-rimmed, her rose-petal mouth screwed up in misery. Fuck me. This isn't what I wanted. To break her even more.

Immediately, I scramble to her side and pull her into my arms. Fuck the sweat. Fuck all of that. I just want her to stop crying. I can't fuckin' take it when she hurts like this.

"Shhhh," I say. "I'm sorry. I'm so fuckin' sorry, baby. I shouldn't have pushed you like that. What was it? The pressure at your neck? The holding you down? Fuck me, I'm so goddamn sorry."

"*No!*" she shouts into my neck, even as her hands cling at my arms, tight enough that her fingernails dig into the skin. Several more sobs wrack through her small body into mine. "Don't be sorry. It's-it's not that," she stutters as her tears slow to a trickle. She looks up and wipes them away angrily. "It's not that. It was...it was fine."

I lean back. "It was?"

She nods. "I'm glad you did it. I sort of hate you right now, but I'm glad I could do it too."

I push a lock of hair out of her face. "Then what is it?"

She sniffs, and when she looks up, the pain blotting her gorgeous blues, as deep as the ocean itself, sends another ripple of hurt through my body.

"I liked it," she admits, even as her lower lip trembles. "It hurt. Your hands around my throat. Holding me down. I hated it. And I fucking liked it too." She shivers. "Love shouldn't hurt, right?" Her voice shakes when she looks up. "That's what I learned from all that mess. *That* wasn't love, and it took me months to figure that out. So why...why do I like it?"

I exhale, not out of frustration, but because finally, *finally* we're getting somewhere. I see it clearly now. She wants what she wants, just like we all do. But she hates herself for it.

"I know why I ended up with someone like that," she whispers. "It's because a part of me...a part of me liked it." She looks up, her blue eyes wide and pained. "Why is that? He kept hurting me, but I kept going back. Just like I did with you."

Her words are straight and true and pierce me like arrows. Because she's right—I did hurt her. Several times, just like she did to me. And like addicts, we both kept coming back to each other, looking for more of that same, bittersweet rush.

"Some of us just learn it like that," I murmur.

I realize that this is one of the few things Layla and I have in common. We might come from totally different worlds, she and I, but we both learned in our own ways that it was normal for people to hurt us.

But maybe that knowledge is also what might set us free.

"You know what I think?" I ask. I stroke the side of her arm, and she closes her eyes. But this time I don't scratch. "I think maybe it's okay to hurt sometimes."

Her eyes open, confused. "What?"

"People like us, well, a lot of people, really...maybe we need a little bitter to make sense of the sweet."

I turn my finger over and press my nail lightly into her skin, just enough for it to bite. The sharp twinge causes the same reaction in her—a shiver of pleasure, and then a pained look on her face. She shudders, but the goose bumps that rise all over her tell me it's not an unpleasant feeling. Her breath hitches, and so does mine.

"You feel this," I say as I draw my hand up her chest.

I place it, palm down, over her heart and thrill in the solid beat of it. She's affected by what I'm doing—that much is clear. Almost immediately, she places her hand in the same spot on my chest, directly over the compass I've had tattooed there since I was nineteen. The same age she was when I met her.

"I'm *never* going to break that again," I tell her. "That's a promise."

"But, you don't know if—"

"*Never*," I cut in.

I don't even blink, urging her to see the truth in my eyes. She searches my face for several moments.

"We can do it in ways that are good for each other. *I* can do that for you, baby. You just gotta tell me: what do you need?"

She swallows, then glances down at the other hand resting on her thigh. Slowly, she covers it with her hand, then clenches her fingers, forcing me to grab her thigh, hard enough that it might actually bruise. And then she kisses me. Hard.

"Ah!" she cries out as I nip her lower lip. But she doesn't pull away. This time she bites back.

"Again," she hisses after she sucks voraciously on my mouth.

And just like that, I'm hard as a fucking rock. It's been over a year of waiting for this, waiting for the moment where we really, truly connect again. I didn't plan for it like this. I didn't plan for the fuckin' bathroom of a shitty nightclub either, or the mat of a boxing gym. But if this is where Layla gets herself back, where we learn to be us again, I'll take it. However it comes.

"Okay," I say. "But only if you give it back."

I give her the rough, almost painful kisses she seeks, knead her legs, her thighs, her ass hard enough to hurt just a little while I grind myself into her. My cock finds her ready, just a few strips of fabric between us. There's nothing more I'd like than to bend her over and take her right now. I'd find her wet and willing, I know it.

But there will be other times like that, when we can go fast and furious. Right now, I need to make sure. I need to make sure it's right.

"What else?" I say as I take another harsh handful of her ass with a light slap. She moans lightly into my mouth. "What else do you want?"

"I want...oh! I want...*more*."

Her hands thread into my hair and yank. That hint of pain shoots down my neck, but it only turns me on more. Her mouth crashes into mine, and we're a sudden tangle of tongues and limbs. It's like a light turned on—my gamble paid off. I opened up a door, and Layla's sprinting through it. Right into me.

"Take—take these off," she says through a few more torrid, biting kisses. She paws at my shorts, and in about two seconds, I've kicked them to the floor along with my boxers. When I look back at her, she's done the same thing with her pants and is in the middle of taking off her top and sports bra. I watch, fuckin' mesmerized, as her breasts bob free. She cups them lightly.

"You said once you were a biter," she says with a sly smile. "Did you forget how?"

On my hands and knees, I cross the mat until I'm positioned over her, with Layla's back to the floor, a lot like we were only a second ago when she threw me off. The knowledge that she can even do that at all makes me want her even more. I bury my face in her breasts, licking, sucking, and even biting. She moans and arches her back.

"Does that seem like I forgot?" I growl before taking one nipple between my teeth and pulling a little.

"More," she beckons, a hand sliding around my head and urging me to one side. "Now."

I take her nipple deeply into my mouth and earn another low, long moan as I suck hard enough for it to pinch. I roll her nipple between my teeth, then bite a little, then a little more, until Layla starts to shake.

"Nico," she whispers, breathy as her legs open under me.

I'm pressed between her strong thighs, hard as one of the steel pipes crisscrossing the ceiling, and her slick heat moistens as I grind into her core. The tip of my cock slips in, and we both jerk as I switch to her other breast and continue that torture she desires. The torture she needs.

"Condom?" she whimpers even as her hips tilt, taking me a little further.

The hands in my hair pull harder, and with her breast still in my mouth, it's all I can do not to shove all the way in and drive her down to the mat. But I swear to God, I really *am* a fuckin' superhero, because I manage to pull out, my cock just hovering at her aching entrance. A different kind of torture. A different kind of sweet.

"Do we..." I pause, weighing the question. "Do we need it?"

Sometimes real closeness hurts a little too. But it's a pain that I crave also, just like she needs it from me. The knowledge that even if they don't, someone could hurt you. Layla's the only girl I've ever been with bare, and I know I'm the same for her. And it's been almost six months since...*him*. More than that for me. We've both been tested, and we talked about birth control before she came back to New York. There's nothing stopping us if this is what we want to do. Which, I realize, I do. I want it more than maybe anything I've ever wanted in my life. Just to be close to her. To know there's literally nothing between us, physically or mentally. To know that we belong to each other so much that our bodies actually become one.

The thought sends a convulsive shiver through me from head to toe.

In response, Layla arches up to kiss me, and her hands reach around to grab my ass and guide me fully inside. She's tight—*so* damn tight—enough that it takes a moment for her to get used to me. I'm not huge or anything, but big enough to stretch her small body. As I push inside her completely, she flops back onto the mat, breathing hard as I take her breast into my mouth again and bite down.

"Nico!" she cries out. It's not a whimper, but a shout. And it echoes, again and again off the cinderblock walls and concrete floors of the gym as I drive into her.

Her voice, its strength, lets loose some animal in me that's been dying to be free. With Layla, I am never anything but my purest self. I have no name. I'm barely a man, but whatever I am was made for her, her essence, her body. Made to devour, pillage, ravage, feast on this body that has only ever fit mine perfectly.

Her muscles tense and her legs squeeze around my waist. The movement squeezes the rest of me too, and it only makes me pound into her that much harder.

"Fuck!" she cries out, hands grasping at the mat while she urges me onward.

"Is it...is this okay?" I can barely get the words out, I'm so fucking overwhelmed with want. Fear. Lust. Passion.

"Nico." I swear to God, if she didn't say it, I wouldn't even be able to remember my own name. But her eyes flash as she swallows. "Harder."

It's the only encouragement I need. In a half second, I have her flipped over onto her hands and knees, two handfuls of her ass in my grip as I yank her hips toward me and impale myself into her waiting warmth.

"Yesssssss!" I hiss as I pound into her.

"Yesssssss!" she cries, her hips pressing back, hit for heavy hit.

"Again!" she shouts.

So I do. Rhythmically, my hand finds the solid flesh of her with a satisfying crack once, twice, a third and final time that causes both of us to fall apart completely. Layla's body starts to convulse as my hands take two harsh handfuls of flesh so I can ram into her for the last time before I fall over her. We come together, and the walls of the gym seem to disappear. I can't see two feet ahead of me. I can't hear a damn thing. All I can do is feel, and what I feel is her. Layla.

CHAPTER SIXTEEN

Layla

"WELL, I GUESS THAT'S IT."

Shama sets her rolling bag by the door, then turns to me with a lopsided smile.

"Here," she says, holding out her key. "For your new roommate, whoever that will be."

I turn the brass piece over and back. I don't have a new roommate yet. Actually, I haven't even started looking, even though I really should. Shama promised to pay rent for at least a month or two until I find someone decent, but I haven't even put an ad on the off-campus housing site or craigslist. Something is stopping me from inviting a stranger into my house. I've been too burned by strangers in this city. I want my home to feel safe.

I shove the key in my pocket and give Shama a hug. Her flight to London is in three hours. There's a cab waiting to take her to the airport, off to embark on her newest adventure. Tears spring to my eyes as Shama returns my tight embrace.

"I'm sorry I can't be there today with you," she says. "I want to see the look on that bastard's face when he gets his."

I step back, swiping away the tears. The truth is, I'm not just upset about her leaving. The DA informed us that Giancarlo's trial was finally moving forward this week after months of delays. So far, he has refused to take a plea, and today the jury will announce the verdict. And on the recommendations of Nico, my therapist in Pasadena, and the counselor I started seeing at the student center, I decided to attend after all. Because like Nico said, I needed to face him on my terms.

Therapy. Self-defense. It's only been a week since our explosive reunion at Frank's, but already I feel like I'm on a better path forward. My fears haven't totally faded. Not even close. But I'm feeling stronger. Like maybe one day I can chase them away.

"It's okay," I say. "It was moved to five, so Nico will be there. And I think Gabe and Maggie are planning to come too."

"You're not alone here, dude," Shama says, like she knows what's going through my head. "You have Special Delivery. You've got his family too. It's not just you."

I shake my head. "He hates being called that, you know."

"I know. It makes me want to do it more now. But seriously, he is kind of special, you know? It fits."

I smile. It's true. Nico *is* special. He's been special since he delivered himself into my life. Inwardly, I can see Nico shaking his head even as his dark eyes dance. Mumbling, *Baby, you are corny as fuck,* even as he leans in for a kiss. The thought just makes me smile more.

"Wear something blue," Shama says. "To make your eyes pop. Then stare that dickhead down as they cart his ass back to jail, say good fucking riddance, and move on with your life."

I nod. She makes it sound so easy. "I'll do my best."

———

At five o'clock, the court is running late, and so is everyone else.

There are several cases being tried today, and the small gallery is mostly full. Giancarlo is being held in the back, waiting for the bailiff to call his name, and I'm alone in the third row of the gallery, my arms wrapped around my waist, feeling much colder than I should in an overheated room full of people.

"It's in your favor," the DA said earlier in the week when she called with an update. "You never know what a jury is going to do, but I doubt this one will be lenient."

They chose to go for the drug crimes instead of domestic violence, since it was easier to prove, and on top of that, the fact that Giancarlo's wounds from Nico had been much worse than the ones I had incurred from Giancarlo made it difficult to prosecute him on that account. He hadn't shown any desire to file charges against Nico, considering the number of witnesses there. But the drugs in the closet were another story adding up to charges of possession, intent to distribute, and trafficking.

The second hand on my watch ticks while I wait—the watch I can't ever look at without remembering how it was taken from me. I squeeze my eyes shut and wait some more. As the courtroom murmurs rise, the colder and colder I feel. I start to rock slightly.

"The here and now," I whisper to myself, keeping my eyes closed. I'm not sure how much more of this I can take, and it hasn't even started. "The here and now."

"Hey, baby."

I open my eyes to find Nico filing into the bench seats, with Maggie and Gabe right behind him. Warmth blooms inside me. Thank God.

Nico wraps an arm around me and pulls me in for a kiss. "You okay? You look a little freaked out over here."

I snuggle into his arms, which I swear have gotten even bigger over the last few months. He's come straight from the academy, still in the uniform, which under normal circumstances, would excite me. He smells slightly of smoke, sweat, and men's deodorant. It's the best smell in the world.

"How was the day?" I ask after I wave hello to Gabe and Maggie.

"Fine, just fine. Two more weeks, and we're done." He sighs and leans back against the bench. "I can't wait. Oh, by the way, they're getting things together for the graduation. You, um, you don't want to come, do you?"

I turn so I can look at him in the face.

"Of *course* I'm coming to your freaking graduation, you goon," I tell him. "I wouldn't miss it."

Nico breaks into a wide smile that injects another shot of warmth into my chilled heart. He practically glows as he kisses me again. It's a chaste kiss—after all, we're in the middle of a courtroom—but it's full of promise of something more later. This is what love is supposed to feel like, I remind myself. Where you feel joy for your partner and only want them to succeed. Where their victories feel like your own. I hope I never forget that again.

But as Nico settles back into his seat again and pulls me close, a bit of tension vibrates through his broad shoulders. It takes me a few minutes to figure out what it is.

"Is this...is this where you were sentenced?" I wonder, looking around the room.

Nico glances at me, clearly surprised.

"No," he says, but the flash in his eyes and his quiet, resigned tone tell me I was right on the money. "It was at the family court in Brooklyn. They handle most of the juvenile offenses there."

"Was it a lot like this, though?" I ask as I look around.

It's a lot like the courtrooms you see on TV: a few rows of pew-like bench seating, a barricaded area for the lawyers and the judge, and a few other designated spots for the jury.

There's a long pause.

"Yeah," he says finally. "It did."

We sit there together silently, collectively lost in thought while Maggie and Gabe are chatting about who's going to babysit Allie next week while Maggie goes to a job interview. I assume Nico's still remembering that day when his life changed forever, the day he offi-cially became the criminal so many think he is.

Except he's not, I think as I toy with the FDNY stitching on his rolled-up, navy-blue sleeve. And honestly, he never really was. I wonder sometimes if the perception of Nico as a criminal is more in his own head than anyone else's. The residue of a single mistake. He's been the savior of so many in his life—his family, his mother. Me. And in just over two weeks, he'll be a bona fide public servant, one of the good guys. The fact has made a visible difference too. He walks different now. Straighter. Taller.

Nico twists some of my hair around one finger, playing with it the same way I'm playing with his sleeve. I don't know if it's just because we're getting used to each other, but I like to think that maybe it's our new normal. I like the constant touching. It provides comfort in a world where I so frequently feel alone. His presence makes me feel like I can overcome almost anything. Maybe both of us will be able to say goodbye to something dark in our pasts today.

"Layla?"

We swivel to the left, to where a woman in a bland gray suit beck-ons. I recognize her voice. Dana Delaney, the district attorney who's been prosecuting the case. She gestures for us to follow her out of the courtroom just as the bailiff calls for everyone to stand, and another defendant enters the room. Maggie and Gabe follow us out, but give us an extra few feet of space.

Outside, we're eclipsed by the echoing stone corridors of city hall. The DA ushers Nico and me to a quiet corner and gives me a regretful look.

"He took a plea," she says frankly, flipping a pen between her fingers. "It's done."

Everything in me wilts. I hadn't realized until now how much I'd been counting on this. A moment to face him, my attacker, and put the demons to rest while the jury gave him what was coming to him. He was going to be served justice. He just had to be. I had been building myself up for this all week. And for what? To be told in the end that he was going to walk away?

"What's the deal?" Nico's strong, deep voice, breaks through my internal cacophony. He pulls on the bill of his hat, and it doesn't escape me the way the DA's gaze flickers appreciatively over his broad, trim body.

"It was last minute," she says. "But the Argentinians came through for him. It's complicated, involving a four-part exchange that basically gets the U.S. government a nasty member of a Mexican drug cartel in exchange for some intelligence and Giancarlo. I can't really go into details, but what you need to know is that his trial is going to Argentinian courts, and he's being escorted to the next flight out of New York." She shrugs. "I'm sure I don't have to tell you that his father had a bit to do with it. I'm sorry."

I wilt even further. It doesn't take a genius to realize that this means salvation for Giancarlo. He's the son of one of the wealthiest families in Buenos Aires, and his father has his fingers in plenty of politicians' pockets there. He'll get a slap on the wrist, if he's even tried to begin with. So much for justice.

I sag into Nico's side, and he mutters a few expletives under his breath.

"Hey." The attorney pulls my attention back. "He won't be allowed back in the country. As far as the USA is concerned, he's a *persona non grata*. The marshals are escorting him to holding now, and from there he'll be put on a flight out of here. That's something."

Nico's hand squeezes my shoulder.

I nod. "Yeah. It is."

A heavy door down the hall opens, and as if on cue, Giancarlo comes out, rubbing his wrists that must have been cuffed moments ago. He's flanked on either side by two agents—likely the marshals the DA was just talking about.

"I'm fine. I'm *fine*," Giancarlo spits as one of the marshals tries to escort him via the elbow. He shakes the man off as they approach the exit.

I'm frozen as I watch him, and next to me, Nico stiffens. As if he knows I'm there, Giancarlo straightens and turns his head.

"You!" he shouts from across the hall.

Nico moves in front of me, but for some reason I push him back. Giancarlo points a finger at me, and like he's suddenly acquired some kind of superhuman strength, breaks free of his captors and comes charging toward me at a run.

"You have *ruined* me!" he shouts. "You stupid whore! Do you know what will happen to me in Buenos Aires? Do you know what my father will do?"

He lunges forward, and beside me Nico tenses like a spring, his fists balled, one foot shifting automatically as Giancarlo approaches. The marshals sprint to catch up.

But before Nico can pounce, my right arm shoots out like a snake and strikes him in the belly. Giancarlo isn't hard like Nico—he's long and lean, but was always a little soft. The last thing he expects is for my fist to catch him in the belly, and the effect causes him to keel over immediately, like he's had the wind knocked out of him.

"Bitch!" he wheezes even as he drops to the floor, clutching his stomach. "You will pay for that!"

"No," I state clearly, staring down at him. "You don't get to hurt me anymore."

With a black look, Giancarlo scrambles to his feet, but before he can lunge again, the marshals grab him by both arms and haul him away, this time in handcuffs.

"You ruined me!" Giancarlo shouts again and again, his voice a chorus down the arched stone hall.

I open my mouth to reply, but think better of it, only now letting Nico wrap a strong forearm around me, almost like he's holding me back more than protecting me. We watch the marshals hustle Giancarlo down to the other end of the hall, out the double doors. New York, with its incessant noise and constant movement, swallows him up.

————

As if he knows that I need some kind of outlet, Nico takes me up to Frank's, where we spend the next hour grappling, fighting the demons that seem to follow us wherever we go. Despite the "knock-out" I managed to deliver in city hall, I feel even more defeated.

Giancarlo's gone. I'll never see him again.

But strangely, I still feel some compassion for him, regardless of what he did. I did care about him once. Giancarlo isn't totally evil. Some terrible darkness swallowed him up, but from time to time I saw glimpses of vulnerability. It was around that vulnerability that we connected. It was what made me stay with him for as long as I did. Now I find myself wondering what made him the way he is. Where his darkness came from to begin with.

It's well past eight by the time Nico and I flop back on the mat after over two hours of sparring together. He's taught me several other moves I could use in the event of another attack, although I think it's more to soothe his own worries than mine. He's been quiet all evening, letting me process the events at the courthouse, but also maybe processing his own thoughts. There was no vicious love-making on the mat this time around. It was all business; we barely spoke, going at it until we were both literally falling down from exhaustion.

"You want to get something to eat, sweetie?" Nico asks as we exit the gym.

I nod, taking his hand. I'm hungry, and we can pick up something quick. But I have something else in mind first.

I tow us down Ninth Avenue until I find the exact thing I'm looking for.

"A tattoo parlor?" Nico looks at me, confused. "Seriously?" He fingers my hand, then drops it so he can cup my cheek. "Tattoos... they don't go away, baby."

I lean into his touch. The warmth that has nothing to do with his body temperature seeps through me, balm to my wounds, thaw to my frozen insides. Nico heals me, just like he always does. Just like he always will.

"I need to do something more," I say. "Something that makes this day more than just about the day my ex tried to kill me. Again."

Nico's mouth is a straight line. "He wouldn't have touched you. *I* would have killed him first." Then he looks down. "I don't know if today is the best day to be making snap decisions, NYU. Especially with something permanent."

I shake my head. I'm saying this wrong.

"It's not like that. It's more like..." I tip my head to the side, trying to come up with the right words. I tug down Nico's shirt collar so I can see the edge of the big compass tattoo over his heart. "Why did you get this?"

He's told me this story, but he reiterates it anyway. "It was to remember," he says. "Not to lose track of who I was. My direction."

"Do you remember my bruises? The cuts on my face?"

His face darkens. "How could I forget?"

I chew on my lip. "This city, other people. My dad. Giancarlo. Other people marked me. Today, I want to mark myself. I want the next intense thing I feel to be because *I* wanted it, not because someone else did it to me. Does that make sense?"

Nico watches me for a moment, his black eyes burning under the streetlight. "You want control," he says softly, in a voice that's almost dangerous.

Slowly, I nod.

Nico examines me for a few more moments, like he's trying to figure out some other puzzle about me. Finally he nods back and pulls the brim of his Yankees hat down low.

He glances at the shop, then takes my hand. "If you're going to do this, we're doing it right," he says. "Come on. I know a much better place."

CHAPTER SEVENTEEN

Nico

Fifteen minutes later, we're standing in front of the tattoo shop on Second Avenue where my friend Milo has worked since we finished high school. Milo did my ink back then too, when he was an apprentice still learning his trade. Most of the art on my shoulder and half sleeve was me providing a canvas for him to practice on. I'd sketch, he'd trace, and I'd zone out on his table, half-enjoying the pinch of his needle. I figured I was already a fuckup, so I might as well get some badass art to look like it. My mom freaked when she first saw the swirling lines that Milo put all over my shoulder and arm. She said it made me look like a thug.

"Isn't that what I am?" I asked her at the time.

"*No,*" she replied, in both Spanish and English so I'd know she really meant it. Even if it's the same word in both languages, my mother has a way of making them sound different. Again and again and again.

Turns out, of course, that she was right. But I didn't really believe it until I met the girl standing next to me, a person in the same exact place I was when I stood outside these doors, back for Milo to put the compass on my chest. I had just gotten my first legit job, the one with FedEx. I wanted something that was *mine*.

I don't regret any of my tattoos, and I'll probably get more one day. They're a map of who I am, who I thought I was, what I wanted. Reminders of a life I wanted to put behind me, and another I wanted to have. If Layla wants that grounding, I'll help her get it. And I won't have her do it alone.

The bell above the door to the shop jingles when we enter. A white girl with blue hair, dime-sized gauges in her ears, and skinny arms full of multicolored tattoos, some of which I recognize as Milo's designs, is paging through a book at the glass counter.

She gives us both a bored look. "Can I help you?"

"Is Milo free?" I ask. Layla drifts away to check out the tattoo designs on the walls

"WHO THE FUCK IS THAT?" A loud voice calls from behind the red curtains that protect the rest of the shop from prying eyes.

I roll my eyes at the gauges girl. "Looks like he found us."

She shrugs and turns back to her magazine. Layla comes to my side as Milo charges through the curtain in the doorway.

Average height, wearing a white t-shirt, jeans, and a red backward Giants hat, Milo looks pretty much like your average Irish kid, with the exception of one thing: everything but his face is completely covered in tattoos, including his fingers and neck.

"What the fuck. Nico fuckin' Soltero—how you been, man?"

I slap my friend's palm and let him pull me in for a quick embrace before he steps back to look me over.

"I heard about you and the FDNY," he says, noticing my uniform. "That's the shit, Nico. Congratulations."

"Thanks, man." I shrug, like it's no big deal, but I don't know if I'll ever get tired of hearing people say this. Talk to me with that kind of admiration. Beside me, Layla grins. Yeah, I'll never get tired of that either.

"And who's this?" Milo sticks a hand out to Layla, who shyly takes it. "How're you doin'?"

"Milo, this is my girl, Layla. Layla, this is Milo. He's the talented bastard who did all of my work."

Layla brightens at the mention of my tattoos, and I stifle a grin. She never says anything, but I can tell she likes them by the way her eyes light up whenever I take off my shirt, or the way she traces the black lines with her fingers.

"Nice to meet you," she says. "I, um, I'm an admirer."

Milo leers. "Yeah, I bet you are, sweetie. But you know I just put down the ink. Your man here is the one with the real talent. You ever seen him sketch?"

Layla immediately blushes. She's thinking of some of my sketches of her; I'd bet money on it. She then turns beet red when I lay a kiss on her cheek.

Milo winks at her, then turns to me. "So what are we doing? Are you looking to add to your sleeve? I have this crazy new pattern I've been wanting to try out. If you want something new."

I shake my head. "Maybe after I graduate. Today we're paying customers. Actually, Layla's the one who wants something."

I look down at her, asking wordlessly if she still wants to do this. Her full lips quirk into a half smile before she turns to Milo, who's looking her over more appreciatively. I just focus on her.

"All right," he says. "Come on back. I'm pretty much done for the night, so I think we can figure something out."

We follow him behind the curtain to his booth in the back of the shop. It contains a padded table that's curtained off for privacy and the various equipment Milo needs to do his thing. He gestures for Layla to take a seat on the table, and she hops up while I lean back against it next to her, my hand on her thigh.

"So," Milo says as he leans against the counter across from us. "What are we doing today, pretty? Something on the wall?"

"Easy," I warn him, but my friend just rolls his eyes.

"You gotta keep this guy on his toes," he tells Layla. "Now that I know he's going to get all big bad wolf on me, I'm going to have to flirt with you all day. You down with that, honey?"

I growl. I can't help it. Layla just laughs and drapes her arm around my neck.

"I'm okay with it," she says before she kisses my temple. "I kind of like the big bad wolf sometimes. But he knows deep down that he's the only one that matters anyway."

I know he's joking—they're both joking—but her words still calm me, and I relax into her touch. I can save my growls for later, when we're alone.

"I...want a script," Layla says. "I was looking at some of the ones on the wall, but actually..." She shifts uncomfortably, and I turn to find her blue eyes wide and uncertain. "I was hoping you'd write it for me."

I frown and turn completely so I'm facing her. "You want my shitty chicken scratch on your body?"

Layla strokes my cheek lightly. She opens her mouth, then glances at Milo, like she's not sure she wants him in the room. Then she swallows and speaks in a low voice.

"I want *you* on my body. You're already there. Knowing you has changed me. You make me stronger. Your *love* and belief in me makes me stronger. I..."

She blinks, and for a split-second, a slight shimmer glosses her eyes. She's trying not to cry in front of Milo, and damn if it doesn't make me choke up too.

Layla looks straight at me. "I don't *ever* want to forget it."

For several seconds, I can't speak. It feels like my heart is lodged in my throat while every emotion I have buried inside is rushing to my head.

"I love you," Layla whispers. "*So* much."

"Fuck," I finally breathe, sliding my hands around her waist and pulling her flush to me. "You have no idea, *mami*. No fuckin' idea how much I love you."

We stand like that for a few moments until Milo clears his throat behind us. I swallow and turn around.

"I guess I'm writing something down," I tell him.

Milo chuckles and shakes his head. He's looking at me the way we used to look at our other friends who paired off with girls. Like they were jokers, the poor schmucks, totally pussy-whipped. And maybe I am. But I couldn't be happier about it.

Milo gets me a piece of paper and a Sharpie. "Don't worry about size," he says. "I can blow it up before I make the trace. Just make sure it's written the way she wants it." He glances at Layla. "Don't forget, pretty. This ain't comin' off."

Layla smiles shyly. "I know."

Milo leaves to get the materials to do the trace for the tattoo, and I turn to Layla with the paper and pen. "What am I writing, baby?"

Layla bites her lip, then leans over the paper with me. "Three words. The first word is spelled s-a-u-d-a-d-e."

It's not until I've written out the letters that I realize what I've spelled. I look up.

"Saudade?"

Layla nods shyly. "And then write, *para tí*."

I finish scratching out the words on the paper, then stare at the uneven black letters as I register what she's telling me. A little over a year ago, right before everything went to hell, Layla and I sat together on a beach in California and confessed what was in our hearts. At the time, it felt like there was nothing to lose. We were apart, with no real future ahead of us. It was a moment, just a recognition of what we were. How we really felt.

———

"Brazilians have a word for that, you know," she said as she played with my fingers. "Saudade. It's...it's hard to explain because there isn't a translation. But the way I had it explained to me, it's like when you yearn for something or someone. Like your heart speaks to their heart,

and when they're gone, it's that emptiness that remains. It's a longing, maybe for something that never even happened."

In Portuguese, they say it: "eu tenho saudade." *And to that, I whispered in Spanish:* "para ti." *For you.*

———

I blink, pulling myself back to the present.

"But you have me now," I wonder aloud. "How can you miss something you have? Because you do have me, Layla. I ain't going nowhere."

Layla shrugs, her cheeks flushed. "I'll always miss you a little," she says. "The bitter and the sweet, right?"

I watch her for a moment as I begin to understand. She's right. No matter how much I love Layla, no matter how close she lets me come, a part of me will always want to be closer, will always want more of her. It's the feeling I have when our bodies are joined, when I'm buried so deep in her I think she might split in two. We devour each other, again and again, and still my heart, my soul, my entire fucking being shouts for more.

Saudade. A longing that never leaves. The bitter *and* the sweet. Just like us.

"Okay," I say. Then I hand her the pen. "Then you have to write it too. How do you say 'for you' in Portuguese?"

Layla's soft pink lips quirk into a half smile. "Are you...?"

"If you're doing this, I am too," I tell her. "It's something we *both* have, right? Write it down."

With another shy smile, Layla writes out the phrase "*saudade de voce*" in her neat, slanted cursive. Her handwriting is delicate and curling, unlike mine. I run a finger over it, and when Milo comes back in, I hand him the paper.

"We're doing two," I tell him as he examines the paper. "That one's hers. The other's mine."

Milo nods, not even bothering to challenge me. He knows me too well. "Where are they going?"

"Right here," Layla pipes up. She points to her ribs, the side of her torso, just under her arm.

Milo bares his teeth. "You sure about that, pretty? That spot is really, really painful. I wouldn't recommend it for your first time."

Layla presses her lips together and nods vehemently. "I want to *feel* it," she says fiercely as she looks at me.

I nod, then turn to my friend. "Me too," I tell him. "Let's do it."

———

Thirty minutes later, after Milo's enlarged and then sketched our messy writing onto the transfer paper, my words are stamped on Layla's side. She lies on the table in only her bra, side up, while Milo scoots on his stool next to her as he snaps on a pair of thick latex gloves.

"Are you sure you want to do this?" I ask again.

Layla props up on her elbows, which pushes her breasts together, putting some *very* inappropriate thoughts in my head. It's been a long time since that night at Frank's. I'm not exactly crazy about the fact that my buddy is seeing her like this, and unfortunately, the wild look in her big blue eyes is only making the effect that much worse. I shift awkwardly on my chair, trying to adjust myself without giving it away.

"Do you think it will look stupid?" she asks.

"No!" I protest. "As it happens, I think you'd look fuckin' hot with a little body art," I answer before I can stop myself. Well, it's the truth. "I just don't want you to hurt."

"Well, that's just the reality, man," Milo puts in. "You know that better than anyone. But I don't think you've had anything as bad as the ribs, to be honest."

He turns on the needle. The buzz fills the small space, enclosed by the red curtains.

Layla looks back at Milo. "I said I *want* to feel it," she says clearly over the buzz, both to him and me. "I'm not going to hide from pain anymore. Do it."

Milo looks at me. I nod, even though my stomach clenches. Here we go.

Layla flinches the second the needle meets her skin, and I flinch with her as I watch. Her sweet face screws up as Milo starts drawing over her delicate skin and moves across bone. It's a feeling I know well. The slight pinch when the needle first sinks into your skin, followed by a slight burning as the area around it reacts. It's a shock at first, but slowly, your body acclimates until it moves over a nerve or a particularly sensitive spot. But until then, the pain doesn't fade. It just regulates, steady like the hum of the needle.

"It hurts," Layla whispers, even though just moments before she was demanding the pain.

She extends a hand, clearly struggling to keep still as the needle digs into her ribs.

But for a second, I'm not sure if she's actually talking about Milo's needle. Her eyes are wide, and her lip trembles. Yeah, baby, I know, I want to say. This life we chose together was never going to be easy. And I'll never stop feeling guilty about that.

But then her gaze drops to my mouth, and there's a very different thought practically shimmering across her face. Take it away, those baby blues seem to say. Or maybe...balance it out.

I take her hand between mine and press my lips to her knuckles.

"Ow," she whimpers as the needle passes over her ribs again.

I wince myself. They say it's closest to the bone that hurts the most. I wouldn't know—mine are all over muscle.

"Hey," Milo puts in when Layla jerks again. "I'm going to screw it up if you keep doing that." He looks to me. "Can you help her stay still?"

I look back at Layla. She wants this, I know. So when Milo's needle starts buzzing again, I do the only thing I can think of to distract her, to take the pain away. I kiss her.

Almost immediately, she sighs, and her fingers relax their iron grips. Deep down, this is Layla's sweet spot, just like it is mine. For better or for worse, neither of us ever learned to take the good without the bad, the pleasure without a bit of pain. Love always had to hurt a little.

She moans as our tongues twist together. Suddenly I don't care that my buddy is two feet from us with his face six inches from Layla's breasts, close enough that he can smell her flowery scent or know the curves of her body. I don't care that we're sitting in a "room" divided only by flimsy fabric, surrounded by an entire shop of people who can hear everything we do. I can feel the vibration with her, feel the sting of the needle along with the sweetness of her kiss. And the combination is like a powder keg that's just been lit.

"All right," Milo says several minutes later. "I'm done."

Layla blinks at me as I pull away. "What? Already?"

She sits up, her long, dark hair falling like a waterfall over her shoulder. Her wet, pink mouth falls open, and just like that, I'm zero to sixty. Jesus, she's so fuckin' beautiful. And it's a *really* good thing I'm sitting down.

Milo smirks. "Maybe you should make out with all my clients when they get something painful," he says. "She went stone-still after you started with that."

"I don't think so," I say with a grin. "Layla's the only one I'm kissing anymore."

"Lucky you," he replies.

Layla blushes while Milo applies a bit of Vaseline and then a light bandage over her new tattoo, and then scrambles back into her t-shirt. She hops off the table, and I whip off my shirt and take her spot almost as quickly.

"All right," I tell Milo as he reaches for the other transfer. "My turn."

I sit still, watching Layla's eyes light up as her handwriting is printed onto my ribs, the opposite side as hers, so that when we stand together our words will face each other. Milo hums as he presses the paper down, and then removes it a few seconds later.

"All good?" he asks.

I check myself in the mirror on the opposite wall. "All good."

The machine starts again as I lie on my side.

"Come here, beautiful," I say, pulling Layla down for another kiss just as Milo's needle starts to pinch. "I'm going to need you to help me bear this pain too."

CHAPTER EIGHTEEN

Layla

IT'S LATE BY THE TIME WE GET BACK TO MY APARTMENT. AFTER grabbing some food by the tattoo shop, we meander in a quiet daze, hand in hand down Second until it morphs from the hipster crowd of the East Village past Houston, where the street sign turns to Chrystie, and the tattoo parlors turn to laundromats and kitchen supplies. As we approach Delancey, we pass an open basement door that seems to be housing some kind of banquet. Shouts in an Eastern European language tumble into the night.

New York gets a reputation for loneliness, for being one of the most cutthroat cities in the world. People come here, and they get chewed up and spit out; I know that better than anyone. Places like this force you to find your tribe, because if you don't, you might not last. You'll become cold, bitter, jaded. Maybe you don't even survive. Nico wraps a big arm around me and I smile up at him, grateful that he's adopted me into his tribe. If he hadn't...I might not have survived.

We cross Delancey and eventually come to a stop in front of my building.

"You want to go up?" Nico asks. "Or do you want to keep walking?"

I hesitate, staring through the thick glass door toward the vacant stairwell. Most of the apartments are still empty, since the landlord's only just finished remodeling them. They'll be rented soon, but for now, the building is big and silent.

"Baby?"

"I don't want you to leave." The words fall out of my mouth, quick and heavy.

When I look at him, Nico's brows are lifted in surprise. "Well, I kind of assumed I'd be staying the night, if that's cool with you. I have to get up early to get things done tomorrow, but I don't mind."

I blink, shaking my head. "No, I mean I don't want you to leave at all." I rub my face. This day has been exhausting, and I'm screwing this up. "Nico, I—"

Nico gently pulls my hand from my face. "Baby, it's okay. Let's just go upstairs. We'll watch a movie or something and crash on the couch." He rubs my shoulder and cocks his head. "You look like you're about to fall over."

I shake my head again, causing my hair to toss around my face. There's still one more thing I want to do. Say. A thought that's been swirling around my mind since Nico kissed me in the shop. If I'm being honest, it's probably been there since I stepped off the plane. But for some reason I can't quite get it out.

So instead of trying to speak, I pull out the key that's been in my back pocket since Shama handed it to me this morning. Wordlessly, I hold it out. The brass gleams under the streetlight.

Slowly Nico takes it. "What's this?" he asks, although cautious understanding is already spreading over his face as he examines the small piece of metal.

"It's Shama's key. Well...maybe your key. If you want it."

Nico looks back up, but I can't quite read the expression on his face. For a few moments, we just blink at each other like a pair of owls, and I'm struck again, like always, by just how handsome he really is. His beat-up Yankees cap is turned backward, allowing the lights above us to cast shadows under his chiseled jawbones, dusted slightly with black stubble. When he blinks, his eyelashes, a thick fringe, sweep across his cheeks. But it's always his eyes that really transfix. Almond-shaped and so dark brown they almost look black, they are fathomless. I was lost in them from the start.

"Just to be clear," he says slowly. "When you say mine...do you mean the key? Or...the apartment?"

I tug on the ends of my hair. "It's..." Just say it, you chicken. "Look, I don't want another roommate. I want...I want you. You're living on a couch right now. You should come live on my bed. Um, *our* bed. If you want it to be ours, I mean. Shit."

Nico's eyes widen as I trail off.

"You just...Nico, when I come home at night, I want to come home to you." Finally, I force myself to look back at him, terrified of what I might find. "Is that—is that crazy?"

He's still, a statue on this empty street corner. Beside us, cars are racing up and down Delancey, but we might as well be in a vacuum, the way the noise is rushing out of my head. Nico's full mouth is open. Still, he doesn't move.

"It's too soon," I murmur, more to myself than to him.

My heart drops in my chest, and I steady against the wave of disappointment that's coming with the realization. I hadn't known just how badly I wanted this until I actually said it out loud. Oh my God, what if I lose him because of this? What if he turns and runs from the crazy girl who's given him nothing but grief and drama, and who now wants him to play house with her?

"God. I'm so sorry. Nico, I'm not trying to pressure you at all, I swear. I know it's only been maybe a month since I got back, and we've been taking it kind of slow, and oh my God, I'm screwing this up, aren't I—"

I'm cut off with a kiss as Nico yanks me close and covers my babbling mouth with his. It's the same kiss from the tattoo shop, the one that burned deeper than any needle. The one that spurred me through the pain that's still burning slightly on my side.

"Stop," he says, breathless, his broad chest heaving, though he refuses to let me move away. "Just stop. Honest to God, baby. I thought you'd never fuckin' ask."

On this lonely corner, a golden halo of warmth surrounds us.

"Yeah?" I whisper, suddenly unsure. Did he really say what I think he said?

"What's the word?" Nico asks after he kisses me again. "Home?" He tightens the arm around my waist, careful to avoid the tattoo, and lifts me so that only my toes graze the ground. "That's what we are together, Layla. Home." He kisses me again. "Now come on. Let's christen *our* new place. Together."

———

A few minutes later, we're practically tearing down my door. Nico uses his new key to open it, and as soon as it's shut, he's dropped his bag to the floor and pulled me in for another kiss, the kind of kiss that might get us arrested if we ever did it in public. His hands are everywhere—up and down my arms, cupping my breasts, squeezing my ass, and without a thought, mine are flung around his shoulders, pulling him tight against me.

We just want to be close. As close as we can possibly get. For the first time, there are no ghosts threatening us from far away. It's just him. It's just me. Just...us.

Keeping his lips fused to mine, Nico guides us toward the bedroom, shedding clothing as we shuffle. His shirt. My shoes. His belt. My jacket. By the time we cross the threshold, there's a trail of clothing from the front door through the living room, up to my bed, and we're standing before each other in nothing but our underwear. Nico in those black boxer briefs that fit him like a second skin; me in plain black underwear and a bra, our matching white bandages skimming our sides.

Nico cups my face and kisses me again. In the blueish light that streams through my window—no, *our* window—his smooth skin glistens, and his black eyes shine with love.

I run my hands over his body, taking my time, just enjoying the feel of it when my fingers graze the frayed edge of athletic tape over a piece of gauze on his chest. I break away and look down.

"What is that?"

Nico looks down to where I'm staring at a small white bandage at the top of the hand-sized compass over his heart. He looks back at me.

"I, um, had Milo do one other thing while you were up front paying. You...you want to see it?"

I nod. Nico swallows heavily, then slowly peels the bandage off. He turns to toss the bandaging into the trash bin under my desk, but when he turns back, I can see the black script clearly: *layla.*

My name. Nothing more. In small, almost unintelligible letters, right where the missing North symbol should have been on his compass. But it's there, for anyone to see.

"Why?" The word slips out, even as tears start to cloud my vision.

"Because that's what you are," he says softly, pressing my hand firmly over the small, reddened words. It can't feel good—it's a fresh wound, just barely scabbed over. But he holds my hand firmly, and his gaze doesn't waver as he speaks. "Layla, I knew it before I came back to New York. A part of me even knew it before I met you."

I shake my head, unable to speak. This is...*he* is so utterly overwhelming.

"Do you remember your trip to New York with your dad? When you were, I don't know, maybe in junior high?"

It was a long time ago. I was thirteen, and my dad took me to New York for a birthday present when he had to attend a conference. I spent most of the time in his hotel doing homework, but we went out at night to restaurants and shows. Even a Broadway musical.

"You went to see *Phantom of the Opera*, right?" Nico asks softly.

I frown. "How did you know that?"

"Because I was there, baby. I was on my way to the subway with K.C. and Flaco. Flaco told me right then that I had gotten the job at FedEx. My first real job that wasn't hustling at some nightclub or helping my mom clean houses." He cocks his head and traces his thumb across my cheekbones. "We were going to celebrate, and the first stop was the tattoo shop, where Milo gave me my compass. I bumped into this girl. She was kind of awkward, and she had a mouthful of braces. But her eyes were like the bluest sky I'd ever seen. And even though she didn't say a word, I knew she saw right through me."

The memory rushes back with the force of a tidal wave. The trio of boys, maybe nineteen or twenty, laughing and joking loudly in the street with a mix of Spanish and English. "Ruffians," my father had called them, mostly referring to their backward hats and low-slung jeans. One bumped into me, then grabbed my arm to steady my fall. He was thinner back then, without quite the same level of swagger, but still strong and solid. His deep-black eyes and bright white smile cut through me, and I was stuck there on the sidewalk, staring at him until my father pulled me into the theater.

I blink, suddenly unable to stop the tears that have been threatening since Nico started talking. How could I have forgotten that moment? Something had always called me back to New York since those first visits...but I had never been able to say exactly what it was. What if it was him? What if it was Nico from the start?

"Every good thing that's ever happened to me has had you in it," Nico says as he brushes hair from my face. His thumbs wipe away the tears that spill, one by one. "I knew that one day I would find my true north. I just never imagined that would be a woman. The she would be this beautiful, inside and out. I never imagined she would be you."

"Nico," I whisper as he pulls me close again. His skin is so warm. He practically glows.

"It's you, Layla," he whispers back before he fits his mouth over mine. "It's always been you."

My mouth opens naturally to his as he literally sweeps me off my feet and lays me down in the bed. Our tongues tangle, lips grapple, but his touch is soft, floating over my skin like a feather. His kisses drift down my body as he removes my bra and underwear, and I watch, lovesick, when he stands up to remove his boxers. I forget sometimes what a work of art he really is. The way years of training have sculpted his body into perfectly cut lines, marred slightly with a few scars here and there, accented by the tattoos on his chest and arm. And now, of course, the words on his side and my name over his heart.

"Come here," he rumbles as he peppers my neck and chest with kisses. He sucks one nipple, then another into his mouth with vigor and just a little bite, but I don't shy. I don't need to. There is no one here but us.

"Fuck, you're ready," he groans as his hard, eager cock brushes against my entrance. "Always so goddamn ready for me."

I hiss lightly as his hand tickles over my bandage. He pulls away, looking down with concern. In response, I push him to his back, rolling over so I'm straddling him.

When he looks up at me, his eyes are big and open. "I don't want to be rough tonight," he says softly as his hands grasp my thighs.

His thumbs come together over that most sensitive spot at the juncture of my legs, and he presses lightly, eliciting a moan from deep in my chest. I rock into his touch, my eyes closed.

"Layla." His deep voice beckons. "Please tell me it doesn't have to be rough."

My chest tightens to the point where it almost hurts, but it's not a pain I hate. It's a pain I love. This is what it feels like to love someone so much you want to burst. The heart can only take so much, but what I feel for this man overflows any vessel.

I know that this time I won't need him to grab my skin so hard it bruises or bite my neck, shoulder, breasts like a beast. I won't need to claw at him or wrestle with him across the floor. We won't need to be rough, because we already did it to ourselves. Today. Yesterday. Most of our lives. I float a finger over his chest, hovering down over the bandage still on his side, the one that matches mine. These are wounds we've given ourselves on purpose. Wounds that, like all the others, will make us stronger. Together.

"It doesn't have to be rough," I say as I lower, slowly, surely, taking him inside.

His other hand finds mine, entwining our fingers as he sucks in a breath. The words on my side—his words—burn slightly, but I don't feel them. As I start to move, all I feel is him.

Nico tips his head back and shudders as I sink lower, taking him further inside me. I rock back and forth, luxuriating in the friction between us, even as his thumbs continue to circle my clit in time with the movement. We watch each other as I move, letting the sounds of our bodies joining, our hitched breaths, skin meeting skin, fill the room. Black eyes meet blue. Dark hands meet light.

I wonder now why I've been so scared to do this, to open myself to him this way. But at the same time, it's totally clear. Here, naked with him, body and soul, I am my most vulnerable. No one can hurt me like he can; maybe no one has. But I also know without a shadow of a doubt that he'll protect me with everything he has. He shelters my heart. He's more than just a lover. He's a partner. And there's nothing for me to fear in that.

"Come," I murmur as the knowledge flows through me, a river of pleasure channeling straight to where we join. It's fast. It's furious. And it's approaching faster than I anticipated. "I want you to come with me."

"Already?" Nico wonders, though I'm already starting to shake.

"Y-yes," I manage as I tip my head back, rocking my hips downward to take him even deeper. Oh *God*, he feels good.

Suddenly, Nico sits up like it's nothing, the rows of hard abdominal muscles flexing until his chest meets mine.

"Ah!" I flinch as his arms encircle my waist, landing on the fresh tattoo.

He tries to pull away, but I keep his hands where they are,

"No." I clasp his face between my hands. "I like it."

And I do. I start to move again, rotating my hips slightly to take him deeper with every movement. Nico groans, pressing his face into my breasts as his hands drop to my hips to guide my movements.

"Layla," he murmurs as I start to move faster. He tips his head up again, seeking my mouth like a drowning man.

"Nico," I whisper in between long, torrid kisses.

Balanced on one hand while the other maintains its iron grip around my waist, he meets each movement, pounding into me from below while I take him deeper, from above. He penetrates me. My heart. My body. All of me, in ways no one else ever will.

"Layla," he chokes out. "Fuck, baby. I'm...oh, God, I'm *here!*"

His teeth find my shoulder, and he bites down as he starts to shake. The slight sting is my undoing, and together we come apart in our own beautiful corona that banishes the cold glare of the city. It's the knowledge of that warmth that keeps me going, and builds my strength. If I am his true north, then he is mine. Together, we'll never lose our way again.

II

VALIÓ LA PENA

CHAPTER NINETEEN

JANUARY 2005

Layla

ALL WEEK. ALL FREAKING WEEK I'VE BEEN WAITING FOR THIS. It's been five days since we saw each other at the airport, when I came home from a very long month in Pasadena for Christmas. It was... nice. Safe. Boring. Sure, it was perfectly pleasant to take a break once my semester was over and spend some quality time at my grandparents' pool. My mom and I have continued to grow closer, and Dr. Parker agreed that I didn't need another prescription for Valium. Apparently Nico is all I need to sleep well at night, even though no one in California is currently aware that he's been acting as that cure for close to three months now.

But even after that month, it's still been another five days since Nico had to take an extra forty-eight hour shift at the firehouse in order to get this weekend off. Five days since our first fumbled coupling at 7 a.m. after he picked me up from my red-eye flight. Five days since he left me in bed that morning, desperate for more of him, but drowsy in the knowledge that there would be more, so much more, for as long as I wanted it. Five days of tapping my pencil irritably on my desk and squeezing my legs together in anticipation. Five days of texting and talking here and there before another bell went off and he had to dash out to be a hero.

In other words, it's been five days of pure torture.

Somehow, since October, this neighborhood, this tiny slice of New York that's not quite Chinatown and not quite Little Italy, became more than just an apartment. Nico moved in the weekend after Giancarlo's trial, and it was the perfect way to close that chapter of my life and start a new one based on *us*. We've celebrated multiple milestones there already: his twenty-eighth birthday with all of his friends and family crammed into the little two bedroom. Just before that, his graduation from the fire academy, which was much, much bigger.

It was a sight I'll never, ever forget. Nico stood on the bleachers with the other two hundred or so cadets in his graduating class. They were all kitted out in their dress blues—formal, navy-blue suits with the military-style hats that should have looked stiff, but instead just made me want to do very dirty things to my man. Nico stood taller, much taller than his not-quite-six feet. I sat with Carmen in the front row, and she held my hand on one side and Gabe's on the other while Maggie and Selena whistled loudly with Allie straddled across their laps. And after the presiding officers called everyone's names and shook their hands, Nico ran down the stairs and swept me up in a giant kiss before the rest of his family crowded around him with hugs, kisses. This man vibrated happiness and pride—more, I think, than he'd ever felt in his life. And therefore, so did I.

But that was months ago, and since then, he's lived the life of a rookie FDNY firefighter. He's stationed in Queens, which means long commutes from our place in lower Manhattan. He works forty-eight and seventy-two hour shifts for low pay, which he'll continue to supplement with shifts at AJ's until next year, when his probationary period is up, and he'll start making a real salary. It means that sometimes we barely see each other, particularly if his off days fall on an exam week for me. I'm one semester away from finishing school, and I spent the majority of November and December taking the GRE and applying for graduate school. In three months or so, I'll find out whether or not I'll be going to the school of social work at Columbia, Fordham, or NYU, or if I'll be waiting tables for a year while I try again.

Social work. Not law school. Because the other relief of living with someone who supports me and cultivates this feeling of safety is that I felt confident enough to pursue a future that isn't the one planned for me. My father, who still has barely spoken to me for most of the past year, has no idea about the change of plans, and my mother hasn't asked. But watching Nico's family's frustrations over Carmen's status inspired me more, especially when I compare it to my father's relatively easy naturalization. The more I see them struggle, the more I understand just how much of my family's fortune is just that: fortunate. Not just a product of hard work, but one of luck. I want to give back, but that's going to take work. And time. And probably a lot of debt.

So our lives aren't exactly easy. They're busy and our budget is tight, especially when we consider just how we are going to afford this apartment after I'm finished with school and my mom won't be paying my half anymore. But those are concerns for a few months from now, and these days, we both get to come home to each other. That's what counts.

I practically skip out of the 6 station on Spring Street, knowing he's at the apartment waiting for me. Normally I slow down, enjoying the eclectic window displays. On this block alone, there's a bodega, a rice pudding shop, an antique furniture store, and a kimono designer whose royal textiles loom over the sidewalk like emperors. But today, I'm practically running.

My phone buzzes in my pocket, and I pull it out as I dodge around a couple perusing a restaurant menu. They give me a dirty look. I ignore them.

"Hey, baby. You almost here? I forgot my key."

The anticipation in his deep voice vibrates against my cheek. It's that same feeling that spiraled between us, between coasts, for the last month. It thrums between us like a guitar string that's just been plucked, pulling me closer and closer to him. To Nico.

"T-two blocks," I stutter just as I turn down Elizabeth. God, I can barely speak.

I turn onto Delancey, the massive boulevard that cuts across Lower Manhattan, pouring across the Williamsburg Bridge into Brooklyn. I can see the corner of the six-story walk-up with the Chinese laundromat on the bottom, facing the still-green trees of Delancey Park. But I can't see Nico yet.

"Hurry," he says, his voice suddenly breathy and a little hoarse. "I'm...cold."

He's not cold. It's unseasonably warm for late January, and the man is a furnace. Whenever he's not out on a call, he spends most of his time in the firehouse gym. His metabolism could power all of lower Manhattan.

"I'm here," I tell him as I reach the corner. "I see you."

Across the street, he turns around. He's still in FDNY-issued navy pants and a t-shirt that pulls across the taut lines of his chest under his thick black jacket. He could change at the firehouse, but he rarely does because he knows how much I love seeing him in uniform. His favorite Yankees cap, curled tightly over his brow, casts a shadow over his eyes.

When he spots me, though, that hat doesn't hide his smile as he claps his phone shut and shoves it in his pocket. It's a bright, shining beacon; its light emanates, calling me to him. Calling me home.

"Baby! What the fuck are you waiting for?" he shouts, laughing. "Get your ass over here!"

He looks up and down Delancey. The big street, for once, is somewhat empty, the next round of cars at least four blocks away. Unable to stifle my grin, I jog across the six lanes, right into his arms just as another rush of cars arrives.

"You," he says as he pulls me close, "have been on the West Coast too fuckin' long, NYU. Waiting for streetlights. Pssh."

I can't help but grin. No one in New York waits for lights to turn to cross an empty street. But I don't even care that he's teasing. That's how happy I am to see him.

We stare at each other, until our mutual smiles start to fall, eyes drift to mouths, and the street corner, despite being mostly empty, starts to feel crowded. Too crowded.

Nico exhales heavily through his nose, chewing on his lip as he stares at mine. Every cell in my body vibrates for him.

"Um—come on," I manage. "Let's go inside."

He blinks, like some kind of spell was broken, then follows me to the door of our building. Behind me, he hovers, his broad hands at my waist while I pull out my keys.

"Stop that," I murmur as he nuzzles into my neck. "I can't get the keys into the lock when you're doing that."

"Mmmm." His deep voice rumbles against my neck. "I can't help it—you smell crazy good, and *fuuuuck*, I've been thinking about this all week." His tongue slips out, causing us both to shudder. "Baby, open the fuckin' door. I'm not waiting more than a minute, and then I swear to God, I'm taking you right here."

I smirk, even though the sudden hard length pressed into my back makes my hands fumble all over again. If anything, the last three months have made this yearning worse, rather than better. He's ready for me too. It's been a month of heavy breathing, daydreaming, and phone sex. And then another week of classes and training, with only a city between us. He wants me? I'm about ready to combust.

"Nico!" I squeal when his fingers travel under the waistband of my jeans.

His fingertips brush the elastic of my underwear, dipping a little further to tease at the dampness already building there before he pulls them out. Then, before I know it, I'm spun around and pressed to the glass door, and Nico's mouth is on mine. Warm, open-mouthed, and demanding, his kiss encompasses me completely, renders me starving in about a quarter of a second. My hands knock his bill up his forehead and grab his thick black hair. We're eating each other alive, right in front of my building, while more than one person passes us with hushed whispers and even a wolf whistle.

"Oooh, look at them."

I couldn't tell you who said it. Nico reaches around, pulls me into him and grinds into my waist while he messes with my keys. I can't even think. His taste consumes me.

Then with a click, the lock opens, and we topple inside. Jesus. I don't even care that the door is transparent. He could take me right here on the stairs if he wanted to, in front of all the neighbors that have slowly filled up our building, and I wouldn't argue one bit.

"Up," I mumbled in between kisses. "Up. Stairs."

"Fuck the stairs," Nico growls, and in a single, fluid motion, he squats down and hoists me over his shoulder like a sack of potatoes.

"Aah!" I whoop in surprise, but he's too busy stomping up the stairs like a caveman to answer.

From my vantage point, I have the privilege of watching his extremely round ass as it moves. Back and forth, back and forth. I reach down with one hand and squeeze, which only causes him to yelp and jog faster.

One of my neighbors' doors opens as we pass the fourth floor.

"Hi, Mrs. Dukakis!" I call through a bout of laughter as Nico continues his stampede.

"Are you all right, dear?" she asks as she follows our stumbling forms.

"She's fine, Mrs. Dukakis!" Nico shouts as he starts on the fifth flight. He's not even breaking a sweat. Apparently being a firefighter has given him some serious stamina.

"Is the door locked?" he asks as we climb the last set, his voice only slightly winded from his little run with an extra hundred and twenty pounds slung over his shoulder.

"Of course it's locked."

With another exuberant growl, Nico winds his way around the

final post and charges to our door, which he practically kicks in after he unlocks it.

"What's so funny?" he asks after he hauls me inside and dumps me on the couch.

I can't stop giggling—I've been laughing all the way up. I yank him down to me, and his hat topples to the floor along with my purse, allowing me to sink my fingers into his flattened curls. Everything is forgotten. I'm not even sure we closed the front door.

"It's nothing," I say between kisses. "Just that I've literally wanted you to do that since the first time I met you." His tongue is slick and urgent, and I open to it completely. "I remember thinking that your shoulders would be really good at carrying a girl some place."

Nico pushes himself up to examine my face. When he realizes I'm serious, he rewards me with a grin, this one is even broader than before. It lights up my room, even in the dark. My body hums in response.

"Baby," he said as he leans back down, "you only had to ask."

CHAPTER TWENTY

Layla

"Should we order some takeout?"

I open my eyes lazily. After conking out for about two hours after our little "reunion," Nico and I are only barely starting to wake up. And if the grumbling under my ear is any indication, so is his stomach.

Mine responds with a loud growl. I prop up onto my elbow and look at Nico, who's peeking at me through one open, squinted eye. I grin.

"Want me to get Chinese?" he asks. "I'll even get dressed and go pick up those dumplings you like instead of calling the place that delivers."

I pinch his side. "You don't want me to cook for you? I thought maybe you would have missed my skills in the kitchen."

He flops back onto the pillow. "Hmm. Did I miss chicken strips cooked in straight vinegar? Lemme think about that...I mean, it did almost blind me when I got home that night."

He twists his full mouth around, like he's really weighing the option, which makes me want to sock him and kiss him at the same time. Okay, so I'm not the greatest cook. I elbow him in the gut, causing him to keel over laughing. He grabs me and starts tickling my side, which he discovered about six weeks ago is incredibly sensitive.

"Okay, okay!" I shout as I thrash around. "I give, I give! Uncle! *Tío!* You win! I'm a terrible cook, and you didn't need to miss any of it!"

When Nico releases me, he's straddling my waist, naked in all his glory and laughing like a maniac. I sigh. I could probably go another round...but I need sustenance first.

"I missed *you*," he says leaning down for a kiss. "Like fuckin' crazy. But it's a good thing I can make chicken and rice, is all I'm saying."

I roll my eyes, but we're both still chuckling as we clamber off the bed and get dressed. The bedroom is ours now—my desk was moved into the other room, across from the other desk and easel that turned into a sort of studio for Nico. He usually has a few days off a week when he's not at the firehouse, and when he's not sleeping or taking care of stuff for his family, sometimes he'll escape to the other room and draw for a while. Most of the time those drawings end up looking a lot like me, but I don't like to pry. When he's ready to show them to me, he will. Which usually it ends up with us on the floor, since I can't help myself after I see them.

"Sesame chicken?" Nico calls from the kitchen, where he's dialing our favorite Chinese place on the next block.

"Egg drop soup for me. It's freezing outside. I still need to warm up."

I pull my hair into a messy bun, then walk into the living room just as Nico's flipping on the Knicks game, kicking his heels on the coffee table in a pair of joggers and a t-shirt that's threadbare enough I can see his tattoos right through the thin white cotton. He looks comfortable, and totally at home. It makes me want to pounce on him all over again.

The open space has changed a lot since he moved in. As soon as we had a little extra cash, we went to a consignment shop and bought a small dining set, a TV to replace Shama's, and a coffee table to go in front of the couch. The walls have a weird mix of both of our belongings—a few art posters I had from my dorm, the tribal masks Nico had hanging in his old room uptown, and a few small pictures of St. Mary and St. Christopher that Carmen gave us and Nico surprised me by hanging right away.

"It's good mojo," he said with a casual shrug.

I didn't argue. It seems to have been working.

The cupboards aren't empty anymore either. Nico, I discovered, is an incredibly clean eater and a reasonably competent chef. Remnants of his boxing training. He'll splurge once a week or so to eat out, but when he cooks, it's usually something simple: chicken and salad, or fish and a vegetable, but always tasty. Considering that I'm not much of a cook at all, I'm usually happy to do the dishes on the nights when he's home, and grab something cheap out on the nights he's not.

"You're going to ruin your liver if you keep eating that crap," Nico says as I flop down onto the couch with an open bag of Doritos and a book. But he grabs a handful of chips for himself and plucks the book from my hand, flipping through it for a second before handing it back. "Borges, huh? Sounds like some nice light reading. I liked the Neruda you read last semester better."

When he wasn't at the firehouse, Nico basically took half my classes with me last semester, browsing through almost all of my books as I finished the first term of my senior year of college. He bent over my shoulder while I wrote my essay on Caribbean trade patterns and another on Cuban immigration history (he was *very* interested in that one). He quizzed me before I took the GRE exam in December and read and reread the admissions essays I sent out for graduate school.

"What did Ileana say last week?" I ask as I snuggle into Nico's side. I inhale his scent, which is warm and a little smoky. He must have been called to a live fire today.

Nico's hand drifts over my shoulder, and he starts playing with my hair. He likes it curly because he can twist it around his fingers. I think he finds it soothing.

"We're still waiting on Gabe's application," he says. "It's been almost three months. We should hear back any day."

He rubs his face. After resubmitting the application for a travel license to go to Cuba, this time on an informational license, he and his family have been waiting on pins and needles for the Treasury to get back to them. It's a long shot, Ileana said back in October. Since they weren't journalists or government employees, it was unlikely an informational visit would be granted. But they still had to try. And keep trying. Otherwise, Carmen would be at the mercy of an immigration judge who may or may not believe her claim to Cuban nationality. And if they didn't, Ileana said, it wasn't a given she would be allowed to stay. That entirely depended on the judge.

"I don't know," he says sadly. "I'm starting to think I should just try to sneak in. I've heard of people doing that. They fly through Venezuela or some place like that and change their money there so they don't break U.S. law by spending money in Cuba."

I frown. "Couldn't you get in trouble for doing that?"

Nico shrugs. "I don't know. But I doubt it would be worse than my mother being deported."

We sit there quietly for a bit, letting the basketball game fill the awkward silence. He's tense, and I hate that there's no way for me to solve this problem for him. I've been doing my best to pay attention to the things I've learned in school about Cuban immigration, but it always comes down to one thing: to guarantee residency, Carmen needs documentation of her birthplace, or else she has to risk court. But getting those documents is another matter entirely, and I'm not sure I like the idea of Nico risking everything he's worked for to do that.

"So, I forgot to ask you earlier since we were, ah, busy," Nico says as I flip through my mail I still haven't gone through from the last month. His fingers draw absent circles around my shoulder.

"What did your mom say when you told her we were living together?"

I gulp. This has been a sore spot for a while. Nico has been patient, knowing that I wanted to tell her face-to-face after we spent some time together again. As far as my conservative mother knows, I have a roommate, but it's another NYU student. She likes Nico, but she wouldn't be so keen on him if she knew we were living together without being married. I don't want to think about what my father would do if he found out. We may barely speak these days, but I'm pretty sure the idea of his daughter living in sin would have him on a plane within twenty-four hours.

"Layla."

I sit up and turn to him. The guarded look on his face tells me he already knows what I'm going to say.

"I'm sorry," I squeak out. "I just...I couldn't. Not yet."

His face falls. And it just about kills me.

"Layla," he says. "Two months I've had to pretend I'm not here when she calls. Had to listen to you tell her about another roommate. It's fucked up, baby."

I hang my head. "I know." I sigh. "But, come on, you know how it goes. Your mom is Catholic too."

It's a stupid excuse, and the look on Nico's face tells me he thinks so too. "Yeah, she is. And she knows exactly where I'm living. She lights a candle, prays for our forgiveness, and is done with it."

"Yeah, but your mom doesn't pay your rent and your tuition."

"Maybe your mom shouldn't either, then."

We stare at each other, wrapped in a standoff. I feel terrible. I know hiding this is the wrong thing to do, and I hate it.

"Is that what you want?" I ask quietly. "I'll do it. But it will make things really hard. I'll have to drop out, probably. Apply for loans until summer or maybe fall semester and graduate then. I'll have to delay graduate school for another year if I do that."

Nico blinks, and the hardness in his face softens. "Would your dad really cut off your tuition if he knew?"

I shrug. "He's threatened it for a lot less."

"And you think your mom would tell him?"

I bite my lip. "Nico, it's just that my mom thinks I'm only barely able to stand up again by myself. She sees my last relationship as one that I need a lot of space from. If she knew that I had jumped right into living with you"—I pause when I see another round of hurt fly across his face—"not that *I* think that, but you know how she would get, well...she might...Nico, it probably would be the reason she'd finally call my dad."

Nico opens his mouth like he wants to say something else, but then his eyes drop, and he closes it.

"Fine," he says as he gets up. "I'm going to go get dinner. You have a bunch of other mail on the table, by the way."

"Please don't leave mad," I say, grabbing for his hand as he sidles around me.

He stops, and again, the hardness in his face melts a little as he looks at me. He leans down and gives me a kiss on the forehead.

"How the fuck can I be mad at a face like that?" he murmurs. Then, with a quick squeeze of my hand, he swipes his jacket off the floor and leaves.

My stomach is still in knots when I get off the couch to retrieve the rest of my mail. I hate that I made him look like that. There's nothing in the world I want to do more than shout to everyone I meet that I hit the freaking jackpot in New York City with Nico Soltero.

But my parents are a different story. On top of being conservative, Catholic, and, in my dad's case, ridiculously strict, they're also bitter after going through their own painful separation this last year. My mom likes Nico okay since she knows his role in extracting me from Giancarlo last spring, but she's definitely not too keen on seeing me jump back into anything serious. Since moving back to Brazil, my dad went from being overbearing to virtually absent in my life. I can only imagine him roaring back in with a vengeance if he found out I was living in sin with a firefighter seven years my senior.

The thought makes me tingle. And probably in a way my parents would *definitely* not like.

I flip through the mail I missed last month, sorting out spam from bills until coming to a large, stiff envelope. But it's not the weight of it that stops me. It's the familiar handwriting on the front.

The apartment door opens, and Nico comes back in carrying a plastic bag containing my soup and his beef broccoli. He sets it on the kitchenette counter and starts grabbing plates, only stopping when he realizes I haven't moved from the table.

"Hey," he says. "Everything all right over there?"

"I'm...I'm not sure." I shuffle into the kitchenette and hand him the letter. Nico squints, stumbling a little as he reads aloud my father's terse, slanted script.

Layla,

It has been too long since I have seen my daughter. Your cousin Luciano graduates from medical school at the end of summer term, and there will be a celebration before *Carnaval*. You should be here too, to be a part of your family. Everything has been arranged. It is the right thing to do.

I look forward to seeing you soon.

Your *pai*

Nico hands back the letter, and for a moment, I run my finger over the word "*pai*," the Brazilian term for "dad." My father has never used it with me. We visited his family once when I was in high school, and after hearing my cousins call their fathers the same thing, I tried it with him and was shot down immediately. "Father," he always insisted, but when that eventually failed, he accepted "Dad."

After he proclaimed most of my life that I am American, not Brazilian, it seems that now he's finally ready to open up that side of his life to me. Maybe he really did need to leave in order to do it.

"When is *Carnaval*?" Nico asks as he opens up his box of beef broccoli and starts eating directly from the container. "And what did he mean by 'everything has been arranged'?"

"He means this, I think." I pull out an airplane ticket, the old-fashioned kind that are still printed on card stock, hand it to Nico.

He flips it over and back again, examining it. "This is three weeks from now."

I nod.

Nico's mouth quirks a little. "You leave the day before Valentine's Day."

I glance down, suddenly guilty. I shouldn't go. It's Nico's and my second anniversary of sorts. Our first one since coming back together. I'm not going to miss that.

"Layla." Nico's deep voice calls me back. "You should go. Brazil? Of *course* you should go. This is great, baby. You should be happy."

Happy. It's a funny word. But as I look at the sturdy, mint-green paper of the ticket, all I feel is dread. Trepidation. There's an inquisition waiting for me in another hemisphere, and he has a barrel chest and responds to "Dad." He'll look at all of the progress I've made over the last six or seven months and rip it to shreds. To my dad, I'm never quite enough.

We bring our food to the dining table and sit down, and before we've eaten anything, I know what I want to do.

"You should come with me," I blurt out.

Nico frowns through a big bite of broccoli. "What, to Brazil?"

I brighten, full of vision. "It's the perfect idea. He can't say no to someone who just flew four thousand miles to meet him. Even my dad would have to admit that's a pretty great thing to do."

"And what am I supposed to do when I get there?"

I grin. Yes. I like this idea. I *more* than like this idea. Suddenly, facing my father again without Nico next to me sounds impossible.

"You're supposed to tell him how much you love me. And then we'll tell him that we're living together, and there isn't a damn thing he can do about it."

His black brow arches high. "You must really think I'm whipped, don't you?"

My mouth drops. "Oh, I..." Shit. I hadn't thought about that. I didn't mean to imply that he was at my beck and call or anything like that. Anything but.

Nico chuckles. "I'm just playin', baby. But honestly, even if I get the money together for a ticket, I don't know if I can swing the time off. Rookies don't really get their pick of the schedule, and I have no vacation time. *Nada*."

"What if I paid?"

With a mouthful of rice, Nico gawks. "Hmm?"

I nod, even more convinced. "I have enough in my savings. I could swing it, and you could pay me back later if you really want to. Everything else would be taken care of, like he said. We'll probably stay at his apartment, or maybe my aunt's if there isn't room. We'll eat with them, so there won't be a bunch of extra expenses. No car, we'll be right by the beach. We'll go to my cousin's thing, and then come back. Or, you know, you could do stuff on your own if you wanted a break—"

"Layla." Nico pushes his food to the side, stands up, then lifts me bodily onto the table so that he's standing between my legs, my hands on his shoulders. "Do you really think I'd go with you to Brazil and then ditch you?"

I push my fingers through his thick black hair, so densely curled I almost can't do it.

"Please don't make me go alone," I whisper. "I want him to meet you. I want him to know the real man in my life these days. The one I can't live without."

Nico gazes up at me, his dark eyes wide and uncertain. Then he presses his forehead to mine and sighs.

"Fuck," he mutters. "It's those damn Bambi eyes. I can't say no."

I blink when he pulls away. "Does that mean you'll come?"

He sighs, even though his mouth quirks on both sides. "It means I'll try." Then his eyes drift down to my lips, which I just happen to lick at that moment.

There's that hunger again—not for food, but for something else. Something in both of us that we can't ever seem to sate completely.

Nico traces his nose across my chest and places a kiss on my sternum. "If I go." Another kiss on the shoulder. "You'll tell him?" One more on my neck. "And your mom too?"

He looks up with gleaming, hopeful eyes, and I clasp his face gently.

"We can tell him together," I say.

Nico's face is blank while he chews on his lower lip. He looks scared. It's not a look I recognize.

"Would you believe I'm not usually the guy girls want to take home to meet daddy?" he jokes as he presses his nose to mine. "Seriously, NYU. What's he going to think?"

"He'll think you're the kind of man who takes care of his girl," I say. "And if he doesn't, he can stay in his hemisphere when we go back to New York together. Because he might have everything to say about my life...but I belong here. With *you*."

"And what would he think if he knew I was doing this to his daughter, huh?" A big hand snakes underneath my pajama shorts and takes a thick handful of flesh that makes me hiss.

"I don't know," I purr as I tip my face up to his waiting lips. "What would Carmen think if she knew the things I do to you?"

A low chuckle emerges from the back of Nico's throat, but he maintains the kiss for a few more seconds.

"Why do you think my mother goes to Mass three, four times a week, NYU?" he asks just before slipping his tongue around mine in that dance I know so well. "She's praying for my poor, corrupted soul. And now, yours too." He kisses me again. "Welcome to the family, baby."

CHAPTER TWENTY-ONE

Nico

THE NEXT DAY, MY BROTHER, TWO SISTERS, LAYLA, AND I ARE all crowded into one tiny office at Family Immigration Services, which is housed in the third floor of a walk-up in Spanish Harlem. Ileana, the caseworker assigned to our mom, is holding the newest letter from the Treasury Department, tapping insistently on her beaten-up desk with a pencil. She looks pretty much the way you'd expect a social worker to look: a granola-eating white lady wearing a wrinkled blouse and a sweater that looks like she borrowed it from her grandfather, with mousey brown hair and a mouth that moves too fast.

Layla sits next to her desk, watching with keen interest as Ileana flips through all of the paperwork we've submitted trying to get this damn permit. I can't help but chuckle a little bit when I think of the fact that this is going to be Layla in a few more years. My girl has absolutely no idea how gorgeous she is. Inside this ugly, tiny room, she shines like a diamond.

Layla catches me watching her and gives me a shy smile. I wink, give her body a look up-and-down, and she immediately blushes.

"*Coño*," Maggie puts in, shoving me hard in the shoulder. "Stop undressing her with your eyes. You're embarrassing yourself." She turns to Selena, who's trying hard not to laugh. "He acts like no one is here. I feel dirty."

"*Gata*, I didn't say anything. You always gotta read so much into things, don't you?" I retort, though I don't drop my gaze. I'm enjoying the way Layla's biting her lip and squeezing her thighs together.

"Ahem." Ileana calls our attention as she sets down the paper.

And as much as I'd like to keep flirting, I turn to the desk along with the rest of my siblings, all dirty thoughts flying out of my head. This is too important.

"It's bad, isn't it?" asks Gabe. He rubs his chin, which is showing signs of a goatee. I smirk. My little brother is actually starting to get some facial hair.

"It's not great," Ileana says frankly.

She leans back in her chair and surveys all of us, looking everyone in the eye. It's one of the things I like about this chick—she might look like a mouse, but she's a firebrand, and she's never treated anyone in my family with anything less than respect.

"Look," she continues. "We had a window last spring, because the new adjustments were passed in June. But they didn't process the family license before then, and since June, the administration has pushed through much stronger restrictions. Basically, they're grand-standing, you know? Creating conflict where there is none to get people all riled up. You know, so we'll conveniently forget about the human rights violations they're committing all over the Middle East."

Maggie and I raised our brows at each other as if to say "here we go again" while Gabe shakes his head. We've all heard Ileana go off about the current president more than once, usually about the current war. I don't know. It's not really pertinent to our situation.

"So, what's left?" Layla asks as she picks up the different letters of rejection. "What else can we do to help Carmen? She has every right to be here by U.S. law. It's ridiculous that losing a piece of paper when she was two will force her to live in the shadows for the rest of her life, especially when she has every legal right to be here!"

The passion in her voice ignites a warmth in my chest. It's fucked up, but I love watching Layla get riled up like this about my mom, my family, her blue eyes full of fire. I have to stop myself from kissing her right there. I meant what I said last night: she is part of the family now. Moments like this show it more than anything else.

But Ileana sighs, and blows all of those good feelings out of the room.

"I'm sorry," she says. "I'll keep researching, but we're running out of options. The best way would be to find someone who actually has living family in Cuba to do this for you. Otherwise, it might be time to start putting together a case for relief. You mom doesn't know any Cubans in New York?"

Beside me, Layla brightens at the idea, but Maggie shakes her head.

"*Mami* came here with a Puerto Rican family. She's been sheltered by Puerto Ricans her whole life. All her friends are Puerto Rican, other than David..."

She trails off, looking at me and Gabe uneasily. David, Gabe's father, is Dominican, but I haven't seen or spoken to the guy since I beat his ass and kicked him out of our apartment for beating on Ma and the rest of us one too many times. That was over ten years ago now, but it's the family's worst kept secret that sometimes our mom would still find her way up to the Bronx to see him in a moment of weakness. Maybe she still does. None of us really know or want to know.

"What about Luis? Isn't he Cuban?" Gabe pipes up, giving Maggie a dark look at the mention of David. I know he speaks to his dad sometimes, but he doesn't mention it to me, knowing there is no lack of bad blood between me and that violent asshole.

I sigh. Everyone in my family has a big damn mouth, but we still keep too many secrets.

Maggie and Selena both look like they want to beat Gabe's ass at the mention of their father, Luis, who hasn't been seen since Selena was about three. He's Cuban, it's true, but the dude dropped off the face of the earth.

Yeah, you could say our family has some daddy issues. One more thing Layla has in common with us, as it happens. She doesn't exactly get along with her father either. The dad she wants me to meet. I press my face into my palms. I have no idea how I would be able to do that without punching the guy who broke his daughter's heart last year.

"One of the girls in my Spanish class has some family in Havana," Layla pipes up. "I don't really know her, but she seems nice. I bet she would be willing to go to Cuba over spring break or something if we could get her the permit."

"Has she gone in the last three years?" Ileana asks.

"Yeah, she went last summer to visit her grandparents."

"Then she's out. The new laws only permit visits once every three years anyway." Ileana looks at the rest of us. "And let's be clear. Your mother says she was born in Santiago, not Havana like you originally thought, and they aren't exactly close. You can't substitute one for the other. What about the rest of you? Do you know *any*one with family in Cuba?"

I shake my head, and beside me, Maggie rolls her eyes at Selena. I could see it all too easily—someone taking our money, a free trip to Cuba, and disappearing on us. Scammers in New York are a dime a dozen; no one in this room other than the two white girls think that's even an option.

"Then it's either keep trying with a family application for one you," Ileana says in a resigned, stern voice, "or we need to turn your case over to a lawyer and get you ready for court. You never know, they might allow one of you a permit. Or else, and I'm not officially suggesting this, you understand, you could also fly there from another country. There's no guarantees you won't get caught, and spending any U.S. currency there is illegal, but you can get there from somewhere like Venezuela. Maybe Toronto or Montreal."

"I'll do it."

Gabe glances around the room, his voice grim and determined while he toys with the bottom of his blue t-shirt. The glasses he started wearing this year are slightly crooked over a fierce expression.

I frown. "*Mano,* you don't have to do that. We'll keep applying. Ma's all right staying at Alba's. They're practically having a slumber party over there, you know?"

"Ma and Alba are driving each other up the wall," Maggie puts in. "I was there yesterday, and I thought they were going to toss each other over the balcony. I don't care how much you love your best friend. After a while, you need some space."

"There was a rumor of some immigrations people sniffing around the church last week too," Selena mentions.

I jerk my head at her. "*What?*"

Selena shrugs. "We heard about it from the priest, who said some of the other parishioners were talking about it outside. I don't know if anyone was taken, but..."

I exhale forcibly. "Sel, you can't be taking Ma to a church where there are fuckin' immigrations officers hanging out!"

"I'm sorry, but have you met our mother? *You* try getting Carmen Soltero to attend any other church but St. Andrew's."

"Fuckin' *fine,*" I spit. "But anyway, we can't just get all crazy because of some rumors. I hope you didn't tell Ma about those."

Selena shrinks a little. "She was there, Nico. What the fuck did you want me to do? Cover her ears, like we do to Allie?"

"Not unless you want a slipper," Maggie murmurs, setting off another round of snickering between her and Sel. I fall forward onto my knees, burying my head in my hands and relaxing only slightly when Layla starts to massage my neck.

"What about Brazil? Can you fly to Cuba from there?"

Layla's sweet voice cuts through the bickering, and everyone quiets as they turn to her. She casts me a nervous glance.

"No," I say automatically.

"That's an idea," Ileana murmurs. "You're going to Brazil?"

"Who's going to Brazil?" Maggie asks sharply.

"I am," Layla says. "And maybe Nico too, if he can get the time off. To visit my dad. I don't know if they have travel restrictions to Cuba, but if they don't, maybe we could work a trip in. I, um, could probably cover the cost..."

She drifts off, no longer meeting everyone's gazes. I know it's because Layla doesn't like to talk about money in front of my family. She thinks it makes her sound like a rich girl, like the *blanquita* people sometimes call her when they first meet her. She hasn't figured out that keeping silent about that sort of thing is a rich girl thing to do. Nothing says you have money like pretending it doesn't exist.

"No," I say again, but it's like no one in the office hears me.

"Nico, I could probably go," Layla says. "I have dual citizenship because of my father, so I could travel with a Brazilian passport—"

"*No.*" I stand up in a rush. "I'm not sending you to fucking Cuba by yourself, Layla. End of fucking story."

I grab her hand and pull her up with me. This office that smells like stale coffee and french fries suddenly feels like a strait jacket. I want to get out of here before this conversation ends the way I think it will.

I glare at Ileana, who's still looking at Layla thoughtfully. "Resubmit the applications under all of our names," I bark at her. "One for each. You need anything else?"

Ileana frowns. I'm acting like a caveman, but I can't help it. I've had enough of this office. I've had enough of doors being shut in my family's faces our entire fuckin' lives. I've had enough of being told no. So now *I'm* the one who's going to say it.

"I'll get that paperwork going again," she says carefully.

"I'm sorry about him," Maggie's saying. "He's just worried."

For some reason the apologies make me even angrier. "Come on," I say as I tow Layla behind me. "Let's get the fuck out of here."

CHAPTER TWENTY-TWO

Nico

LAYLA'S QUIET AS WE WALK THROUGH ASTORIA, MARCHING down the icy sidewalk toward the subway. I'm being an asshole, I know. And Layla, reading my mood, keeps trying to give me space. But every time she steps away, my hand only tightens its grip, as if by reflex.

I take an automatic sharp right off the main street.

"I forgot my charger at the firehouse yesterday," I say shortly before Layla can ask where we're going. "I'll just run in and get it."

Layla frowns. My next shift starts tomorrow afternoon—I could just borrow hers, like I did last night.

I'm helpless. It's a feeling I know too well, one I was slowly starting to think might finally be fading out of my life. But all I learned from that meeting was that there's not a damn thing I can do to help my mother, and it's killing me.

The firehouse, on the other hand, hasn't quite lost its gleam. Three months after I graduated from the academy and was assigned a station in Queens, I still get a little thrill every time I arrive. The door to helping my mom get residency still might be glued shut, but this one finally opened. My job. My girl. If I can just focus on the good stuff, maybe I'll be able to pick that last lock.

"I'm sorry for being such a dick back there," I say as we stop.

Layla looks up at the three-story brick building, her eyes bright in the cold winter sunshine. It's her first time here. With the business of the semester and then her leaving for Christmas, she never got the chance to come up and see it, but I know she's been curious.

"I think you owe Ileana the apology," she says. "You weren't very nice to her."

I sigh. "Yeah. I know. I wouldn't blame her if she told us to fuck off."

"She's not going to do that. But you should make it right too." Layla looks up at the firehouse. "This is so cool. Can you show me around?"

The look on her face—the pure, unadulterated pride—lifts me out of my shitty mood in about ten seconds.

I grin back. "You fuckin' bet."

Still holding her hand, we cross the street, and I push open the heavy door.

"It's one of the oldest firehouses in the city," I tell her proudly as I walk her around the bottom floor. "They used it on a set of some movie, but I forget which one."

Layla's all eyes as I give her the grand tour through the downstairs, showing her the lockers where we keep our stuff, the dispatch room. I lead her into the big garage, where we keep the trucks. She walks around curiously, examining the interactive map on one side of the room, the rows of helmets and jackets hanging on the walls, the boots with pants bunched around them, ready to be pulled on as soon as an alarm goes off. She drags her fingers over the red paint of one of the trucks in awe. It reminds me a little of my first day on the job. I'd been in the trucks at the academy plenty of times before, but on that day, I was starstruck. I stared at the ladder I was assigned to for a solid ten minutes before I could do anything else.

Layla takes a look at the ladder eagerly. "This is *so* cool, Nico. So if the bell rang, everyone would come racing down here?"

I shove my hands in my coat pockets and nod. "And they'd probably thank us to get the fuck out of the way too."

I glance around the garage nervously. I'm a rookie, so I'm still getting used to the way things work, although the job is beginning to commit itself to muscle memory. Still, I'm pretty sure I'd catch some serious fuckin' heat if the chief caught me in here with my girlfriend when they get a call.

"Come on, sweetie," I say, nodding toward the door. "There's more."

I take her up the stairs to where most of the guys are crowded in the kitchen. Mike, who's about the same size as the industrial-sized refrigerator behind him, is stirring a big pot of sauce while pasta boils on another burner. Four other guys are leaning over the counter with Cokes, probably wishing they were beers. They're laughing, teasing Mike about his bad habit of putting too many onions in his sauce. On the other side of the kitchen, a few other guys are watching a basketball game in the lounge area. It's a typical scene. I never knew how much of this job was just waiting around for something to happen.

"Rooooook," Joe, a younger guy from Staten Island who's on his fourth year, calls from his spot at the counter, starting off a round of the same calls all around the room.

Layla grins until the chorus ends. They all sound like dogs barking at the damn moon. I'm rolling my eyes, but I'm not going to lie. I kind of like it.

"You just can't stay away, can you, rook?" Mike says as he ambles over. "What the fuck? Are you obsessed with us, or something? Are you like that chick Herrera's dating, the one that shows up at the firehouse at all times of the night and day?"

A bunch of other guys chuckle while Damien Herrera, the guy in question, rolls his eyes from the couch. He's the butt of a lot of jokes like that, but the dude really does bring it on himself. His woman is a legit psycho.

"And who is this beautiful thing?" Mike asks as he looks over Layla frankly. "And what the hell is the rookie doing with a girl as fine as you, sweetheart? He should know better than to bring you around here with all of these hooligans."

"Hey, hey, take it easy," I warn him. "This is my girl, Layla."

"We got a live wire, I see. How you doin', sweetheart?"

Mike waggles his eyebrows as he kisses Layla's hand. He's a teddy bear of a dude, and he's just giving me shit, but that doesn't make me like another guy hitting on my girl. I shake my head. I'm not jealous by nature, but I think a part of me might always feel that way a little bit with her.

"Yeah, you can stop that now," I retort, unable to help myself completely as I tug Layla out of Mike's reach. I don't care that technically he's my superior, the ranking lieutenant in the house tonight. I just want him to stop fucking touching my woman.

Fuck. Maybe coming here was a bad idea. I was all excited to show the place off to Layla, but now it's just making me tenser.

"Is there more?" Layla asks, having been pulled tightly into my side.

She looks up at me, and the teasing and laughter surrounding us dies. Suddenly, the only thing I want to do is go home, lose myself in her gorgeous body for an hour or two, and reset my mind.

I soften. "Yeah, there's more. I'll show you the upstairs, grab my charger, and then we'll go."

We bid our farewells to the guys as I take her up the third flight of stairs to the sleeping quarters and the small weight room where I work out between calls. About half of the small single beds have sheets on them, dressed for the people who are currently on live shifts overnight. The rest are just plain vinyl mattresses, waiting for the next shift to come.

Layla turns and leans against one of the beds without anything. "It kind of reminds me of a fraternity house," she remarks.

I nod, although I've never been in one. "Do they sleep twenty to a room like this?" I joke. "We're like sardines in here."

But Layla nods. "Sometimes. It depends on the frat and school, obviously. The ones at NYU are basically just on a floor of one of the dorms, but a few have pretty big common dormitory rooms. At least you don't have bunk beds." She looks around. "Which one is yours?"

I raise a brow. "You tryin' to get me into bed, NYU?"

Right on cue, Layla blushes, sending a familiar flutter through my stomach. I could make her do that all damn day.

"You're terrible," she says. "I was just curious."

I walk up to her so we're standing close enough to be nose to nose. "It's right..."

I bend and trace my nose down her neck, just under her collar. Just a taste, I tell myself. In her tight black jeans and clingy sweater, she's looking particularly fuckable at the moment, but I'm not going to do that here. I shouldn't. Not with all the guys downstairs. Not when Layla can't always control her voice when I'm in her. No, I won't. Even if the look in her eyes tells me that she really, really wants to.

"Here," I say, as I tap the bedpost just behind her and stand up.

The pupils of Layla's eyes have dilated slightly. "Do you ever think about...you know? Getting busy when you're in here without me?"

Honest? Pretty much never. Late at night, when we're all mostly asleep in here, it's a chorus of snores, grunts, all of the sounds men make when they're asleep. Pretty much the unsexiest thing on the planet.

But right now, with the room empty, the door closed, and the afternoon sunlight making Layla's hair glow like that... We shouldn't do anything. I know that. But I'm also not so sure I can wait until we're home. And by the way she's chewing on her lower lip right now, I don't think she can either.

"What's the chance anyone is going to come up here right now?" she asks, her voice low and throaty as she links two fingers through my belt loops and pulls me closer.

"Unlikely," I say. "No one comes in here except at night."

My mouth hovers over hers, not quite taking what I want. I'm teasing myself here, but I couldn't care less. Sometimes half the fun is anticipation.

Layla glances at the door, which is still cracked closed, then looks at me and licks her lip. And when I say licks it, I mean runs her tongue slowly around her plump, pink mouth until it shines, ready to be kissed.

Jesus Christ.

"Keep lookout," she says, and before I can ask what she means, she's sliding down to her knees, unzipping my jeans, and freeing the pipe I've had going down there since I watched her walk up the stairs in front of me.

"Layla, you don't have to—oh, *shit*, that feels fuckin' good."

Her mouth slides over me, with her small hand gripping around my base where her lips don't quite reach. My head falls back as I lose myself in the sensation of her sweet mouth, and it takes me a few seconds to remember that we're not in the privacy of our bedroom and I need to be watching the door.

"Fuck," I hiss as she takes me even deeper. Her mouth is fucking magic. "I—Jesus, Layla. Baby, I—" I'm practically incoherent, but something's missing. I want more. I *need* more.

Suddenly, I'm acting completely on instinct. I pull her off me and yank her up my body. Layla's mouth, warm and wet, hangs open as her heated gaze drags over me. The uncurbed desire in her bright eyes just gets me that much harder.

"Nico—" she starts to say, but I cover her mouth with mine as I walk her backward a few steps, rip open her jeans, and shove them down her legs before she topples backward onto the empty mattress I usually claim for myself.

"I don't want to come in your mouth," I say as I sweep her legs across me so she's facing me on her side.

Her pants, still twisted around her ankles, keep her thighs together, but that just makes her that much tighter when my cock finds her slick passage. She's basically bound sideways as I hold her down, her sweet, full body open for me to do what I want.

I close my eyes in half-pain, half-pleasure as I slide into her warmth. *Fuck.* It really never stops. It doesn't matter how many times we do this—her tightness, her depth, the way she squeezes around me as I fill her completely—it feels better every time.

"Why?" she whispers, barely able to get the words out as I start to move. She shudders, and I get even harder knowing I have the same effect on her.

I lean down to kiss her again, needing to taste her in that moment more than I need anything else—food, water, air. I need Layla more. I pull out, teasing her slightly with just the tip. Her breathing grows shallow as I look down, entranced by that scant few inches where our bodies are joined.

"Because," I say as I shove back in with one hard thrust. "I want to come in you."

It's hard to make jokes when we're like this, but Layla still manages one, breathy and light. "But you would have."

She shudders when I deliver another punishing thrust. I give her the wickedest smile I can, thrilling in the way her entire body responds, then deliver a quick slap across her ass. Her nipples perk, even through her sweater, her back arches, her muscles tense, and she tilts her hips slightly to take me even deeper.

"Yeah," I tell her in between more unforgiving thrusts. "But this way, I get to feel you come too."

My hand reaches between her thighs to find that warm, soft spot that I know will push her over the edge. I circle my thumb over it, working in tandem with my hips. I'm close—if we were at home, I'd stop, change positions, bring her to the edge and take her back down three, four, five times before letting us both explode together. But here we could get caught at any time.

My brothers could walk in at any second, find me eight inches deep in the sweetest pussy in New York. And you know what? I'd have no fuckin' regrets.

But for her sake, I wrap it up fast. Press a little harder until her body starts to shake and she loses a bit of its control, unable to keep as quiet as before.

"You know it's better like this, don't you, baby?" I ask, bending down and keeping my voice low so only she can hear me. The sounds of the guys' voices filter from downstairs, and it only turns me on more. "When you get to feel my cock in your tight, wet pussy? When I get to feel you squeeze and shudder around my dick?"

"Ummmmm," Layla groans into my neck, her teeth biting into my skin. She's robbed of speech at this point, that slight pain brings me even closer.

"*Fuck*," I swear as I pound into her. "This body was made for me, you know that? I fuckin' *dream* about this body, Layla. I don't care who sees me, baby. All they would see is the way I *own* this gorgeous. Fucking. Body. *Whenever. Wherever.*"

"Nico!" she gasps, now clawing hard. Her nails are going to leave marks, and I couldn't be happier about it.

I take her clit between my fingers, and watch as she falls apart completely. Her entire body seizes, a lithe line of muscle quivering around my hips, squeezing me like a fuckin' vise.

"Nico," she whimpers as she holds on for her life, taking pound after punishing pound. "Please."

"Fuuuuuuuucccck," I growl as I follow her into oblivion.

Layla opens her mouth to cry, and I stifle both our moans with one last demanding kiss that matches the final few thrusts of my cock. *This* is what I needed for the last hour. This banishes the last of my hopelessness, because when I do this for Layla, when I do this for both of us, I feel like I could rock the whole fucking world with what we are together.

If only it would last.

I work out the rest of my orgasm and hers until slowly, slowly, the room comes back into focus. Her body softens into mine, and I lean my head on her shoulder as I catch my breath. The sounds of the city call from the other side of the window, and the guys' voices filter up the stairs. My mind puts itself back together. I can lose myself in Layla for sure, but when we're done, the world is always waiting.

Slowly, I pull out, then point Layla into the bathroom to clean herself up when she asks. We haven't used protection in months; things get a little messy. When she's done, she comes right back to where I'm leaning against the window at the far end of the dormitory and lets me fold her into my chest. My hands float down and rest on her ass—that sweet curve that's always seemed like it was molded for my palms.

"Yo." I squeeze lightly. "You're filling out a little more here, huh?"

"*What?*" Layla arches back to stare at me open-mouthed. "I'm *what?*"

I look her up and down, not even bothering to mask my open leering, and squeeze her ass again. "I know this ass like I know my own name, Layla. We've been eating well, huh?"

"Oh. My. *God!* You just told me I'm getting fat!"

Layla smacks me on the shoulder, and I can't help but start laughing, which only makes her smack me harder.

"I didn't say anything like that!" I shout, turning her around and binding her arms down in front of me. "And besides, I like it. More of you to love, right?"

"Ewwwww!" she cries, and now I'm practically wheezing because I'm laughing so hard. I'm being a dick, teasing her about a few extra pounds. I grew up with girls—I know better than to say a damn thing about their bodies at all, much less something that's not exactly complimentary.

"We'll see what you have to say when I start pointing out how you're losing your six-pack," she retorts, reaching down to pinch at the nonexistent layers of fat around my belly. "You're going to be thirty in two years, old man. Time waits for no one."

I just deliver another grin, the kind that always makes her stumble a little, and pull up my shirt. "These ain't goin' nowhere, baby. As long as you look at me like that, I'll be doing my sit-ups every night before bed. That's a promise."

Layla's mouth drops a little as she looks over my abs, and then she bites her lip all over again. *Fuck.* The problem with teasing my girl is that her response usually gets me even more hot and bothered. And since we already tested our luck in here once, I'm not about to tempt fate by bending her over the mattress again, as much as I want to.

"I'm sorry," I say as I nuzzle close for a kiss. She's tight-lipped at first, but then she gives in, sucking gently on my lower lip. "I'm just teasing. You look perfect, sweetie. You always do."

And yet. She does look a little different. What do they call it? Puppy love pounds, or something corny like that? I noticed it last night too. It's a good thing—she never did gain back all the weight she lost when she got sick, and she seemed to lose some last year too. Not much of a surprise, considering what kind of stress she was under.

I search for the words to tell her what I mean. Because really, she's even more beautiful than she ever was. Luscious. A little fuller. The word ripe keeps tripping off my tongue, but I'm pretty sure if I used any kind of word that could also be applied to produce, I'd earn myself another punch, and Layla's starting to punch hard these days after training at Frank's with me once a week or so.

So instead I fold her against me again, her back to my front while I rest my chin on her shoulder and enjoy the way her breasts— which, yeah, I think are a little bigger now too—push up under my forearms.

"You know I think you're beautiful," I murmur before inhaling deeply. Layla's sweet scent surrounds me, and immediately, I feel at peace. "You'll always be beautiful to me. No matter what."

Layla sighs and relaxes in my arms as we look out the window, over the rooftops of Queens toward the taller buildings of Manhattan.

"Let me do this for you," she murmurs.

I sigh. She's not talking about sex anymore, I had a feeling she was going to bring it up eventually. Layla and I have been living together long enough now that we're starting to know some of each other's patterns. I know when something triggers her back to Giancarlo, and a little clowning around with some well-placed kisses can usually nip a full-on panic-attack in the bud.

She, on the other hand, has an uncanny habit of knowing exactly when I feel like the world is trying to bury me, and that my instinct is to fight back. Hard. Sometimes I lash out, and that's usually when I have to walk away from people before I hurt them.

But Layla never lets me walk alone. And sometimes she can steer me back to the bedroom to distract me from my worst thoughts. Two handfuls of my favorite body part usually solve that problem, and Layla is usually all too happy to let me lose myself in her until my mind is clear enough to think straight and listen to whatever she wanted to say to begin with. Like right now.

"It would be a simple trip," she says as she leans into my neck. "Get there, go to the records office, go home. That's it. Ileana can walk me through it."

And then, of course, that's usually when she lays down her predictably clear logic. I press a light kiss into her hair as my breathing returns to normal. But when it does, and the pounding of my heart lessens, that heaviness is still there. I'd risk a lot for my mom. I'll put myself, my record, all of it on the line for her. But there's no way I'm risking Layla.

"No," I say quietly, hugging her a little tighter. "I love you for wanting to, baby, but the answer is no. We'll find another way."

CHAPTER TWENTY-THREE

FEBRUARY 2005

Layla

THERE'S SOMETHING THAT HAPPENS WHEN YOU STEP OFF THE plane in a foreign country. It doesn't even matter if it's the same climate—something in the air shifts. A smell. A weight. Something changes, and you know you're in a completely different place.

As we walk down the steps of the small plane and follow the line of passengers across the runway toward the Vitória terminal, Nico's head is on a swivel. This is the first time he's ever been out of the country, which I didn't realize until we had gotten on the second leg of our flight in Miami.

It took a lot of trades, overtime, and basically giving up every holiday for the rest of the year, but Nico managed to get a week off to come with me to visit my dad. He basically worked nonstop for the past three weeks while I did extra credit in my classes so I'd be able to leave too. It's not an easy trip to be making for either of us, but I'm definitely glad we're here.

"It smells..." Nico wrinkles his nose adorably, looking around for something, then back at me, confused. "Sweet. What is that?"

I grin. "Chocolate. There's a factory a few miles from here. *Garoto* is like the Brazilian version of Willy Wonka."

Nico grins. "Oompa Loompa? Brazilian style?" He leers at me. "I would doompity-do you right now, baby. Jesus *fuck* it's good not to be on an airplane anymore." Even with his backpack, he jogs a second next to me. For someone as active as Nico, sitting for fifteen hours straight was tantamount to torture.

"Oh my God, you're corny." I nudge him in the shoulder. "Only you could make a song by tiny orange men sound dirty."

Nico leans in to nip my ear. "I could make a *lot* of things dirty with you, baby. 'Specially after having to sit next to you for that long without so much as a kiss. Who knew joining the mile-high club would be so damn hard?"

Nico drapes his arm around me, tipping his head up to the sun so its light can shine under the brim of his Yankees cap. In New York, it's freezing, with snow on the ground and another round predicted while we're gone. Here, Brazil is in the middle of summer, and it's hot here on the coast.

I'm laughing and blushing at the same time as we head into the airport terminal. That is, until I see the person standing with his arms crossed on the other side of the small barrier.

Tall, stolid, with thick black hair threaded with only a few strands of silver. Wearing an impeccably ironed blue button-down shirt and neat slacks in spite of the heat. He's the kind of man who looks about six inches taller than he is only because of his stern presence. Who's had frown lines since his twenties because of how little he smiles. Whose fingers tap impatiently even when he's not waiting for someone.

My father.

Nico's arm falls from my shoulder, and I take his hand as we follow the crowd through the glass doors and into the terminal. He squeezes, but whether it's to comfort me or himself isn't clear. Nico, my strong, unflappable New Yorker, has a sweaty palm.

"Dad," I say as we approach the barrier between people waiting for passengers and the tiny baggage claim area. "Hi."

My father leans over the barrier and gives me kisses on each cheek, Brazilian style, barely even grazing my skin. It's like he's greeting a stranger for the first time. There's no hug, no smile. He's not a particularly affectionate man, but I had at least hoped for some thawing of his normally stern personality, considering we haven't seen each other in over a year and a half. But it looks like any chance of that happening vanished when he caught sight of the tattooed, backward-cap-wearing bad boy walking beside me.

"*Alô, Senhor Barros*," Nico pronounces, working extra hard on the Brazilian pronunciation of the name that I taught him on the way over. "*Tudo bem?*"

"Who is this?" Dad asks me abruptly, reverting back to his terse English, more heavily accented now than I remember.

I frown. "Dad. I told you weeks ago that Nico was coming. This is Nico Soltero, my boyfriend." I know I shouldn't like the way that sounds so much, but I do. I really do.

Nico's face has suddenly turned blank. Shit, I know that expression. It's the same one he wears when he sees cops on the street or when security guards follow him around a store. It's the face he wears when he feels trapped. Stereotyped. Pigeonholed.

"Nico," I say, reaching for his hand to tug him over next to me. "Babe, this is my father, Sergio Barros."

"*Doctor* Barros," Dad corrects me, though his gray eyes don't stray from their stern perusal of Nico.

I'm basically witnessing one of those nature videos when two male lions are facing off. My dad puffs out his chest, but keeps his arms firmly crossed while he stares, unblinking. His sooty eyes, with their dark circles that I get, which almost make him look like he's been rubbing his eyes with ashes, are unwavering. Nico, to his credit, also refuses to look away, and if it weren't for the way his hand squeezes mine almost hard enough to hurt, I wouldn't even know he was bothered. The thick silence between them actually stunts some of the other chatter around us as people look up from greeting each other to watch the standoff.

Slowly, Nico extends a hand again. Dad looks at it as if Nico's offering him a dead fish. Then, slowly, he takes it, and they commence a white-knuckled handshake that seems to last about an hour. When they finally let go, both of them flex their fingers, relieving the pressure.

"Soltero," Dad says. "And what kind of name is that?"

"Dad!"

The last thing I need is my dad fishing around for Nico's pedigree. I'm already mortified by his frosty reception, although I don't know why I expected this to be better. There was a reason I never had a real boyfriend through high school. Still, Nico's going to be on the next plane out of here if things don't perk up.

"My mother's from Cuba, sir," Nico answers gamely. "My dad was Puerto Rican and Italian."

"Was?" Dad asks. "What do you mean, 'was'?"

A muscle in Nico's jaw ticks, but otherwise he maintains his plain, open expression. "I guess is. I don't really know, sir. Honestly, I've only met him a few times, and not since I was a kid."

An awkward silence falls. Nico really, *really* doesn't like to focus on the fact that his dad was one of the first who dropped his mother and her kids like a hot potato as soon as he got the chance. I will him to know the truth—that I couldn't care less. None of that changes who he's become. In fact, it might have contributed to it.

"Well," Dad says finally, dragging his harsh gaze back to me. "Where are your bags?"

I look down at my small carry-on and the beat-up duffle Nico has over his shoulder. "This is it. We're only here for a week, so we didn't want to check anything."

Dad frowns as he starts walking toward the end of the barrier, where the gate opens. "That's it? Did you forget the banquet?"

Nico and I follow him, shuffling by other passengers in the crowded airport.

I frown. "Of course I didn't forget it, Dad. Don't worry, we brought some dress clothes. We'll just need an iron, that's all."

Dad darts a narrow-eyed look at Nico's duffel bag. "What kind of man packs his tuxedo in a sack?"

"Tuxedo?" Nico asks. He glances at me. "I was supposed to bring a tux?" He holds up the garment bag that was slung over his other shoulder. "I brought a suit. I hope that's okay. I guess I could rent something..."

"The banquet is black tie," Dad responds, not even bothering to look up as he checks his watch. "Layla, I tell you these things so you will listen. Does that expensive school teach you anything? How to read a basic email?"

Nico just glances at me, alarmed, but I shake my head, willing him to trust that I'll figure it all out. My father said absolutely no such thing. And even if he did, it doesn't really matter. I doubt that Nico will be the only one to show up in a suit instead of a tux.

We walk around to the other side of the barrier, and I set down my bag, ready, finally to embrace my father the way everyone else in the terminal seems to be doing. But even though it's been more than a year and a half since I last saw him, Dad just keeps walking toward the exit, his step as brisk as ever. It's only when he notices we've fallen behind that he stops and turns around.

"Layla," Dad barks, loud enough to startle a few clusters of passengers. "Are you coming?"

Without waiting for an answer, he walks out of the airport. I take a deep breath. A hand slides around my waist, and Nico pulls me protectively into his side.

"Your dad could host a comedy show," he mutters. "He's like a real bundle of laughs."

I chuckle, but lay my head on Nico's broad shoulder and inhale. "I'm so sorry. We've been here two minutes, and he's already being an asshole."

"He just loves you. I'd probably freak out if my daughter walked up with a guy who looks like me too."

"Stop. If our daughter ended up with someone like you, I'd be over the moon."

Nico freezes, and it takes me a second to realize what I just said.

"Shit," I say. "Don't freak out. I didn't mean anything by it."

But instead, I'm rewarded with a sweet smile that sets my insides alight.

"Relax. You're good. I got you," Nico murmurs into my ear.

His scent and the warmth of his breath on my neck immediately cause my shoulders to fall back to their normal position. I sink into him slightly and recharge for a moment before standing up straight and turning my face toward his.

"Thanks," I whisper, giving him a quick kiss. "I got you too."

"Anytime, baby." Nico smiles into my lips. "Now let's catch up with your dad before he drop-kicks my ass onto the next flight home."

———

We drive through Vitória in silence while my dad listens to the news, which, in its rapid Portuguese, is mostly incomprehensible. Nico and I just gaze out our windows, taking in the sights. The airport sits on the north side of Vitória, and we'll have to drive all the way through the island in the center of the C-shaped bay to get to Vila Velha, the twin city on the other side of the bay. Nico and I sit together in the back of my dad's Mercedes, since his front seat is full of paperwork he couldn't be bothered to move. I don't mind. I actually preferred to be close to Nico, even after spending a whole day straight on three different planes together.

There isn't much to see for the first part of the drive. The green foliage that surrounds the narrow highway hides a lot of the houses lurking beyond. Nico smiles when we pass the Garoto factory and starts humming the Oompa Loompa song until Dad clears his throat loudly enough to make him stop.

Eventually the highway curves into the city, and we start zooming through the hills of crumbling housing that encircle the low-lying island on which Vitória is built, where the beaches and high-rise buildings are. Occasionally Nico points to things and asks me what they are, but honestly, I don't know much more about the city than him, having only been here once in my life. I know that my dad's sister, whose son is the one graduating this week, lives in Vitória proper, in an apartment looking over a beach called Praia da Camburi. My dad lives on the other side of the massive arched bridge that crosses the bay into Vila Velha. I know from pictures that his apartment is also beachfront, on the sixteenth floor of a building in the shopping district of Praia da Costa.

"How do I say that?" Nico points to a road sign for Vila Velha, as we start crossing the bridge. "Vee-la Vel-ha?"

I shake my head. "The 'h' is pronounced kind of like a 'y' when it's paired with a vowel like that. That's why when you see it after the n, it's pronounced like ñ in Spanish. *Claro, Senhor* Soltero?"

Nico gives me an almost wicked look in response to my sudden Portuguese, one that has me wishing very badly we'd just gotten a hotel for at least one night instead of spending the whole week in my dad's apartment. There is absolutely no way we'll be allowed to share a bed. When Nico catches my hand, scratching his finger on the inside of my palm. It sends a shiver down my back.

"You're so damn smart," he whispers as he squeezes my hand, then turns and keeps looking out the window at the city fading away behind us and the other one approaching as we descend the tall arch. He nods at the hills that are piled with ramshackle housing that resembles multicolored cinder blocks stacked on top of one another. "Projects, right?" he asks with a half smile. "What did you call them?"

My lips quirk in response as I remember one of our early conversations together on the subway, passing some of the public housing projects on the way up to Nico's apartment at the time. It was during the first weekend we spent together, just after our first date. The first time Nico began showing me sides of New York, of himself, that I'd never been exposed to.

"Those neighborhoods are called *favelas*. But 'projects is just a word,' you know," I repeat his own words from one of our first dates.

That earns me a full-on grin, and Nico lifts my hand to kiss my knuckles.

"No doubt," he murmurs.

We both lapse into silence as we continue the ride—me lost in my thoughts as I watch my dad through the rearview mirror, and Nico murmuring to himself from time to time. It's only after I listen for a bit that I realize he's reading signs to himself, followed by the translations in Spanish.

"*Praia. La playa*," he says before he catches me watching him. "Beach, right?"

I nod. "Yep, you got it."

He looks back out the window, taking in the even mix of palm trees and tall buildings that make up one of Brazil's smaller cities. "Spanish and Portuguese aren't really so different, once you figure out the little things."

"They are *completely* different." My father's voice cuts in from the front, and he narrows his eyes at Nico through the rearview mirror. "If they were the same, they would be one language, not two."

"Actually, they are pretty close structurally, Dad," I say. "I've been taking both for my program, remember? It doesn't really feel like I'm learning two completely different languages. They share almost all of the same roots and cognates."

"Still," Dad says. He continues to stare bullets at Nico, who shifts uncomfortably in his seat. "Different enough."

CHAPTER TWENTY-FOUR

Nico

Dr. Barros pulls the car into the underground parking garage of a giant high-rise that's basically beachfront. It's right across the 4-lane thoroughfare that runs alongside one of the major beaches in Vila Velha right on the main Praia da Costa, according to all of the street signs. The two cities, like Layla told me earlier, separated by only a small bay, are basically one big one. Each side is probably about the size of one of the boroughs in New York.

Praia da Costa is on the other side of a giant—and I mean *giant*—arched bridge that towers over the bay and drops down into Vila Velha, next to a big white building that looks like some kind of church, perched on one of the egg-shaped hills that seem to rise everywhere up and down the coast.

"We should walk up there tomorrow," Layla says as she points to it. "It's this old convent. Nico, it's *so* pretty."

I nod. I wouldn't mind jogging up that hill right about now. I just spent way too many hours crammed into three square feet on three different airplanes. My body needs movement. But first things first: I gotta get this guy to stop looking at me like he wants to toss me off that bridge we just drove over.

I've known him for less than an hour, but I don't like Dr. Barros. I don't like the way he's barely said hello to his daughter even though he hasn't seen her for eighteen months. I don't like the fact that he keeps correcting and chiding her like she's seven years old. I don't like the fact that he keeps glaring at the tattoos on my arm like I have 666 printed on my bicep.

And I *really* don't like the sad way Layla keeps looking at him—like a beautiful, blue-eyed puppy begging to be pet. Yeah, it's taken me all of twenty fuckin' minutes to understand how a girl like Layla got wrapped up with that asshole last fall, and it has everything to do with *this* asshole in front of me.

You could say I'm having a hard time giving the guy a fair chance.

"So, you must be really proud of Layla, Dr. Barros," I venture as we take our bags up the elevator from the garage.

Dr. Barros turns around with an arched brow. "Proud? Of what?"

Beside me, Layla wilts, and I have to smother the growl in my chest. Is it fucked up that I want to punch that smug look off his face? What the fuck does he mean, "proud of what?" Layla's a fucking incredible person, and you'd think the guy who fucking raised her would understand that. Dick.

"Well, to start, she's killing it in school," I say, receiving a grateful smile from Layla. "You know every school of social work in the state is going to be throwing money at her for next year."

"Social work?"

The elevator doors ring open, but no one leaves. Dr. Barros steps in between them so they won't close, then turns to face his daughter.

"What is he talking about?" he asks.

Beside me, Layla shrinks into my shoulder. Fuck. I didn't want to get her into trouble with her dad—I was just trying to focus on the good stuff. I thought she would have told him about her applications by now. A quick glance at her, and she shakes her head imperceptibly

—no, her dad did not know anything about her plans to switch to social work. And clearly, he's not happy about it.

"Answer the question, Layla."

She sighs. "Do you think we could talk about this somewhere else besides the elevator, Dad?"

Dr. Barros worries his jaw back and forth a bit before exhaling heavily through his nose.

"Bring in your things," he says in a much lower voice. "Take a rest. And then we will *talk* about whatever this... 'social work'...is."

He walks out without another word, and Layla gulps.

"Sorry," I whisper.

She gives me a weak smile and shrugs. "It's my fault. We don't talk enough, and I was too chicken to tell him before. *I'm* sorry he's being so rude."

"Please," I say. "Like I ain't seen scarier dudes than your dad a hundred times before."

I'm not about to tell her that even though I don't like her dad, and I'm positive I could take him in a fight, I actually find the guy pretty fuckin' intimidating. Sergio Barros isn't a slouch. He's obviously intelligent, ambitious, and successful. You don't have to see his nice car or his fancy degrees to know he's the kind of dude who doesn't settle for less. And I already know he extends those expectations to his daughter. More than that, though, his opinions matter to her.

Yeah. That makes me nervous.

But instead of stressing out my girl, I shrug back and stamp a quick kiss on her cheek when he's not looking. Layla giggles, and I relax a little. In the end, it doesn't really matter if any of the Barros family likes me at all. Layla is the one whose opinion counts.

We walk into one of the nicest apartments I've ever seen, and that's saying something. I may have grown up in a crappy little place, but I've seen some sweet digs in New York. This place is nicer than some of the posh spots my mom used to clean on the Upper East Side. Nicer than K.C.'s townhouse in Hoboken or Alba's view on the West Side. This place is huge. Apparently a plastic surgeon's salary buys you an entire floor of beachfront property in Brazil. It has me wondering why I wanted to be a firefighter.

The living room alone is bigger than Layla's and my entire apartment, covered with dark wood floors that aren't even a little scuffed. The room has not one, but two sitting areas that include a bunch of spotless white furniture, including some arranged around a fireplace. Why would you ever need a fireplace in Brazil?

The walls are decorated with tasteful and expensive-looking modern art. Not really my preference, to be honest, but it definitely looks nice. No chintzy religious pictures or movie posters for this guy. But I also can't help but notice the lack of pictures. No photos of his daughter or family. No mementos of his travel or knickknacks that show anything about his personality.

I don't know...Dr. Barros might be the kind of guy who likes interior design, but I'm betting he had this place decorated for him. This is the kind of place that screams high maintenance and makes me miss our secondhand couch and beat-up dining table. I'm here for less than five minutes, and I already want to get back to me and Layla. Our small piece of New York. *Home.*

"Dad. Wow. This place is amazing."

Layla's even taken aback as she stares around the giant living room, with its picture windows that look out over the promenade and hills rising to the southeast. Is it weird I'm glad she's impressed? That she's not really used to this kind of luxury?

"Remove your shoes. Then come."

Dr. Barros waves us down a long hallway off the other side of the living room, but as Layla and I awkwardly take off our sneakers, I can't help but notice that her dad keeps his on. I follow them down the hall, holding my beat-up Converse like a bum while Dr. Barros gives us a lightning-quick tour of a bathroom, his bedroom, another bathroom, his housekeeper's quarters (holy *shit*, this guy has a live-in housekeeper?), and the three more rooms at the end of the hall.

"You will stay here," he says to Layla, pointing through an open door to a simple bedroom with a double bed and a dresser. "Guest room." He gestures at me, but doesn't make eye contact. "I didn't know you were coming, but I will have the maid make up this room."

Dr. Barros jerks his head toward another room, which looks like some kind of rec room, with a TV and a couch. No bed.

"*My* bedroom is here. In the middle." He gives me a knowing look. "I am a light sleeper."

It takes everything I have not to look away, but I'm not going to be ashamed. I want to tell him that if I grew up sneaking out on creaky New York fire escapes, he's not going to hear shit if I want to sneak into Layla's room. I want to tell his smug face that I already know his daughter Biblically in every sense of the word, that we share a bed every single night. But I'm pretty sure I wouldn't be allowed to know her that way ever again if I spilled that secret for her. Not right now.

"Couch sounds great, Mr. Barros."

I give him the biggest grin I can manage—the one that Layla calls my lady killer when she thinks I'm not listening to her talk to Shama. It's the one that shows my dimples, and I enjoy the way that Layla blushes when she sees it. I also enjoy the way Dr. Barros scowls when he notices his daughter's reaction.

He frowns, the lines on his forehead deepening. "*Doctor.* It's Dr. Barros."

I grin even wider and nod. Yeah, asshole, I know. Some people just need to be fucked with.

Dr. Barros turns to Layla, clearly about to launch into a new tirade, probably about the little bomb I dropped in the elevator. But just as his mouth opens to reveal two silver fillings, the pager on his belt goes off.

Dr. Barros mutters to himself in Portuguese, something that I'd guess isn't too polite by the look on Layla's face. He looks up, twisting his mouth around into another deep scowl. I swear to God, it's like a frown is this dude's default expression. I wonder if he goes out of his way to make himself look like an asshole.

"I have to return to the hospital," he says. "I will be back, maybe for dinner. Benedita is doing the shopping, I think, but she will have the cooking done by eight." He looks up. "Layla, there is a key for you in your room. I already told the guards downstairs your name. Can you give your...*his* name to them if he leaves?"

Dr. Barros tips his head at me, like I'm not even there, and I'm practically grinding my teeth to keep from shouting, "Nico, you arrogant fuck! My *fuckin'* name is Nico!"

Layla sighs and nods. "Yeah. I think my Portuguese is good enough to do that."

Dr. Barros clears his throat while he glares between us. "And no... you do not go into her room. This is a *decent* house. You are not alone. *Entende?*" He lapses into Portuguese, like he almost can't help himself. Like the very thought of his daughter being defiled by the likes of me makes him lose his mind.

And you know what's fucked up? I like it. It makes me a dick, but I *like* that the one thing that really disturbs this cocky asshole's perfect cool is his awareness that his only daughter is probably getting it good on the regular from a tattooed, working-class *me*.

We glare at each other, and I stand as tall as I can. I can't help it. I arch one eyebrow, and Dr. Barros sucks in a breath. He knows *exactly* what I'm thinking.

"Dad."

Layla's voice breaks the standoff. We both turn to her, and suddenly, it's very clear my girl is ready to drop. And of course she is. We've been traveling for way too long, starting with a red-eye out of New York. Her eyes are bloodshot, and her skin is pale. As badly as I might want to fuck with her dad by fooling around with Layla while he's gone, there's obviously no way she's going to do anything but sleep in his absence.

Dr. Barros seems to know it too. For the first time, a little softness crosses his face as he looks—really looks—at his daughter for the first time since she arrived. His eyes travel over her weary body, taking in her rumpled t-shirt, the way her hair is piled atop her head, the dark circles, a lot like his, that have gotten worse for lack of sleep. He reaches out a hand and gently strokes her cheek. And as if she can't help it, Layla closes her eyes and leans into his palm.

Fuck. It physically hurts to see how badly she wants her dad's love. And honestly, who doesn't? I remember when I was a kid, when I tracked down my dad at the grocery store in the Bronx where he worked. I was dying for his attention, and when he barely looked at me, it just about killed me. I can't imagine how painful it is to have someone turn their back on you when they spent the first eighteen years of your life actually being present.

And yeah. It makes me hate the dude that much more.

"Go rest, *linda*," he tells her, and then, with another nasty look at me, he leaves.

When the elevator doors close behind him, Layla practically melts into the doorway. The high of landing in Brazil and seeing her dad is gone now, and what's left is exhaustion.

"Shit, sweetie," I say as I pull her against me. "Come on. Let's get you into bed."

She lets me tow her into her room, despite the fact that her dad just told me explicitly *not* to enter. But despite the fact that her body feels as good in my arms as it ever does, I just help her lie down on the bed and sit next to her, stroking her hair back from her face as she looks drowsily up at me, her blue eyes the only light in the darkened room.

"Sorry my dad was such a jerk," she murmurs, one hand clasped lazily around my wrist.

I smile down at her. "Don't worry about it. I'm sorry I blew your news, baby."

She sighs and shakes her head. "It's fine. He needed to know anyway. I keep too many secrets from him."

Like me, I want to say. Like the fact that I'm not just your boyfriend, not just some dude you go on dates with. Like the fact that I'm the love of your life, right? That we live together? That we're starting to make a real life together?

Aren't we?

It's kind of crazy how much I liked what she said at the airport. The idea of having a daughter of my own one day scares the shit out of me, but the idea of Layla pregnant, our kid growing inside her... yeah. I probably like that too much. And it didn't escape me how quickly she walked it back.

So I try not to overthink why Layla hasn't told her parents about the real extent of our relationship yet. I try not to wonder if maybe, just maybe, she hasn't really told them because she's ashamed of me. Because maybe she doesn't really think we'll be together forever.

The thoughts press like a knife that's always poised right over my heart, holding me hostage, and these doubts are the blade. Nothing's cut through. But the possibility is always there.

Just ask her, cabrón. K.C. is sitting on my shoulder again, telling me not to be such a pussy. Flaco and Gabe are right behind him, shaking their heads and muttering to each other that I need to get my head out of my ass. *After all that you've been through, what the fuck are you waiting for?*

Ask her what? I want to say back. How she feels? If she really loves me? She tells me that every day, multiple times a day. Should I cut off my own balls too, just to make it clear that I have no fuckin' ability to restrain myself when it comes to this girl?

I open my mouth to let it out, because why the fuck not? I'm here. And if I want her to be honest, maybe I need to start doing that too.

Layla sighs as her eyelids flutter shut. I close my mouth and stroke her hair back again. She leans into my hand, just like she did with her dad, but now her expression is peaceful, without any trace of pain. She knows I love her. She doesn't worry about that anymore.

So, once she's asleep, I decide to do what I normally do when shit gets a little too much to handle. Something I feel like I'm going to have to do a lot while we're here.

I work out.

CHAPTER TWENTY-FIVE

Nico

Layla sleeps through most of the afternoon and into the night. My girl was *tired*, and any idea I had about sneaking across the hall into her room late at night was put straight to rest by those circles under her eyes. So in the morning, when I get up and run awkwardly into Dr. Barros in the kitchen, where his housekeeper is serving him, I'm a little irritated by the suspicious looks I'm getting. Fuck that. I'm behaving like an altar boy.

Benedita, the housekeeper, gives me a hooded look, like she knows me, even if she doesn't really. She looks over my faded shirt, my sweat-stained hat, my running shoes that haven't been white for a really long time. It's like she knows we're cut from the same cloth; that my mother cleans up rich people's shit for a living too. Like she knows I'm not really supposed to be here.

"*Cafe?*" Dr. Barros asks, gesturing at the shiny silver set on his bright white tablecloth, at the rolls, cut papaya, some kind of creamy white cheese kept in a jar, and a square loaf of something that looks like jelly. He shakes out his newspaper, but doesn't look at me. He's being polite and rude at the same time, in a way only rich people seem to know how to do.

"*Obrigado*, but I'm good. Just going to go for a run."

At that, he looks up. "Another run?" He looks me up and down, like he's appraising my body. He's a doctor, so I can't help but wonder what he's looking for.

The coffee smells good, but I need to exercise before this day starts. First up is Mass with Layla's entire family, followed by some giant barbecue at her aunt's house, with cousins. If the Barros clan is anything like Layla's dad, I'm going to need to run at least ten miles just to relax. I ran a quick couple of miles up and down the promenade last night before coming back to the house. But I'd forgotten to have Layla call down to the doorman for me, and he made me sit on the front steps until Dr. Barros showed up sometime past eight and approved me so I could follow his shiny black Benz into the garage. He wasn't too happy that I was loitering outside "like a common street urchin," as he put it. Well, he didn't give me much of a choice, did he? And who the fuck talks like that except Disney villains?

I grab my ankle to stretch out my quad, lingering in the doorway. "Yeah, I tend to be pretty disciplined about it. If I don't do something most days, I get a little cranky? What do you guys say? Everyone is supposed to get an hour a day?"

I don't mention that if I don't exercise, my version of "cranky" isn't the nicest thing in the world. Running. Boxing. Lifting. These are things I realized a *long* time ago that I needed to keep the darkness in my life from swallowing me up.

"Some people need to be very...physical," is all Dr. Barros says.

I choose not to respond, even though it's clear what he's trying to say: that I'm the kind of person who uses my body because I probably don't have a mind.

"We leave for the church at nine thirty, is that right?" I ask him.

"Nine," he says, and with another loud shake of his paper, turns back to his coffee. "We will not wait, either."

"Don't worry, Mr. Barros. I'm never late."

And before he can correct his title, I jog out.

I make my way up and down the promenade in front of the beach, the same run I did yesterday, but the relatively short distance isn't enough for what I need. To start, there are too many people. Even at this time of the morning, it's packed with other joggers, rollerbladers, cyclists, and people just walking around the busy neighborhood. But really, it's the equivalent of running around the Upper East Side, and considering I'm going to get enough of *that* side of Brazil over the next few days, I wouldn't mind taking a break when I can.

The cities here are really different than New York, or even LA. The rich people are packed down on the beaches in thin strips of high-rise buildings that block out the hills behind them, covered with poorer neighborhoods. But you can't get away from the poor here. In New York, you actually have to get out of the wealthy neighborhoods to see the city's poverty, or even just peel back a layer or two to realize it's right there with you, like my family's apartment. But despite their proximity, the poor go out of their way to stay nice and hidden.

Here, poverty looms all around, staring down at you from the hills that surround the low-lying beaches. People like Layla's dad might live in high-rise buildings, but they can't block out the *favelas*.

So as soon as I finish jogging down the promenade and back up, I turn off the main drag and start exploring the interior of Vila Velha.

I jog up side streets, vaguely noticing the way the buildings slowly morph from the glossy apartments into smaller, plainer structures that house businesses and shops, and eventually to places that basically look like stacked, multicolored cinder blocks, terraced up the hills that stick up from the land like fingertips. They look familiar, like the pictures of the slum in San Juan where K.C.'s family (and my mom) originally lived. Eventually there are fewer cars on the street and more bikes, sometimes a flimsy motorcycle or two. I actually pass a donkey around one corner. It's still busy up here. People are passing back and forth between their houses; others look to be on their way to work. But although I get a few curious looks, most of them are friendly, nodding their *"alôs"* or *"bom dias"* as I pass.

It takes a while before I realize why I feel more comfortable up here than down on the beach. This isn't a good part of town. Most of the people I pass wear clothes that are dirty and stained, several of the compartments have dirty floors and graffiti on the outside, and more than one kid glances at me from windows with hardened eyes. The farther I go, the fewer kids have shoes.

But unlike down on the beach, the people in this part of town don't give me a second look. The reason is clear: I look a hell of a lot more like them than I do any of the rich, light-skinned *brasileros* jogging up and down the promenade. Most of the people in this neighborhood are mixed like me, with skin colors that range from light brown to black. It's a neighborhood that's about as diverse as my own back home. A neighborhood where I don't look or feel out of place, even though I've never been here before.

Layla told me about this. That Brazil, maybe even more than the U.S., has its own racialized caste system. Up in the north, it's more common to see black people, especially in states like Bahia, which, according to Layla, has a stronger African community, though it's definitely not reflected in their politicians or leadership. Just like back home, most of the people in power here call themselves white, even if by American standards, they aren't. Still, Layla and her family look like they just walked off the boat from Portugal or Italy, and so do most of the people living down there by the beach.

One thing's for sure, though: soccer really is a national sport here. Whether it's on the beach or on top of this hill, I've counted at last six different soccer games this morning, all played with balls in worse condition the farther up the hill I go. The last one looks like it's missing most of its air and got into a dogfight a while back, but the kids seem to be having a good time with it.

Yet another ball comes flying at me as I round a corner close to the top of the hill. I just manage to stop it with my foot before it goes rolling down the street behind me, and I look up to find four little kids, all barefoot, watching me, their hands on their hips.

"*Chute!*"

The littlest one of the four jumps up and down on the rough pavement, waving his hands at me. Skinny, with a few teeth missing and a mop of light-brown hair that sticks out in a few different directions, he looks like he can't be much older than five, though his large brown eyes look much older.

I kick the ball back, and he passes it to his friends, but he's obviously lost interest in their game. He shuffles down the street to me, not seeming to care much about the fact that his little feet are kicking loose rocks on the dirt road or that he's just ditched his friends to come talk to a strange man.

He spits a quick stream of Portuguese at me, but I have no idea what the fuck he's saying. Sometimes when Layla's dad speaks, I can recognize a few of the words, but this kid speaks something much less formal. Something that belongs to the streets.

"What's that, little man?" I ask in English, and then, thinking better of it, in Spanish. Something tells me these kids aren't exactly in school all day long learning the English alphabet.

His eyes pop open. "*Americano?*"

Ah. That I understood.

"Yeah, man," I say as I sit down next to him on one of the blocks of concrete that's been set up around their little makeshift field. "*De Nueva York.*"

His eyes get even bigger at the words. Everyone knows where New York is, even clear on the other side of the planet. John Lennon wasn't wrong when he called it the center of the universe.

I hold up my fist for him to bump, and he stares at it for a second, before mimicking the action. When he knocks his knuckles against mine, I spread my fingers and imitate the sound of a bomb blowing up. The kid's face lights up with a grin.

"So, what's your name, *papi?*" I ask him, venturing into Spanish.

"*Tu nombre?*" When the word doesn't seem familiar to him, I tap my chest. "Nico." Then I point to him. "*Tú?*"

"Ahhhh." The kid nods in clear understanding. He slams his palms down on his chest with more force than I would think a little squirt like him would be capable of. "Bruno."

I grin. "That's a big name for a little man, Bruno. You better grow up to be strong, you got that?"

Bruno just nods, even though he has no idea what I said. Instead, he's absorbed with my arm, which is bare in the tank top I'm wearing.

"*Isso.*" Bruno floats a little finger over the swirls of my tattoo. He rattles off another long round of Portuguese, and when it's clear I don't understand what he means, he just says, "*Tatuagem?* Ouch?"

It's not really that hard to communicate in different languages if you can keep everything to one-word sentences.

I nod. "Yeah, man, they hurt. But they were worth it. They remind me who I am. To be strong. *Fuerte. For-te?*" I'm guessing at the potential translation again, and the second version seems to work. I flex my arm for good measure, and Bruno's eye pop open again.

"*Forte,*" Bruno repeats with a nod, though he pronounces it like "foh-chee" instead of the way I did: "for-tay."

"*Forte,*" I echo him, and we fall silent as he examines the tattoo some more.

"Bruno!"

A woman's voice calls from across the field, and Bruno's head spins around.

I might have grown up in a building with doors that locked, but I know what it's like to have my mother call for me like that, with fear threaded through her voice, looking out the window to where her kid is running around a neighborhood full of junkies and gang members. Ma had about as much choice as this kid's mother does. There was no way you could keep four kids confined to five hundred square feet, as much as she would have liked to. She had to work, and she had no way to watch out for us other than to teach the difference between right and wrong and hope we'd stay out of trouble. It's funny. I didn't think about it much then, just stayed away from needles we'd sometimes find on the sidewalks, or walk down the middle of the street whenever we saw dealers or junkies crowding the sidewalks. But now that I'm older, the idea of raising my own kid in a place like that scares the shit out of me. Just one more reason my mother is a fuck lot stronger than I ever imagined.

Bruno stands up and waves to his mom, and I wave at her too, trying to be friendly, let her know I'm not a bad guy. Let her know that right now, at least, she doesn't have to worry. Her expression softens, but she doesn't stop watching. Then Bruno turns back to me with another long round of Portuguese that I can't understand.

"*Eu vai*," he says simply, which is close enough to the Spanish for "go" that I get it.

He points his little thumb toward his mother, who is watching us impatiently with her hands on her hips. The action causes his t-shirt sleeve to fall down his arm, revealing just how skinny he really is.

"Ah, here. Hold on, man."

I stand up and fish a few *reais* out of my shorts pockets. It's all I brought with me—maybe the equivalent of ten U.S. dollars, in case I got lost somewhere and needed a cab or a bus back to Praia da Costa.

But it's obviously a lot more than this kid has seen in a while, or ever, if his wide-eyed gaze is to be trusted. He turns, obviously to gloat to his friends, but I pull him back toward me.

"Hey," I say.

Bruno blinks up at me.

"That's for your mom," I tell him. "*Para tu mamá, entiendes?*"

It's close enough to the Portuguese that he gets what I'm saying and nods immediately.

"Go, give it to her now," I tell him, nodding again toward the woman who is looking at us curiously. "*Ahora.*"

Bruno nods again, but before he leaves, he opens his little mouth. "Thank you," he says in clear English. "*Tchau*, Nico!"

He scurries over to his mother, who takes the awkward collection of coins and small bills before looking to me with surprise. Her features aren't any less hardened, and are maybe a little bit ashamed, but she nods before she puts the money in her pocket. It's another combination of expressions I also know very well. The same look my mom had every time we stopped at the food bank, or when Alba or one of her friends would slip a few extra dollars into her pocket. Gratitude. Surprise. Relief. Shame.

Before he follows his mom back into their house, though, Bruno looks at me one last time. He sticks his little chest out, and gazes at me with emotions that are so different from his mother's. Pride. Curiosity. Intelligence. Determination. Features that this neighborhood will probably do its best to erase, but if he's lucky, won't be snuffed out completely.

I wave at him, and he disappears, but his expression stays with me. He's so damn tiny, but such a strong reminder that people are so much more than where they come from. That no one is born being nothing.

It's easy to forget sometimes. But, I realize, maybe more important to remember than anything else.

I stand there for a few more minutes, looking out over the two cities spread out below. I examine the arched bridges that connect the two sides of the bay, the green hills in the distance that are mirrored by the ones closer to the city, the ones covered by houses just like these, kids just like these. It's just one city, but it seems so vast from up here. A king's view from the poorest seat. And this country is filled with them.

For the first time in my life, the world seems much, much bigger than New York. But I'm also seeing how many of the differences I've always taken for granted maybe don't matter that much at all.

CHAPTER TWENTY-SIX

Layla

NICO WAS QUIET THROUGH MOST OF THE MASS. HE ARRIVED from his run about thirty minutes before we were supposed to leave, much to my dad's obvious irritation, and with a quick kiss on my cheek (also to Dad's irritation, which I think Nico intended), jumped in the shower and changed into a nice pair of gray pants and a white button-down before stealing some bread and guava jelly at the table. I should be annoyed that he's going out of his way to bug my dad, but weirdly, I'm not. No one gives my father shit.

He sat next to me in the car, looking up at the hills as we drove out of Vila Velha to Guarapari, a suburb where my aunt keeps a vacation house by the beach. He was lost in thought as we filed into the small chapel where my family goes to church, and he only gave distant smiles when we wave hello to my aunt, uncle, and their kids: David, their oldest son, Luciano, the new graduate, and Carolina, their daughter, who is only a few years older than me. David, an engineer, is even older than Nico and has a kid of his own and another on the way. Nico remained quiet through the rest of the proceedings, watching the priest lead the small congregation through service that was just about exactly the same, speaking only when prompted by the familiar rhythm of the rites and liturgies, except saying the words in Spanish instead of the unfamiliar Portuguese.

We linger a little after the ceremony, telling everyone we want to explore the small chapel, even though really we just want a minute to ourselves before facing the inevitable barrage of curious faces at my aunt's.

"Ma would like this," Nico finally remarks as we look over one of the stained-glass windows, a portrait of St. Christopher. "Do you think they have postcards or anything? I want to send her one."

It's hard not to kiss him for wanting to send his mom a memento. But this is a tiny church, and doesn't have the same array of pamphlets and cards you find at the bigger cathedrals.

"Ah, well," Nico says with a shrug when I say so. "I can take a picture and light a candle for her instead."

My heels echo on the stone floors as we walk toward a small apse where there is an array of prayer candles. Another thing that doesn't change, no matter where you are in the world.

Nico lights a few of the candles and murmurs a prayer under his breath, then crosses himself. If I'm counting right, it looks like he lit four in all: one for each family member back home. He kisses his fingers before dropping a few *reais* in the donation box.

"Are you feeling okay?" he asks me as we continue to walk around the church. "You didn't seem to eat much at breakfast this morning when I got back."

I shrug. The truth is, I haven't really been feeling that great since we landed. I'm guessing I picked up something on one of the planes on the way down. Those things are disease incubators.

"I'm all right," I say as we continue to walk down the aisle on the other side. "I just wasn't that hungry. You've been pretty quiet, though."

Nico shrugs. "I like this place." He looks around, taking in the tall stone walls and the rows of pews.

"Yeah?" I look around, enjoying the simplicity of the space. "I was worried you were bored since you couldn't understand much."

Sun shines in the arched windows on one side, casting blocked rays of light onto Nico and a few other places. He smiles, and the room is suddenly even brighter.

"I understood enough," he says as he swings our hands slightly between us. "I've sat through enough of those to know what's happening. The Eucharist is the Eucharist no matter where you go, *verdad*?"

I smile at his casual use of Spanish. It's another word that's only different from its Portuguese cousin by a single letter. "*Verdade*. So it is."

I gaze around the chapel. It's stark and relatively bare, so unlike my father's ornate apartment or the bigger cathedrals you might find in Rio or São Paulo. But I know from my last visit to my grandparents' house that my dad's family hasn't always been rich. My grandparents still live in the same house on a farm in Colatina, a small town about two hours north of Vitória. *Vovô* made his fortune growing tobacco and coffee, enough to send his children to a private Catholic school that allowed both of them to qualify for Brazil's notoriously difficult public universities. Now most of the farm has been sold, and the old house, the *fazenda*, and a few acres of land around it, are all that's left. It's a long way from the glossy surfaces and rich textures of my father's home. Much, much closer to this church.

"When I saw this place the other time I came, I dreamed I'd get married here," I remark absently as I draw my free hand over the polished wood of the pews.

It's only after it's out there that I realize the gravity of that kind of statement to Nico. Super smooth, Layla. Ugh, he's going to think I'm dropping hints or something crazy like that. I ignore the fact that I *do* imagine getting married to him sometimes. It's a daydream that's *way* too easy to fall into.

I open my mouth to apologize, but instead find Nico looking at me softly.

"Did you?" he remarks. He lifts my hand to his lips in a motion that's strangely chivalric, even for him, but fits the ancient setting of the church. His black eyes twinkle, but not just from the sunlight. "It's not a bad dream. I kind of like it, you know." He looks around at the simple beauty. "It fits you, this place."

We watch each other for a minute, tension and some other kind of strange magic building between us. Nico opens his full mouth, like he wants to say something else. My chest constricts—why, I'm not sure. But neither of us looks away; neither of us even blinks. It's the same feeling I get when I want to kiss him, but even now, it's something more. Something that goes so much deeper than what my body does with him. From the start, everything with Nico has been on a cellular level. Past the body. When he looks at me like this, he penetrates my soul.

"Layla—" he begins, but is cut off when the heavy doors to the church open, and my father strides in with his customary frown as his footsteps echo off the high ceilings.

I look to Nico and mouth "sorry." He shrugs and gives me a lopsided smile, as if to say, "What can you do?" Dad immediately zeroes in on our joined hands as he approaches.

"Layla," he barks, giving Nico a dirty look. "*É uma igreja. Respeito!*"

I'm annoyed by that enough that I barely even care that he spoke to me in Portuguese for one of the first times in my life. "Dad. We're just holding hands."

As if in response, Nico's fingers tighten their grip instead of pulling away. I know it's partly just to get under my dad's skin, but I'm feeling kind of territorial myself. I don't like the way my dad acts around the love of my life. Especially when he's interrupting moments that are important.

Dad glowers, and Nico mutters "*Oye, tranquiló, viejo*" under his breath. I give him a wide-eyed look, and he winks at me so I have to stifle a smile.

"What was that?" Dad demands.

I gulp. I doubt my dad would appreciate being told to calm down. Or being called "old man."

Nico just blinks innocently. Well, as innocent as he ever really looks. Then, deliberately, he holds up my hand and drops it. "I just said we need to go, Dr. Barros," he says. "It's also disrespectful to be late, right?"

With a huff, Dad spins around and leaves, but when Nico follows, I tug him back. He turns around, a shit-eating grin on his handsome face that makes me start laughing.

"Dude," I chide, though I'm still giggling. "You have got to cut it out. You sound like a troublemaker caught at the principal's office."

Nico snorts. "I'll cut it out when he stops talking to us like we're high school students. Until then, he's lucky I haven't started calling him Principal Skinner. Now, come on. I wasn't kidding about not wanting to be late. I might like busting your dad's balls a little since he's never going to like me that much anyway. But I don't want to piss off the rest of your family."

———

For all his bravado, though, Nico grows quiet again as we drive with my dad to my aunt and uncle's house, a big place in a gated community down by the beach. It's a really quiet neighborhood. Most of the people here only use their houses as vacation homes, places where they come on the weekends after working in the city during the week. But Fabiana—known to me and the more extended branches of my dad's family as Bibi—and her husband, my uncle Manuel, moved here semi-permanently after their kids left for university, although Manuel still uses their apartment in Vitória a few days a week when he's working.

The two-story house is big and airy, with the downstairs walls all opening through four different French doors onto a large yard bearing a cashew tree, a small pool, and patio where we'll eat lunch. When we arrive, all of the doors are open to reveal the Spanish-tiled ground floor, and Bibi's selection of comfortable, lounge-ready furniture. The barbecue on the side of the house has been started up while their cook and a maid hurry dishes to and from the kitchen to the patio table.

"Damn," Nico mutters as he takes in the spread already laid out. "That looks...amazing."

It really does. Bibi's gone all out, using our presence as an excuse to make real *churrasco* this afternoon for her family and a bunch of her neighbors. There is a big shank of meat rotating over a rotisserie, and the man at the grill is flipping sausages and smaller pieces of meats and fish. On the table I spot the classics of Brazilian barbecue: *feijoada* (black beans stewed with pieces of sausages and pork), *farofa* (a ground yucca dish made with beans, pork rinds, and egg), fried plantains, a massive fruit salad, and pitchers of mango and cashew juice. My aunt, uncle, and cousins are mingling with neighbors, and I recognize a few other faces from church.

"*Linda!*" Bibi's high-pitched cry sounds from the other side of the patio, and my father's magnanimous older sister practically sprints across the yard to greet us, closely followed by Manuel, her husband. "I saw you in the church, but we had to come back here so quickly. Come, let me look at my baby!"

Her exuberance makes me smile despite the fact that I've only met my aunt twice. Trips to and from Brazil are expensive, and considering that she and Manuel had three kids, they only managed to visit us in Seattle once when I was little. The other time, of course, was only a few years ago, when Dad, Mom, and I visited for *Carnaval*.

The memory hurts. It was a whirlwind trip, but I wonder now if it was the start of Dad's change of heart about his country. He hadn't been back for so many years. Maybe it was that visit that catalyzed his decision to leave.

Bibi hugs me tightly and kisses both my cheeks before passing me off to my uncle, a sober, smaller man whose personality seems to be the opposite of his vivacious wife. I wonder how she and my dad can possibly be related. They seem to be polar opposites.

"*Tudo bem*," Manuel greets me kindly as he kisses my cheeks.

"*Tudo boa*," I answer automatically. "Good to see you again, *Tio*."

Bibi pats her carefully coiffed black hair, which looks like it's slightly tinted red in the sun, and winks while Manuel nods at Nico, then ambles away to say hello to other men closer to his age.

"Now, *who* is this?" Bibi asks, looking Nico up and down. She grins, her red lips tugging slyly and her black eyes sparkling. "Do all the men in New York look like this? Carolina, you might want to visit your cousin in New York. *Gua*-po!"

Nico leans in to accept her kisses on his cheek. "*Brigada, senhora*," he murmurs, and grins when my aunt pretty much trills like a bird in response.

"*Oi*, my *good*ness, that voice! He sounds just like...who is that singer? That one with the low voice? Did you hear that voice, Lina?"

"*Sim, Mãe*," replies a crabby voice in Portuguese. "I heard it. And it does not sound like Barry White at all. Stop embarrassing yourself."

Nico and I both turn toward my cousin Carolina, who is the closest to me in age at twenty-four. Tall, willowy, and blonde (a hair color that is definitely not natural, given all of our family's dark hair), she stands with the slouch that only certain girls affected with wealth and beauty can pull off.

"*Oi, tudo bem*." She greets me with another round of kisses on the cheeks while I murmur "*tudo boa*" in return. She follows the same process with Nico. "Don't pay her attention. She just likes to make trouble."

"Stop," Bibi chides her daughter. "He's so handsome! And polite! Sergio, *você não está feliz que sua filha tenha um homem tão forte e guapo?*"

My father, who is walking around our little party, just strikes up a cigarette and grunts before he walks away to join a few other men sitting around a table by the pool. I watch for a moment, slightly astounded by the sight. My dad never smoked when I was growing up. He obviously knew how terrible it is for you, not to mention how bad it looks for a doctor to be a smoker in the first place. But here, it's different. Almost everyone smokes. There doesn't seem to be the same kind of stigma, even for health professionals.

Nico chuckles at Bibi's remarks, and I just shake my head. We both know my dad is not particularly happy that his daughter has "such a strong and handsome man," as Bibi said. But I'm glad to know the rest of my family doesn't necessarily feel the same way.

"Come on," I say to Nico, taking his hand in mine to guide him through the rest of the party. "We need to say hi to everyone else. And then we're going to eat."

———

Forty-five minutes later, we've been thoroughly welcomed into the fold. Even Dad seems to have forgotten that Nico is with us, since he's happily entrenched in conversation with my uncle and a bunch of other men from the neighborhood.

I sit at the end of the long table, watching as Nico lets my cousins and some of the other younger men usher him into a game of horse-shoes at the other end of the lawn. Bibi takes a seat next to me, carrying a pitcher of water.

"It's too hot to eat so much without a drink," she says. "You want wine? I can get wine."

"No, no, Bibi, I'm fine. Thank you though."

A burst of laughter erupts from the horseshoe players, where Nico turns triumphant after making his first score. He blows me a kiss before starting another turn, and I finger my straw, enjoying the warm feeling his bright smile puts in my belly.

"I like him," Bibi says.

I turn to her and smile. "I know. You made that pretty clear earlier, Bibi. I think he still has lipstick on his face."

She smiles as she lights a cigarette, but shakes her head. "That was...well, yes, he is very handsome. But mostly I just like to, how do you say, tease your father. But I watch. And now, I like *him*. He is kind, yes?"

I swallow and nod. "Yes. Very kind."

Her eyes soften, the slight wrinkles around them become a little less pronounced. With all of her glamor, it's hard to remember sometimes that my aunt is actually in her sixties. She looks and acts like a woman much younger.

"And he is smart?"

Again, I nod. Strangely, I'm a little teary. I hadn't realized how badly I wanted people besides me to recognize all of Nico's amazing qualities.

"And he is good to you, yes?"

I use my index finger to swipe away the tears threatening to fall. "Very. He's the best, Bibi."

She nods, satisfied as she takes another puff. "Good. Then I like him the best too."

I sigh. "I just wish Dad felt the same way. He doesn't like him at all. He treats him like he's dangerous, or like he's going to corrupt me."

In response, Bibi produces a very unladylike snort. "My little brother is a fool some days, Layla. He only act this way because he was the same, you know."

I raise a skeptical brow. "I don't remember Dad having any tattoos, Bibi."

She waves away the thought with her cigarette, causing ash to fly into the air along with the snaking lines of smoke. "He didn't need them. He was bad enough. Out all the night, chasing the girls. Sergio, he was *so* handsome, *so* charming when he was younger. All the girls, they love him. And then, he go to America, and...things, they change. But not so much. That was when he meet your mother."

I don't reply, sensing a story coming. Bibi takes a long drag of her cigarette as she watches my dad. Of all the men standing around the table, he has the most presence. Late fifties, yes, but with a full head of hair, olive skin, and dark eyes. He makes a joke, and the other five or six men around him burst into laughter. He might be my dad, but his charisma is obvious, even to me.

"Sergio is hungry," Bibi says. "He was *always* hungry. You know, we grow up okay, but not with so much money, not like this. He made our father very angry when he did not want to run the farm. But then he go to university, and after that, to America, to Stanford. And he becomes a big doctor, and he meet your mother...he thought he has everything. But still, it was never home. There, he was foreign, you know? And I think that after a long time, it make him bitter. This man..." She waves her cigarette toward my father, who has resumed his normal scowl. "He is not my brother. My brother is still coming back sometimes."

We watch them for a bit more while I pick at my food, and Bibi puffs away.

"So, maybe he sees himself in your Nico," she remarks. "Maybe he worry that in time, you will be with a man who will be bitter too."

I frown, staring down at my juice while I swirl the straw around meditatively. Is that it? Is that why Dad hates Nico?

From across the yard, Nico catches my eye. He winks, and that familiar warm feeling spreads again.

"Yeah, but Nico doesn't have to go anywhere to find home, Bibi," I tell her. "Neither of us will. Because his home is me. And mine is him."

Bibi is quiet for a moment while she finishes her cigarette, then lights another. She watches Nico with me, and her red mouth quirks when he laughs with her sons as one of them makes another score. He turns to me for another grin. Unaware of my aunt watching him, Nico mouths, "I love you" before he turns back to his game.

"Yes," my aunt says with an approving nod. "I see it."

———

"Oh, God."

One slice of steak, two sausages, and countless scoops of *feijoada*, *farofa*, and fruit salad later, I am stuffed. Sated.

And losing just about all of it in my aunt's bathroom on the second story.

"This is what happens when you eat too much, Barros," I mutter to myself as the nausea dies. I stand up, flush the toilet, then go to the sink to wash my hands, rinse my mouth, and splash water on my flushed face. It was the weirdest thing—fifteen minutes ago I felt fine. Way too full, but fine. And then suddenly I had to make a beeline up the stairs to the bathroom so that no one would hear me puke up all the delicious food that had been so painstakingly prepared for me.

And now that it's gone...I'm fine again.

"It's your American stomach," I tell my reflection, dabbing a damp cloth over my cheeks.

"Is it?"

I flinch, then turn to find Carolina standing in the doorway. She strides in, her long, lithe form about as droll as her features. She reaches around me to a drawer in the sink, pulls a zipper makeup bag from the back, and removes a plastic-covered pouch that looks like a tampon.

"Here," she says as she flips the package at me.

I frown. "Oh, I'm not—it's not that time of the month for me, yet."

"It's a, how do you say? Pregnant test? Not tampon."

I stare at the flimsy package for a moment, digesting her words. "What?"

Carolina pulls it back. "We have them from when David and Erica were trying to have a baby last year. But you...*oh*. You mean you and your man, you don't..."

"No, um, we do," I admit, somewhat bashfully. My cheeks redden all over again, but for different reasons.

"Good," Carolina says. "Because if I had that at home...I know we are supposed to be good Catholics and stay virgins forever, but come on. It's a new generation." She shrugs. "What do they expect?"

I shrug too, unsure of what to say. I don't really know enough about the sexual politics of Brazil to know what I should say and what to keep to myself.

"How long since your last, you know?" Carolina checks her reflection and messes with a few strands of hair.

"My..." I start counting the days back since my last period, and slowly it dawns on me that I'm late. And not just a few days. It's been...close to two months.

I freeze.

Carolina clicks her tongue and holds out the test expectantly. "Yes. See? Take the test. Better safe than sorry, no?"

With a shaky hand, I take the test and examine it.

"You pee on it," Carolina says. "Then we wait. Don't worry, I will wait with you."

She leans back expectantly on the counter. Through my suddenly addled brain, I remember that it's one of the differences I noticed last time in Brazil—the way women, especially my cousins, have no shame about their bodies in front of each other. Bathrooms. Changing rooms. Locker rooms. Women here don't have secrets.

"Ah...okay," I say as I move awkwardly back to the toilet and proceed to pee on the stick, as directed, while Carolina watches matter-of-factly. When I'm done, she gestures to a few paper napkins she's laid on the counter.

"Put it there," she says. "We will wait."

CHAPTER TWENTY-SEVEN

Layla

"You are okay?"

Carolina pauses as she strides back into the bathroom. I'm sitting on the toilet, my hands braced on my knees while I try to breathe properly. This explains so much. The slight weight gain. The tiny changes in my body. The fatigue. The sudden nausea.

Carolina looks alarmed. "Should I go get *Tio?*"

"No. *No.* Do *not* get my dad. I'm fine. I'm just..." I swallow, barely able to believe it myself. I stare at the test where it's perched on the edge of the bathtub. The two pink lines cross over each other in a terrible parody of chastity. "I am pregnant. You were right."

Carolina looks at me sympathetically, then sits down on the edge of the tub, careful not to disturb the test. She pats me on the knee.

"Don't worry," she says. "I won't say anything. At least you are lucky. In America, you don't have to keep, no?"

I frown. That is literally the last thing on my mind at the moment.

"Um, no," I say. "We don't *have* to keep." But obviously what I'm thinking is all over my face. "Not keeping" is not an option. Not for me. Not in this world. Not in any.

"Ahhh," Carolina says and gives me a sweet smile. "Well, I will not say anything to *Tio* either. We don't want him to kill your man before you can marry him, no?"

Oh, God. Marry? Is that the only other option?

"It's okay," Carolina soothes, but I can barely hear her voice as the thoughts continue to rush through my head all at once.

Nico barely makes enough to live on by himself, and what little extra he has goes to taking care of his mother and siblings. Raising a baby in New York City can't be anything but crazy expensive, and I'm supposed to be going to graduate school next year. He's going to freak. *I'm* going to freak. Holy shit, what are we going to do? What is *Nico* going to do when he finds out he's going to be a father?

Numbly, I follow Carolina out of the bathroom after shoving the test, wrapped in its plastic, into my purse. Carolina babbles something more about bad contraception methods and how long I have until people realize I was pregnant before we got married instead of after. If we get married at all. Do I even want to get married? Would Nico?

My head is spinning, and suddenly, I can't take it anymore. Halfway down the stairs, I stop her, tugging on her arm so she'll face me.

"Hey," I say. "Carolina? No more, okay? This...this is just our secret for now. *Secreto*," I add in Portuguese, just for good measure, even though my cousin speaks decent enough English.

Her brown eyes, which haven't shown much more than droll curiosity since she walked upstairs, perk a little sympathetically.

"*Sim*," she says with a nod that sends her blonde tresses waving. "Of course."

We enter the patio to find everyone mostly where we left them—the boys still goofing around the yard as they finish another game, the older men having moved inside a bit to check the latest soccer scores, the women chatting around the tables by the pool with their cigarettes and coffee.

I slip around the back of the house before anyone catches me. I need a minute to myself.

There's no one back here, only a small concrete walkway that leads to the circuit breaker and a generator, along with vines that cover the hillside leading almost directly up from the house. I step over the vines, breathing deeply from air that isn't laced with cigarette smoke or chlorine, and when I reach the concrete, I lean against the wall and bury my face in my hands.

Immediately, several faces start flashing through my head. They're all disappointed. My mom. My friends. Nico. My dad. All of them frowning with concern. Disdain. Dread.

I can hear their voices too.

This isn't you, Layla.

I thought you were better than this.

What kind of girl are you?

But the thing is, I don't feel the dread I should. I'm scared, of course. Terrified. I have no idea what's going to happen—if I can afford this, do it on my own if I have to. I don't even know if I'll be a decent parent at all.

Still...I can't regret anything I'd ever make with him. Nico is my heart. My air. My breath. Even if he can't deal with this—and I know deep down that it will probably terrify him too, more so than it scares me—he'd never abandon us.

Right?

He did leave you for LA.

It's a small voice, adding to the others, but somehow it echoes even louder.

He did leave you once.

My hands clench the thin fabric of my sundress, and I keep my eyes squeezed shut as I will the doubts away. It's not fair to me. It's not fair to him.

But instead, they grow louder.

"There you are!"

I open my eyes to find Nico bounding through the vines, a broad smile on his face. His slacks are wrinkled from too much play, and his shirt, with its sleeves rolled up to his elbows, has a couple of grass stains on it. But he looks perfect. Happy.

"Holy *shit!*" he crows. "I just took your cousin to *town*, baby. Straight up owned his ass in horseshoes, my first time out!" He pulls a wad of crumpled Brazilian currency out of his pocket and shows off his spoils. "Fifty-five *reais*, yo! Steak dinner on me!"

I can't help it. I giggle, looking down at the bills and back up at him. "You know that's about fifteen dollars, right?"

Nico's face falls slightly, but he gives me a horsey grin anyway before he tackles me with another hug and a bunch of kisses around the neck. Whether it's the thrill of competition or just having fun, he's definitely riled up. Within a few seconds, so am I.

"Beers on the beach, then," he says as his tongue flickers against my neck. "Damn, you smell good. Are you wearing something new?"

"I think it's the flowers back here. Bibi loves jasmine."

"No, it's you." He continues to trail his nose down my neck. "Do you know how long it's been?" he asks in between kisses that grow longer every time. I open to them, taking him deeper. Each one works to banish my doubts.

"Um, about three days?" I wonder as I wrap my arms around his neck, amazed, as I always am, at just how easily he's able to distract me from my worries.

"Baby, are you losing your memory?" Nico leans back and frames my face with his hands. "I had to do three straight shifts back to back to get this time off, remember?"

I grin. Oh, I remember. Three straight shifts meant nine days of barely seeing him. It meant me hoofing it up to the station twice just to sneak kisses in the bunkroom. Both times we'd been interrupted by a call, and then we were on a plane to Brazil. It has actually been a *very* long time, at least by our standards.

I pop on my toes so I can kiss him, long and hard, enjoying the faint tastes of beer and barbecue that mingle with his unique flavor.

"Mr. Soltero," I say. "Who do you think you're talking to? It's been exactly twelve days." Kiss. "Four hours." Kiss. "Twenty-four minutes." Kiss. "And thirteen seconds since you were last inside me."

Nico raises an eyebrow. "Where's your stopwatch?"

I giggle. "Okay, maybe I made up the last three. But it has been over twelve days."

His teeth graze my jawline before he fixes his mouth on the skin just under my ear and sucks, hard, until it pops from his mouth. "Exactly," he murmurs as he traces his tongue around to the other side. "Too. Fuckin'. Long."

He takes my hand and places it on the tented front of his pants. He's hard and long, and I take hold of him and squeeze, enjoying the way he moans in my mouth as I do it.

"Tell me you need it," he says, his voice lowering half an octave as I squeeze again. "Shit."

"Need what?" I squeeze again. This time he groans slightly.

"You need what?" he repeats. "Don't play with me here, baby. Just fuckin' say it, Layla. I need to hear you say it."

I *should* say what I came out here to mull over. I should tell him the news I only just found out a few minutes ago myself. But like always, I'm not thinking clearly when he's pressed between my legs, when his full mouth is working that strange voodoo on my lips, my jaw, my earlobe, my neck.

"Your cock," I mutter as he drops kisses down my chest, testing the collar of my dress to find the sensitive hollow between my breasts. "Fuck, Nico, I need your cock."

I don't know if it's pregnancy hormones or what, but I'm all over the map. One minute I'm about ready to cry out of anxiety and fear, and the next, I can only think of tearing off this man's pants. It doesn't matter that my family is literally on the other side of the house. It doesn't matter that I can still hear their voices clearly filtering through the late afternoon breeze. I need this man. Inside me. Freaking yesterday.

"Your wish is my command, baby," Nico growls before capturing my lips in yet another soul-searing kiss as his hands drop down to take two harsh handfuls of his favorite part of my body.

"Nico." I try to push him away, but it's hard, too hard. Especially when I'm also half-clawing at his shirt, grabbing him by the collar and yanking him closer. He just groans and kisses me like a starving man, practically eating me alive right there in the yard.

"What in the *hell* is going on here?"

Nico and I fly apart to either side of the patio, but neither of us can hide our flushed faces, swollen lips, the way Nico's shirt is half-untucked and unbuttoned a bit too low, or the way my dress strap is falling off my shoulder.

My father glares at us, then marches through the vines, kicking them away viciously. "*What* were you doing to her?" he demands of Nico.

Nico, to his credit, stands his ground as my dad approaches. He doesn't run or skulk away like a naughty teenager. He holds his chest out firm and crosses his arms over it, like he's ready for anything my dad has to say.

"Dad, calm down," I try weakly. "Nothing was going to happen." Other than the fact that something definitely already has, of course.

"*Nothing* was going to happen?" Dad growls. "His hands are all over you, and *nothing* was going to happen?"

"He's my boyfriend!" I cut back without thinking. "What do you think we do? Hold hands and stare at each other all day?"

Nico snorts, but immediately shuts up when my father practically castrates him with a hard, black glare. Still, Nico says nothing—just continues to meet that stare head-on.

"What are you doing with him?" Dad asks me. "This is not my daughter. My daughter does not sneak away with boys at a family party. This is not what our family does!"

I can't help an eye roll. "Seriously? Go check the pantry, Dad.

Pretty sure Luciano and his girlfriend are having a *really* good time in there."

"Well, *my* daughter does not!" Dad roars. "Especially not with this...this..."

"This what?" Nico's voice is low, but I can hear it shaking. "This what, Dr. Barros?"

My heart rises in my throat. It didn't take long, but it's been clear this confrontation was going to happen all along. I had just hoped to push it until the end.

Dad looks Nico up and down, dragging his gaze over his faded pants, his rumpled shirt, the tattoos peeking out from under his sleeves.

"Keep your hands off my daughter."

Nico steps forward, his chest puffing out slightly. "With all due respect, sir... No."

Dad stomps his foot hard enough that I swear the ground shakes a little. "This is *my* family's house. My family's property. And if you cannot respect me, if you cannot respect *them*, you can leave. I will pay for your ticket back to New York myself."

"And if I don't?"

Dad opens his mouth again, his face twisted deeply with his anger. And then his pager pierces the air. A few seconds later, he starts, as if he has just realized what's happening. Slowly, gradually, the flush falls from his face, and he pulls his pager off his belt to check the number. With a long exhale and a death glare at Nico, he whips his cell phone off his belt and flips it open to dial the number that's appeared.

"*Alô,*" he says when a voice answers almost immediately.

Nico and I stand silently while Dad speaks in rapid Portuguese to the other person, too fast for me to follow. There's too much specialized language for me to understand. I'm guessing it's medical jargon. They continue a brief exchange, which clearly doesn't please my father, because by the time he hangs up the phone, his face is back to being bright red.

"What's going on?" I ask, suddenly aware that he's pulling his car keys out of his pocket. "We're not going, are we? We just got here a few hours ago."

I look back at Nico, who shrugs. Fifteen minutes ago, he had the biggest smile on his face that I've seen in weeks. He's actually having a good time, and the last thing I want him to do is have to jump into a car with a man who looks like he would rather just take him to the airport and damn the cost of a ticket back to the States.

Dad wrinkles his nose and blows out another long exhale. "I have to go," he says curtly. "To São Paulo for a surgery. I will be back tomorrow." He frowns at us. "You will stay here in Guarapari with Bibi and Manuel and your cousins until the party. I will be back for that."

Nico raises his brows slightly at me, and immediately I know he's thinking the same thing. With my dad gone, we'd have the apartment to ourselves, with only the housemaid. We'd have space to do...a lot of things.

To tell him, an internal voice says. Okay, sure, that's totally what I was thinking about, looking at the way Nico's broad shoulders and chest muscles ripple through his button-down shirt. Absolutely.

I turn back to my dad. "That's okay. We can just stay in Vila Velha with Benedita. You can ask her to chaperone if you really need that."

"*You will stay in Guarapari,*" Dad practically spits out. "Clearly someone needs to keep an eye on you, and Benedita is not up to the challenge. Manuel will take me to the airport, and he will pick up your bags on his way back."

"Dad, come on," I try again. "Please don't make a big deal about this."

He glares at me. "You cannot possibly think I would allow my unmarried daughter to stay alone at my apartment...with *him*. Don't be a fool, Layla!" He pushes a hand through his thick salt-and-peppered hair. "Although, maybe it's too late for that."

I wilt, crossing an arm over my stomach reflexively. If this is what he has to say about a kiss in the garden, a child out of wedlock will probably get me disowned. Although, honestly, I'm starting not to care what he thinks of me anymore.

"Dr. Barros." Nico's deep voice cuts across the yard, turning my dad's deadly glare on him. My cousins, clearly used to my father's temper, quiet at the sound of the conflict. "I think that's enough, sir," Nico says in a tone that is calmer, lower than my dad's, but somehow just as threatening. He takes my hand, and squeezes. "We got it."

"Stay *here*," Dad spits, and then turns on his heel and leaves.

CHAPTER TWENTY-EIGHT

Nico

As upset as Layla is when her dad leaves for São Paulo, I'm not a bit sorry he's gone for a few days, even if the whole point of coming here was to see him in the first place. I can't pussyfoot around it anymore. The dude's a straight-up asshole.

I don't care that he dealt with some bullshit when he was younger. Looking around what his family has here, what he had back in the States, I can promise I dealt with a lot more. And I don't fuckin' treat people the way he treats his daughter. Period.

So yeah, it probably wasn't the best thing in the world for him to see me getting handsy with Layla. And yeah, he might have seen a lot more if he had interrupted about a minute and a half later. I'd probably be facedown in the pool right now, or on my way back to the airport.

But I also kind of don't give a shit. It's fucked up, but I kind of wanted the guy to know she doesn't belong to him anymore. Shit, she doesn't belong to me either, but she's mine just the same. And if I want to mess around behind some palm trees, I know she will too. So he can fuck off about it.

Now that he's gone for a bit, Layla and I are both able to relax a little, even if it is with a bunch of other cousins around. Most of the neighbors clear out before dinner, which ends up being the leftover spread that we just pick at while we spend the rest of the evening lounging around the open-air living room, watching soccer with her cousins. It reminds me a lot of my family, the way they tease, laugh, and shout at each other over the table. The older ones have started families of their own, so there are a few little kids around. Luciano and David, Bibi's sons, have pretty much accepted me—a hell of a lot more than their uncle has, anyway. Bibi keeps finding excuses to kiss my cheek. If it weren't for Dr. Barros and his shitty attitude, I'd probably like this side of Layla's family. A lot.

Layla starts to relax too after her dad leaves. She lounges with Carolina and Marcella, Luciano's girlfriend, joking around in stunted Portuguese that, from what I can tell, is better than she thinks. I can only catch maybe fifteen percent of what's said, but I'm proud of my girl. Layla laughs as she takes in her aunt's stories, giggles when one of her cousins makes a crazy joke. Her happiness shines. She's practically glowing.

So I'm not even mad when Bibi sticks me on a stiff trundle in Luciano's room and Layla on the floor in another with Carolina and Marcella. This house is packed for the rest of the weekend, with three or four people shoved into the four bedrooms while everyone prepares for the banquet coming up. Even though I'm dying to finish what we started behind the house, I actually don't want to go around disrespecting Bibi and Manuel for the same reason I kind of want to get it on in Dr. Barros's apartment just to piss him off. It's just about how they treat Layla and me—with basic goddamn respect. It's also obvious that every second Layla spends getting to know her family erases some of the sad-puppy look that comes when her dad snaps at her. So, yeah. I'll take all the blue balls in the world if it keeps making my girl shine.

As luck would have it, the next day Bibi and her kids are pretty much consumed with prepping for Luciano's graduation party. Apparently this kind of thing is a really big deal here. They have to leave all day, and although they invite us to come tag along to their clothes fittings and last-minute shopping, it's clear they would probably get it done faster without us. Manuel stays behind, but is too absorbed with watching soccer to do more than wave when Layla and I tell him we're going to the nearby beach for the day. Dr. Barros seems to be the only one who gives a damn about us having a chaperone.

Which is how I end up walking on a mostly deserted stretch of fuckin' paradise, hand in hand with my girl. Since, like she told me, most of the people in this neighborhood work in the city during the week, everywhere on the beach that the mostly empty neighborhood borders is pretty much deserted. Just dunes and cliffs of yellow-white sand, bright blue water rippling through lagoons, and gullies that lead out to a wider beach and the ocean beyond. And nobody here but me and my girl. Me and Layla.

"You okay, baby?" I ask her after we choose a spot to hang out for a while at the base of one of the dunes, next to a lagoon so clear I can see all the way to the bottom.

I don't know why. But I haven't been able to shake the feeling like something is up with her. She's been happy, but also looks...I don't know. Preoccupied.

Layla pauses. "I'm fine. Why?"

I pull a corner of one of the big beach towels tight and give her a look. "Layla. I know you better than anyone else. I know when that beautiful brain is moving like crazy, and you've been thinking up a storm all morning. So, *que pa'o, mami?*"

Layla's rose-petal mouth quirks a little at the Spanish. She likes it when I call her *mami*, of all things. It's not like the other women I've known, the ones who think it's exotic or some shit like that. Layla's been around my family and me enough to know it's the most common word in the world. Some men use it for every girl they know: their mom, their sisters, their friends, their lovers. Layla's been in New York long enough that *some* random dude has probably called her *mami* on the street. But hopefully she knows that from me, it means she's family. At least, that's what I hope I'm seeing when her eyes sparkle like that.

"I just..." She sits down on the towel and leans back, draping one arm over her stomach. "Do you think it's weird that I like it better when he's not around?"

I sit down on the towel next to her, and then, by habit, move through a set of sit-ups while we talk. I went on another long run this morning before everyone got up, but my belly is gonna turn to mush with all of this rich food if I'm not careful.

"Who?" I ask as I touch an elbow to my knee. "Your dad? No, I don't. I'm not gonna lie, sweetie. I think he's a dick, especially to you. But I don't have to like him because I'm not his daughter."

Layla's eyes brighten as she watches me push through a bunch of Russian twists. "What? Oh. Yeah."

I stop moving and grin up at her. "Should I stop doing this while we're talking, blue eyes?"

She blushes and looks away toward the ocean. "No. I can handle it."

She doesn't *look* like she can handle it if her flushed skin is any indication. Even just being here a few days is giving her a glow, even more than before. But I like the effect too much to stop, so I start doing some boat raises instead.

"What's a chan-cle-ra?" Layla asks a few minutes later.

I do three more reps, then stop. "What's a what?"

"A... whatever your sister says when Allie's being naughty. Sometimes you tell her she better be careful or your mom might come after her with it too."

I sit all the way up and scrunch up my face for a moment, then burst out laughing as I finally figure out what the hell she's talking about. "Oh! You mean a *chancleta?*"

"Yeah," Layla says, nudging me on the shoulder. "What's that?"

I grin. "It's a house slipper. Like your shoes." I gesture toward her flip-flops. "It's sort of a joke, something Puerto Ricans say, right? You do something bad, your mom's gonna smack you with her *chancleta, la chancla*. You talk in church, you're gonna get slapped. You say something rude, she'll fling it across the room at your head. And it always hits, no matter what."

"So it's just a joke?"

I turn my head from side to side, considering. "No. I mean, it's mostly a joke. We make it a joke. But we all got smacked with that or plenty of other things when we misbehaved. I'm sure Maggie does it with Allie. She always gets spooked if you bring it up, you know?"

Layla nods. "I get that. My dad...he used to do that with the kitchen spoons. The wooden ones. He did it until I was about ten or so."

For a second, it feels like the glory of the day dims a little. I don't know what Sergio did. I don't know what Layla did. If you asked me yesterday if I thought people spanking their kids was okay, I would have said sure, even thought getting smacked by a foam sandal is a lot different than a wooden kitchen implement. I would have said there are going to be times where your four-year-old probably isn't going to listen to reason.

But I also get what it feels like to have the shit kicked out of you when you're a kid. I get what it feels like to be scared of the people who are supposed to take care of you. There's a thin line between discipline and abuse for some—and people like Layla and me don't always know completely where it is. That confusion starts young.

Layla shrugs and wraps her arms around her knees, hugging them close. "It is what it is."

I'm quiet for a second. "It's shitty, is what it is." I shake my head. "A lot of Latino men are like that. We grow up in a culture that tells us, like, being a man means being to be stronger than other people. To dominate, especially the women in our lives. Macho bullshit."

"I *never* want to hit my child," Layla murmurs fiercely as she stares out at the water. "With anything." When she turns to me, there's a look of desperation on her sweet face, one I'm not sure I totally understand.

But I do know one thing: I'm there with her. I'm there with her all the fuckin' way.

"Never," I tell her, reaching into her lap to take one of her hands. She looks at our hands linked. "We'll never do that. I promise."

Layla lays her head on my shoulder and sighs. Her shoulders relax, and she hums a little.

"My counselor," she starts to say, pausing a little, like she's trying not to stumble over the words. "She says...she says we learn how to love and be loved by our parents."

I nod. "It makes sense." It's something we've talked about before. The fact that neither of us ever really learned how to be loved the right way. The way it made it so hard for us to believe that we even deserved to be loved. That it always had to be painful. Hard.

"Really, who's easy to love at all?" Layla wonders, so softly I think maybe she didn't mean for me to hear it.

But I do.

"You are."

I can't help the shake in my voice. I hate that she questions this about herself. She knows her dad is the reason why she's gone through what she has. Why she lets so many people walk over her, treat her like she's nothing. The fucked-up thing is that I think Dr. Barros actually does believe in his daughter. He knows she's smart, knows she can do great things with her life. But her failure to meet his expectations drowns out anything good he sees. And it makes Layla see herself as less than she is.

"You are," I say again. But my head drops. Because I know I can't blame all of this on Dr. Barros. "I know I left you too," I say as I stare at the bright blue patterns in the towel. "And, Layla, fuck...you have no idea, baby. If I hadn't...I think about..."

A tear drops down my cheek before I can help it. Not too many things make me break, but the memory of Layla, battered and broken last spring is one of them. I'll die before I let that happen again. I squeeze her hand tight enough that her fingertips turn a little white.

"Stop," she says quietly, squeezing right back. She's crying now a little too, but her voice is steadier than mine. "It's done. That's all done. It wasn't your fault, and then you brought me back, Nico. You saved me, over and over again."

"Ah, shit," I mutter as I let go of her hand to swipe away another few tears. Fuck. She really does turn me to mush.

But there's one more thing I need to say. Something I need her to know more than I need water to drink, air to breathe. I slide a hand around her neck and pull her close so our foreheads touch and our breathing mingles on the sea breeze.

"You listen to me, baby," I say, willing her to feel every word down to her bones.

Layla inhales through her teeth and closes her eyes while I speak.

"*No one* is easier to love than you. You're right, baby. Some people are easier to love than others. But *no one* is easier to love than you."

———

Sometime, maybe a few minutes, maybe an hour later, I wake up as the sun is falling below the cliffs behind us and the houses perched on top of them. I stare up at the palm trees that hang over us, their wide leaves casting shadows across the sand, and a breeze floats through the hot air.

I'm not tired. No sirens are going off. No blare of traffic outside my window. No crazy people trying to get out of my way.

The only time I've ever really spent outside the city was in upstate New York, when I was confined to the youth jail. The country there was so silent it was deafening, and for years I avoided that kind of quiet like the plague.

But here...with the heat and the sun. The lapping of water a few yards away. Here with my girl, the love of my life...this is fucking paradise. And I never thought I'd live to see it.

I turn to tell her just that, but my girl is nowhere to be found. I push up, looking up and down the beach to see where she might have gone, but it's not until I'm on my feet that I finally spot her.

Layla floats in a sea of aqua, her sun-kissed body cradled in the calm waters of the lagoon. The late afternoon sun blinks off the water, clear down to the sandy bottom, and she lies on her back, eyes closed, arms akimbo while she drifts.

The sight of her takes my breath away. I mean, literally, I can't breathe, and all the air in my chest exits at once. But it's not just her physical beauty that does it, even though she is and always will be a work of art to me. It's the look on her face as she floats. The circles under her eyes have disappeared, and her full mouth quirks to the sides with a small, secret smile that's only for her.

Here, together, in this perfect space, just her and me...my girl is finally happy. She's finally at peace. It's a look I thought I'd never see again.

Her eyes blink open, and they are bluer than the water that surrounds her. She smiles, then twists onto her belly and dives below, touching the bottom like a porpoise before she surfaces again. I watch, my voice caught in my throat as she emerges again, then swims closer until she can stand up fully. The water rises only to under her breasts, and I watch, transfixed, as droplets of water roll over her shoulders and down her chest, hanging for a second off her curves before slipping the rest of the way to the water. She's an angel dipped in gold, a woman from dreams I never knew I had...until I met her.

And she's smiling. At me. Like a man under a spell, I get up and wade out to meet her.

How the fuck did I *ever* get so lucky?

"Hey," she says, waving her hands through the water. "I just went for a swim. When did you finally wake up?"

"Marry me."

The words tumble out of my mouth before I can even register the thought. Like they've been waiting in the wings, ready to charge forward the second my vocal chords could release them. And now that they're out, it's like I've been waiting since before I knew her to say them.

Layla stills, her hands floating palms-down in the water. "Wha-what?"

"I..."

I swallow. Holy fucking shit. Did I really just say that? Everything blurs.

"I...shit. That was not at all how I was going to ask you that."

"You were going to ask me?"

"No. Yes. I...I don't know..."

I look up, and her blue eyes are glossy and worried. They shimmer like the water.

"Layla," I say softly, taking her hand under the water. I thread our fingers together, then pull them up so I can kiss her fingers. "Hey."

She finally looks at me, and though her eyes are still uncertain, there's love there too. She looks at me the way I never knew anyone could. The way I know I look at her.

"Marry me," I whisper again. And this time, it doesn't catch me by surprise. This time I fucking mean it.

CHAPTER TWENTY-NINE

Nico

Her wide blue eyes are as big as the ocean.

I swallow, suddenly terrified. "It's not how I planned to ask, you know."

I keep going, babbling the way Layla usually does when she's nervous. I'm glad that out here in the water, she can't feel my palms, the way I'm sure they're sweating right now. I take her other hand now for good measure. Otherwise, I'm honestly scared I might fall over.

"I was going to...maybe in a few years or something like that. Save up for a ring, do it right, you know?" I glance around, the water swishing with the movement. *Coño*, what the fuck am I looking for? A fuckin' fish to come save me? "Shit, I can't even kneel here, can I? Fuck...but, baby, I..."

I drift off when I look back at her. Her eyes are still shining, but the surprise and shock from before is gone. Instead, she looks the same way I feel whenever I look at her—really look at her. Like she can't breathe. Like her happiness threatens to swallow her whole.

Her slender hand is over her chest, and the one still in mine is clutching it so hard her knuckles are white.

"You...you okay, baby?" I ask, stepping closer.

"Say it again," she whispers. "All of it."

There's a warmth in my chest whenever I look at Layla. Before I met her, the world felt cold most of the time. Now it expands, so much I feel like I could burst.

"Layla," I whisper, taking one last step closer so I can pick up her other hand. We're almost nose to nose now, but I don't want her to turn away. "I never...you are...how do I say it? I'm not smart like you, baby. I don't have the words. But when I look at you..." I swallow. "I see the world differently because of you, Layla. And I swear to God, if you give me a chance to make you happy, I'll never stop try—"

My awkward words are swallowed by her kiss. Her lips are soft, just a little salty from the ocean, but they open quickly, welcoming me home. And that's really what this is. I want to marry Layla, because she's already my home. That's what we are and always have been for each other.

"Yes," she whispers against my mouth. It's so soft, and at first I'm not actually sure that I heard her.

"What?"

I can feel her mouth spread against mine, a wide smile that makes that warmth in my chest expand even more. "Yes," she pronounces, and then she laughs.

It's not a giggle, even though I fucking love that sound too. But this one is even better. It's a full-bodied laugh that bounces off the rocks and waves. It's full of life, and calls back to the girl I first met over two years ago. Someone who wasn't afraid to open herself up to a stranger. Someone who showed me what it meant to love.

"Yes?" I ask her, suddenly picking her up by her waist. I swing her around in the water, making her laugh even harder. "Yes? *Yes?!*"

I ask again and again, because I really can't believe that someone like Layla Barros wants to marry someone like me. Or maybe I can. Because really, that's what Layla has been teaching me all along.

That maybe I'm not such a bad idea after all. That together, we're the best idea in the whole fuckin' world.

"Yes," she repeats every time. We settle into the water, submerging our bodies as she wraps her legs around my waist. Her arms rest around my neck, and our noses touch. "A million times, yes, Nico Soltero. I'll marry you."

I close my eyes, so caught up in the moment, in the gravity of what the fuck we are about to do, that I can't speak. Marry. Wife. Husband. It's what we were always meant to be. But *holy shit*. Still.

"Nico?"

When I open my eyes, I still can't speak. The low, golden light of the sunset casts around her like a halo, lighting up even the darkest corners of her tortured heart. *Our* tortured hearts. I have never wanted my sketchbook so badly, but even so, I know I'll never forget the way she looks right now.

Her black hair lies glossy and wet over her shoulders, and her fair skin, flushed from a day outside, gleams as the light skims its wet surface. The thin blue material of her bikini hugs her body as the light shimmers over her curves, and I know it's not the warm breeze floating around us that has her nipples—which somehow seem fuller, a little riper than normal—pressing through the fabric. Her blue eyes fucking glow. The electricity crackles between us. The lines between lust and love are really, really thin. Right now, I genuinely can't tell the difference.

"Jesus," I finally exhale. "Holy shit. I just...sometimes I can't believe you're really mine, Layla."

Her legs drop, and I tug her forward so she's standing between my knees. I run my hands up her bare, smooth legs until my fingertips meet the fabric of her bikini. My heart feels like it's about to explode, along with something else that just got hard as a rock. Thirteen days now it's been. *Fuck*.

I bury my face in her neck and inhale her scent. It's not strong—something a little flowery—a soap she likes, blended with something a little sweet that's only hers, something evident with the salt water glistening on her skin. It's a smell that makes me feel warm and home and turned on all at once.

"Um, Nico?"

Her hands rest lightly on my shoulders. I pull back. "Yeah?"

"Can you...do you think..."

"What is it, sweetie?"

She peers down at me with a fuckin' adorably determined look on her face. Then she sucks on her lower lip, causing it to puff slightly when she releases it from between her teeth. She watches me watching her. I know she's nervous. I know I should say something. But she's so goddamn beautiful, I can't think straight, much less say anything coherent. And she's all fuckin' mine.

"Can you just kiss me again, please?" she finally asks. "And this time...don't stop."

I blink in surprise. Of course. Don't fuck this up again, you pussy. Especially since there are no asshole fathers lurking around the next corner. This tiny lagoon is deserted. It's just me and her.

Layla shivers as my hands wrap around her tiny waist, but I doubt it's because she's cold. The water out here is like bath water, and even with the sun starting to sink, it's probably close to ninety degrees outside.

She tips her head back, waiting for me to do what she asked. So I do. I start gentle; trying to keep from eating her alive like I did behind the house. I want to savor her, worship her, treat her like the queen she is to me. She needs it slow, teasing. She needs me to tease her mouth open like this, lead a sweet slow dance with our tongues as we unravel bit by bit. At her speed, not mine.

Remind her that she's worth it.

Her fingers thread into my hair, and the slight pull sends a current of need through me. *Fuck.* God, this girl makes me manic. One second I'm trying to pull away, let her cry on my shoulder again if she needs to. The next I'm a fuckin' animal.

Slowly, because I don't want to scare her, I unhook the front straps of her bikini and let them fall down her back, then pull down the front so her breasts bob free in the water, allowing me to suck one nipple, then the other into my mouth.

Part of me wants to rip the whole thing off her, but I'm pretty sure she wouldn't be too happy if she had to walk back in nothing but that scrap of fabric she calls a cover-up. Gentle, I keep telling myself, even though all I want to do is lift her up and take her against the rocks a few feet away. I want to spread her legs and drive into her, make sure she knows deep down within that she's mine, leave my mark, my seed, my essence or whatever the fuck you want to call it. I understand now what makes men want to do things like hide their girls' pills and creepy shit like that. It's primal, the need to leave something of yourself inside your woman. Make the two of you truly one.

Layla moans as I drift back to her other breast, biting a little at the end before I release it from my mouth with a slight pop. But I keep my eyes shut, because I know if I actually look at her, I'll lose the tiny bit of control I have left. Her legs are locked around my waist again. I'm hard and pressed against the core of her, and she's already rubbing up and down the whole fuckin' length of me. She wants this as bad as I do.

My fingers play over the slightly raised edges of the tattoo along her ribs, the one that matches mine. *Saudade*, they both say. A yearning for something you never knew. Something we both wanted before we ever even met.

I feel the curve of her waist. The swell of her hips. Her ass, oh *God*, that ass that I dreamed about for months when we were apart. That I'll probably dream about for the rest of my life.

"Oh!" she cries, breathy and light as I grab just a little bit harder. Her hips roll into me, and I groan into her mouth.

"You like that?" I ask before I land a kiss on her neck, then draw my tongue to lick the tiny drops of salt water away.

She shivers again, so I do it again. And again. When I graze my teeth like this, she usually moans a little. She likes it when I bite too, when I pulled just enough on her nipples to make it hurt. A tug, a nip, the casual use of my teeth on her earlobe, and then with a well-placed growl, my girl starts panting for me to fuck her. And god*damn*, do I ever.

But not right now. This is about love, not lust. I saw the look on her face after her dad caught us yesterday. She was scared. Terrified. Right now she needs it soft and slow, and that's okay. I don't care how I get to be with her as long as I just get to be with her.

"Nico."

Layla's voice, sharp and cutting, stills my mouth on her shoulder. I pull back. *Shit.* I was trying for gentle. Maybe I need to stop with the teeth completely. Like a feather, you asshole. You need to be like a fuckin' feather.

"*Nico*," Layla says again. She grabs my jaw and forces me to look straight at her.

I blink. "Fuck, I'm sorry. What is it, baby? I'm being too rough, aren't I? Tell me what you need, okay? I'll do whatever you want..."

Layla frowns. "Stop treating me like a china doll."

"What?"

Quickly, while I stare in disbelief, she reaches down the front of my shorts and grabs hold of my cock. There's no question in her firm grip, no nerves in the way her thumb circles lightly over the tip. A shudder, the best kind, ripples through every muscle I have.

"I think you know," she says, and her eyes, a darker blue than I've ever seen them, dare me to look away. "Stop it."

―――――――

Layla

His cock twitches in my hand. I squeeze a little harder, and his whole body shakes. I'm not going to lie; the power is a little thrilling. He wants this just as badly as I do.

"Nico," I say as evenly as I can. "Just fuck me already. Or did you forget how in the last two weeks?"

A change filters over his body. His muscles tighten. His shoulders straighten. His black brow rises slyly, and his half smile matches it while his hand slides around my waist, and I'm wrapped around him like a cobra while his cock stiffens even more in my hand.

"I would *never* forget how to do that, NYU," he growls before he takes my mouth again.

His kiss consumes me, even more than it did moments before. But where that was a kiss of gratitude, of wonder, this is one of pent-up lust and frustration, the kind that both of us have been feeling for days. The last remnants of his self-control disintegrate, and suddenly Nico's hands are everywhere: my arms, my waist, sliding down to take two solid handfuls of my ass again and squeeze. *Hard.*

"*Fuck,*" he groans as he kneads my skin. His cock, iron between us, bulges through his pants. "Are you—are you sure..."

"Sure about what?" I mutter as his teeth graze my neck. "That I want to fuck my future husband? Out here? Where anyone could see us?" I lean back to look him in the eye. "You bet I am, *papi.*"

With nothing more than a sly smile that lights up his face—whether because of my casual use of Spanish or because he can see just how badly I want him—Nico slams his mouth onto mine. His arms wrap around my waist and shoulders as his tongue and lips invade, while his cock, stiff and ready, teases between my legs.

"Say it again," he murmurs as he takes one breathless kiss, then another, all the while reaching down, around my legs, to tug my bikini bottoms to the side.

As he suckles my lower lip, his hips rock forward, and the tip of his cock, eager to bury itself in my depths, makes us both shudder.

"I...need...you," I whisper as he pushes forward, teasing me ever so slightly, even while his hands maintain their death grip around my thighs.

Nico closes his eyes, taking a deep breath before he latches his mouth to my neck, my ear, my jaw.

"Not," he croaks, his voice a current. "Not like I need you."

He consumes me like a starving man, his lips, his teeth, his hands, anywhere and everywhere, all over my body while my hips rock automatically, seeking the angle to take him deeply, that angle he never quite permits.

"Nico!" I cry as his teeth find my breast again and bite, harder than before. In that way that only he understands, Nico walks the line between pleasure and pain.

"Touch yourself," Nico rumbles into my neck as his cock continues to tease. "I want to watch you come."

"I...can't," I whimper into his neck. The tension ebbs and flows, a current that will take down a waterfall, just slightly out of reach. I want to fall, I do. But I need him to do it.

"Yes, you can, baby," Nico says.

He shelters me with his body, dipping down to lick my collarbone or worry a nipple between his teeth while he urges my hand down between us. But his lips always find mine again, and his tongue twists and turns, driving the tension that my hand begins to match until that edge approaches far faster than I ever thought possible.

"I feel it," he says as my fingers move a little faster, press a little harder. "You're shaking, baby. You're so fucking close. Can you feel it too?"

"Mmmmm," I groan into his lips, sucking on the lower one like it's a piece of candy. "I want to feel *you*."

"Yeah?" he murmurs before taking another kiss, this one much, *much* deeper than before.

"Yeah." And before he can respond, I take hold of his long length and guide him back to that slick, dark space where he fits best.

"*Shhhhiiiittt.*" Nico's breath is hoarse, guttural as he slides inside, so deep, so...home. Then he starts to move.

"Tell me again," he says, lifting one of my legs to wrap around his waist while his other hand slides between our grinding bodies, finding that spot I need for release.

I arch backward into the water, thrusting my breast toward his waiting mouth. But his name is the only word I can say. "Nico."

"Tell me," he insists. His eyes squeeze shut as he moves; this is all instinct for him. For both of us.

But he needs to hear it. He needs to hear that thing I could never say to anyone else. Because it was only ever the truth with him.

"I need you," I whisper, threading my hands into his hair and pulling him close. He fills me, body and soul, so deep, so strong. With him, I am stronger. He is the reason I can be what I never was before.

My body starts to shake. I'm close, so close. "I need you," I whisper again. "Nico...I....oh, God...I do, I *need* you!"

"Fuck!" he shouts. His hips move a little faster, a little more erratically. He drives deeper, harder than he had intended. But I take it, every delicious, punishing blow. The hand at my hip slides up my body and behind my head. He thrusts even deeper, and as I lift my head to meet his hungry kisses, Nico winds my hair around his fist. And then he pulls.

"Nico!" I shout, as my legs squeeze his waist impossibly tight. My body seizes, up toward the sky, a world as limitless as us. With his kiss, this pull, the ultimate pleasure blended with just the tiniest prick of pain, Nico makes me fly right along with him.

"Layla!"

His groans echoes around the sandstone cliffs as he loses himself completely. The hand in my hair keeps the knot in its unrelenting grip as he buries his face into my neck and shouts out the rest of his release.

Slowly, surely, we come back to earth. Back to these waters that drift around us, as peaceful as before. Back to these palm trees, that whisper a little with the wind. Nico's broad, strong body keeps me afloat, lifeless except for the slight twitches of his muscles as they slowly release their tension.

"Fuck," he breathes. "God, I love you."

The words sing through me, though I'm almost too dazed to hear them.

"I'm sorry," he mumbles.

My eyes close. "Huh? Why?"

He leans back so he's looking at me. "I...I kind of lost myself there."

The concern on his face is so sweet. And it only strengthens my resolve that one day I'll convince him I'm strong again. Enough for him. Enough for our baby.

"Yeah, but if we lose ourselves, at least we do it together," I say.

My hand drifts up and down the length of his back. Nico sighs in contentment and pulls me back down to lie on his shoulder. Then he presses one last sweet, soft kiss to the top of my head. "Well, thank God for that."

———

Nico

We swim for a bit longer, but as the sun starts to fall a little lower, Layla throws on her cover-up and suggests we walk through the town to get back to her aunt's house, where everyone will be arriving for dinner.

I just want her. I'm thinking I'm going to have to figure out a way to sneak her to a hotel tonight, even if it's just for a few hours. Fucking her—if that's what you can even call it—in the lagoon didn't do anything to quench the thirst I've been feeling for days. If anything, it just made it worse. We're engaged. She's going to be my wife. And fucking *hell* if I don't want to celebrate that.

But instead, we walk back through the rural part of Guarapari, hand in hand or with our arms around each other's waists as we wander in and out of shops. In one, Layla ducks into a dressing room with a handful of sundresses, leaving me to linger uncomfortably around the register, waiting for her.

"You are American?" the salesgirl asks me, taking in the tattoos on my arm and sticking out the top of my tank top. It's something I've noticed here—there aren't as many people with body art. It's the first time I've been in a place where I look the same as so many other people, but even so, I stick out. No one else has an arm full of tattoos.

But that's not what I'm thinking about when a glint of gold catches my eye.

"Yeah," I answer her as I lean over the glass counter. "Yo, how much is that one? *Combien?*"

I point to a gold ring that's wedged with a bunch of others in a velvet display. I glance over my shoulder, but Layla's still busy behind the curtain. When I turn around, the salesgirl has already pulled it out and set it on a small plate.

The ring is small, but obviously nice. Its metal has been spun so finely that it almost looks like lace. There are no stones in it, no diamonds or rubies or anything like that. I couldn't afford them anyway. I won't be able to get Layla a real engagement ring for a long time, and even then it won't be anything impressive. But maybe while she waits, she could wear something like this. Something beautiful and pure, just like her.

"Is it real?" I ask the girl. I look up sharply. "Like her finger's not going to turn green or anything, will it?"

The salesgirl's face screws up in confusion. "Ahhh..."

"*Verde*," I repeat in Spanish. Shit, how do they say that in Portuguese? I have no fuckin' clue. I try my luck again in Spanish, slowly. "*Debido al metal, entiende?*"

Luckily, it seems to be close enough to Portuguese that she understands—it dawns across her face, as she vigorously shakes her head. "Ah! No, no. No green, gold. We buy from Ouro Preto, you know?"

I shrug. I have no idea what she's talking about. Instead, I examine the ring more, even scratching a little with my thumbnail to see if anything comes off. But she seems to be telling the truth.

"All gold," the salesgirl repeats. "All gold."

I look up. "How much?"

That one, she knows. After looking down a list of prices next to the register, she scratches out a number on a piece of paper and turns it around. I do the mental calculation in my head of converting *reais* to dollars. It's not cheap, but it's a song compared to what something like this would fetch in New York.

Without thinking about it too much, I pull out my wallet and thumb through the cash I have left. "Ummmm," I say. I take out about half of it. We leave in a few more days. I'll just have to be frugal. "Here. And you can put the rest on this?"

I hand her my credit card, the one with a tiny limit that I only have for emergencies. I glance over my shoulder, checking to see if Layla's coming out yet. "Can you hurry, please? *Por favor?*"

The salesgirl nods with a wink and continues processing the payment. She puts the ring in a little cardboard box, and I shove it in my pocket and sign the receipt like a crazy man. And it's just as well, since as soon as I'm done, Layla walks out with two dresses over her arm.

"You can't look," she says as she shields them from me. "They're a surprise."

Surprise? She has no idea.

I do my best to look casual and totally normal as she pays for the dresses. But all I'm thinking is that now that I finally have a ring to give her, how am I going to ask her to wear it?

CHAPTER THIRTY

Layla

"*O QUE VOCÊ ACHA?*"

The hairdresser spins me around so I can see myself fully in the mirror.

It's a small salon, almost completely full of all of the women in my extended family—Bibi, Carolina, her sons and their significant others. Even my grandparents came from Colatina for the big party tonight. She's having her ancient gray strands set into curls around her head. It's more pomp and circumstance than I've seen for anything other than a wedding, but apparently this is totally normal in Brazil, at least in a certain set. The night before, when Carolina mentioned taking the day to get ready for the banquet, and I'd mentioned Nico's and my plans to go to the beach again before the graduation Mass and ceremony the next day, my cousin had looked at me like I should be committed, and then promptly dragged me downstairs while shouting for her mother.

Which is how I found myself in the salon for almost the entire afternoon following Luciano's graduation ceremony. After attending yet another Mass and then watching my cousin receive his degree along with the other twenty or so members of his class also graduating at the end of the summer term, I'd been swept into a car with Carolina and everyone else to be primped for the banquet tonight. Though I'd tried to be demure the day before, not wanting to be a burden or lose more precious time with Nico, Bibi took one look at me, windswept, sand-covered, with my hair a curly windblown mess from the salt water and hours spent at the beach, and informed me that she wasn't taking no for an answer. And as much as I like Bibi, I don't think she was doing it to be nice. This was one of those events, apparently, where her family would be *seen*.

But now I'm glad I went. It was only after watching all of the women in my extended family get waxed, buffed, and primped like it was no strange thing to have all of this done for a relatively small event, that I realized just how out of place I would be if I *didn't* do it. Compared to them, I'd end up looking like a cavewoman. I don't want to admit that a small part of me doesn't want to disappoint my dad either. Or, at least, I don't need another reason beyond the one growing in my belly.

His daughter. Pregnant. Out of wedlock. It sounds bad enough as it is, but when you add to the equation that my father is so Catholic he refuses to divorce his estranged wife who lives in a total other country...well, it's basically going to be like splitting an atom inside my father's head.

Of course, I need to tell Nico first. Sitting in the chair while a woman from Recife paints my toenails, I twitch my ring finger, imagining a ring, any ring, on it. Nico isn't rich—neither of us are—and I hope he doesn't think he has to get me anything expensive, or anything at all. All I want is him, as I've told him time and time again. He gives me so much more than any of this. Just like he'll give our baby.

My hand drifts over my still-flat belly from time to time, and occasionally Carolina looks knowingly from the other side of the room, where she's having her roots touched up. She's wondering if

I've told him, I'm sure. Wondering if I've told anyone. But for now, this secret is mine. Just me and whatever it is. A little bean, a little creature, a little something made of love and nothing else. Whatever happens in the next few days before we go back to New York, I'll never forget that.

I look at my reflection. My hair has been blown into soft, silky waves, which the hairdresser has braided into a fishtail look over one shoulder, leaving a few escaped tendrils to frame my face. It's a style that looks a lot less complicated than it is, considering the number of pins and amount of hairspray she used. But the overall effect is ethereal and romantic, and fits the floaty white gown with the gold threaded embroidery over the bodice and down the skirt that's hanging in the salon's dressing room. Bibi brought it back after yesterday's shopping expedition with equally adamant insistence that I wear it instead of the four-year-old dress I still had from my senior prom. I fought it at first. After all, I used to love the light-blue dress with the sparkly fabric and color made my eyes pop. But it was the kind of dress that a high school student would buy, made of cheap polyester materials in a trendy design, more like dress-up than real life.

Bibi's dress is for a woman, not a girl. And when I tried it on, saw the way the embroidered chiffon floated over my curves, accentuating without looking tacky, and the way the combination of white and gold actually made my eyes look even bluer than normal, I knew one thing: Nico needed to see me in this dress.

"*Eu gosto,*" I tell the hairdresser, giving her the thumbs-up. "I love it."

She nods, then points to the smaller station in the far corner of the salon where one of my cousins is having her makeup done and says something in Portuguese. It's a little faster than I'm used to, but the meaning is clear: I'm next.

———

The banquet takes place at a rented hall close to Luciano's university, in a circular building with open-air walls through which we can see into a park that surrounds it. In the center of the room, a DJ is spinning all the greatest hits from the last few decades, while most of the graduates and their families are still mingling, getting drinks from the open bar on one side or enjoying hors d'oeuvres from the buffet at the other. Even though the class had all of twenty-five people in it, it seems like the entire law school and their families showed up to celebrate. It's true what they say. Brazilians like to party.

I stand a bit awkwardly with my cousins around one of the tables that are laid around the dance floor in the center of the room. It's empty, but Carolina has assured me it will fill soon, once everyone is drunk enough. The boys are nowhere to be seen. We're a little early, having come straight from the salon.

"You almost look like a bride," Carolina says, looking me over again critically. "Your eyes...gah! Do you wear contacts?"

I shake my head.

Carolina exhales again. "I'm *so* jealous. I wanted to get contact to make my eyes blue like yours, but *Mamãe*, she says no, not while I live with her. For now, anyway."

I look down at my dress, then back up. I look good—I know that—but I haven't been this dressed up in ages, maybe not ever. I look like money in this expensive dress and the diamond earrings my aunt lent me. But that's not what I care about anymore. If I ever did.

"You don't think it's too much?" I wonder, suddenly worried she can see past the light chiffon to the truth. Nico and I haven't told anyone about our new engagement. So far it's just been our sweet secret. I'll have to tell my dad before I leave, but right now, it's been nice to just have it between us.

Carolina shakes her head. "No, no, it's perfect. I was just teasing, you know?"

I exhale. "Okay. Do you know when the boys will be showing up?"

Carolina shrugs. "They were coming from Guarapari, so it's hard to say. Maybe they find some traffic, I don't know."

"Wow."

His deep voice, the only one speaking English, curves through the air and wraps me in its warm embrace. I turn around and I'm immediately blown away. I forget sometimes how well Nico cleans up. And...wow is right. For him, not me.

Unlike most of the other men in the room, who are dressed, as my father stated, in standard black-tie regalia—black tuxedos with white shirts—Nico's in his all black suit, with a matching shirt, tie, and vest. I've seen this suit before. It's his only one, the all-black ensemble he wore at Thanksgiving, which was also his uniform when he worked at a swanky club in LA. But I haven't seen it since he moved back.

He should be a shadow, but instead the monochromatic outfit just makes his skin glow. His thick black hair has been tamed a bit, swept off to the side slightly, and the sole bit of color in his outfit is a red pocket square. He looks elegant. Maybe a little dangerous. And he's all mine.

His gaze burns over me as he takes in my dress, my hair, the jewelry, even the dainty gold cross gifted from Bibi.

"Damn," he murmurs under his breath, pulling slightly at his collar. When his eyes finally meet mine again, they gleam. "Wow. You look insane, baby. For real, you look *amazing*."

I blush under the heat of his gaze. He doesn't hold back, just continues to stare in awe—an emotion he rarely hides when he feels it, but which I haven't seen this naked before.

"Thanks," I whisper. "You—you look—I mean...gah."

Behind me, Carolina laughs. "I think she mean you look nice too," she clarifies before walking away.

Nico takes my left hand and strokes my knuckles, lingering over the bare ring finger. "Sorry I'm late."

I shake my head a little. "Please. There's nothing to be sorry for."

"We had to wait for your dad to get back from the airport. And then, well...let's just say he wasn't too happy when he remembered I didn't have a tux." Nico's mouth twists sardonically as he remembers. "He cares a lot about what other people think, huh?"

The clouded expression makes my fists clench. I hate that look, that lingering insecurity that comes out every now and then. I hate anything or anyone who makes Nico feel like anything less than the amazing person he is.

"He cares too much," I tell him. "It's his Achilles' heel. *I* think you look incredible. Isn't that what matters?"

Nico brightens, a shy smile replacing the frown. "You bet your ass it is, sweetie. So riddle me this: do you care too? Or would you be willing to dance with me on an empty floor?"

I glance at the dance floor, which is indeed mostly empty with the exception of a few younger attendees and an older couple swaying off to the side.

I turn back. "I am *always* willing to dance with you, Mr. Soltero."

———

An hour later, the dance floor has filled up along with us, and we're both a little sweaty and worn out after dancing to song after song that could probably be pulled from cheesy pop albums of the eighties and nineties.

"I gotta say," Nico calls before he spins around on his heel. "I wasn't expecting to get down to Shania Twain on my first trip to Brazil. It's like they didn't get out of the nineties pop hell, huh? K.C. would be freaking out down here."

I giggle. "I think it's just this DJ. You don't 'feel like a woman'?"

Nico grins. "Nah. But I liked watching you scream it with everyone else. You're so cute when you sing, baby. Off key, but really damn cute."

I shove him in the shoulder, which he just takes as an excuse to pull me closer. As if on cue, the Spice Girls stop singing, and for the first time, the DJ puts on a slower song. Mariah Carey's "Honey" isn't anything that's going to kill the mood, but the tempo, a little slinkier than the manic pop songs, gives Nico an excuse to pull me closer, swaying me back and forth to the lazy rhythm.

"What is it with you tonight?" he murmurs as he starts to roll his hips in a way that obviously comes from the years of practicing salsa in his mom's kitchen growing up. "You look...you look different. Something's different." He spins me out, then pulls me back in. He looks across the room to make sure my dad is still engrossed in a conversation with a few other men, then sneaks a quick kiss. "You're fucking glowing, baby."

Now is the time. I should tell him now, right? But before I can, Nico stops dancing and reaches into his jacket pocket, though his other hand remains firmly on my back, keeping me close.

"I, uh, picked something up the other day," he says as he withdraws his hand. "I saw it and thought of you. I was going to wait until we were back home, but..." He looks over me again, taking in the apparent beauty he hasn't stopped talking about for the last hour solid. "I don't know. Something...I feel inspired. I want you to have it now."

He opens his hand, and what I see makes my heart stop.

It's a ring. A simple gold ring that gleams against the fine lines in his palm. It's delicately engraved, like the gold has been spun together to weave an imperfect, yet perfect design all the way around the thin band.

I look up. "Nico..."

Nico chews on his upper lip for a second, then gives me a shy smile. "I know it's not a diamond, Layla. One day I'll get you one, I promise. If that's what you want, baby, I'll do whatever I need to do to buy you the biggest diamond in Manhattan, I swear to God. Layla, I just want to make you happy. That's it—"

I lay my hand over the ring, a gesture that stops his babbling.

"I don't want a diamond," I tell him, keeping our eye contact solid so he knows I mean it. Then I look down. "I want this. It's so perfect, Nico. It's simple and beautiful. It's so us."

"I want you to have it," he says. "I didn't do it the right way the other day. I didn't get to tell you how beautiful you are to me, inside and out. How brave. How much I love the way you open your heart to the world, again and again. How much you want to make it better. How you inspire *me* to be better, every damn day."

His words make me giggle, the awkward kind that only happens when you feel so much your chest might split open. I reach up to swipe away a few errant tears that spring unbidden—not from sadness, but from joy.

"Layla," Nico says, tugging me just a little closer. "Will you marry me?"

I bite my lip, then hold out my left hand. "Of course I'll marry you, Nico Soltero. Tonight. Tomorrow. I'm yours, body and soul. Don't you know that by now?"

He slides the ring on my finger, and it fits, just like I knew it would. Nico knows me sometimes better than I know myself—why would my ring size be any different?

"What are you thinking?" he asks tentatively.

I look back up at him to find, even now, a little insecurity playing across his chiseled features. "I think I'm the luckiest freaking woman on the planet right now," I say honestly.

Nico grins, that signature smile that lights up every room he's in. That lights me up. "I think we need to celebrate. I'm going to get some champagne from the bar."

He turns to leave, but I tug his sleeve back. "Just...just water for me, okay? I don't want to drink."

His face screws up with immediate concern. "Baby, you're not going to go crazy if you have a glass of champagne with me. Come on, it's our engagement. We should toast, don't you think?"

I shake my head. He thinks I'm stopping him because I'm afraid of taking a step backward, to that dark, crazy time when I was spiraling without him. That I'm so scared of going there that I won't even have a cocktail. But that's not it.

"Layla," Nico says, taking a step closer. "What is it?"

He waits patiently, the expression on his face kind and open.

And I know in that moment, that nothing I could tell him would ever push him away. Nico loves me, loves *us*, unabashedly, with all that he is. There's nothing to fear.

So I open my mouth to tell him the truth, the news that's going to change both of our lives. The news that has me petrified and over-joyed all at once. That I'm dying to share and at the same time, terri-fied to say out loud.

"I'm—"

"*What* is that on your finger?"

Before I can say a word, my father comes charging through the crowd, his voice booming over the music. He storms between Nico and me and grabs my hand, the one with the gleaming new piece of delicate gold jewelry, practically ripping it off my arm Behind him, Nico's face turns black. He *really* doesn't like my dad, and clearly he's not cool with the way he's touching me at the moment.

My father, however, doesn't care. He shakes my finger, and the two veins over his temples look like they are about to burst.

"Layla," he demands. "*What*. Is the meaning. Of this?"

CHAPTER THIRTY-ONE

Nico

I FREEZE. WE BOTH FREEZE. BUT I DON'T MISS THE WAY LAYLA takes a step toward me, like she's looking for shelter. I hate that her own father makes her feel that way, but I get it. Goddamn, do I get it.

"*What?*" Dr. Barros shakes Layla's hand, then drops it like it's burning.

He takes a long drink of something that looks like whiskey, then sets his empty glass on a nearby table before standing up, swaying a bit. Great. He's mad *and* shitfaced.

"What is the meaning of this?" He lets out a long string of Portuguese, and from the way some people's eye bug out, I'm guessing it's pretty foul.

"W-we're getting married," Layla says.

She holds out her hand with the simple ring that barely stands out in this room full of rich, flashy ladies with even flashier jewelry. But the gold on her finger still gleams in the light.

"Nico asked me. And I said yes, of course," she tells Dr. Barros, sticking her chin out a little in this fuckin' adorable away that would make me want to kiss the living shit out of her if I wasn't so worried about her dad right now.

Because I know that look. I've worn it a few too many times myself. It's the look you get when you're about to explode.

"Married," Dr. Barros repeats, and I can practically see the steam coming off his head. "To—*this*?" He gestures at me like I'm a piece of fuckin' furniture. Like I'm a thing, not a person. "No. I forbid it."

"Well, that's too damn bad," I pipe up. I can't help it. I'm so tired of this guy treating me like I'm less than him, treating Layla like she's a fucking puppet. He has no fuckin' right. "Last I checked, Layla and I are both adults. And I'm pretty sure you haven't given a shit about her for the last year and a half anyway."

Layla shakes her head at me, clearly telling me to shut the fuck up. "Dad," she says. "Please. Let's just talk about this somewhere quiet..."

"He's a criminal," Dr. Barros states a little too loudly, and the word causes another few onlookers to murmur a little. Slowly, people around us are taking in what's happening. The dance floor is growing still, even with Montell Jordan blasting on the speakers.

It takes everything I have not to stare at the floor when the English speakers in the crowd look at me with renewed, slightly fearful interest. No. I'm not guilty of anything but falling in love. That's not who I am anymore. It's not who I've been for a long time now. Maybe I never was.

"What are you talking about? Of course he's not," Layla snaps as she comes to stand in front of me. It makes me proud. My baby is valiant, guarding me from her dad. In her white and gold, she's an angel, but the good kind, like Gabriel—the kind that don't fuck around, you know?

"You think I don't look him up? You think I don't find that he was in jail?" Dr. Barros demands wildly, his English uncharacteristically sloppy, the work of a few too many scotches. "Layla, he is nothing. He comes from nothing. He is becoming nothing. He is not good enough for you!"

"He's a hero!" Layla hisses defiantly, reaching behind to take my hand. "He's a firefighter in the best city in the world. He saves *lives*, every day, and he definitely saved mine. What do you do besides give women bigger tits?"

A laugh bursts out of my chest before I can stop myself. I should be angry—fuck, I *am* angry. But the look on Dr. Barros's face when his daughter says the word "tits" in front of a whole bunch of fancy rich Brazilians is fuckin' priceless.

"That's enough!" he shouts. His face reddens even more as he looks around. Yeah, the dude has definitely been pitching back the sauce. "We are leaving. Now."

"No," Layla replies.

"*Sim.*"

"No!"

"Layla, we are *going!*"

Dr. Barros grabs for Layla's wrist and jerks her forward, twisting her arm painfully and forcing her to kneel slightly next to him. Any trace of humor disappears completely, and just as fast, blood roars in my ears when Layla tries to fight it, her face contorted in pain as she does.

Oh. Hell. Fuckin'. No.

It takes me less than a second to dart in between Layla and her dad, grab his wrist, and twist it enough that he has to let hers go. I thrust him away from her, allowing Layla to step backward behind me, suddenly released. Out of the corner of my eye, I notice her rubbing her wrist where he had grabbed it. Now I'm the one barely holding onto my temper.

"Get out of my way," Dr. Barros orders. "This doesn't concern you. This is a *family* matter."

"Well, then it does concern me, Dr. Barros," I say. "Since Layla *is* my family, sir. And I'm hers."

He turns to me with a face full of rage, and surprises me when he walks close enough to make us almost nose to nose.

"*You* will never be her family," he informs me through capped, white teeth. "*Never*. Not you. *Never* someone like you."

I grind my teeth. I don't like this guy at all, but I never wanted him to hate me. This isn't someone Layla may ever be able to walk away from. You just can't ask someone to do that with their own dad. I don't want Layla to hate me either for messing up their relationship more. Because when I look at her, see her blue eyes full of curiosity, fear, but always, always trust in me. In us. I don't doubt it anymore. In fact, the insinuation that we're *not* inextricably bound together makes me pretty fuckin' angry.

"Is that right, *Doctor* Barros? Well, where the fuck were you last year, or the year before that, sir?" I take a step forward, forcing him one step back. "Because I'm the one who's been there. I'm the one that carried your daughter out of some asshole's apartment after he had beaten her black and blue. *I'm* the one who talked her into going home even though I wanted her with me. Your daughter is my heart and soul, sir. I would do anything for her. Lay down my life for her in a heartbeat. So there ain't *no fuckin' way* that anyone gets to talk shit about her, about *us* like that. Not while I'm alive." I pull myself up as tall as my five feet, almost eleven inches will let me. "I don't care if you're her father. I don't care if you're the Pope. You mess with Layla, you mess with me."

Dr. Barros blinks, his dark, shadowed eyes burning into me and everyone else. Into his daughter. But my words fly right by him. Maybe he's too angry to really hear them in the first place.

"Layla," he tries again, straining, it's clear, to keep his voice down. "We go. Now."

"No, Dad."

Dr. Barros gulps, hard enough that it makes his bow tie twitch. "Layla," he tries again.

"She doesn't want to go with you," I tell him.

And then I make my biggest mistake, one that in all my years of training with fighters, of living in bad neighborhoods, of growing up in a city where you *always* look over your shoulder, I should have learned by now. I turn my back.

"Come on, baby," I say, taking Layla's hand and pulling her close. I press a kiss to her forehead, willing her to know that whatever happens tonight, I'm still here for her. I'm always here for her. "Let's get out of here."

Maybe it's the kiss, innocent as it was. Or maybe it's the way that his daughter is looking at me, with big blue eyes full of love, the kind that drives me every day to be something better than I am. Whatever it is, Dr. Barros sees something that sets him off. And he attacks with a roar.

"NOOOOO!"

In a split-second, I'm wrenched away from Layla, and I've got a pair of slim, well-groomed hands flying at me. One cuffs me on the jaw, a sucker punch I'd be able to dodge on literally any other day, any other moment.

"Sergio!" screams Layla's aunt.

"Dad!" Layla shouts.

But I don't know where they're coming from, because I'm too busy fighting off the best of Brazilian society right now. Frank, my old trainer and mentor, used to say that half a good fighter is skill, and the other half is adrenaline. And that if you pit one against the other, adrenaline wins every time.

Dr. Barros might be older and weaker than me, but he's got fury on his side.

Still, I've got a little of that too. A well of it, really, that will probably never totally go away. And when I think of the way he looks at his daughter like she's nothing, that anger bubbles up in no time, and I'm ready to swing back.

"Dad!" Layla shouts as Dr. Barros scrambles at me again, his fists flying toward my face.

The guy is no fighter. His hands are soft, the slim fingers of a surgeon, not a soldier. I duck easily, parry him away as the crowd naturally spreads into a circle around the dance floor. He comes at me again, and this time, I parry away his fist, deliver an easy cross to his cheekbone, and as he falls back, grab hold of his wrist and twist him neatly into a half-nelson under my much bigger shoulder. I'm an inch or two shorter than the guy, but that means nothing in a situation like this.

"How does it feel?" I growl at him, close enough to his ear that only he can hear me. "How does it feel to be yanked around like you're nothing, huh? You like it? Because I sure as fuck know your daughter doesn't."

People are shouting in Portuguese all around us—calling for help, for someone to grab me, grab the thug American beating up the eminent surgeon, no doubt. I figure I have about two more minutes of this until I'm going to have to sprint for the door.

"Let...me...go!" Dr. Barros shouts, jerking his chest two and fro, his face turning red like a tomato.

"You gonna calm down, *culo*?" I ask, unable to keep the profanity from slipping out. Somehow swearing in Spanish is worse here than at home, but I can't help it. I don't want to use his title. I don't feel anything resembling respect for the guy anymore.

Dr. Barros stiffens, which tells me he knows exactly what it means. "*This* is what you call respect?" he shouts, his face screwed up as he continues to thrash around. "*This* is how you wanted to ingratiate yourself to me?"

"You're not leaving me much of a choice," I reply evenly as I struggle to maintain my hold. I'm stronger, but my anger is fading. His, however, is going strong. But not strong enough. "If you calm down, I'll let you go."

My arms are straining, but I'm immovable. He's going to hurt himself if he doesn't stop. But then again, I'm not sure I care.

"You will *never* be with my daughter!" he howls. "I will die before allowing some filthy, *moleque* to pervert my family! You will *never* deserve her! You will *never* end up with her—over my dead body!"

"But it's already done."

The crowd and Dr. Barros hush at the sound of Layla's voice.

"What does that mean?" he hisses, still struggling against

my hold.

Layla steps forward, suddenly having found her voice. She glances around nervously, then zeroes in on her dad. "I'm pregnant."

The word ricochets around the room like one of those pinballs at an arcade. I should know, because it basically hits me in the head. The DJ shut off the music long ago, probably hoping the absence would shut down the fight. And within a few seconds, the only sound is a light murmur as the people around us digest what Layla's just said.

And when I do...I can't feel a thing. Dr. Barros and I both freeze, and a half second later, he flops to the floor with a thump while my hands fall limp to my sides. Dr. Barros lies on the tile for a few more seconds before he sits up, rubbing his head, as if he's not sure he heard what he just heard. But I just stare, unable to move. Did I hear what I thought I just heard?

"I'm pregnant," Layla repeats softly, this time only to me. She steps closer, her eyes bright and wide. The people around us strain to hear, but these words are for me. "I only found out a few days ago, at the barbecue...I was planning to tell you when we got back to New York." She swallows, looking guilty. "I'm sorry, I just...needed some time to digest it myself."

At the sound of her voice—her sweet, kind, unsure voice, I jerk. "You're...pregnant?"

Layla nods. "I am."

I take a step back—not because I want to, but because I'm having a problem standing up straight. Pregnant. Holy shit. A baby. *My* baby. Holy shit.

Dr. Barros stumbles off the floor, pushing people away so he can make his exit as quickly as possible. Before I can say anything, Layla reaches out to me, her eyes eager and scared all at once.

"Nico?" she whispers. "Say something."

But when I open my mouth, nothing comes out. Not a sound. Not a breath. I look at her, and then I look at the people still watching us openly. And then I turn around and walk out of the building.

CHAPTER THIRTY-TWO

Layla

I watch as my father stumbles one way, bloody-mouthed and hunched over in the direction of the parking lot, and Nico strides in the other, toward the beach that's only a block or two away. Whatever I was expecting when I dropped this news—from either of them —this wasn't it. These are the men in my life who are supposed to love me more than anyone. This isn't how I wanted to tell either of them, by dropping the word "pregnant" like a bomb in the middle of this glitzy party. I'm lucky that only a few people around us probably really understood what was going on. But even those few are enough to bring shame on my family.

I stand in one place, swiveling between the two directions aimlessly until Bibi approaches and puts her hand on my shoulder.

"Go to him," she says.

She looks at me kindly, and her brown-eyed gaze, so like my father's, but invested with humor and kindness I've never seen from him, drops to my stomach, over which my hand lies. There's nothing there to cup yet. It's a flat expanse that's more of a dream still than a reality.

I don't know whom she's referring to. But I know whom I need to follow. So I turn toward the beach and make my exit.

The pavilion that's housing the party sits in the middle of a grassy park, crisscrossed with the looming, sharp-ended shadows of palm trees, while the bougainvillea climbing the walls sneaks up the sides, black against the glare of the moonlight. The grass eventually opens onto the promenade in front of this beach, like all the others. When I step into the light, I can see the outline of Nico's broad shoulders across the four-lane street as he strides, head down, toward the ocean. He pauses for a second on a rise in the sand, stares out at the waves, and then falls, ungracefully, to sit and shoves his head in his hands.

Even from here, little more than a shadow, he's so beautiful. Streetlights glint off the sheen of his hair, and the broadness of his shoulders still captivates me from afar. They sag, though, clearly feeling once more the weight of the world.

I never meant to add to his burdens.

I make my way across the street, ignoring the whistles out of the cars that pass, and remove my high-heeled shoes before crossing the beach to where he sits. Once I'm there, I sink into the sand quietly.

He hasn't looked up at me yet, but he knows I'm there. He always knows I'm there—he probably knew I was watching him from across the street.

For a while, we sit in relative silence, listening to the low roar of the cars behind us filling the air along with the sound of the waves beating the surf.

I wonder where my father has gone. If he went back to his apartment, just over the big bridge in the distance, to continue drinking himself silly while he ruminates on his daughter's shame. He was already drunk at the party. I doubt he would have made such a scene otherwise. And then I had to add to it by admitting to being pregnant out of wedlock in a roomful of staunch Brazilian Catholics. To my father, to his family, it doesn't get much worse than that. It's not like it doesn't happen; it happens all the time. But the appropriate way to deal with it would be to get married quietly, before anyone could notice completely, or else get rid of it, equally as quiet.

What must my father be thinking now? He left the United States to escape social castigation. And here I am, bringing it to his feet. All my life I've tried to make him proud. He'll never look at me the same way again. He'll never forgive me.

It occurs to me, right then, that I legitimately may never speak to him again. This isn't the kind of thing he would ever be able to forget.

Nico shifts where he sits, bringing me out of my dark thoughts. He lifts his head to look out toward the ocean, and I see waves of worry flowing from his beautiful, strong face. He rubs his hand over his eyes, down his rounded nose, over his full lips and up his chiseled jaw. Then he sighs, long and low.

What my dad thinks no longer matters. What's most important to me is right here, I realize, with some measure of peace. What matters is the man next to me, the man who owns my heart. What matters is us. Our future. Together.

If we still have one.

"What am I going to do?" Nico wonders softly, so low his voice almost has the same timbre as the waves on the shore.

My heart drops, heavy at his words. I say nothing at first, just wait patiently until Nico leans his head on my shoulder. It's warm, solid, though I can feel him shaking.

"Are you...so you're upset then?" I ask, unable to stop my voice from quaking slightly. I toy with my ring, twisting it around my finger. Maybe he'll want it back.

The idea crushes me. My chest feels like it's caving in. I know I'm too young. I know it's too soon for us. I know to everyone else, we're just a couple of poor, crazy kids who have no business jumping into a marriage, much less starting a family.

But even with that, a part of me had hoped that Nico would be happy about this news that we had created something out of the bond between us. I've only carried this knowledge with me for a few days, but already it's a part of me. Already, I would do anything for it.

"Upset?" he repeats. "No, baby. I'm not upset."

I turn to look at him, take in his beautiful profile—the jaw that could cut glass, sprinkled with the slightest stubble. The nose that's rounded at the end, just a little too long, but which fits his face. The dark eyes, lined with thick lashes, that look at everything with so much soul.

"So...what are you?" I wonder.

Nico just stares out at the ocean for what seems like an interminable amount of time. Then, finally, he turns to me with eyes so wide they could swallow me whole.

"Layla," he whispers as a lone tear tracks down his cheek. "I'm so fuckin' happy I feel like my chest is about to split open. But, baby, I can hardly speak, I'm so scared."

His calm is eerie. I want him to do something. Laugh. Run. Cry. Shout. Anything but this strange stillness that seems to have taken over.

"I just...fuck. I don't know how to be a dad," Nico says, his voice shaking slightly. "I never had one. The closest thing I saw was David, Gabe's dad, who..."

He closes his eyes, as if in pain as he trails off, pressing his forehead into his arms. He doesn't want to voice those memories out loud. I know the feeling.

"I know," I say. "Your mom told me. After Giancarlo." He's alluded to it as well. David was abusive. He would take things out on his kid, the mother of his son, and her other children. It was Nico who chased him out for good. But with violence. That I know. It was always with violence.

It's a side of him I've only had glimpses of, but never seen until tonight. But I'm not scared. I could never be scared of him.

Nico turns his head on his forearms and gazes at me, eyes slightly glossed over. Fear shines through their black depths. "What if...what if I end up like that?"

Oh.

"Nico," I begin. "You would never—"

"Hush," he cuts me off, taking my hand in his.

In the bright moonlight, gleaming off the waves, the contrasts between us seem to be that much starker. Nico plays with his fingers, his darker skin weaving with my lighter. The glow of the moon blinks off the gold embroidery of my gown, the watch on my wrist, and probably from the diamond earrings hanging from my ears. His suit, which is slightly threadbare at the hems from years of use, swallows the light instead.

His eyes, dark though they are, still shine brighter than any diamond.

"I'm not a nice man," Nico states plainly. "Why would I be a nice father?"

"Nico—" I try again.

"No," he says. "Look."

He flexes his right hand. There's a bruise already spreading across his knuckles and a cut on the middle one. And on top of that, the evidence of other tiny nicks, calluses, and other marks of heavy labor are evident. It's the hand of a warrior, in more ways than one.

"Do you see that?" he asks quietly. "Baby, that's the hand of someone who is violent, just like your dad says. I just hit my future father-in-law in the face, Layla. In front of a whole crowd of people. What if—what if I did that to our kid?" His eyes finally meet mine, and his lower lip trembles. "I don't think I could live with myself if I ever did that. But what if that's all I know? What if, I don't know... what if I'm like your dad? Or Gabe's dad? What if I get mad at it or something and I just...snap?"

He clenches his fist suddenly, then drops it to the sand. His eyes squeeze shut, as if he's in pain, and my heart squeezes right along with them. I hate that he sees himself like this. Doubts himself so much. And I hate that my family made him do it again.

"Can I ask you something?" I venture.

He looks up. "What's that, sweetie?"

I tip my head. "Have you ever hurt someone for any other reason than protecting someone else?"

Nico rubs his neck and sighs. "When I was in high school, right after I got out of juvie...there was this kid, Jaden. He was...well, let's just say he was partly responsible for me being in the joint in the first place. What they locked me up for—he was the one who did it."

I nod, somewhat familiar with the story. We had only known each other a short time when he revealed his past—the fact that he had been sent to a detention facility for two years for a violent crime that would always blemish his public record. It isn't fair really, holding someone hostage for the rest of their life for something they did when they were only fifteen. And while he certainly had a dark side, Nico wasn't even the one who had actually beaten the bodega owner with a crowbar while he and two other kids had robbed it. He was just the one holding the weapon when the police arrived on the scene.

"Anyway, Jaden was always a bully, and he was even worse when I got out. I remember seeing him steal this kid's hat in school, this kid who couldn't do anything, couldn't stop him. Later that day, Flaco, K.C., and I saw him walking down the street. And I don't know...I just flipped."

Nico looks up, his brow furrowed with the memory. He folds his hands into casual fists, and the movement causes the muscles in his forearms to ripple.

"What kind of man does that?" he wonders. "I beat the shit out of a kid for stealing some guy's hat. I lost it, Layla, plain and simple. And two months later, I did the same thing to David, Gabe's dad. Told him to stay away from my family, or I'd kill him." He turns to me with a steely glare. "And I meant it, too."

I take a second to digest the story. But one thing is clear.

"So the answer is no," I say. "It doesn't sound like you've ever been violent just to be violent. You just...Nico, you protect. That's what you do."

"Baby, the way I felt back then...it's nothing to what I feel for you.

For...her. Him. Whoever that is inside you." He swallows, and the movement makes a muscle in his jaw flutter. "I would do *anything* to keep the two of you safe. It scares me. That day with Giancarlo... Layla, I would have killed him if you hadn't called me back, I know I would have. What if my anger goes the wrong way? What if...what if I hurt our kid?"

Relief and sorrow flood through me. Because if that's all this is, just a fear that he won't be a good father because he never had one himself, then I have nothing to worry about at all. If anyone in the world could be a good parent, it's Nico. I have no doubt about that. I just wish he could see it too.

"Don't you know?" I ask him as I gently stroke his cheek.

His eyes close with my touch. "Know what, sweetie?"

"You said..." I pause, trying as hard to swallow the warbling in my voice as to put the right words together. "You said that no one was easier to love than me? Well, no one loves like you. Nico, it's what you do. It's who you are. You are the most giving, thoughtful, loyal, big-hearted person I have ever met. No one could have rescued me, rescued your family, the way you did, and I'm talking about in here"—I tap my chest lightly—"and out there. Nico, there is no doubt in my mind you would be an incredible father to our baby. You might be scared, but honestly? I'm not."

He's quiet for a minute or two as my words sink in. Slowly, his breathing grows more regular, and his chest doesn't rise and fall quite as intensely. He turns his head.

"We're going to have a baby?" he asks again, like he's not sure this is really happening. But this time, his voice is full of awe. Wonder. Joy.

I nod, and bite my lip, unable to stop smiling.

"And you still want to marry me?"

I fling my arms around his neck, and we topple backward into the sand. Nico barks a laugh as his arms come around me.

"A million times over," I whisper as I burrow into his neck. "I'd marry you every single day if I could. And I can't *wait* to start our family. Together."

We lie there for a moment, oblivious to the fact that we're getting sand all over our nice clothes, in our hair, and everywhere else. Above us, the stars are slightly blocked out by the lights of the city, just like they are in New York. But farther out, over the dark ocean, they twinkle clearly, harbingers of some brighter, unknown future.

"A baby," Nico murmurs, over and over to himself. He pulls me into his chest. "You and me. That's all we really need, huh?"

I tip my head for a kiss, and he delivers, his mouth warm and inviting, his tongue gentle and sweet.

"It's all we need," I agree. "But we have so much more."

His chest rumbles with agreement as he kisses me again. "I love you. So fuckin' much."

I smile against his lips. "*Te amo tambien.* I'm going to have to learn Spanish better now. I want our baby to be fluent. Like you."

My poor Spanish earns me another ear-splitting grin and an even deeper kiss. When he's done, Nico sits us back up and brushes sand out of my hair and off my dress.

"Portuguese too," he says with a lopsided smile. "Come on. We better go face the music with your family. And then...I think it's time to go home."

CHAPTER THIRTY-THREE

Layla

It's close to midnight when we creep back into my dad's apartment. He and Nico had brought all of our things from Bibi's house before coming to the party. All we have to do is pack up, and we can leave in the morning.

"There's got to be some way to get on an earlier flight," Nico says as the elevator doors open onto the living room. "If your dad doesn't want us here, do you think your aunt would let us sleep at her apartment? Or maybe there's a hotel near the airport or something."

Our tickets aren't scheduled for another day, but he's right. It's time to go home.

But I don't reply, caught instead by the sight of my father sitting in one of his lounge chairs in the living room, a crystal glass half full of brown liquid—probably more whiskey—in his hands.

He looks up at our entrance, and his eyes are bloodshot, with a big bruise blooming across his left cheek where Nico punched him. He glances between us, landing where our hands are joined. He opens his mouth, then sighs and takes another large gulp of his drink.

"We just came to get our things," Nico says stiffly, keeping me close to his side. "We'll stay at a hotel. It's fine."

But it's not fine. Nico wants to protect me, but this is my father. He's in pain, and I hate the fact that I caused it, even if his anger hurts me too.

"Dad?" I whisper. I release Nico's hand and walk toward my father, then squat down next to his chair so we are eye level. "Daddy?"

When he looks at me, his eyes are full of hurt and sorrow. "*Meu docinha*," he murmurs, with a gaze that's softer than anything I've seen from him in years. "*Linda*."

I don't respond, just hold still as he reaches out slowly to brush a few stray hairs out of my face. His hand lingers on my cheek, a tender touch I haven't gotten from my father for longer than I can remember. A tear trickles down my face, followed by another as one falls down his as well.

My father. Crying.

"You're not mine anymore, are you?" he asks sadly. "Not my daughter anymore."

More tears fall, but I don't deny his words. Because it's true. Although I'm his daughter, through and through, I don't belong to him anymore. Not since he left my mother and effectively left me too. Really, not since I left him and moved to New York.

"What happened?" he asks hoarsely.

I brush a few more tears away. "What do you mean?"

"He said he found you in an apartment...beaten, he said." Dad sits up and swipes the damp tracks off his cheeks. "What happened to you?"

"Dad..." I twist some of the fabric in my dress. This isn't a story I can tell easily, even to a therapist.

"Tell me." It's not a request.

Nico takes a step forward, and my dad looks up wearily.

"I deserve to know," he says, his voice creaking slightly, "what happened to my daughter. At least give me that."

I open my mouth to tell him he doesn't deserve anything. That he left Mom and me last year to fend for ourselves. That he called maybe three times for an entire year, and basically abdicated any rights he had as a father. That it's because of that hurt, that neglect, that I chased people and places all last year to ignore the pain and loneliness I was feeling inside.

But instead I move to the couch that faces the chair. Nico automatically comes to sit next to me, wrapping a protective arm around me that clearly announces his role as my protector all over again. Dad glares at the hand clasping my shoulder, but says nothing.

"It was last year. Just after you went back to Brazil," I begin. "I met a man—"

I'm interrupted almost immediately by Nico muttering, "Please. Ain't no *man* that I saw."

I elbow him in the side, and he casts me a lopsided smile before tugging me closer.

"Sorry," he says. "It's the truth, though."

I roll my eyes and turn back to my dad, who tips back more of his drink.

"Was he American?" Dad asks.

I shake my head. "No. He was from Buenos Aires. He was studying business at CUNY and lived close to where Nico used to, up by Harlem. He..."

I drift off. I don't want to go through the details anymore. I've spent most of the last year combing through them, recovering from the trauma of that short relationship. What it did to my body. My heart. My mind. It's only been in the last few months that I've really started to feel like myself.

But my father needs to know. He needs to know because he's partly responsible.

"He was a lot like you, actually," I say.

Dad's head whips up and he winces, like it gives him a headache. His eye is already turning black. "What do you mean, he was like me?"

I gulp, and Nico squeezes my shoulder encouragingly.

"Proud. South American. He came from a strict, wealthy family, and he was very, uh, bossy. Hard to please. He was...familiar to me. I didn't understand that at the time, but I do now."

I look directly at my father, forcing myself not to look away as he studies me and ingests my description. But it's true. Giancarlo was, in many ways, a placeholder for the other authoritarian in my life. The order and control he exerted over me, the manipulations, echoed the normality of my father's control, and so, in a fucked-up way, made me feel loved. In my confused heart, one that was already in pieces after Nico had left, after my father had left, that attention made sense. And for a while, it felt better than nothing.

Until it felt so much worse.

"And so what happened?" my father inquires. "How did you end up..." He trails off, unable to complete the sentence before he has to take another drink.

I exhale heavily. "He was...not good to me," I say quietly.

Beside me, Nico tenses.

"What do you mean, 'not good'? Layla, be more specific."

"I mean like that!" I blurt out. "He would yell at me, just like you do. Demean me. Talk down to me, all the time. He'd make me second-guess myself and all the important relationships in my life. I never felt so alone until I was with him, and at the end, when I fought him about it, he took it out on me physically!"

My voice is shaking at this point, as if I never knew how much I really did blame my father for all of this. Would I have been attracted to someone like Giancarlo if I hadn't learned this kind of thing at home? I'll never know. But maybe not. Maybe...

"He hit me here." I point to my cheek, while tears start to roll down it all over again. "And here." To my eyebrow. "And cut himself too, and bled all over me. And tried to force himself on me. He would have succeeded too if N-Nico hadn't shown up when he did."

By the time I finish, my voice is almost a whisper, and the tears are flowing freely. Nico's arm drops to my waist so he can hug me as close as possible. He presses a long, lingering kiss to my forehead, like he's trying to absorb the memories and take them away.

He doesn't have to say those three words he does when I'm scared, but I feel them anyway. *I got you.* And he does, he always does.

Dad, however, has no idea. He flashes an angry look at Nico. "And where were *you* this whole time?" he demands. "You say you love my daughter. You want to protect her. Why did you only come at the end?"

"You are *not* trying to blame this on him, Dad," I put in.

Nico inhales, but keeps his arm tightly wrapped around me. "I was in Los Angeles, trying to make an honest living. A future instead of being a nobody," he says, recalling Dad's harsh words from earlier. There's no more pretense in his voice. No more "Dr. Barros" or "sir." Things are real now, and he has nothing to lose.

"Nico saved me," I say. "Dad. Dad!"

Finally, my father turns back to me, and it's then he sees the truth in my eyes.

"I'd be dead without him," I say. "You owe him my life. *I* owe him my life."

Dad tips back the rest of his liquor, then sets the glass on the side table with an audible clink. I can't imagine what he's feeling, discovering all of this about his daughter on top of the fact that she's marrying a tatted-up bad boy from Hell's Kitchen and carrying his child.

"You know he's a criminal too?" he asks. "First day you were here, I did a background check. I knew you were no good. He beat a store clerk within an inch of his life, just like he did to me. Do you know this, Layla? Does that make him a hero too?"

Nico wilts slightly beside me—the motion is so small, that I can barely sense it. But I can. I know him too well. I slide my hand to Nico's knee and squeeze. *I love you,* I try to convey.

"Dad, I know about Nico's record. And for what it's worth, he didn't do the crime he was convicted for. Either way, it's in the past.

He was just a teenager. Should we hold all of the indiscretions of your youth against you?"

"That's not the point," Dad spits. "He's not good enough for you, *linda*. You deserve the best, not a boy who, good as he might be, only wants you for your money." He glares at Nico. "How do we know he's not still wrapped up in some kind of criminal organization? You are so naive, Layla. I know how these things work. You do not."

"What the fuck..." Nico says, but before he can reply, I sit forward so I can look my father in the eye.

"You are intoxicated, which is the only reason I'm not walking out the door right now," I say clearly. "But if you want me in your life, you need to stop. Stop making up stories. Stop trash-talking the very best person in my life, a person to whom you actually owe a great debt. Just *stop*."

Dad swallows, looking between us, taking in our connection. We are unbreakable. Internally, I beg him to know it.

"I'll cut off your tuition," he says, though his voice is already weakening. "I'll cancel my check for this semester. I won't pay for your school next year, or any year after. You want to go to this silly school so you can take care of poor people like this? I won't do it. Not if you are with him."

"Then I won't go to school next year," I say. "I'll work and pay for it myself."

"*We'll* pay for it ourselves," Nico adds beside me. He sits up a little straighter. "Layla's going to finish school, with or without you, Sergio."

At the sound of his Christian name echoing through the room, Dad winces again. But he doesn't argue with it.

"I'm not leaving New York, Dad," I say. "I'm not leaving Nico. We're a family, he and I. That's what we are now. Maybe what we've always been." I stand up, and Nico follows suit. "You can be a part of it or not," I tell my father. "I hope you will. But if you're going to be in it, you can't boss me around anymore. And you need to treat my fiancé, your grandchild's father, with respect. Otherwise...that's it. We'll live our lives, and you can live yours."

I exhale the breath I didn't know I'd been holding at the end of all of it. It's the hardest thing I've ever done, putting my foot down with my father. All my life I've been his little girl. Someone he coddled early, but disciplined more and more, trying to make into something he could never be: someone he was satisfied with. But all it taught me was that I was never enough. It made me scared. It kept me from understanding what love was.

Until I met Nico.

Like a magnet, Nico moves close, wrapping both of his strong arms around my waist as he pulls me against his front. It's a move that's typically affectionate for him, but given the context, in front of my father, marks me as his as much as I've named him mine. In this room, we are a unit, more so than I have ever been with my parents.

Nico flattens his palms over my middle, over the child that's still barely more than an idea yet. But it's there, nonetheless. And now it's all that matters.

My father sighs. He's a man beaten, withered. And for the first time in my life, he looks old. He gazes at us for a long time, tapping his lips like he's wishing for a cigarette or something to take off the edge. Then he sighs, long and low, and says something that genuinely shocks me.

"Thank you," he says formally. He stands up, and to my surprise, extends a hand to Nico. "For my daughter's life."

Nico stares for a minute, then unwraps his right hand from my waist and accepts the handshake.

"Right," he murmurs. "You're, ah, welcome."

"I'll never be happy about this marriage, you know," Dad says. "She's too good for you."

I cringe, but Nico just tucks both arms back around me.

"She is," he agrees. "But that never stopped me from loving her. It's happening whether you like it or not, Sergio. We're a family now, like she says. That's all there is to it."

Dad's weary eyes drop to my stomach. They float over me, over Nico, as if for the first time registering us together. Whole.

"Yes," he says. "*Deos me ajude...I know.*"

And with a squeeze of my shoulder, he turns and trudges down the hall, a man defeated, but I hope, a man who is also learning to accept what he can't change.

Nico and I watch until Dad disappears into the darkness. My chest feels hollow, but I'm also strangely calm. I may never fully have peace with my father. You can't undo twenty-some years of anger, control, and abandonment in a few minutes. But the catharsis feels good. Right. And maybe we can both move forward.

"Let's get some sleep, baby," says Nico, rubbing my shoulder sympathetically. But before I can ask whether or not he thinks we should keep sleeping separately or risk my dad's continued wrath by sleeping in the same room, his phone rings.

It rings. At one o'clock in the morning. And the number is from New York. Where they're only an hour behind. Everyone we know understands we're in Brazil right now, where cell phone roaming charges are ridiculously high.

"What the fuck..." Nico murmurs as he flips it open. "Maggie. What's going on?"

I watch as he collapses back onto the couch and thrusts a hand through his hair. His sister's voice is as loud and insistent as ever; though I can't understand her, I hear her urgency. Her fear.

"Fuck," Nico keeps whispering as she talks. "Okay, calm down. Mags, I said *calm the fuck down.* Listen, I'll be back as soon as I can, okay? First flight out tomorrow. *Gata*, don't worry. It's gonna be fine."

She says a few more things, and I fall next to Nico. He clutches my hand while he listens.

"Tomorrow," Nico reassures her. "Okay. Yeah, call Ileana. I don't care if it's late. Blow her shit up until she answers. We'll figure this out. Okay, bye."

"What's going on?" I ask as soon as he closes his phone.

When he turns to me, most of the color in his beautiful tan face is gone. The fierce light, the sparkle in his eyes is gone, replaced by utter hopelessness.

"They got her," he whispers. "My mom. Immigration arrested her tonight. She's...they got her."

And that's all my strong man can say as his greatest fear comes true: Carmen, his mother, who was brought illegally to Puerto Rico and then to the United States when she was just a small girl, has finally been discovered after more than thirty years of living in the shadows of New York.

Without thinking and while my father watches, utterly confused, I pull my phone out of my clutch and start dialing automatically. Nico's face is blank. There's not much I can do, but one plan of action lies before me. My father is probably passed out by now, and unlikely to help at any rate. But there's one other person who understands what Nico has done for me. Maybe, just maybe she'll help.

"Mom?" I ask when I hear her familiar voice. "It's Layla. I'm still in Brazil. But, Mom...I need your help. Nico needs our help."

CHAPTER THIRTY-FOUR

Nico

"I don't want you to go. It should be me."

"Shhhh. We've been over this." Layla looks up from checking her passports and tickets and strokes my face. "This is the quickest option if you don't want to be tied up in court for months or even years."

I have to hand it to my girl. While I sat there in a daze, getting sand all over her dad's fancy white couch, she was on the phone with her mom for at least two hours, giving her the details on the situation and figuring out a solution. It was clear at first that Cheryl didn't want to help. She wanted to wait until the morning and talk to Ileana. But in the end, I wonder if Layla didn't call her mother first just to get her dad to spring into action. Because as soon as the dude realized Layla was on the phone with his wife, he shot out of his bedroom, not giving a shit that it was almost three in the morning at that point. He snatched the phone from Layla and took over the situation immediately, and we just sat back while the two of them argued about who was going to help us the most.

Which is how we found ourselves here at the airport the next morning, me holding one ticket back to the States, and Layla clutching another for Santiago.

I hate this. I fuckin' hate this, and so does Sergio. But, as Ileana confirmed when we talked to her this morning, it was probably the easiest way. Layla has dual citizenship, so she doesn't need a special permit to fly to Cuba from Brazil. So the plan is for her to do just that: fly to Santiago, get a copy of my mother's birth certificate, then go to Montreal and on to New York. Sergio helpfully upgraded her flights to first class all the way and shoved a credit card into her hand, along with a massive pile of Cuban pesos that he got from the bank on the way here.

"Fifty if they hassle you," he reminds her as her flight to Rio echoes over the airport loudspeaker. I smirk. For all his polish, Sergio Barros is clearly a man familiar with the art of bribery. "One hundred to speak to a supervisor. Say it with authority. You're *my* daughter, Layla. Don't forget this."

Layla blinks up at him. "I won't, Dad. I promise."

"You don't have to do this," I tell her again. "I'll do it. I'll sneak in through Venezuela or somewhere like that. Some place where they won't stop Americans."

Layla places her hand on my arm. "Stop. I'll be fine. I'm not violating any laws here, and I'll meet you in New York in a few days, okay? I promise."

I sigh. This is so damn wrong. Here I am, sending my brand-new fiancée and my unborn baby on a plane to a country where U.S. citizens aren't supposed to go. And to top it all off, Layla doesn't even really speak the language. They're going to take one look at her big blue eyes and trusting face and eat her alive. *Fuck.*

It goes against everything I know to be right. And yet...it's the only thing to do.

"*Nico*," she says again, pulling me out of my misery. "Take care of your mother. I'll be there in a few days."

The loudspeaker calls the number and the boarding information of her flight one last time. Layla presses a final kiss to my lips, and I pull her closer, taking a little more. I'd rather walk through fire than put her in danger. But this is how it has to be.

"Three days," I murmur against her lips. "If you're not back in three days, I'm coming after you myself." My hand drifts up her side to where, underneath her thin t-shirt, the words "*saudade para ti*" are etched over her ribs—just like the Portuguese equivalent is on mine. Fuck. I miss her already, and she's not even gone.

She bites my lower lip softly. "Promise. I love you."

"You have no idea."

And then, because I can't not do it, I pick her clear up off the floor and kiss her again, the kind of kiss that I shouldn't do in front of her father or any polite company. Fear. Love. Lust. Worry. I kiss her until we're both breathless, ignoring the whistles flying around the terminal, the glares from her dad, the fact that the flight attendants are making the last boarding call right now.

And when I finally put her down, those big blue eyes see straight through me. They always have. She clasps my face and presses one last kiss on my lips.

"I know," she murmurs. "I know."

And with a touch of her forehead to mine, she turns and leaves.

"Baby!" I call out when she's halfway out the door, about to follow the last of the passengers toward the small plane waiting on the runway.

She turns and looks at me.

"Be good!" I call out.

As the words register, Layla grins—that bright smile that shot an arrow through me the first time we met. And for the first time all day, I think that maybe things might really turn out all right. Because who could resist a smile like that?

And then it's just her dad and me, standing side by side as Layla's plane taxis around the runway and eventually takes off with the woman we both love. When it finally disappears, Sergio turns to me, his face sagging with guilt. I get it. Layla isn't someone who is ever easy to say goodbye to. And as much of an asshole as he is, I also know that deep down, Sergio loves his daughter.

"Your flight," he says. "It leaves..."

"In an hour," I tell him.

His relief is obvious. He's glad he won't have to share his apartment with me for another night, and he won't have to keep me company much longer either. Well, I feel about the same. The guy is a dick. He's a sorry dick right about now. He realizes, on some level, that he pretty much lost his daughter, and to the kind of guy he never wanted her to be with in the first place. Well, fuckin' tough. I'm done being made to feel like I'm not good enough for her.

I wasn't able to fly with Layla to Rio. The quickest way back to New York that I could still afford was routed through São Paulo—though how going an hour and a half in the wrong fuckin' direction is quicker, I'll never know. But it is what it is.

Sergio turns, and to my surprise, holds out his hand. I pause for a second, then take it. He squeezes it tight, more tightly than I would have thought someone with such slim hands could. Skilled hands. A surgeon's hands.

"Thank you," he says again. "For what you did for her."

I don't say anything, just nod. I wonder if he remembers thanking me for the same thing the night before, or if he was too drunk. But I don't say anything, because what else is there to say? He still has a nasty purple bruise on his face from where I hit him, and my right knuckles have a nice scab building from where they split on his cheekbone. And the thing is, I'm still not sorry.

"Will we see you at the wedding?" I ask.

He blinks, like he's forgotten all about that. Then he closes his eyes, almost as if he's in pain, and rubs his forehead. Whiskey makes for a hell of a hangover.

"Yes," he says in the end. "Of course. Yes, I will be there."

"Good," I say. I couldn't care less if he came, but I know Layla will. It's important to have your dad there when you get married. I get that.

He nods, then turns to go.

"Take care, Dr. Barros," I call after him, sending a quick wave. I figure I can give him that. He's not Dr. Barros in my head anymore, but I can pay him the small respect he asked for in the beginning. It's the least I can do for taking away his daughter.

He pauses, frowns a little, then surprises me.

"Sergio," he replies. "My name is Sergio."

And then he's gone.

————

From there, I take three of the longest fuckin' flights of my life. The hour and a half to São Paulo feels like four, and the eight and a half to Miami feel like twenty. By the time I stumble off the last three-hour flight into the arrivals gate at JFK, I've been traveling for close to twenty-four hours. Twenty-four hours, and I have no fuckin' clue what happened to Layla after she left. There isn't much in the way of cell phone service in Cuba, and what little they have sure as shit doesn't service American cell phones.

For now, there's nothing on my voicemail. Not a hey, I'm good. Don't fuckin' worry. Nothing.

I dial Maggie's number as soon as I'm off the plane, but it goes straight to voicemail. Next up is Gabe, who picks up right away.

"*Coño!*" he shouts so loud I have to hold the phone away from my ear. "There you fuckin' are. We've been waiting for hours for you to land."

I yank my duffel and garment bag over my shoulder as I truck out to the curbside, looking for the shuttles into town. It's more expensive, but there's no way I'm taking the train back into the city. I need to be able to communicate with everyone and get up to speed.

"My flight was delayed in Miami," I tell him. "But I'm here now. What's good?"

Gabe gives me the low-down on Ma's situation. "She's being held in a detainment facility upstate," he says. "In Albany."

"Albany? Are you fuckin' kidding me? With all the illegals in New York, immigration doesn't have a holding center in the city?"

I hand a porter the fare and let him take my bags, then board a bus headed for Manhattan.

Gabe's laughing in my ear. "Real estate, *mano*," he says. "That's what Ileana said. Too expensive."

I'm glad he's laughing because I'm fuckin' not. Not while my mother is locked in a fuckin' detainment center hours away, ironically close to the other facility where I wasted two years of my life. I shiver. I remember what it was like to be carted away in some shitty van. I'd never left the city before. And suddenly I was in the middle of nowhere, staring at vacant lots of snow, tiny towns full of trailers and bare-branched trees. It was the perfect place to send criminals. A place where they could abandon you. Forget you.

I imagine my mother, who hasn't left New York since she first arrived in the mid sixties, when she was maybe ten, at most. She's a woman who barely speaks English, who's lived her life behind the thick curtain of the Puerto Rican community in New York for fear of exactly what is happening to her right now. I imagine what she must be feeling, and *fuck*, it makes me want to hit something. Because for the first time, I can't get to her. I can't protect her.

I never should have gone to Brazil.

"It's going to be okay," Gabe's saying, breaking me out of my thoughts. "Ileana's up there now. She says the deportation officer set a bond, and—"

"A bond?" I ask. "They can do that? I thought if you were caught, that was it."

"*Claro*, they can," Gabe replies. "And they do. Her hearing is set three weeks from now downtown. She has to appear before a judge, I guess, just like any other charge."

"So they had to cart her all the way up to Albany just to assign her a court date back in New York? That makes no fuckin' sense." I shake my head.

Gabe chuckles again. "That's the government, right? That's why they shipped you upstate too instead of Spofford, am I right?"

I snort. A few more people get onto the bus, and eventually the porter swings on and shuts the door behind him, calling out the stops in Manhattan coming up.

"So where are you?" I ask as the van starts moving. "Give me the address, and I'll meet you there. We can go get Ma together."

Gabe just laughs, and in the background, I swear I can hear the sound of my sisters cackling.

"I don't think that's going to happen, bro," he says plainly. "We're on a bus to Albany. Me, Maggie, Selena, and even Allie."

"What?!" I practically explode out of my seat.

"Shhh. You're going to wake up Allie, man. She's asleep. It's just a little road trip," Gabe says, way the fuck more playfully than he should, considering. "Go home. Get some sleep. We'll be back tonight, and Ma will be with us. Don't worry, *mano*. We got this."

———

It's almost dark by the time I finally get back to the apartment on Chrystie Street. My mind is still working a million miles a minute, but all of the thoughts are sloshing together, lost in a haze of jet lag and worry. Gabe and my sisters will stay the night in Albany. There's no way they'll be able to get up there soon enough to get Ma out tonight. Which means I'm stuck here like a buster, playing the waiting game for everyone else to fix shit.

Not a role I'm used to.

I trudge up the five flights of stairs and unlock the door, breathing in the familiar scents as I do. They're stale, since the apartment has been shut up for a week, but still there: leftover coffee, a little bit of Lysol, linens and towels, and the vanilla-scented candles Layla likes. It's barely been a week, but I'm glad to be back. I don't know why it surprises me still that this place feels so much like home. But not now, I realize. Not without her in it.

"There you are."

"*Jesusfuckin'Christ!*" I practically jump out of my skin at the sound of a low, female voice coming from the couch on the far side of the living room.

The voice laughs lightly as I turn around, and then Cheryl Barros stands up and smooths out the front of her pants.

"What the..."

I stare, dumbfounded, until she's standing in front of me: Layla's mother.

"You look tired," she says. "It's a terrible flight, isn't it? I always hated going there, just for that reason alone. Did you go to the farm too?"

Wordlessly, I shake my head. What the fuck is happening?

Cheryl shrugs. "You didn't miss much. It's awful. Two hours of winding roads up a river, and the place is absolutely swarming with mosquitos. Layla liked it when we visited, of course, but I could never sleep well in a house without screens on the windows."

My mouth works, but still, no words come out. I don't even know what she's doing here. How she got in here. But...*of course.*

This apartment is in Cheryl's name. It's her lease. Of course she has a key. Of course she can get in. Of fucking course.

"I came to help," she says. "But also because my husband had some very interesting things to tell me after the two of you caught your flights." She walks around the couch, takes a seat at the dining table, drums her fingernails on the lacquered wood, and looks expectantly at me.

"I think," she says, "you'd better come sit down. And tell me exactly where my daughter and grandchild are at the moment. And how it is you came to have a key to her apartment in the first place."

CHAPTER THIRTY-FIVE

Layla

THE CITY HALL BUILDING IS OLD, WHITE, AND THE STUCCO
gleams under the bright Caribbean sun. Unlike many of the buildings
I passed while riding in the back of the 1950s taxi here, it's relatively
well maintained, with its Spanish-style architecture that lords over
the palm tree-laden square. It's not the picture that we're often
painted of Cuba in the U.S.—a dilapidated country full of old cars
and inadequate systems. There is certainly some of that; I've seen
more vintage cars here than I ever thought existed in the world. But
this building stands tall and bright. There's nothing dilapidated about
it. If anything, it's pretty intimidating.

Not for the first time, I shake my head, wishing Nico were here. It
feels wrong, somehow, that I'm seeing the country where his mother
was born before him. Of course, I'm barely seeing it, I'm so tired. It
took me three flights to get here. Vitória to Rio to Santo Domingo to,
finally, Santiago at about 10 a.m. I left my bag at the small *casa*, one
of the common local accommodations that are kind of like bed and
breakfasts run out of people's houses, where the Brazilian travel agent

booked me. Then I went straight to the registry after receiving directions from the house owner. I've been traveling for almost twenty-four hours straight, and I'm exhausted. But my flight to Montreal is tomorrow, and then it's home. I just need this piece of paper. And the office here in Santiago, where Nico's mother was born, is open.

It takes a while to find the correct room inside the city hall, while I skirt past several men and two women in green uniforms, all with guns holstered to their waists. It's not uncommon to see a military presence in Brazil, and there were some in the airport in Santo Domingo too. But here in Cuba, the military seems stronger, or at least more ubiquitous. I was warned before coming not to take pictures of them or talk to anyone about politics. The last thing I want is to be accused of spying or insurgency.

I know I've got the right door when I walk into a room containing a single clerk at a desk in front of a back room filled with filing cabinets. Filing cabinets mean one thing: records. It reminds me of one of the NYU libraries—austere, poorly lit, and badly ventilated. A few people are slumped in the chairs scattered around the perimeter of the waiting room; others lean against the wall, while others are just sitting on the floor, looking half-asleep. I take my place at the end of the line and wait. And wait. And...wait.

When it's finally my turn, the clerk is abrupt.

"How can I help you?" she asks in Spanish that is so clipped around the consonants, I can barely understand her. But her meaning is clear enough.

"*Necesito un certificato del navidad,*" I state in my awkward Spanish. I'm not as bad as I was a year ago, but I know my pronunciation is poor. "*Para mi madre.*"

The clerk frowns. I'm guessing she gets this request a lot. I've already been informed by multiple people at the *casa* that getting records here is difficult, particularly since technically people are not allowed to take them out of the country. The process, therefore, usually requires extra money to grease the wheels. Luckily, I have a stack of that.

I take out a set of bills in the approved Cuban tourist currency, and lay them on the counter for her.

"For the fee," I say, though she hasn't mentioned anything of the sort.

The clerk examines the stack, like she's trying to evaluate what I'm doing. Everything about her expression is suspicious, and again, I'm desperately wishing that Nico were here with me. He knows how to read people so much better than me. He'd take one look at this woman, wink and make some crazy joke in Spanish that would put her at ease, and ten minutes later he'd probably have flirted ten birth certificates out of her instead of just the one I need.

The clerk reaches out slowly and taps a finger on the bills. Then she pushes it back to me and whips out a faded form before rattling something in Spanish that I'm guessing means roughly "fill this out, you idiot American."

I take the paper and pen and tuck the bills back in my bag. I'll try again in a minute. This has to work. It has to.

An hour later, I wait through the line again to hand her the paper. Again, I set the stack of bills on the counter while she goes over the paper. But this time, her response is almost immediate. She stamps a clear red mark across the top of the paper: *Negado*. Denied.

"What? No! Please, I've come all this way!" I pull out another wad of cash from my purse and slap it on the counter. What else can I do? "Please! *Por favor*. I'll pay extra, I will. *Pagaré...mucho*," I translate poorly, lacking the vocabulary I need to make my point.

But she knows what I mean. She just doesn't want to do it. For whatever reason, the clerk shakes her head and starts waving the money away, almost like she doesn't want to look at it.

"*Por favor*," I try again, this time more calmly. "It's not for me. It's for my fiancé's mother—*la madre de mi novio*. She needs the certificate so she can live legally in New York. She's been there since she was a girl, and now she's in custody with immigration. If I don't bring back the document tomorrow, they'll deport her. Please!"

The woman looks me over, her sharp eye slanted with doubt. "She is in America?" she asks in clear, obvious English.

I swallow with relief, and a little bit of irritation. She let me go through all of that terrible Spanish when she speaks perfectly good English? "Yes. Yes, she is. Please, she's been there for more than thirty years."

Again, her sharp gaze drops down over me, lingering on the watch that encircles my wrist, then travels back up to look me in the eye. "Then maybe it's time for her to come home."

My entire being droops as I turn from the desk. I failed. I have six people waiting for me to return to New York with the document that will keep their family intact, and I have no idea what to do next. This was the end of the line, and there are no other choices, other than Carmen begging clemency from the court system. The money I have didn't work. What the hell am I going to do?

"Layla."

I look up, and to my surprise, find my father standing in the doorway of the office. His face is covered with a sheen of sweat, like he ran all the way here from Brazil, but otherwise, he is dressed the same as always, in a button-up shirt and slacks. Relief slides over his face when I turn around.

"Dad?" I wonder. "What-what are you doing here?"

He shrugs. "I took the next plane after you. Your mother wouldn't have it any other way, and she was correct. You left. The boy left. And I..." Before I can say anything, he goes on. "I wondered what in the hell I was doing, allowing my daughter to travel to a strange country like this by herself. Not when I could come and help her."

I stare at him for a moment, and then, by instinct, fall against his chest to give him a hug. He's still at first, then wraps his arms around me and strokes my hair, the same way he did when I was a child. I have to focus on breathing not to cry into his shirt. The people in the office are all watching us curiously, and I don't think crying in the middle of the vital records office is going to help anything.

I'm so angry at him. I was ready to leave Brazil and never come back. I was ready to leave my father, cut him out of my life since all he wanted to do was control it.

And yet...now that he's here, I've never been happier to see him in my life.

"Please," I say, handing him the paper. "Help."

He examines the denied application, then faces the clerk, who is watching him curiously out of the corner of her eye. I sometimes forget that for an older man, my dad is still quite handsome. That women notice him.

I roll my eyes. It cannot possibly be as easy as that.

And then I watch as he strides up to the counter like he owns it, cutting in front of the three other people waiting, and starts speaking in Spanish—a language I didn't even know he spoke!

No. They're not going to let him get away with this. I can't hear what he's saying, but I watch the clerk as she listens, watch the people behind him standing with their arms crossed, watch my father smile and laugh and gesture at me and the paper like he's sitting across from the woman at an adorable bistro table instead of a dank government office.

At one point, the woman laughs. My father reaches out a long finger and strokes her chin. The woman blushes, and I'm sickened slightly by the sight of my father being more affectionate with a stranger than he's ever been with me or my mother in my life. A smile brightens his stern face, and for a moment, he looks pleasant. Kind. Handsome.

I can't hear what they're saying, but the woman twists and turns from side to side, playing with her curly hair like a schoolgirl flirting with her crush. She keeps shaking her head, saying no, but her smile and body language clearly say otherwise. With his other hand dropped below the counter, my father beckons to me with a flick of his fingers. It takes a second for me to understand what he wants, but as soon as it registers, I glance around, then take some of the cash out of my purse and set it in his hand.

He flips it onto the counter between him and the woman. She examines it for a moment, and my father whispers something else. I catch the word *linda* float on the air, and watch as the woman grins again and then slides the money under the counter. Then my father stands expectantly while she turns and disappears into a back room. He turns to me and winks. I'm still too shocked to reply.

A few minutes later, the woman returns holding a flimsy envelope. She clutches the birth certificate against her chest for a moment, and a flash of fear crosses her face.

"You can't take it out of the coun—" she starts, but stops talking when my dad lays another stack of bills from his pocket on the counter.

He leans back across the counter, and slowly traces a finger up her forearm. Even from my place on the opposite wall, I can see her shiver with desire.

"*Creo que está perdido, no?*" he asks with a sly smile.

The clerk bites her lip, then after looking around to see that no one else is watching, pulls the money across the counter and below with the rest. "*Sí,*" she says. "I think it *was* lost."

Dad plucks the birth certificate out of her hand and gives it to me. I promptly tuck it into a folder in my purse, treating it like the gold it is: Carmen's salvation.

"*Gracias, linda,*" Dad says to the clerk, who proceeds to blush all over the place. But to me, he resumes his stern mask. "Let's go."

An hour later, I find myself sitting in a wicker chair in a square a few blocks away from the *casa* where now both my dad and I will be staying the night before the flight we are apparently both taking to Montreal in the morning. He's taking no chances, or so he said, of making sure his daughter gets home safe. I sort of wonder if it's because he wants to speak his mind one last time to Nico, but for whatever reason, he's insisted on coming with me, seeing my apartment, inspecting the life I'm now living. I'm not sure what I think about it, but I accept. For the first time in a few years, my dad is actually showing some interest in my life again. Now it will have to be more on my terms, but I'm willing to try if he is.

Music floats down the street, the casual cadence of Cuban salsa, with drums. There is music everywhere in this city. Every time we turned a corner to get here, I would hear it, swimming through doorways and out of open widows. It's not quite the same type you would hear in the Bronx, but the rhythms are similar and remind me of the parties at Alba's apartment. I wish I were there now.

The waitress drops a glass of rum for my dad and a coffee for me on the table before she winks at him. I roll my eyes. The attention he gets from women here really is ridiculous.

We sit for a minute, and I watch as my dad pulls out a pack of cigarettes and lights one.

"I can't believe you smoke now," I say, watching the habit that's been so strange to me since arriving in Brazil.

He looks up, curious. "You are? Everyone smokes in Brazil. Here too."

"Yeah, but you're a doctor. You know exactly what that's doing to your body."

He takes another drag, then examines the cigarette carefully, like he's never really considered what it does to him.

"I do," he admits. "But...do you know, I do not think I care so much. Everyone is going to die in the end."

We lapse into silence again as we drink and my dad smokes, and I do my best to ignore his newfound nihilism.

"We could have been like this," he says in a low voice, gesturing around the square.

There's another cluster of military personnel in one corner, loitering in their green uniforms and berets, and a group of students in the other. It's not a bad scene. People are laughing, cars are driving by. But it is strangely...quiet...for such a public place. Not silent. But you'd expect it to be a little louder.

"Who?" I ask. "The U.S., you mean?"

He darts a warning look at me that clearly says I need to be quiet.

"No," he says quickly. "Brazil."

I blink, unsure of what he means. In my classes, we learned about some of the destabilizing events of the sixties and seventies in South America, including the military coup in Brazil that was sponsored by the United States. But it's a history that was always a little unclear. The coup ended the rise of socialism in Brazil, I thought. But then it became a military state for the next twenty.

"When I was starting university," my father continues as he sips on his rum, "that was when Jango was overthrown."

I nod, somewhat familiar with the events from my classes. João Goulart, also known as Jango, was the president during the early sixties, one whose proposal to nationalize a variety of social services earned him the ire of right-wing nationalists and the military.

"My professor last year thought that was a reflexive maneuver," I said. "He thought it was more because the U.S. saw it as another situation like, well...here."

I was hesitant to say Cuba out loud. Talking politics was frowned upon.

Dad shrugged. "It was. I remember being very angry about it at the time, actually. My father, he supported it. But, like so many young people, I was very interested in what was happening here in Cuba and in Colombia. I liked the idea of people receiving free healthcare. Better social services." He looks at me pointedly. "When I first became a doctor, I wanted to help, you know. I wanted to do more than clean up scar tissue or help women, ah, enhance themselves."

I smirk. I can practically hear Nico on my shoulder, urging me to say "tits" again in front of my dad.

"So you wish that the coup hadn't happened?" I wondered. "Do you wish that Jango had stayed in power?"

Dad looks around, like he's evaluating the state of the country. I've read plenty about Cuba, what information is available to Americans. My professor, clearly a leftist thinker, was always careful to temper the critiques of Fidel Castro with other facts: like that Cuba has some of the best public health records and highest literacy rates in the world. Its economic conditions, he argued, were due to the embargoes by the U.S., not because of the way that Castro and the communists actually ran the country. I didn't know. It was hard to say one way or another. A country where people had to watch what they said for fear of being accused of being a government usurper also seems oppressive.

Dad just shrugs again and finishes his rum. "Fifty years is a long time for one man to be in power," is all he says, and I know he's referring to Fidel. Then he turns to me. "I was angry, yes. But then we watched what happened in Argentina. In Chile. We watched as people disappeared, again and again. And I looked at my government, at the men who guarded every building with their guns, and the people who were scared to talk out loud...just like here. And I decided I would leave before maybe they wouldn't let me."

It turned out to be unnecessary. Because, as I knew, Brazil held elections again in 1985, two years after I was born. But by that point, my father was well into establishing a practice in Seattle. He had married my mother, gotten his citizenship, started a life in America. A life that gave us all so much, but isolated him even more despite the freedoms he sought.

It was a strange paradox. And one that explains his tight-fisted grip on our lives. He sought stability. He sought reassurance. He sought the knowledge that his family would never have to struggle the way he did.

"Why did you come here?" I ask finally. "Besides to keep me safe, I mean. You didn't have to help with the records. You don't like Nico at all. And you don't even know his mother."

Dad's dark eyes soften. "You speak as if keeping you safe isn't the most important thing. I am your father, Layla. That is all that matters to me."

I don't say anything. My other questions still stand.

Dad clears his throat. "I know what it's like to grow up in a country toyed with like a figure in a game," he says. "I don't know this Carmen, but why should she have to come to a country she's never known? A country her father left for the same reason I did—because in the end, it was being enchained by a country that claims to be the land of the free?" He shrugs and takes a long pull of his cigarette. "Free for itself, maybe. But at the expense of everyone else."

I frown. "Do you really think it's as simple as that?"

He shakes his head. Of course it's not. But as he stubs out his cigarette and stands up, resignation falls over his stern face. It's strange. This is the most honest conversation I've ever had with my father. It's the first time he's admitted that maybe his decisions in the past were less than perfect. That things didn't always turn out the way he planned.

"I don't know this woman, this Carmen," he repeats. "But everyone deserves to be free."

CHAPTER THIRTY-SIX

Nico

YOU KNOW THAT SAYING, "LIKE SITTING DUCKS?" IT'S A DUMB saying. I've barely ever seen ducks sitting. They're usually paddling or waddling around Central Park. Sometimes they quack at you because you had the balls to interfere with their fishing or whatever. Maybe they fly south for the winter, or just across the pond. But they don't really sit, and if they do, it's in some bushes or someplace like that where people won't be able to get them. They don't just sit there, waiting around like idiots for the firing squad.

But right now, that's what I feel like, sitting with my family in a row that feels strangely like a church pew, while we wait for my mother's case to be called into the small courtroom. The room is packed, full of other people also waiting for their fates to be sealed by the few judges who sit on the city's immigration court.

It's two o'clock. Layla's flight was supposed to arrive early this morning from Montreal, but I haven't heard from her in more than four days. Her phone must be dead. The calls have been going straight to voicemail since we left.

I rub my chest, the spot where her name is tattooed over my compass. I miss her like crazy, but it's really the not knowing what's about to happen that's the worst part of all. Is she okay? Is my mom going to be okay? The only thing I had to do the last few days was work, pulling a forty-eight-hour shift at the firehouse. I have twelve hours off, but then I'm right back on at midnight for another three days. I should be tired—well, I *am*—but I wouldn't have been able to sleep anyway.

"Somebody tell me again how the fuck this happened?" I whisper to Gabe.

That earns me a sharp look from Ma, who's sitting quietly with the lawyer that Cheryl hired to represent her. I have to hand it to Cheryl. For someone who's basically just been a housewife for the last twenty years, she knows how to come in and put shit together. And damn, it really is a whole different story when you have money for someone to go to bat for you. Christina, the lawyer, got the court date moved up several weeks to today.

She rolled her eyes a little at the plan to get the birth certificate, which made me want to punch through a wall all over again. Ma was probably eligible for relief, she said. The bigger issue would be that she had worked under the table for so many years and hadn't paid taxes. Still, documentation wouldn't do anything but help, and if my mother can prove she's a Cuban citizen, she's covered under the Cuban Adjustment Act to apply for permanent residency.

But, of course, that means my girl needs to get here fast. Because if this hearing starts and we don't have documentation...that means more court dates. More lawyers we can't afford. More possibilities that in the end, my mother might still be forced to leave.

Fuck. I can't think about that right now.

"Relax," Gabe says. "Christina said even if they start deportation proceedings, it takes months, maybe even years. And unlike Ileana, she actually thinks she has a good shot at getting relief because she's been here for so long."

"No," I say. "I mean, how did we end up here? I want to know how *exactly* immigration ended up tagging Ma."

It's a story I've asked for over and over, and no one seems to be able to give me a good answer. Maggie was at home with Allie. Selena was at work. Gabe was in class. We know that at some point after attending a Wednesday Mass by herself, which she doesn't normally do, Ma was cornered and arrested in the space of five minutes on her walk back to Alba's apartment. And from there, a message was left on Gabe's cell phone before she was taken to Albany.

When she came back with Gabe and my sisters, she didn't want to talk about it. Shut herself up in her room at Alba's for over an hour before she would come out.

She's ashamed. After being careful for so many years, she's ashamed that she was caught. That she's putting us all through this. But most of all, more than I've ever seen her, my mother's scared.

I glance down the row, to where she's sitting in her Sunday best, flanked on one side by Maggie and by the lawyer on the other. On the other side of the lawyer sits Cheryl, blonde and stiff while she looks over the room. She looks taller than everyone else, but it's only because she sits up straight, whereas most of the people in here are slumped. Fear does things to your posture, I guess.

Cheryl and I still haven't quite figured each other out. Layla's mom is a lot like her—soft spoken and a good listener, and the kind of person who looks you right in the eye. She wasn't surprised, for instance, when I told her about the engagement or about the fact that Layla is pregnant, since Dr. Barros called her that night. She was, however, pretty damn surprised to find out that I had been Layla's new roommate for almost four months.

———

"If it wasn't a problem, why do you think she hasn't told me?" she kept asking as she walked around the apartment that, slowly, Layla and I made our own.

I hopped up on the counter after getting myself a big glass of water and watched her pace, trying to see what she sees. It wasn't the empty place she left Layla with in August. We'd hung pictures. Bought a few more pieces of old furniture. We had mail on the counter and food in the cupboards. Coats hanging from hooks I installed after Christmas, and a bunch of framed photos of the two of us placed on bookshelves and a few windowsills. We made it a home. Our home.

Cheryl picked up one of the pictures—one of me and Layla at another of Alba's parties, just before Christmas. Layla loves my family's parties. In the weeks before, I taught her some more salsa moves so we could rip it up a little. I didn't even care that my sisters teased me like crazy because I fell in love with a girl who likes Marc Anthony now as much as they do. I just really, really liked the way Layla sways her hips.

I looked around the apartment, suddenly aching for my girl. It wasn't right, being there without her.

"So my twenty-one-year-old daughter is suddenly pregnant and engaged. And now Bibi tells me she's in Cuba," Cheryl said. "Alone."

She looked up, and her blue eyes pierced, just like her daughter's. It was unnerving, if you want to know the truth.

I hung my head. Hating myself for letting her go to Cuba without me. Hating that I didn't know where she was. If she was safe. Convinced I really was the worst person in the world.

"Which is why," Cheryl continued, "I told Sergio to do the right thing and follow her."

I practically fell off the counter when she said that. I smacked my hand on my forehead, causing my baseball cap to fall into the sink. "What? Is he there now? Can we call them?"

Cheryl sighed. "I've been trying. But the last time I tried to call him, he was already gone. He should be in Santiago by now."

I slid off the counter. "Jesus. I mean, geez." It's not like Cheryl hadn't heard me swear or anything, but I figured I shouldn't test my luck.

She tapped her fingernails on the table and slid her lower lip around her teeth. It was another habit she gave her daughter, and it was unnerving as fuck to watch another woman do it.

"Yes. Well. Apparently he does love his daughter after all." Cheryl turned that deceptively deep stare of hers on me again. "And now I think you had better tell me exactly what my daughter is marrying into that requires her to fly on your behalf to a country where Americans are not supposed to go."

I told her everything and then some. After all, she was right. Layla and I were family, even if we weren't married yet. There was a piece of me growing inside her, so no matter what, her family and mine were linked forever now.

To her credit, Cheryl didn't say anything while I told her my mother's story, much more than Layla gave up when they spoke. She just took a calm seat at our scratched dining table and listened, occasionally cocking her head a little when I came to an exciting part.

And at the end, she asked only a few questions. Who was Ileana? Where exactly were we getting our information from? And when exactly was the court date? Once she had that information, she picked up her phone and proceeded to hire our family a real lawyer. The other stuff—the baby, the engagement, the fact that I'd been living with her daughter in sin—would have to wait for later.

Finally, I can't take the waiting any more. Gabe watches curiously when I get up and start pacing around the room. I can't sit still. I feel like a trapped animal.

"Nico!" Maggie hisses at me. "You look like a psycho. Stop!"

"I can't help it." I really can't. I don't know if I've ever been this worried in my life.

Christina looks over with an understanding smile. "You know, we probably have about an hour or more."

At the end of the row, Cheryl catches my eye, and a slim, blonde brow rises. Cheryl seems to read me well for someone who barely knows me. Too well. Maybe it's in the genes.

"Go take a walk," she tells me, in words that barely float down the row to where I'm about ready to combust. She holds up her cell phone. "Stay in the building. I'll call."

I hesitate, glancing at Ma. With her hands clasped in her lap, avoiding Cheryl's gaze, all of our gazes, she watches me with tired eyes. She's scared too, a lot more than me, and suddenly I feel bad for going as crazy as I am. But I also see plainly that I'm not helping shit treading holes through the cheap carpet. A walk would be good—for me and for her.

"Okay," I say. "I'll be back in fifteen minutes."

"Take thirty," says Christina.

"Take an hour," mutters Maggie, causing Gabe and Selena to laugh. Even Cheryl quirks a smile.

I decide instead to jog up and down one of the big concrete stairwells on either end of the building. I zigzag up, then back down, doing it again until I land on the second floor and start walking, not really knowing where I'm going.

I need her here. Layla always knows how to cool me down, how to find my center. But what if something happened to her? What if she's lost somewhere in Cuba, with no money, no phone, no way to get back? What if she's hurt? What if someone hurt her?

The nervous energy doubles and triples over again. Fuck. Maybe walking wasn't the way to go.

I stop in front of an office, but it takes me a second before I can actually read the words written on the glass door: "Marriage Licenses."

I stare at them for a long, long time. I don't know how long it takes to get a marriage license in New York. Maybe they'll make us wait months. Years. Maybe they'll want her to have enough time to think it over, decide it's a terrible mistake to marry a bad idea like me.

Except I'm not. For once, it's not Layla's voice saying that—it's mine. It's the one thing I've come to understand since I met her. To Layla, I'm somebody, and the longer I've known her the more I've realized that I'm somebody to other people too. She did that. She does that every day. And now I'm actually starting to believe it.

I push open the door.

There are four other couples in the waiting room for the judge, three of them dressed in their little white dresses and rented tuxedos. They look gooey and in love. It just makes me miss my girl even more.

"Can I help you?"

I turn to the desk, where a clerk is looking at me impatiently over a pair of aviator glasses straight out of the seventies. I approach the desk nervously.

"I, um. I'd like to apply for a marriage license."

The clerk looks around. "Who you gonna marry, honey? Yourself?"

I swallow. I don't know what the fuck I'm doing here, but now that the words are out of my mouth, I know what I want.

"No," I say. "I have a fiancée, thanks. I just wanted to get the forms, so we could, you know, do this?" I chew on my lower lip for a second. "*Can* we do this today?"

The clerk tips her head and gives me a smile, the kind you'd give a little kid pretending to be a policeman. "You have to wait twenty-four hours after you're granted a license," she tells me. "Your fiancée. Is she here, honey?"

I shake my head, pulling on my hat. "No. But she will be. Could we...could we just get it started?"

The clerk gives me a look like she feels sorry for me, then reaches out and taps my hand. "Sorry, hon. The law says both parties must be present to apply for a license. No exceptions. When she gets here, come back. In the meantime, take the application and fill it out so everything is ready to go." She looks me up and down, takes in my uniform, the jacket with the FDNY patch, the letters embroidered on my hat. "Tell her to hurry too, honey. Because if she doesn't want to marry you, I just might take her place."

I gotta give it to her, the lady can make me grin. I tip my hat, and take the application to a table to fill out, while the giggly couples get called back, one at a time. I smile at them as they go, thinking to myself that maybe, just maybe, that might be me in twenty-four hours. If Layla wants a big wedding, wants to spend every penny we have on dresses and cakes and flowers and food, we'll do it. Because I don't want to wait. I want Layla Barros to be my wife as soon as fuckin' possible.

If she can just get here.

As I finish the last line of information that I can, my phone buzzes in my pocket.

Cheryl: It's time.

"Thanks," I tell the clerk as I take off at a jog. "I'll be back." And she smiles, like she knows I will.

———

I enter the formal courtroom just as my mother is sitting down at the table in front of the judge on the other side of the barrier. The lawyer sits next to her, while a government attorney sits on her other side. The lawyer already explained to us how today would go. The judge would confirm the claims of the state and confirm that they were there in response to the charges. Ma would have to sit in a witness stand, like it's a trial, and from there she would be questioned by both attorneys. The judge would then decide whether there needs to be another hearing, or if the case could be dismissed.

I slide into another pew (I can't think of them as anything else) next to Gabe, then turn around to greet the other members of my family who have arrived: Alba, K.C., Flaco, and a few other extended aunties and uncles who showed up to support my mother. This isn't anything compared to everyone in New York City who considers Carmen Soltero family. If this were the final hearing, I know that half of Hell's Kitchen would be here to speak on her behalf. She doesn't just have a village—she's got a city of millions. The knowledge gives me faith that everything is going to be all right.

In a bored voice, the judge announces herself to the court, then, just as Christina said, confirms the case and then has Ma swear in. The representative from ICE stands and drones a quick statement about Carmen Soltero entering the country illegally and requesting deportment proceedings to begin. With every word, my mom shrinks into her seat. And at the end, she's practically a child again, that little girl who first came off a plane in the sixties, following a family who had adopted her because she didn't have any of her own.

"Counselor?" The judge turns to Christina, who stands.

Christina proceeds to inform the judge that under the terms of the Cuban Adjustment Act, my mother has every right to be in the United States. "As a national of Cuba and having resided in the United States for a duration longer than two years, she is legally entitled to permanent residency status under the terms of the Cuban Adjustment Act," she states.

The judge takes a deep breath, and with a raised brow, turns to Ma. "Ms. Soltero, would you like to say anything?"

Shakily, Ma nods. Next to me, Maggie starts chanting the Hail Mary under her breath, and down the row, I catch Alba crossing herself. Ma's English still isn't great, but we've all been practicing with her for months now—even Layla.

"I come to New York when I am ten," she states in a clear, shaky voice. "With a family from San Juan de Puerto Rico." She turns and smiles at Alba, who waves. "That is Alba Ortiz, my sister from this family. Her parents are not alive anymore, but she come with me in the plane."

The judge looks between them. "But you were born in Cuba?"

Ma nods. "Yes. I was born in Santiago de Cuba. My mother, she died when I was a baby. When I was two, almost three, my father had saved enough for us to take a boat. This was after Fidel came into power."

The whole room is silent as she tells this story, to the point where every shake of her voice vibrates through the air.

"I don't remember the boat except for the last part. I remember the ocean. The waves, they were very big. The boat, it went up and down, side and side." She mimics the motions with her hands. "It make me sick. My father, he put me under the boat, in a tiny room. Then he go away. Maybe to help. I don't know. But I lose him in that storm. And when we come to Puerto Rico, I was alone."

She blinks several times, and I can tell she's trying not to cry. I've maybe seen my mother cry twice in my life. Once when I was sent away. Once when I came back. But now the judge is asking my mother to remember things she keeps buried. Stories she never wants to tell.

"Alba's family...I don't know how I come to them. I remember I was scared. And a woman bringing me to their house in San Juan." She clears her throat. "They took me in. Make me part of their family. And when they come to New York, I come with them."

"Without identification," the judge murmurs more to herself than anyone else. "And I don't suppose you had a birth certificate on you at two or three years old." She looks up. "How do you actually know you're from Cuba to begin with? You were so young. A lot of people come by boat to Puerto Rico. You could be Dominican or from somewhere else."

"My father told the men of the boat," Ma says. "They tell *Señor* Ortiz. He tell me."

She shrugs, but my eyes are on the judge. I wonder how anyone could hear this story and deny her is beyond me. But thousands of people have similar stories. How many people come here looking for a better life, trying to escape countries ripped up by wars and poverty, so much of it caused by this country and others like it? I've known plenty. New York is full of them.

"I come to New York without a family," Ma says, her voice a little stronger now. "And so I make my own. There they are. All my children. My granddaughter."

She turns around and points to us: me, Maggie, Selena, Gabe. Even Allie on Maggie's lap. Maggie grips my hand hard enough that I'm going to bruise, and Selena is practically plastered to Gabe.

"Please," Ma says. "Don't break up my family. In Cuba, I have nothing. Everything I have is here."

The judge looks over all of us, her eyes plainly sympathetic.

"I'm sorry," she says. "But, Ms. Soltero, unless you can provide documentation of the fact that you are a Cuban national, I cannot grant relief based on this evidence. Therefore, we will schedule another hearing to give you enough time to procure documentation—a birth certificate, for instance."

"But she has one!"

The judge looks up, both curious and annoyed. A murmur rises in the court, everyone wondering who would have the balls to interrupt a federal judge. But I know who it is. The second I hear her voice, a wave of relief washes over me. She's all right. She's here.

I twist around, and there's Layla, striding down the aisle with Sergio following behind her as she whips a yellowed piece of paper out of her backpack. She stretches across the barrier to hand the paper to the lawyer. With a brief clasp of my mother's wrist, Layla backs away until I can grab her hand and pull her onto the bench next to me.

"Hey," she greets me with a short, thorough kiss. The circles under her blue eyes are darker than normal. She's tired, and not just because of traveling for three days straight, I realize with guilt. Traveling for three days straight can't be good for the baby.

I pull her tight, nosing her and placing a hand on her stomach. "Hey, *mami*. You okay?"

Blue eyes shining, she nods. "I got it," she whispers fiercely as I wrap an arm around her shoulders, eager to feel her body, know she's safe. Know she's real.

"Shall we continue?" asks the judge in an irritated voice.

Christina looks up from the document. "Your Honor, permission to approach the bench?"

The judge nods, and Christina and the government attorney walk up to the judge. We strain to hear them, but none of their conversation is clear from our perspective. All that's left to do is wait.

After a few minutes, both lawyers return to their tables, while the judge continues examining the birth certificate.

"All right," says the judge. "In light of the evidence at hand, I believe we have a different outcome. I hereby cancel removal proceedings for Carmen Soltero and order the immediate processing of her application for permanent residency under the Cuban Adjustment Act."

With a bang of a gavel, she closes the session, and the bailiff stands up to call the next case. In the meantime, my mother gathers her birth certificate and returns to the gallery, where she's immediately embraced by all of her children. Layla lets me go long enough to sweep my mother up in a bear hug. She's crying. We're all crying. Every single one of us a big teary mess as we shuttle out of the room so we stop interrupting the court.

Once all ten of us are in the hall, my mother locates Layla and pulls her close. Layla's crying too, her big blue eyes glossy with relief and happiness. My girl is part of this family too. She knows it. Everyone knows it.

"Thank you," my mother says, again and again as she strokes her hair softly, the same way she used to do to all of her kids when we were small. "My other daughter, you know that? I am so, so happy you come into my boy's life."

"Me too," Layla whispers as she returns the embrace. "Me too."

When at last she's released, I pull her close and kiss her the way I wanted the second I knew she was there.

"I'm glad I came into your life too," Layla says as I practically squeeze the life out of her.

I nuzzle her, touching our noses and close my eyes. My heart might truly explode. I never knew this kind of happiness, this kind of peace, was possible, and it's all because of this girl.

"Me too, baby," I whisper, squeezing my eyes shut as the tears keep coming. "Me too."

CHAPTER THIRTY-SEVEN

Layla

IF THERE IS ONE THING NICO'S FAMILY KNOWS HOW TO DO quickly, it's throw a party. Literally as soon as we're outside city hall, Alba, Flaco, K.C., Carmen, and *all* of the Soltero kids practically explode right there on the sidewalk, cheering and jumping on each other like it's the Fourth of July.

"You fuckin' did it!" Nico cries as he lifts me into the air, then pulls me back down to kiss me again, longer this time.

I'm immediately grabbed and hugged and kissed by everyone, their joyful tears rubbing on my cheeks as they pass me around.

"It wasn't me," I'm finally able to get out with K.C.'s arm slung around my shoulder. He grew up with Nico. To him, Carmen is like a second mother.

"What's that, NYU?" he asks me, rubbing my head like a kid.

"Easy," Nico warns playfully, but he still pulls me back to that familiar place under his arm. I can feel his concern in the clutch of his hands. He's still checking to make sure I'm here for real. My man was scared while I was gone.

I turn to where my parents are standing awkwardly together on the sidewalk. They're both smiling a little, bemused by the Solteros' open displays of affections, but basically statues compared to the boisterous display of joy going on. They take in the movement of this family, and my mother in particular studies Nico's mother and sisters. Why, I'm not so sure.

"It was my dad," I say, and when I say it, Dad meets my gaze.

His dark eyes are as tired as mine, and he looks much different from his usual polished self. His clothes, after wearing them for two days straight, are as rumpled as my pants and jacket—his usual white button-down creased into oblivion, his gray slacks wrinkled terribly. He clutches his thin blazer around his body, a poor ward against the mid-February wind.

"What do you mean?" Nico asks, his brow furrowed in confusion. He pulls his hat backward so he can see me clearly, and for a moment, I'm taken aback by the beauty of his face, even in its confusion. The curl of his lashes, the almond-shaped eyes. The carved cheekbones and full lips. It's not a face I'll ever tire of.

I clear my throat. Okay, pregnancy is seriously doing things to my libido. I've barely slept in two days, we've just accomplished a major victory in his mother's life, and all I can think about is getting this man into bed. Where are my priorities?

"Well, I tried," I say. "But the clerk really didn't want to give me the birth certificate. She said no, rejected the money I brought. I was freaking out, and then...my dad showed up."

I look at Dad, who actually looks somewhat bashful. It's a weird look for him. His olive skin is slightly flushed, and for the first time, he can't totally make eye contact with me. It's...sweet.

"She didn't like me," I tell Nico. "But she liked my dad."

Everyone else listens to the story as I relay the rest as best I can, considering I didn't completely understand the entire exchange. But in the end, the meaning is clear, and everyone, even my mom, is gazing at my dad with gratitude.

"You did good, Serge," Mom murmurs, earning a soft look from my dad. Huh.

Nico steps forward, and his family quiets a little, despite the hum of the city moving around us. Nico extends his hand—the same hand that gave my dad the bruise over his cheek.

"Thank you," he says solemnly. "I mean it. Me, my family. We're in your debt, Sergio."

They shake hands for what seems like an eternity, and it really does seem like something passes between them. Something big.

Carmen pushes her way through her kids to stand in front of my father.

"*Dios le bendiga,*" she says. God bless you. "Dr. Barros. Thank you."

Dad blinks, a sheen clear over his deep-set eyes. He shakes his head—something about the blessing got to him, but I'm not sure what it is. She beckons him down, and to my surprise, he obeys, allowing her to kiss him on both cheeks on a busy street in the middle of New York.

"'*Brigado,*" he murmurs, seemingly unaware that he's lapsed into Portuguese instead of Spanish.

"Time to celebrate!" calls out Alba. "My house, now! Food, everything. It will be perfect. K.C., you go pick up some pizzas, okay?"

K.C. shrugs, like he's not a semi-famous DJ at this point, just a kid who takes orders from his mother. "Sure, Ma. Whatever you say."

"Come on. Sergio and Cheryl, you too!" Alba calls. And before my parents can answer, she gets into a cab with K.C., followed soon after by the rest of us.

———

"So, *habla español*, huh?" Nico asks my dad as they both sprinkle their slices with extra hot chili flakes.

Mom watches as Nico folds his massive slice in half lengthwise so he can hold it without it flopping over, then gingerly does the same with what's probably the first piece of pizza she's had in ten years.

Dad quirks a sardonic smile and gives a brief nod. "Some, yes. I learned in Argentina when I was a boy. Not so bad for a *culo*, eh?"

Nico raises a brow, though he has to suppress a smile. "Good to know. Now if the baby's first language is Spanish, you'll be able to speak to it."

Dad looks less than pleased by the idea, but he says nothing. Mom just takes another tiny bite of her pizza and pretends not to have heard anything.

Nico looks at me. "What do you think, baby? Should we try to speak Spanish at home?"

I shrug. "I mean, sure. I bet just having Carmen as its grandma guarantees the baby will be fluent, don't you think?"

"Baby?" Carmen's voice cuts through the clamor around Alba's big table. "*Quién va tener un bebé, papito?*"

Nico pauses mid-bite, his face slightly reddened. I immediately flush everywhere. *Oh.* Of course. In the craze of everything, no one knows our big news.

He swallows heavily, then sets his slice down on his paper plate. "Ah, well, *Mami...*" He reaches out an errant hand, and immediately I take it in my lap and squeeze. "We found out in Brazil that...well, Layla's pregnant. And while we were there, well, I asked her to marry me, and"—he grins—"she said yes."

"What?" Selena cries out.

"That's amazing!" Maggie shouts, just as Gabe reaches around me to slap Nico's shoulder. Immediately, almost everyone in Nico's family is on their feet, and we are too, accepting another round of kisses and congratulations and hugs like crazy from everyone in the room. Allie immediately jumps up and demands to be the flower girl, while Alba starts talking about dates with Carmen. I grin at Nico over K.C.'s shoulder. His eyes shine with happiness.

"Was it a shotgun proposal, Dr. Barros?" K.C. jokes.

Everyone turns to my dad, who still hasn't gotten up. My mom sits next to him, blank-faced, though clearly she already knew. There is no surprise on her face. My heart falls. *No, Dad*, I will him. I know what's coming.

"No, asshole," Nico shoots back at K.C. "I asked her before, if you really have to know." He turns to me and presses a sweet kiss on my lips. "So we're getting married. Soon, I hope."

There's a loud clearing of a throat. I shut my eyes. *Shit.*

"No, you're not."

Just like that, all of the joy in the room vanishes as everyone turns once again to my father. Dad pushes a hand through his hair, then crosses his arms over his chest. His pizza sits on his plate, growing cold. I doubt it's going to get eaten now.

"I am sorry," he says slowly, looking at me, not everyone else. "I didn't want to do this now. Not with the celebration and everything. But you're too young, Layla. He is...even with the baby, he is...this boy is not a good fit for you. He will not be able to give you the same life you have. The life you know. You are too...different."

He gestures toward Nico, like there is something there that I should see in him that's self-evident. Whether it's the tattoo on his arm or the darker color of his skin, the fact that he has a delinquent record or that he grew up in relative poverty...it's all just surface. None of it matters.

His arm still around my shoulders, Nico shrinks. His eyelashes sweep across his cheeks as he looks down.

No. Absolutely not. I am *not* having that.

I turn to my dad, ready to tell him to get the hell out, but Nico's family beats me to it.

"Are you *kidding* me?"

"Who the fuck do you think you are, man?"

"*Coño*, who the fuck *is* this dude, huh?"

Nico's family and friends all speak at once, practically jumping over themselves to shout at my dad. Maggie looks like she's about ten seconds from taking off her earrings, and even Carmen looks like she wants to take a swing at my dad for insulting her son.

But it's the last voice that surprises me the most.

"Sergio, that's absolutely ridiculous."

My mother's voice drops through the cacophony and cuts them all off at the knees. In utter shock, Dad turns to his wife—if you can even call her that, since they've lived apart for close to two years now. But if I'm not mistaken, looking at her pains him a little. I wonder if, despite everything they said, the church wasn't the only reason they didn't want to divorce.

"You don't know, Serge," Mom says, speaking directly to him in a voice that is stronger than I've ever heard her use with my dad. "We owe that boy Layla's life."

Sergio glares at Nico, but his anger fades when he turns back to Mom. "So he says. But we don't know *really* that—"

"*I* do," she corrects him. "Layla stepped off that plane utterly broken, Sergio. Her face. Her soul. She had a cut from here to here." With a delicate hand, Mom gestures across her eyebrow and up her forehead. I actually still have a delicate scar there, but the surgeon Mom took me to see did good work last spring. You can barely tell anything is there.

Nico buries his nose in my hair, but I can feel him vibrating next to me.

"A man did that to our little girl, Serge," Mom continues, like there isn't an audience of nine staring at her. "And would have done worse, I'm *sure* of it, if this boy hadn't stepped in! And she would be an absolutely shell of herself if he hadn't been there for her every day since." Her voice is shaking now, and then she turns to Nico. "I never thanked you properly," she tells him. "But I'm doing it now."

"Cheryl, let's talk about this another time."

"We'll talk about it *now*," Mom bites out. "Before you insult Layla's new family even more."

Dad bites his lip, but has the courtesy to look contrite.

"What I know is this," Mom says. "This boy is the kind of *man* who would step in and do what needed to be done...when we were too wrapped up in ourselves to see what was going on." She pauses and darts a glance at Nico again. "We are very lucky, I think, to have someone like this, like *all* of the Soltero family, love our daughter. I don't think we could ask for more."

I swallow a sob, and behind her, I see both of Nico's sisters swiping at their eyes. It means a lot to this family to have the oldest of the kids, their caretaker—the one other people always seemed to see the worst in, but in whom they see and have the best—validated like this. Nico clenches my hand like he'll never let it go. He's watching my mom now too, and to my surprise, his eyes are also glossed over. This means more to him than he'd ever want to admit.

Mom clears her throat. "And if you don't think so, well, I'll just have to make sure they don't *need* your approval to live. You're not the only one who can pay tuition, Sergio."

I turn to Nico, willing him to look at me, to see the belief in us that I have in my eyes. There is *nothing* I know better than the fact that we are supposed to be together. I would go to hell and back for this man. I would give up everything I know to follow him anywhere. He just needs to see it.

"Where's the license?" I ask quietly.

His black brows quirk, and the side of his mouth twitches. Damn. I *really* want to kiss him—actually, I want to do a lot more than that. Freaking pregnancy hormones! Focus, Layla!

Nico pulls out the piece of paper we got at the clerk's office today, when everyone thought we were going to the restroom after leaving the courthouse. We weren't.

"*Let's do it now,*" he whispered in between kisses as his black eyes shined with happiness. "*I don't want to wait. Today's a day for new beginnings, baby. I want ours to start right now.*"

I grinned and pressed my nose to his. "*Show me the way.*"

The memory still fresh in my mind, I unfold the paper and hand it to my dad.

"Tomorrow," I say, then turn to everyone else, speaking loudly, though my voice shakes. "We're getting married tomorrow. We decided to elope, and we're getting married at city hall in exactly twenty-two hours and forty minutes. Dad, I really want you there. I understand if you can't. It's a lot to take. But this baby deserves to have its family intact when it comes into the world. So now...it's your choice. Support us. Don't support us. But this is my family too now. And if you can't treat them with the respect they deserve, then maybe you shouldn't be here at all."

Dad looks at me for a long time, then glances between the two of us. Eventually the energy in the room subsides, but no one moves from the table. Finally, Dad stands with a screech of the chair leg on the floor and comes to stand in front of me.

"Come," he says, draping an around over my shoulder and pulling me close.

Nico releases my hand, and I stand up to lean into my father's embrace. His familiar scent—Hugo Boss cologne, scotch, and a hint of cigarette smoke—overwhelms me. My eyes well up. When I look up, my father's eyes are closed.

"This is what you want?" he asks. "This life? It won't be what you grew up with, Layla. Not like the one I made for you."

I shake my head. Like that matters. Like any of that ever mattered at all. "I don't need you to make a life for me, Dad. I want to make it for myself."

He gazes down at me for a long time with a look I barely remember: one of pride.

"With him?" he asks.

"He's the best man I've ever met," I whisper fiercely. I don't have to say the rest of what I mean. It lingers anyway: *even better than you.*

Dad winces, but holds me that much tighter. "I guess..." He sighs. "Tomorrow, then. But you're not getting married at city hall, *linda*. Do it right. We'll find a church, okay?"

"*Sí, sí!*" Carmen cuts in on top of my dad. I hear, rather than see her smack Nico on the shoulder. "You were not getting married in a church?" she demands in Spanish. "I raised you better than that!"

I'm released, and when I turn around, Nico is grinning while he fights off his mother's light smacks on his shoulder. He gives me a lopsided smile, as if to say, "What did you expect?" When we had planned to run off and get married, we hadn't counted on having our two very religious parents fighting our every step.

"Well, we do already have the license," he says to me.

I shrug. I don't really care where we get married—just that we do.

Nico turns to his mother and my dad, who have unwittingly bonded over the one thing the both of them care about most: being good Catholics.

"You find us a church by tomorrow," he tells them, "and we'll show up. Otherwise, it's city hall. Because I'm not waiting more than a few days, and neither is she."

CHAPTER THIRTY-EIGHT

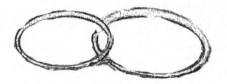

Nico

I should be nervous, but I'm not. Cold feet, that's what they call it, right? Well, as I let my mom fix a new red tie around my neck, my feet are anything but cold. They're perfectly warm and ready to take off at a run the four blocks to the church where I went almost every Sunday for Mass my entire life.

I don't know how she did it, but somehow Cheryl managed to convince the priest to officiate a wedding before the six o'clock Mass, the day after Layla and I applied for a marriage license. Turns out that if Layla's dad has a way with clerks, her mom has a way with priests. And I can't tell you how fuckin' awkward it was hearing about Cheryl charming the pants off Father Boylan. Layla said the man actually blushed.

Layla and Cheryl stayed at our apartment the last few nights while her dad got a hotel close by, and I went back to work another seventy-two-hour shift that ended this morning. So I haven't seen Layla in three days, and when I do see her again, I'm going to marry her.

Cold feet? Try blazing hot.

"Ma, it's *fine*," I tell her, batting her hands away.

I straighten the knot in front of the mirror, then spread everything down. It's the same suit I've been wearing for years, but I splurged for a new white shirt, and was surprised when Sergio presented me with a gift from him and Cheryl this afternoon—the red tie.

"*Ay, bendito*," Ma murmurs behind me as I check over everything. "You look so handsome, *papi*."

I turn around to face her, and I soften when she reaches up to smooth back my hair.

"*Un hombre*," she says as her hand drifts over my chest.

I smile. It's the same thing she said to me when I got dressed for my first real job. I was eighteen and trying to knot a tie for the first time in my life. The new job as a part-time doorman was a step up then, at a time when I wondered if I'd ever be able to get a real job. But slowly, I came to realize that my past didn't have to define me. That it doesn't have to define any of us.

I look over my mother's shoulder to where my sister plays dominoes with Allie. My niece is about to start school next year, a scholarship spot at a private school on the Upper East Side. Maggie catches me watching them and winks. They're both dressed up, Allie in her little red dress so she can be our impromptu flower girl, and Maggie in a flowery green thing that makes her look really pretty. I don't normally think of my sister that way, but she is. She's strong and solid, just like our mom, and usually doesn't have time to bother with things like getting her hair done or wearing the kinds of clothes that get her a lot of attention. But today, she really does look beautiful.

Gabe strides out of the back room, fixing his glasses and his tie, followed by Selena, who's just as gussied up as the rest of us. We're all in more than our Sunday best. But then again, this isn't any normal Sunday.

"I look like a penguin," Gabe says as he comes to stand next to me and look in the mirror. He's wearing the same as me: a black suit, white shirt, but his tie is black.

"No, you don't," I tell him. "You look like a waiter."

"*Pare*," Ma orders us. "All of my children look beautiful today." She surveys us, real joy beaming out of her face. "Every single one." She turns to the kitchen, where Alba and K.C. are having a drink, and beckons Alba to take our picture.

"Ma!" Selena protests. "I hate having my picture taken!"

"Sel, hush," I tell her, already moving toward the picture window that looks over New York. "Come on. I'm getting married. Pictures are a requirement."

With only a little bit of groaning, we assemble together, the four of us standing on either side of our mom. Ma comes to just above my shoulder, taller than I remember her being before. The flowers she put in her hair today tickle my nose; the smell of gardenias filters all around us. But then I realize that for the first time, my mother is standing up straight. She's not cowered down, trying to hide from the world. Instead, she stands with her head held up, her chest out, looking straight at the camera with an unabashed grin on her face. The realization makes me stand tall too—it makes all of us do it. I toss an arm around Gabe on the other side and pull my sisters close. We're all grinning already, and it's not because Alba's telling us to. Our smiles are real. Even Allie, clutched by her grandmother, can't stop giggling.

This feeling won't last. Life is like that—bad things happen. People get sick. They lose their jobs. Shit happens that make things hard, but they also make the sweet moments like this that much better. My family has dealt with the bitter for a long time. I close my eyes for a second. For just a moment, we finally get to enjoy a little bit of the sweet.

———

We walk the four blocks to the church, where the priest is setting up for Mass. It's the same church where I was baptized and was confirmed. The same place where my mom found solace for so many years, and the same place where we thought our family was going to be split apart.

Cheryl scurries around lighting candles in the sconces, but most of the dim light in the church actually comes from the rows of prayer candles in the apses, where people light candles for their loved ones. Their well wishes float through the air and all around us. We have thirty minutes to do this, but that's about twenty-five minutes more than I need. I just need to say the words. Tell her I love her. Say: "I do."

There are only a few people here to see us off. My family, Alba, K.C., and Flaco. Cheryl, Sergio, and Vinny, Layla's friend from school, and Shama, who actually flew back from England to be her maid of honor. All the aunties and uncles will be meeting us at Alba's for a party after, but for this, we just wanted it to stay small. Just the people who know us. Who know our story.

"You good, man?" Gabe claps me on the shoulder as I take my place in front of the altar, next to the priest. On his other side stands Shama, holding a small bouquet of tulips—Layla's favorite flower. She gives me a smile, though I notice her glancing every so often to the piano at the side of the chapel, where K.C. is tapping out a soft melody.

I smile to myself. "Yeah," I say. "I'm more than good. Let's do this."

Everyone feels the love at weddings. But not like me. Not like when my girl steps out of the atrium, flanked on either side by her parents. Sergio looks the picture of a patrician, older father, distinguished in what looks like a brand-new suit, and maybe a little sad as he walks his daughter down the aisle. Cheryl is dressed in blue, the same shade as her and Layla's eyes, and her dark-blonde hair shines like a halo. She finds me and nods, and I return the gesture.

But neither of them can hold a candle to my girl. She wears a lace dress that comes down past her knees and hugs her hips. With its delicate sleeves and modest skirt, it's not a dress that puts everything on display, and yet, it frames her curves perfectly. Her hair is down and pulled back from her face, curling around her shoulders in a way that makes me want to pull on it and stroke it all at once. She carries a bouquet of pink tulips that match the color of her lips, and even from the far side of the atrium, her blue eyes find mine and fucking sing.

The wedding is small and perfect. The priest gives a brief speech about the sanctity of marriage, reading out names off the card provided to him an hour before. Layla and I repeat after every vow he states, unblinking as we clutch each other's hands, moving our lips around the sacred words that we both mean with everything we are.

There's no doubt. No fear. Just love. Just the knowledge that everything we've been through in the last two years—no, in all of our lives—has been leading us here, to this moment, and to the future ahead of us.

"Do you take this woman?" the priest asks, but by that point, I can barely see him. All I see is her.

"I do," I whisper. "Always."

Layla's face shines.

The priest smiles, and asks for the rings—the simple gold ring I bought just last week, and another gold band that was gifted from Cheryl and Sergio this morning. Another peace offering of sorts.

We slide the rings onto each other's hands, both of us fighting tears the whole time. A cheer rises as he says those final words I've been waiting for: "You may kiss the bride."

So I do. And I swear to God, before all that is holy, I'll never, ever stop.

―――――

Two hours later, we're back at Alba's house. Just like at her holiday parties, all of the furniture has been cleared out, making space in the living room for all of the aunties and uncles, cousins and friends who've shown up last minute to dance and laugh and eat and wish us well. Everyone is full of *pasteles* and chicken, beer and wine, and whatever else we could rustle up around town. Cheryl bought out half the flower markets in New York. Alba's apartment looks like a florist exploded in here. K.C. set up his turntables in the corner and has been spinning a mix of Latin music that includes both samba, bossa nova, merengue, and salsa—a perfect mix of the two of us.

Even Sergio and Cheryl are having a good time. I've caught Cheryl's laugh a few times when she lets her estranged husband spin her around the floor. Layla watches them closely. I get the feeling she's never seen them let loose like this together. But I get it. The look on their faces tells me they're remembering things that happened long before she was born. They're remembering what it was like to fall in love.

Layla and I sway in the middle of the crowded dance floor, mostly too caught up in each other to follow the beats. My jacket's been long tossed aside, and she lies with her cheek on my shoulder, burrowed into me after we finally finished accepting all of the blessings from everyone here.

Suddenly, she stops moving and pulls away. She looks down, her mouth dropped in shock.

"What?" I ask. "What is it?" Shit. *Shit.* Something's wrong, I know it. We just couldn't have one fucking day to ourselves, could we?

But then Layla bites her lip, and her eyes open with a look of wonder.

"I felt it," she whispers, pulling my hand to her still-flat belly.

I know it's too early to feel kicks. Maggie didn't feel anything with Allie until she looked like she had a mini basketball sticking out of her. But Layla clearly feels something, and who am I to tell her it's anything other than indigestion?

"Like a butterfly," she tells me, keeping my hand pressed under hers. "Can you feel it?"

I shake my head and grin. "No. But I will." I can't wait.

The clear, recognizable notes of a bass line and piano sound through Alba's speakers, and like that the party really starts up. Just try to tell a room full of Puerto Ricans not to sing at the top of their lungs when this dude comes on. I dare you.

Layla tips her head, listening. "Is this Marc Anthony?"

I chuckle. "You've been hanging around Maggie too much. I'm impressed."

She taps her foot, unable to keep her hips from twisting and turning with the beat that's already started. I stare. It doesn't matter how many times I see her do that; the way Layla moves her body is fuckin' mesmerizing.

"You like it," she says. "Don't even pretend."

I laugh. "Now you *really* sound like Maggie."

But she's right. My hips are already moving, feet shuffling back and forth in the familiar rhythm. I can't help it. Salsa is infectious, and it's in my blood. And now that there is a part of me inside Layla, it's in hers too.

I grin and take both of her hands. "Come on, then," I tell her. "Let's show them some new moves."

I start twisting her around in the combinations we've practiced over the last few months, even trying a few new ones that I didn't know I had in me. Layla's laughter filters around the crowd, her happiness beaming through her entire body, just like I know it is through mine. All around us, our family and friends watch with smiles and laughter that joins ours. I know it won't always be like this. I know our life will still be hard sometimes. That we'll fight. Make mistakes. Struggle for money, jobs, places to live, maybe even more when there's a baby.

But no matter what's coming, we'll always have this. We'll always have us. And that knowledge will keep me going for the rest of my life.

"Hey," Layla says as I pull her back in. I kiss her, because I can't not, and she returns it and smiles. But it's a normal smile, because I'm always kissing her.

"What's that?" I reply when I let her go again.

"What does '*valió la pena*' mean anyway?" she asks, quoting the song lyrics.

I cock my head. "It means, 'it was worth it.'"

A slow, knowing smile spreads across Layla's face. "That sounds about right," she says. "It was *definitely* worth it."

She stumbles a little as I take her around a particularly difficult turn. She falls into my arms, and when she looks up, she's breathless.

"It's okay," I assure her as I pull her upright. "I won't let you fall. I got you, baby."

Layla grins, that smile that lights me up, that sets me on the right path every time. The smile that guides me home. My true north.

"I know," she says as she pulls me close. "I got you, too."

EPILOGUE: PART I

MAY 2009

Nico

"WHAT DO YOU THINK, *PAPI*? RED OR PINK?"

Mattie shakes his head, making his black curls flop over his forehead.

"*Violeta*," he pronounces. "Mommy likes the purple best."

My son's Spanish is probably better than mine, courtesy of the fancy-ass preschool he's attending. Thank you, Grandma, although if my mother-in-law ever hears me use that word, Layla says I'll get a drink in my face. Of course, that only makes me want to say it more.

I look back at the rows of flowers, searching for the dusky shade of eggplant he means. It's the color I usually buy my wife, the one I've been bringing her since we first met. I would see it at sidewalk stands just like this one, and the purple, the same color as the flags hung from the downtown buildings owned by her school, would remind me of that sweet, beautiful girl I met in the middle of my delivery route. The one I should have stayed away from. The one I could never forget. The nickname is a joke now, since she graduated almost four years ago, but Layla will always be my NYU.

I turn back to Mattie, who's giving the flower selection the same critical eye. Mateo Christopher Barros Soltero, otherwise known as Mattie (because that name is way too grown up for a person who still can't tie his own shoes), is picky. Too picky for someone who barely comes past my knee.

"*Papi*, they don't have purple," I say, holding out the two bunches again. "Come on, man. We need to meet up with *Abuela* so I have time to pick up Mommy. We got an appointment, and we can't be late."

Mattie scowls at the flowers and shakes his head again. "*No.*"

I sigh. That was a Spanish *no* right there, the kind he learned from Ma and Maggie and Allie and Selena—all of the women in my family who manage to shove "what the fuck are you thinking?" and "are you fuckin' kidding?" and "try again, you idiot" into two tiny letters. This kid has two very strong personality traits: he's stubborn like his aunties, and he fuckin' adores his mother, maybe even more than me. Only the best for her, and he doesn't settle. Even at three.

I put the flowers back. "Okay, okay, fine. You choose. But for real, Mattie, you got two minutes."

Mattie strides up the sidewalk and back to reexamine the selection, his chest sticking out. He's short for his age, but a little soldier, no matter if his shoelaces are always untied or he always has a little bit of chocolate smudged on his cheek.

When he comes back, he's carrying a spray of bright blue flowers that pretty much match his eyes, the ones he inherited from his mother. Everything else on the outside is all me, from the thick black hair to the shoulders that promise to be a little too wide for his frame one day. But his eyes? His heart? That's all Layla.

"These," he says. "Because they match her school now." He frowns. "Wait, is it still her school since she finished yesterday? The funny hat means she was done, right?"

I smile. It's stuff like this that amazes me about this kid. Three years old, and he remembers that the school colors for Columbia are blue and white. I doubt I could have remembered my own name at that age.

"Close enough, man. It's still her school." I take the flowers and hold them up to the vendor. "Yo, man. How much are these?"

"For the hydrangeas? Ten dollars."

I fish a crumpled bill from my wallet and hand it to the guy before turning to Mattie. "All right, kid. Let's go. We got a train to catch."

———

We spend the forty-five-minute subway and then PATH ride across the Hudson into Hoboken chatting about pretty much whatever goes through Mattie's head. Superheroes and why does that guy have a funny ear and how his friend Henry has a superhero cape and he'd like one too and, and, and...

"Daddy?"

"*Que pa'o, papi?*"

I look down at my little man. That's really what Mattie is. Living in the city makes kids grow up faster than they should. I would know. And as much as Layla and I try to keep his innocence intact as best we can, the truth is, you see shit in this city, whether you grow up on Park Avenue or in the projects. I wish Mattie didn't know what it sounds like to have his mom catcalled or see someone with so little they have to sleep on the street. But that's New York. Highs and lows. Skyscrapers and tent cities. You can't tell a three-year-old to keep his eyes closed; just teach him how to understand it all as best you can.

But I'll give him this: you can't tell a three-year-old to be quiet either. And when Mattie sees someone doing wrong, *especially* if it's to his mom, he calls that shit out. I almost fainted when he yelled "GIVE THAT LADY BACK HER WALLET!" across a subway car two months ago, but you know what? The asshole did, and then he was tossed out of the car on the next stop. And then the entire, jam-packed subway car started clapping. For my kid.

Yeah, you could call me a proud dad.

Mattie looks up at me, twisting his lips around in thought. "Why don't you call Mommy Columbia instead of NYU, since that's her school now?"

I mimic his expression. We both do that when we're thinking—make weird shapes with our mouths. Layla laughs at it all the time, which, to be honest, only makes me do it more. I love that sound.

At first I'm not sure how to answer. I mean, I can't really tell Mattie that I call his mom NYU because it makes her turn the color of a ripe peach, the exact color of her skin after I smack her on the ass. I can't tell him that it reminds us both of when we first met, when I'd shove her up against the brick wall of her dorm and kiss her until she'd run out of breath. Or that just a name will sometimes make her do the same thing to me, even after four years of marriage.

"It bugs her," is all I tell him. "And she likes it."

Mattie frowns. He's a very literal little dude, and usually if something doesn't make sense, he'll push me until it does.

Luckily, he doesn't press it this time. A group of panhandlers starts singing at the other end of the train, their rendition of "A Hard Day's Night" a distraction from slightly naughty nicknames and even naughtier memories. The singers are pretty good. You can't be busking for money in this city and not have some talent.

When they're done, Mattie turns to me, and I already know he's going to ask for change. He's so much like his mother—he can't stand to see people hurting, people in need, without doing something to help. Unfortunately, there are a lot of people in New York who need help. My wallet doesn't have enough singles.

"Here," I say, pressing another few bills into his chubby hand.

He grins, and when one of the singers comes around with his hat, Mattie gleefully drops the dollars in it.

"Good song!" he tells the guy, and the man grins, showing a big gold tooth in the back of his mouth along with a few others that look like they need some dental work. Mattie, to his credit, just keeps smiling. It's just another way he's more like his mom than me—he sees the best in people, no matter what.

About twenty minutes later, we get off in Hoboken. At one point, I hoist Mattie up with one arm to help him avoid the rush. Some people are just dicks, through and through—they won't even slow down for a little kid.

"I'm *fine*, Dad," he says, kicking his little legs to be put down when we emerge from the station.

"I know, I know," I tell him as I set him on the sidewalk. "I just gotta look out, you know?"

He brushes out his sweatshirt, then goes about taking off his backpack and digging out his baseball hat—a little black Yankees cap, just like mine. He claps it on, looks back up at me, and grins.

"Now we're twins," he says. "See?"

I nod. I can't help but smile back when my kid looks at me that way. "Yeah, *papi*, we're twins. Come on, everybody's waiting."

We walk the few blocks to K.C.'s townhouse near the river. The girls are all almost ready for the party—there's a bunch of big blue balloons tied to the iron rail of the brownstone. When we enter the apartment upstairs, I'm hit in the face by a giant cluster of blue, white, and gold streamers and a shit ton of tinsel hanging from the doorframe.

"Ah!" I cry, spitting them out while Mattie runs into the decor.

"Be careful!" snaps Maggie as she walks out of the kitchen carrying an armful of blue and white plates.

I toss the streamers over my shoulder and stride in. My sad blue flowers look ridiculous compared to the fuckin' flower shop my sisters —and I'm guessing Cheryl, because some of these bouquets look expensive—have set up in here.

"Maggie, what the fuck—I mean, freak?" I hastily correct myself when Mattie beelines back across the room. Shit. I mean, shoot. It's a habit I still haven't been able to break since having a kid. It doesn't help that everyone in my family swears like sailors, and the guys at the firehouse are twice as bad.

"That was a curse, Daddy," he calls out with his tiny palm turned over. "A dollar for the swear jar at home. I'll put it in my pocket for later."

Maggie snorts. "Please. *Papito*, you gotta bill him more than a dollar if you want your daddy to quit using the f-word. I've been trying to get him to clean his mouth out since Allie was born."

"Please. Like you got any right to call me out. You need to take some Palmolive to your own mouth, *gata*, that's what's up." I roll my eyes, then fish out my last dollar and hand it to Mattie. "Don't tell Mommy," I tell him, and clap him on the head while he runs off to find his cousin.

"Ma's here?" I ask. "Where is she? Or Selena and Alba?"

Maggie tosses her head back toward the kitchen. "Alba and Selena are in there making the rest of the *pasteles*, and Ma went with Scott to the store to get some more fruit for the punch." She clicks her tongue. "I'm glad. They are freaking nauseating."

I snort. After Ma got her green card, the first thing she did was start taking English classes. And wouldn't you know it, she fell for her teacher, Scott. Scott is a nice dude, a retired community college instructor who teaches free ESL classes for immigrants at the library. Apparently Ma was his star student, and since then, they've been pretty much inseparable. Ma moved into his apartment in Queens last summer, and two weeks ago, the dude actually asked my permission for her hand in marriage.

"Head of household," he said, like that was supposed to make a difference.

But the thing is, it does. It matters that for once, my mother found a man who cares enough about her to care what her family thinks of him. It matters that he treats her like gold, like a whole person, not someone to clean his shit and do whatever he says. And it matters, *really* fuckin' matters, that she's happier than I've ever seen her in my life.

So of course I said yes and bought the guy a couple of beers. Now we're just waiting for the announcement.

"Seriously, though," I say as I take the plates from Maggie and bring them over to the table. She takes my flowers and examines them critically. "You don't think this is a bit much? It looks like a *quinceañera* in here. It's just her master's degree. Layla doesn't like this kind of craziness."

"Boy, please. You are not the only person in this family proud of my sister. First person in our family to go to graduate school. And now she's going to do good with it? Your fucking sad little flowers don't cut it. Everyone wanted to do this for her, and she deserves it, so let us throw her a real party."

I look around, waiting for Mattie to charge back in, but he doesn't. Of course not. I'm the only one who ever gets caught cussing.

I can't argue with my sister's words, though—that she considers my wife a sister or that her accomplishments are something to be fuckin' proud of. I can't lie. I was practically busting at the seams when I watched my girl accept her diploma yesterday. I was maybe even prouder than when she graduated from NYU, because this degree was hers in a way that first one wasn't. After Layla was accepted to Columbia, she worked her ass off and won four different scholarships to pay for school and living expenses so she could get her master's in social work instead of going to law school like her dad wanted.

Sergio never stopped bugging her about it. In fact, once he knew his daughter was pregnant, would you believe the asshole actually took a sabbatical and moved to New York for the birth? Three fuckin' months I had to put up with that dickhead poking his controlling face around my apartment, checking on my kid, giving me dirty looks every time I had to pull a two or three-day shift, criticizing every damn thing I did, from the way I put on a diaper to the way I warmed up milk. If it wasn't for how pissed he got every time I called him *Mister* Barros instead of Doctor, I don't know how I would have survived.

But I can't say I wasn't ever grateful, either. Like that time Mattie got croup, Sergio was the only one who knew how to loosen that shit in his throat to keep him from choking to death. Scared the fuck out of me, let me tell you. Or when Mattie got hand, foot, and mouth disease from his first daycare, Sergio was the one to calm us down over and assure us that Mattie wasn't dying of measles.

So, yeah. Maybe the guy's not all bad.

In another year, though, Sergio Barros won't be the only doctor in the family. Gabe has two more years at NYU medical school, and then he'll officially be Dr. Soltero, ready to start an internship in family medicine. And even though I know we'll be throwing a *hell* of a party when he does graduate, Maggie's right. Layla is the first to get some fancy initials after her name. After Soltero. It is something to celebrate.

"Hey." Maggie snaps me out of my thoughts with her fingers two inches in front of my face.

"Yo!" I cry out, batting her hand away. "Why do you *always* have to do that?"

Maggie smirks. "Because you *always* ignore me when I'm talking."

I frown. "What is it?"

"I said, don't you have an appointment you need to get to?"

I blink, then check my watch. Shit, yeah. If I'm going to have time with the graduate herself at home, I have to jam.

I grab the keys to K.C.'s Yukon off the table and start for the door. Mattie won't miss me—he's probably knee-deep in Allie's Barbie collection by now, poor kid.

"K.C. know you're taking his car?" Maggie asks as she heads back to the kitchen.

I jingle the keys. "It's all part of the plan. See you at seven."

"Don't be late!" Maggie shouts, but I'm already halfway out the door.

———

Layla

I glance at the wall clock, but it still says the same time. Still five after two. Still twenty minutes past the time my freaking husband was supposed to be here to pick me up.

I stand up from the couch and smooth out my skirt. After our appointment, Nico and I are meeting with my parents, who both came to town for my graduation last night, for a small celebration. I should probably go change my shirt, a thin cotton tank top that's more comfortable than dressy, but Nico's unreasonable enjoyment at irritating my dad seems to have rubbed off on me. He'll take one look at my outfit, a simple red skirt and cotton tank top, and give me a lecture for lacking appropriateness.

Well, whatever. Going for drinks at the Plaza isn't really my idea of celebrating, especially these days, but it's fine. It's their comfort zone. Really, though, a master's degree isn't *that* big of a deal. Not compared to the fact that Gabe is going to be a freaking doctor in a few more years. It's a two-year degree that I finished with the help of a lot of people. If anyone should be celebrated, it's them.

I glance around our small living room, checking for things out of place. This is the first time in a long time I've actually had some time to myself without the threat of papers to write or housework to catch up on. Since we moved here, I've been in school, balancing the hectic life of having a husband whose job takes him away for days at a time, living with a toddler who would just as soon knock things over as look at them, and trying to get through the intense two-year program that would allow me to do the kind of work I've dreamed of since that day I watched Carmen find her freedom.

My job starts next week, but first things first. As soon as my final paper was submitted, Mom, Carmen, and I went through every piece of junk that Nico and I had accumulated over the past few years and tossed it, getting ready for the changes up ahead. And today I spent the morning cleaning my house.

It's weird to call it that—*my* house. I mean, I'm still not quite twenty-six. Most people my age spend their extra money on drinks or vacations. No one is spending them on a new furnace or toddler clothes.

But honestly, I couldn't be happier. We're so lucky. Our little townhouse is nothing massive, maybe a quarter of the size of the house where I grew up outside of Seattle. But it's a lot bigger than most apartments in New York, with three full bedrooms, an actual living room, even a washer and dryer. Is it weird that a washer and dryer excites me now? There is a *lot* more laundry to do with two boys in my house.

I wouldn't have thought I'd like living this far from Manhattan, but things change when you have a kid. We kept the apartment in Chinatown until Mateo was about a year old, but you get tired of walking up and down five flights of stairs *really* quickly when you're carrying a baby, a stroller, and all the other crap that somehow magically materializes when you have a kid.

Mateo brought other changes too. When he was born, something clicked in both of my parents. They might have finally gotten their act together and finalized their own divorce, but they also realized that this life I had been building in New York wasn't going anywhere. So instead of alienating my new family and distancing themselves from what I had embraced, they gifted Nico and me with a down payment on this place in Riverdale, just in time for our first anniversary. Nico was speechless. Really, he literally couldn't speak for almost an hour.

I wander out the back door, to the tiny patio that makes up our "backyard," if you could even call it that. Having a yard at all in New York City is a luxury. This space was my birthday present last year from Nico and Gabe. Together they landscaped the two hundred square feet of nothing into a mini-paradise, laying down a brick patio, exchanging the chain-link fence for a taller wood one, and building a fire pit in the middle. They planted a few trees that now block out most of the surrounding buildings, and a bunch of different flowers that make it smell sweet in the spring. It's my happy place.

I sit down on one of the lounge chairs and look up through the foliage, past strings of lights to the blue sky that's dappled with clouds. Even from here, you can hear the chatter of the city, although it's quieter in this part of the Bronx. We're not far from the Metro line we both take into Manhattan almost daily, and the sounds of kids playing at the park a half a black away filter through the fence. But the noises blend together with the wind coming off the Hudson and laughing through the trees. It's peaceful, not frenetic. Just what I need.

I close my eyes and listen, turning my face to the sun.

Please, I find myself praying to a God that, over the years, I've come to believe in more and more. *Please protect it. Please don't take it away.*

I listen, but there's no answer. There never is, but I know He's there. He must be.

"I thought you might be out here."

Nico's deep voice seeps into me, and even though I'm annoyed he's late, I'm immediately calmer. That's just what his presence does. It's why, though he'll never know, I'm that much more anxious when he goes to work. Nico's job isn't the safest in the world. As interesting as his stories about climbing into burning buildings or broken sewers are, there's a part of me that doesn't want to hear them. Is it terrible that I kind of wish my husband were the type of firefighter who rescued cats in trees?

But I'd never stop him from talking about his job, one of the loves of his life, because I love every damn bit of himself that Nico Soltero has ever been willing to share with me. Even the scary parts.

I turn and smile. "It's so nice, and the weather is beautiful. We have to enjoy it while we can, right?"

Nico leans against the doorframe, making no move to come get me, though I kind of wish he would. He looks as freaking delectable as ever in his uniform—the navy pants that hug his slim hips and round backside *just* right, the short-sleeved button-down shirt that really doesn't leave enough room for his biceps, the curved-bill Yankees hat that he'll never, ever toss out. He smiles and crosses his arms, making the tattoo sleeve that now extends down his forearm ripple. He let Milo try out a few more patterns, blending several dates into the curving lines. The day he was released from Tryon. The day he graduated high school. Our first date. The day he was accepted into the FDNY academy. The day his mother was granted permanent residency. Two days later, when we got married. Mateo's birthday.

There are others too, etched so small in black you can only see them when you're close enough to kiss them, as I often do. His arm has become a map of his life, and I'm honored to be a part of it.

By the time my gaze drifts back up to meet his, Nico's no longer smiling. Suddenly the air, despite the balmy spring weather, crackles.

Even more than six years after we first met, it's still like that between us. There's an energy, something between us that connects on a cellular level. Something in Nico's body, in his blood, his veins, calls directly to mine. Sure, sometimes it gets swallowed up by everyday life. It's hard to want to jump each other's bones when a baby is crying and you've got a term paper due in two days, or when you've been working for seventy-two hours straight and the water heater's broken. But even so, there are still times when he will just look at me—across the dinner table, over a mountain of laundry, when I walk in the front door—and I swear, it's like the wind was knocked out of me. Every single, solitary part of me reorients toward him. And for just a moment, it feels like there's nothing else.

"You're late," I whisper, although I'm done caring about that. It's occurring to me, just as I'm sure it's occurring to him, that we have the house to ourselves, which almost *never* happens.

Nico smiles again, this time slow and deliberate, gradually baring his bright white teeth in that sly way that hints of something much more wicked. "No, I'm not. I borrowed K.C.'s car. No train today, so we have plenty of time."

His deep-brown eyes, almost black, slide over my body, tracing over the shirt that clings to my breasts and waist and the skirt that stops mid-thigh. It's not a particularly revealing outfit. Comfortable and light, appropriate for the warm May weather. As if on command, though, goose bumps rise all over my skin, down my bare legs. Nico's eyes gleam, and finally, he pushes off the doorway and joins me on the lounge.

"How you doin', Mrs. Soltero?" he asks as he squats down for a kiss. "You're looking pretty fine over here in the sunshine."

"You are so corny. Nice rhyme."

He doesn't answer, just reveals one of his dimples before he slips a big hand around the nape of my neck and plants a long, slow kiss on my lips. His tongue teases them open, and I oblige, eager to taste him thoroughly. We don't often get moments like these when we can take our time.

"Mmm." His voice rumbles low in his throat as he pushes me back into the chair. His other hand drifts down my shoulder to palm one breast. "What the..." He breaks away and looks down. "Baby, you're not wearing a bra."

I raise a brow and bite my lip. "I was home alone. Didn't really see the point."

"Yeah, but..." He licks his lower lip. "Baby, look at you. What if you had to answer the door like that?"

I follow his gaze. Okay, to look at me, you'd probably think I was freezing. But to be fair, that's *his* fault, not mine.

I look back up and grin. "Afraid I'm going to attract the attention of another deliveryman?"

That only elicits a growl and a kiss that's much more possessive than the first. Both hands find my breasts now, knead and caress while mine slide up his neck and into his thick black hair, knocking the baseball cap to the ground. Nico drops his lips down my neck, and then, as he breaks away, plays with the straps of my shirt, pulling one strap over my shoulder, then the other until the entire neckline is below my breasts.

Keeping the straps wound around his fingers, he teases my nipples with the tightened fabric. Up and down over the sensitive nubs until my breath grows shallow, keeping his eyes on mine the entire time. When I moan a little, he drops the straps, and his thumbs feather down over the soft skin of my breasts, then over my nipples, making them rise even more. My back arches into his touch. Then he pinches, and any and all thinking ceases entirely.

"You got jokes, huh?" Nico asks as he tugs lightly on the ends of my aching breasts. They're more sensitive than ever, and I know that feeling is only going to get worse in the months to come. If it's anything like it was with Mattie, I'll be tempted to run to the firehouse in the middle of the night just so Nico can take care of it.

He pulls again, this time harder. My eyes close against that intoxicating combination of pain and pleasure as he pulls again, forcing me to follow the movement and sit completely up until my lips meet his full, eager mouth. He kisses me deeply, pairing a bit of sweetness with the pain he inflicts.

Then, just as suddenly, his hands and mouth pull away, and I'm released back against the chair cushion with a light thump.

My eyes fly open. "Are you kidding?"

Nico sits up, black eyes dancing. "What?"

I shake my head. "There is no way you're going to get me all turned on like that and stop midway. That's just cruel for a woman in my condition."

That wicked smile returns, just like I knew it would.

"And what condition would that be?"

I tip my head. "Pregnant, as you well know. And everyone knows you're supposed to do what your wife tells you. You're not supposed to stress her out, so you have to give her what she wants, whether it's weird foods at three a.m. or sex with her hot firefighter husband."

Nico tips his head back and laughs, and then, before I can say anything else, he slips one big arm under my back and another under my knees, and sweeps me off the lounge against his very broad shoulders. There won't be any carrying me over his shoulder for the next several months, but that won't stop him from picking me up in other ways. He'll do it when I weigh an extra thirty pounds, too, as he proved the last time around. I was honestly scared he was going to break his back, carrying me up six flights of stairs, but the man is stubborn as a mule. Considering our son, it appears to be a family trait.

"We could just stay out here, you know," I suggest as I bury my nose into his neck, inhaling his salty-sweet scent. Soap. Sweat. Smoke. The combination is intoxicating.

"We could," he agrees, though he's already moving toward the house. "But the last time we tried that, Mrs. Mariano gave me dirty looks for a week." He kicks the door shut behind him and gives me a long kiss, full of tongue and promise. "Face it, NYU. You're too damn loud."

I smack him on the shoulder, but I don't argue as he continues carrying me up the stairs and into our bedroom, maintaining our kiss the entire time. The man is seriously talented with that tongue of his. I should have known better than to let him use it when we were outside, where the neighbors could hear.

He lays me on the bed, but when he tries to stand up, I snake a hand around his neck, keeping his face close for a moment more.

"Please," I whisper. "You know. You know how I need it right now."

Nico stands up, clearly checking me over. It's not often I make this request, and when I do, it's usually because I'm scared of something. Sometimes he doesn't know what. The demons that used to visit me from time to time rarely stop by these days, but our life has replaced them with some others. I have more to lose now, just like him.

I stare as he removes his shirt, reveals every delectable muscle, every beautiful line of his chest and stomach, one button at a time. The funny thing is, I don't even think he notices the way I'm drooling over him. He's too busy thinking about what I'm asking, making sure I'm really okay.

"I don't—I don't want to hurt you. Either of you," he says, though I can see by the way his hands are clenching at his sides that he wants to do exactly what I'm asking. Today, we're both scared. We're both searching for a bit of control, in the best way we know.

"If it's going to happen again, it's going to happen again," I say, struggling to keep my voice from warbling. It's one thing to think it to myself, but it's another completely to say it out loud. "But you remember what the doctor said. Sex has nothing to do with it. Neither do any of the other things we normally do. The best thing we can do is just be ourselves. Together."

Nico swallows, causing a muscle in the side of his jaw to tick. His hands flex again. He's dying to do it. Flip me over. Ram inside. Release his frustrations onto my body the same way I'm dying to let him.

But still, he pauses.

He thinks too much. At least, that's what I always tell him. Even though we've been together for as long as we have, Nico still doesn't always believe I completely understand what I'm asking for. Or maybe he still can't believe I like it as much as he does. Nico understands that deep inside, there is always going to be a part of me that burns a little, an anger that needs to be let out, a need to hurt, just a little. He gets it because he feels it too. But that doesn't stop him from feeling bad about it.

Even though he spends most of his down time at the firehouse working out, he still has to take off for Frank's a few times a week just to rid himself of the tension that builds up. Sometimes it's just too much for my man to bear, and hitting something, whether it's one of the heavy bags or Nate's mitts, is one of the only ways to get rid of it.

This is the other. I wish he didn't feel guilty about it, but the reality is, we both get what we need when he takes control, gets a little aggressive. I need to feel just a little pinch of pain. And sometimes he needs to give it.

I get up on my knees and shuffle to the edge of the bed, where I slip off my shirt and skirt so that I'm kneeling in front of him, almost naked. He watches me unbuckle his pants and pull them down so that, after he removes his shoes, he can shimmy out of them the rest of the way. I toy with the elastic of his boxer briefs, but only tug them a little lower than his hip bones. There is something so crazy sexy about the combination of muscle, bone, and tendon that converges right above that band. I lean in and lick the spot, then sit back up to kiss him properly.

"Please," I whisper against his lips. "I'm not going to break. *We're* not going to break."

Then I clap his hand to my ass, which is *still* his favorite part of my body. Seriously, I could probably get this man to do anything I wanted if I kept his hand right here. It's not a privilege I take advantage of a lot, but it's nice to know it's there.

Nico moans into my mouth, and his hand automatically kneads the full flesh.

"Fuck," he breathes before sucking on my lip again with a slight bite. His other hand grabs the other cheek, and he massages them together, pulling me up against his hard length. "Jesus. *Christ.*"

I reach behind and cover his hands with mine. Then I clamp down, grabbing with him, and make him do it hard. Hard enough to leave a bruise.

"Ah!" he bites out.

Suddenly, I'm flipped over so I'm on my knees, my face pressed into the bedding while my hands are held together behind my back. My underwear is dragged down my legs, and before I know it, he's pressed against my entrance, sliding in slowly at first, and then thrusting deeply into that warm, slick place where he still fits so perfectly.

There's no wait. No gentle touch or kisses to get me ready. He doesn't take the time to lick or play with his hand—but he doesn't need to, not today. His little game on the patio had me ready and willing well before he picked me up, and he knows it too.

And he knows I'm looking for something else anyway.

The crack of his hand meeting my flesh echoes through the air, and I shudder, in the best possible way.

"Again," I call, low because my voice is muffled in the sheets. But he hears me.

His hand smacks my ass again and again, alternating between a light, brushing swat, and a full-on smack as he pounds harder, filling me completely with every push, every grunt. I press my elbows down, pushing back against each blow, groaning into the sheets every time his palm lands on my skin. I'll be bright red by the time he's done, and I'm absolutely loving it.

With the last, particularly rough slap, I scream into the sheets, and Nico pauses.

"Layla," he barks. "Up. Now."

I push up awkwardly, and he helps me the rest of the way so that I'm resting against his chest, both of us on our knees together while he remains buried inside. He twists us toward the shelves mounted over the bed, the ones that are doubly reinforced for moments like these, and sets my hands on the edge of the lowest one so that I'm bent at a slight angle, It's one of our favorite positions, one that allows me to take him deeply, yet gives him full access to the front of my body.

He lifts one knee and sets his foot down on the bed, almost in a parody of a proposal, except he's buried seven inches deep and giving me one of the hardest fucks of my life instead of an engagement ring.

"Is that how you want it, baby?" he asks as his hand slams down again. "You want it hard like this?"

"Ummmmmmm, yesssssss!" I shout, holding onto the shelf for dear life. When he takes me this way, I can barely think, much less speak in full sentences.

Nico's hands float up my sides, resting briefly over my ribs, where my half of our matching tattoos stretches over my skin: in his handwriting, *saudade para ti*. His fingers trace the lines as he continues to thrust, harder and harder, while his fingers curl and his nails scrape my skin just a bit as he drops that hand down between my legs.

The effect is instantaneous. He pinches my clit, and it's that tricky combination of pleasure and pain, the one that Nico always manages to find *exactly* right, that sets me off.

I begin to shake. He pulls the hand away.

"Nico!" I cry out hoarsely as my muscles tense. "Oh...*fuck*! Baby, I'm so close, *sooooooo* close."

He slams in again, and again, but his words are no longer intelligible. I can feel him expand within me, growing bigger, longer, harder. It only brings me even closer to that critical edge, the place where I can't hold myself back any more.

"Hold on, baby," he grunts. Thrust. Smack. He winds a hand into my hair and yanks me back up against him. The hand at my clit works a little harder, then pinches a bit and pulls.

"Now, Layla," Nico croaks. "Come with me, baby. *Now!*"

His teeth find my neck, and he bites. Hard.

"FUCK!" I shout as my orgasm launches through me.

My entire body shakes, seizing up against his strong, solid warmth, kept from toppling over by the arm around my hips and the other hand clasping my hair. I don't know how he doesn't come apart too, but it's Nico's strength that keeps us from falling over together. He's shattered too. I can tell by the way every part of him wound around me is flexed, muscle, vein, and tendon all in high relief. His teeth still clamp down hard enough that I swear he's going to draw blood, and he emits a long, almost pained groan against my skin as his release floods me.

Our life together has never been easy. We've had our battles to fight to be together, both coming from inside and outside of ourselves. Money. Family. This city and all the memories it holds.

We both have our outlets, our ways of coping, so that when we come together, we can give each other the best we have to offer. Most days they work, but sometimes they aren't enough.

But this. This connection. This outlet. This heat. This love. This is *always* enough.

————

The End...for now. (Click here for the Extended Epilogue)

EPILOGUE: PART II

Nico

"I'm going to hell," I state clearly about ten minutes later, though I couldn't be happier about it.

"You always say that after we do that."

Layla pushes her hair out of her face. A few strands are stuck to her forehead, which glows a little from what we just did. I don't know if I've ever told her, but she really is most beautiful after sex. Her face is high and flushed, with a glow of happiness that emits around her like a halo, but the fuck if I don't still want to corrupt all that angelic goodness.

"A good man wouldn't think about his pregnant wife this way. And he sure as shit wouldn't do some of the things I do to you." I turn over onto my side and give her a gentle kiss, the kiss she deserves.

"Hush," Layla says. "A good man does *exactly* what his pregnant wife asks for. And you did it. So good job."

I look her over, observing the fullness of her body. She looked like this before too—nipples slightly darker, hips a little fuller. Everything just a little more, I don't know, ripe somehow. She shines, like a piece of fruit that's just been picked. She was sick for a few weeks in the beginning, but now, when she's just beginning to show a little, that she looks fuckin' breathtaking.

Her fingers drift over my chest, playing over the compass under her cheek. Tracing the letters of her name at the top. My true north. That's her, always.

I kiss her again, full of gratitude. Seriously, how the fuck did an asshole like me get this lucky? "So I guess that means I'm perfect, huh?"

Layla smiles. "Perfect for me."

"For us," I confirm.

Then, with a groan, I gently roll her onto the pillow and get out of bed. I could stay in here all day, especially now, after a forty-eight-hour shift, when my bones are so tired I could fall asleep standing up. Sometimes, when I have a day off that lands on a Saturday, we do camp out here for the day. Mattie goes to my mom's, and we get the quality time we desperately need and never seem to find enough of.

But today is not one of those days.

"Come on, *mami*," I tell her, reaching out to help her out of bed. "If we don't get going, we really are going to be late."

Layla takes my hand and stands up, the sheet falling off her naked body, and the fuck if I'm not hard all over again. Damn. We *really* need to get a few more of those lazy Saturdays in before the baby comes.

Layla's mind is already on other things, though, as she moves around the bedroom getting dressed again. I watch her for a few seconds. Looks like sex didn't completely work to distract her from her worries. Not that I can blame her. Today is a big day.

"It's going to be all right," I tell her, though I'm already moving to the closet for a change of clothes. As much as I like the way my girl looks at me when I'm wearing my uniform, after wearing it for three days straight, I'm more than ready for jeans and a t-shirt when I finish my shift. Not this time, though. Layla thinks we're going out to dinner after our appointment, and we usually do a little something to look nice for our "date nights."

I put on a pair of black pants and a sky-blue shirt that Layla bought me last year for my birthday. "Baby," I say again as I tuck it in. "It's going to be fine."

Layla sighs, but just keeps her gaze on the mirror as she brushes out her hair. She has on one of her endless black dresses, a relatively modest one with thread-thin straps that clings to the rest of her body down to her knees. It's totally appropriate what she thinks is a celebratory dinner with her conservative parents, but it still makes me want her. Then again, I'd probably want her if she wore a garbage bag.

I finish putting on my shoes, then walk up behind her so I can wrap my arms around her chest and set my chin on her shoulder. I meet her eyes in the mirror and have to brace myself not to look away when I see the fear pouring out of them.

"*Mami*," I say quietly. "It's going to be okay. I promise."

Her eyes gloss over. "But what if it's not? Nico, what if it's—"

"Shhhh," I cut her off and press a kiss to her cheek. To tell you the truth, I don't even want to think it. I don't want to say it out loud or hear it either. "Let's just go, okay? Let the tech show you herself."

―――――

It doesn't work. We're both silent for most of the ride back into the city, to the midtown offices of the fancy fuckin' specialist that Layla's parents insisted on this time around.

The past still haunts us both. I can tell what she's thinking about, because I'm remembering the same things. The look on her face when she first discovered blood between her legs just before the end of her first trimester. The tears that streamed down her cheeks when the doctor told her what was happening. The way she wept while I held her all the way to the hospital. And the way we sat together, forehead to forehead, clutching each other while the doctors gave her drugs that would help her deliver the baby we'd never know. The little girl who was no longer living.

You don't realize how much you want someone until they're gone. Even if they were never there to begin with.

Saudade, that longing for something that's never happened, never felt more apt than when we lost a child we never really had.

A few days later, when Ma, Maggie, and Selena came over, and even Cheryl flew out to help Layla in ways that I'm pretty sure only women can, Gabe took Mattie for the afternoon while I went down to Milo's tattoo parlor on Second Avenue and had my friend start the next part of my sleeve. That was when we got the idea to ink the dates in between the swirling designs he was printing all over my skin. Grace's birthday was the first—the day my baby girl came into the world and left it at the same time. Next came the others, all the good and the bad, the most important days of my life. Everything that made me who I was.

That was the day I realized I never wanted to forget a thing. That you have to take the bad along with the good, or you'll never make sense of either.

"Hey," I say once I've parked the car, and Layla and I are walking down the sidewalk, hand in hand. "It's going to be all right. The doctor said you were in the clear after twelve. You're at twenty weeks now."

But today is different, and we both know it. This is the full scan. The day we find out the sex of the baby. Look at all its parts. Watch it move. This is the day that things get very real.

Or not.

Layla stays quiet all the way up the elevator, while we wait to be called into the ultrasound, while she changes out of her dress, and while we wait for the technician to arrive.

Even after she does, my girl is tight-lipped, blinking furiously against a tide of emotion that's always threatening and made worse by the crazy hormones circulating her body. She holds my hand with a death grip while the gel is applied to her belly and the probe is placed on top. We both watch the screen, searching the static for the one thing we are desperate to know. That she-it-he-whoever...is still alive.

Ba-dum.

The sound breaks through the technician's chatter and my cloudy thoughts loud and clear. It's a whisper, a rushing rhythm against the static, quick and lively. Layla's mouth is open, and I'm pretty sure mine is too. But I honestly can't tell, since neither of us seems to be breathing.

"God," I whisper as I stare at the screen. Something moves—a hand, a little foot. Some kind of limb that waves back and forth, swiping through the static noise to announce itself to the world.

"Oh, yes," says the tech as she looks at the screen. "I'd say you have a very healthy little girl here."

And at that word—that one little word—I swear to God, my heart drops all fourteen stories back to the asphalt.

"W-what?" I ask. "Did you say we're having a g-girl?"

Layla grins. Usually she's the one who stutters when she's nervous, not me. I kiss her knuckles absently, but I'm focused on the tech. I need to hear this news again to be sure.

"Well, there's always a chance we're not seeing something, but usually it's pretty clear at this point." The tech moves the sensor a little more. "See there? She's doing a great job of showing us what she's got. If it's a boy, you can usually see the penis from a few different angles, but when it's a girl, you really need her to spread her legs nicely, just like she's doing right now."

Layla giggles. I literally have to stifle a growl.

"Miss?"

The tech looks up.

"You're very nice and all," I say. "But I'm going to need you to stop talking about my daughter spreading her anything, okay?"

"Nico!"

Layla swats at my shoulder, but I'm dead serious. Jesus. If this is how I'm feeling about a blip on the screen, I don't even want to think about how I'm going to be when this tiny creature becomes a full-fledged person. As the tech continues moving the stick around and taking pictures of different parts of anatomy and answering Layla's questions, I'm imagining all sorts of things. Not death, but life. Because the baby on that screen is kicking up a fuckin' storm. There ain't nothing on that screen but bold, take-no-prisoners *life*, one cell at a time.

Me. Nico Soltero. With a daughter. Black-haired, blue-eyed, probably going to be even more beautiful than her mother and have more attitude than her aunties. A daughter who will attract every motherfuckin' asshole New York City has to offer.

And just like that, my heart stops all over again and doesn't start beating until the ultrasound is over, Layla's cleaned up, and we're back on the street, walking to the car.

"Hey." Layla tugs my hand, pulling me to a stop somewhere around Lexington and Seventy-Fourth. I think. I really can't tell. "Say something. Are you all right?"

"How are we going to protect her?" I whisper. "How are we going to make sure that she doesn't go through what you did? My mom did? Maggie did?"

Visions of the women I love most in the world with their faces black and blue flash through my head, and right there on the street, I have to stop. I have to lean against the sturdy brick wall of a building to calm my racing heart.

I thought it would kill me when I saw Layla torn up that way. I felt like committing murder, and I came closer to it than I'd like to admit. And to be honest, she's never fully recovered either. When something happens to you like that, you never totally do.

I don't think I'd survive if someone did that to my daughter. I really do think I'd keel over, dead. Right after I buried the fuckin' bastard first.

Layla frames my face with her slim hands and presses her forehead to mine, ignoring the curious looks of New Yorkers walking past us on Lexington Avenue. The touch soothes me, but only just.

"That's not going to happen to her," Layla says. "I know it."

"But how do you know?" I ask. "How?"

She inhales as she pulls back, but doesn't avert her gaze and doesn't move her hands. Those blue eyes could alway see straight through me, and right now, they're holding me up.

"I know," she says, "because she's going to grow up with something different. Baby..." She trails off with that common name, the one I always used to call her, but now she's come to call me too. I like it. No, I love it.

She leans in and touches her nose to mine, then brushes our lips together.

"Don't you see?" she whispers in a voice that would be swept up by the city if we weren't so close.

My hands find her waist to pull her closer. This woman is my lifeline. My everything.

"You and I never knew the kind of love we have now. That's why it took us so long to figure out what we really had." She sighs, then kisses me again. "Our love doesn't just save us, Nico. It saves our kids. Our families. And their families too. That's how we'll protect our daughter. By loving her. But most of all, by loving each other."

It takes a few seconds, but she doesn't look away. Layla holds me with her wide blue gaze, straight and true, until her words nestle deep inside me and bloom with their truth. I pull her even closer, enjoy for a moment the feel of her in my arms. I remind myself that the past is in the past, and this woman has been my present for years now, and God willing, many more to come.

"You," I tell her. "I love you. You know that?"

She smiles against my lips. "I know that. And I love you too. Always."

"You hear that?" I look down at the bump that's barely visible under Layla's dress, then spread my palms over it. "I love your mom, baby girl. And don't you forget it, okay?"

Layla laughs, and the clear sound breaks through the fear and worry clouding my sad, sorry mind. Leave it to her to remind me of how much we have rather than how much we stand to lose. We won't get everything right. We'll make mistakes. But my girl's right about this, one hundred percent. What we are together saves us. Every single time.

———

Layla

"Do we really have to take the car back tonight?" I wonder as Nico steers K.C.'s big Yukon down one of the narrow streets of Hoboken. "I thought K.C. was touring through Europe this summer."

"He is." Nico pulls into a parking space about a block from K.C.'s brownstone and turns off the engine. "He left last week. But, uh, I think Alba needs it for something."

I arch a brow. He's lying—Nico's almost as bad a liar as I am—but I don't know what about. Never in the last five years have I *ever* known Alba to drive K.C.'s car. I'm not even sure she has a valid license, like so many people in this city.

"Come on," Nico says, jangling the keys. "She's inside cleaning for him. We'll just drop these off and go to dinner, okay?"

I get out of the car, and Nico takes my hand, humming a little as we walk, sometimes bouncing on his toes. Something shifted between the ultrasound office and here. Nico is lighter than he was twenty minutes ago. We're both buoyed by the news that the baby is good. That *she* is healthy and happy.

"This will be quick," Nico assures me as he unlocks the door to the apartment, though his eyes sparkle like black diamonds.

What is going on...

"SURPRISE!"

I'm practically tossed back into Nico's chest by the energy of all the people in the room who spring forward, shouting and laughing as we walk in. K.C.'s big living room has been transformed from a sophisticated bachelor pad into a mass of sparkly blue pompoms, covered pretty much floor to ceiling.

We're quickly engulfed by at least fifty different party guests, and it becomes evident just what this is: a graduation party.

In between kisses on the cheeks, I look around to find familiar faces of people I've come to know and love over the years, and some new ones too. Maggie and Allie sweep me up into a hug, and are quickly joined by Selena and Carmen. I return their embraces and kisses wholeheartedly. None of my life would be possible without these incredible, strong women there to support me. They have been the ones who watched Mateo when Nico was at the firehouse and I needed to study. They have been the ones who taught me how to cook well enough that I didn't completely gross out my family or burn down the house. They have been the ones who provided untold emotional support over the years. My life is full and whole because I have them in it.

"You're late."

"Here we go," Maggie mutters to Selena.

I turn around to find Dad weaving through the small crowd. He leans in to gives me a kiss on both cheeks, then, as if thinking better of it, gives me a hug too. Nico rolls his eyes, but I take it. My dad may never be the warmest man in the world, but he's definitely better than he used to be.

When he releases me, I smile. "We're not late. It's my party, right? I'm right on time."

"Where were you?" Dad asks as I give Mom a hug too. She rolls her eyes at me when we finish, as if to say, "I tried to stop him."

I turn to my dad. "We had an appointment with the ultrasound tech, if you must know. It was my twenty-week scan today, on top of all of this."

At the words, my dad's dark eyes bug out. "Layla, I told you I wanted to be there at the scan. You don't know if this technician is any good, *linda*. I'm a doctor. I know things she may not."

"Dad, you're a plastic surgeon, not a perinatologist. Plus, the technician works for the specialist *you* sent me to," I argue gently. "We wanted it to be just us this time, okay? But if you want to look at the ultrasounds, they are in my purse."

"That's not the point, Layla! The point is that we had an agreement, and as your father and a doctor, I have a right to be there—"

"Sergio," Nico breaks in, his voice tightening a little. "Let's let it go, all right? It's done, and ultimately, it was Layla's and my decision to make."

"Serge," Mom adds. "Come on, it's a party..."

Dad turns back to me, frustration and stubbornness warring across his features as he looks down at my stomach and back up to me. He opens his mouth to unleash another tirade, but it's quickly interrupted by another little voice shouting across the room.

"*Vovô! Pare!*"

Mateo comes tearing out of the kitchen, his little legs churning. Dad swivels around toward his voice.

"*Vovô*, you said you would be nice today," Mateo chastises my dad openly in front of at least ten people watching. He shakes his little finger, and behind Dad, my mom has to cover her mouth to keep from laughing.

"You promised," he says again, then tips his face up to his grandfather and waits.

Dad opens and closes his mouth a few times before sighing and squatting down so he's face-to-face with Mateo. Even though Mateo still looks mostly like Nico at this point, I can see little things of me in him too. Other than his blue eyes, which he obviously gets from me and Mom, Mateo gets that same divot between his eyebrows when he frowns that my dad does—right now they are mirroring each other.

"Nice?" Dad repeats.

Mateo nods. "You *promised*, Vovô."

Dad sighs. "Okay, okay. You win." He claps a hand on Mateo's head and stands up. "It's done. And yes, it's a party. We are here to celebrate." He turns to Mom, who is now watching with a raised brow. She's impressed with Mateo's technique. So am I, for that matter.

"Cher, where are the drinks?" Dad asks. "I could use a scotch."

"Come on, Serge," Mom says, pointing toward the refreshments table. "Let's get you sorted."

I turn back to Mateo, who immediately launches himself at me. I reach down to pick him up, but before I can, Nico sweeps him off the floor and brings him eye level with me.

"Whoa there, dude. You got to be careful around *Mami*, all right? She's carrying some precious cargo."

"Stop. Let me hug my love, will you?" I accept Mateo's tight embrace when he tips toward me with outstretched arms. It's then I notice he's carrying a bouquet of ratty hydrangeas that have lost most of their blooms.

"Did we surprise you?" Mateo asks after he's done squeezing my neck.

I kiss him on the cheek and watch his eyelashes flutter. "Yeah, sweets, you did. Did you do this?"

Now content to sit in his dad's strong arms, Mateo nods, his blue eyes the same color as the decorations all around us. "Daddy and I got you these. *I* picked them out though, because Daddy couldn't remember which school you go to."

I take the hydrangeas from Mateo's chubby hands and make a big deal of sniffing them while he watches. They don't smell like anything—the flowers on the street rarely do—but the look on my kiddo's face turns me into the best actress on the planet.

"They are amazing," I assure him. "Thank goodness Daddy had you there to help."

Mateo puffs out his chest proudly and gives Nico a look that clearly says "I told you so." "I helped *Abuela* make the cake too, see?"

He points to a big table at the far end of the room, which is already crowded with people.

I turn to Nico. "Did you do this too?"

My husband grins, that signature smiles of his lighting up the entire room. "I might have had something to do with it."

I look around again. Most of the people here are friends of Alba and Carmen, people Nico considers family just because they are part of the tight community he grew up in. Cousins galore, most of whom are actually related to K.C. directly. Flaco and his parents. Dozens of aunties and uncles, people who have blessed me and my child over and over again. There are other faces I know too. Shama, home from LA, where she took a job with an advertising agency. Gabe, taking a night off studying with his girlfriend, Sarah, another medical student in his cohort. Vinny is back there somewhere, though he won't stay long, usually preferring to spend his weekends bar hopping with other investment bankers.

I turn back to Nico. "This is amazing. It's way too much."

He shrugs. "Try telling my mom that. You know you can't stop her and Alba when they want to throw a party. Add in Cheryl, and things go a bit crazy."

"What are they going to do when you graduate?"

It's hard to tell, but I think my man flushes a little. Just a few weeks ago, we received a letter from CUNY admitting him for fall semester as a part-time engineering student, along with all of his previous community college credits and the prereqs he finished last year. He's nervous, but Nico decided in the end he wanted to do more than just follow orders at his station. Eventually, he wants to be the one giving them, and at some point that requires a degree.

He doesn't even have to answer my question. I already know that I'm going to plan the biggest party this city has ever seen when my man graduates from college. Between me, Carmen, his sisters, Alba, and K.C., it's basically going to be like New Year's Eve times ten.

So Nico just smiles again. "I might be a little proud of you, NYU. Not a lot of people could get their master's while they have a kid running around at home, especially this guy."

"Columbia!" Mateo shouts. "Her school is Columbia, Daddy. See, Mommy, he *still* doesn't know!"

Nico just grins even wider, and though he speaks to Mateo, his twinkling black eyes are still trained on me, with a little more focus, carrying intent for later. When we are alone again. "What'd I say, huh? Mommy is always going to be my NYU."

I blush. I can't help it. Nico sucks on his bottom lip for a second, and my face turns even redder.

"*Ven*," he says, tugging me close so that I'm wrapped up in the two men in my life, big and little arms together, while my husband kisses me. It's not the kind of kiss that anyone would accuse of being inappropriate, but it carries heat nonetheless.

"I love you," he whispers into my ear, his deep voice thrilling down my spine. "And I am proud of you, so you better get used to it, baby."

I don't have to say I love you too—he knows it, every day, all day. But I still want to. That's the thing about love, something that Nico and I always seemed to understand. You want to tell them, every day, because when you really love someone, you want to see them lifted up. You thrive when you make them happy.

So I kiss him again while Mateo watches happily. "I love you too. Thank you."

Nico grins, then sets Mateo down on the floor. "All right, Mattie. Let's get this party started, shall we? First up: let's get your ma some punch."

———

Two hours later, my feet hurt from dancing so much, but I'm still swaying on the floor, held up in a cocoon of my husband's strong arms. Without the benefit of K.C.'s musical stylings, our parents chose the playlist, which basically meant starting the evening with a few hours worth of old-school salsa, followed by the string of bossa nova that's calming everyone down. Mateo is asleep under the table with a bunch of his cousins, and the adults who haven't left or collapsed around the couch in food comas are grooving to the saxophone and piano soothing the room to sleep.

I lay my head on Nico's shoulder, letting him slowly turn us around the middle of the the living room. I haven't had a drop of alcohol, but I feel drunk—with happiness.

Across the room, my parents are dancing, close and in a way they haven't for years. As if sensing the change, Nico follows my gaze.

"Look at that," he murmurs. "Something happening there?"

I turn my face into his neck. "I doubt it. That looks more like goodbye to me."

After five years of separation, my mom finally put her foot down and got the divorce. She hasn't mentioned anything yet, but I suspect she's met someone new. Grandpa died just after Mateo's birth, so it's been just her and Grandma in that big house in Pasadena. I wouldn't blame her at all for wanting something more than country club dinners with her mom.

But still. What kid doesn't like seeing their parents together? I never miss the dreamy look on Mateo's face when he sees Nico and me kiss after a few days apart. Sometimes he's more excited for our reunion than for his own after Nico finishes a long shift.

As if he knows what I'm thinking, Nico rubs a broad hand up and down my back. The simple touch warms me. This is what he does—always takes care of me.

"Not everyone can be as lucky as us," he says.

I close my eyes, content to feel his touch lingering over my neck, shoulders, spine. It's true. We are lucky, incredibly so. And the crazy thing is, I know there's more to come.

Maybe that's why I still feel that melancholy from time to time—that longing, that desire, for something a little more. Brazilians call it *saudade*, the word that's printed on my ribs and Nico's, twin statements of that yearning neither of us can ever quite shake. A desire for something that maybe hasn't even happened. The future that lies before us.

There are so many things coming. My new job, starting as a children's social worker. My entire career will be focused on making sure kids who find themselves here alone don't get lost the way Carmen was. That they always have someone to help them find their way.

Then there's Nico's school, which I know he'll attack with the same gusto he approaches every new thing he sets out to accomplish. Our daughter, on her way, and who will no doubt be as much of a delight and challenge as her big brother.

I long for these events because I know they'll bring us more happiness, more joy, more heartache, more fulfillment.

"I love you," I whisper, lower than the music, low enough that he probably doesn't even hear me.

But he does. Nico hears more than my words. He hears my soul.

The hand at my back moves up to cradle my head to his shoulder, while his other arm remains tight around my waist. He strokes my hair and murmurs something unintelligible in what sounds like Spanish. My own Spanish is good enough now that I'd be able to understand it if I could hear it at all. But it's okay. Right now, I'm content just to feel.

We stand like that for a few more moments, catching the eyes of a few onlookers. All of our parents glance over with clear fondness—it swims out of Carmen, and even my father's normally stern features soften. It's because they know what this is. They know what we are.

Nico hums a little as he plays with my hair, and I feel the truth sink in before he even says the words.

"I love you too," he whispers back, his soft lips dusting lightly over my ear. "Always."

El Fin...O Fim...You get the picture.

Thank you for reading!

If you'd like to know more about Nico's life as a young man, please enjoy the first two chapters of Broken Arrow, the prequel to Bad Idea, below, or click here to download the entire thing: bit.ly/BrokenArrowGiveaway

BROKEN ARROW

CHAPTER ONE
Johnstown, NY

1994

The tall, metal gates bang shut with a clank that echoes across the surrounding fields. I look up at the security cameras that stare at me with black eyes, perched over the curling barbed wire.

Tryon. The detention center where I just wasted the past two years of my life.

I turn to the road, where K.C., my best friend, and Alba, his mother, are waiting. I feel bad that they had to make the trip all the way out here to get me. New York is two bus rides and an expensive cab drive away from Tryon, but I'm still a minor, so the state wouldn't release me without a custodian. And because of my mother's immigration status, that's been her best friend, Alba, my whole life and will be for another three weeks until I turn eighteen.

"Come on, baby," Alba says as she clasps my head briefly.

K.C. punches me playfully in the shoulder, but he's a little shy. It's going to take some time for me to get back to my old self. But we've literally grown up across the hall from each other. K.C. knows me better than anyone else in the world. He'll be patient.

It's over. Two years of being watched by creepy security guards, trying not to get the shit beat out of me by them or other inmates, counting the seconds while I stare at the gray walls of this fuckin' jail for kids—I don't care what they call it; that's what it is. It's over.

The bus ride to New York is quiet. Alba sits up front, working on her knitting and paging through a magazine. K.C. and I lounge in the back, and he lets me take the window seat after I shove my small backpack into the compartment overhead. I don't have much. My sketchbook. The clothes I brought with me, which are now too small. Some pictures of my sisters and my brother. My mother, who I haven't seen in two years.

"How you feelin', Nico?" K.C. asks after the bus gets under way from Albany, and the dull roar of the pavement can mask our conversation.

I blink, almost not recognizing my own name. How many times have I actually been called Nico in the last two years? I barely spoke to any of the other kids—most of them were either too doped up to talk or else spoiling for a fight. When the guards or teachers talked to me, I was always Nicolas, Soltero, or sometimes Mr. Soltero if the teacher decided to try that day. Every now and then Nick, though I wouldn't answer. But never Nico. Never my real name. I never gave them that.

There aren't many people on board. The hum of the tires fills the air, but it's a good sound. Almost soothing. A different kind of quiet from the tension of Tryon.

I sink into the cushioned seats, scratching at the red sweats covering my knees. I didn't have pants I could wear out of the center, so they gave me a pair of the uniforms. I fuckin' hate this color. I will never wear red again for the rest of my life.

It's been a long time since I sat in a chair with cushions. We had our rock-hard mattresses and lumpy pillows at Tryon, but otherwise, everything in the place was hard plastic and metal. Apparently, criminals don't deserve soft seats, even if they're only fifteen.

"I'm good," I say, edging away from him toward the window. I need a little space. I've barely been alone in two years. With someone, whether it was a guard, other inmates, or those assholes they called teachers watching my every move. While I ate. While I brushed my teeth. All day long, right next to someone. My mother's apartment won't be too different—there's five of us that share the tiny one-bedroom—but at least I'll get to take a piss by myself again.

"You look different," K.C. remarks. "Went in lookin' like Chicken

Little, come out lookin' like Rocky. Shit. Nobody's gonna fuck with you now."

I shrug. We've both changed. K.C. came to see me a few times over the last two years, but only when he could save up the money. He's about six inches taller than when I left. Still pale with short black hair, but his light mustache has darkened, and now he has a goatee. He doesn't look like a kid anymore. Now he's a man.

Which I guess I am too. They gave us disposable razors while the guards stood over us. I didn't need them when I arrived, but I started using them almost every day over the summer. I'm not as tall as K.C., but I stand at almost five-eleven now, which is still taller than a lot of people in our neighborhood. At Tryon, a lot of the kids played basketball or walked around the track during rec hours, but I did the boxing program, the same one that produced Mike Tyson, and now my chest and shoulders are filled out. I don't look like the scrawny, scared-shitless kid who left Hell's Kitchen in the back of a secured van. I look like the kind of guy who could beat the shit out of someone. And you know what? I probably could.

But honestly, I just feel tired, like I haven't slept in two years. I've been too scared that someone was going to jump me when I closed my eyes, too worried that I'd wake up with my few things stolen or that one of the guards would unlock the door of my tiny cell in the middle of the night. We all knew what happened to Freddy, the kid from two doors over. We all knew why one kid literally pulled the screws out of the floor and swallowed them. We knew why some kids wanted to kill themselves rather than spend another night in Tryon.

"Get some sleep, *mano*," K.C. says, settling back into his seat.

He gets it. No one knows me like K.C., even if I've been gone. We've known each other our whole lives, since our mothers got pregnant at the same time and raised us together in Alba's living room. He knew me when I started running with a group of kids who used to knock over the local bodegas on dares while he started spinning records in his cousin's basement. He knew me when I got caught the last time and ended up here.

I lean against the window and close my eyes. When I wake up, I'll be back in New York, and it will feel like the last two years were just a bad dream.

~

Other Works by Nicole French
The Spitfire Series

Legally Yours

I had a plan. Finish law school. Start a job. Stay away from men like Brandon Sterling. Cocky, overbearing, and richer than the earth, he thinks the world belongs to him, and that includes me. Yeah, no. Think again. It doesn't matter that his blue eyes look straight into my soul, or that his touch melts my icy reserve. It doesn't even matter that past all that swagger, there's a beautiful, damaged man who has so much to offer beyond private planes and jewelry boxes. But I had a plan: no falling in love. I just have to convince myself.

Keep reading for the first three chapters of Legally Yours.

Chapter 1

I glanced over the top of my cubicle toward a window about ten feet away. Snow was coming down hard, in big, fat flakes that shone white against the black night and stuck to the pane whenever a sudden gust of wind slammed into the building. I looked at the clock on the opposite wall and sighed. You'd never know by the looks of the office that it was almost 9 p.m.

"The Pit," as everyone called the group of cubicles that housed temps and interns, included a pod of hopeful, over-achieving, third-year law students like myself. The four of us still had one week left on the job. After working the standard summer internship at Sterling Grove's full-service firm, I had been asked, along with the other three interns, to stay on when the firm took on a major trial case. The trial had finished up last week, and the firm had won, with some thanks due to the countless hours Steve, Cherie, Eric, and I had put in over the last four months. Our hard work paid off when we were offered full-time positions after we finished school and passed the bar exam. It was no small carrot—the firm was one of the largest in Boston, and the positions some of the most coveted for any new grad.

But unlike the other interns, I wasn't actually sure I wanted to work at Sterling Grove. It wasn't that it wasn't a good firm (despite the first-year associate hours that would be undoubtedly hellacious). There was simply something missing. Two and a half years ago, I had left a job in investment banking for law school, hoping to find a career that would make me feel, well, complete. Law had seemed like a good idea. It was lucrative, analytical, and I had the potential to do more for the world than just stockpiling money. And upon starting my classes, I quickly learned that I loved the philosophical side of justice just as much as the practical. Law school was a practice of existing somewhere in the middle.

The difficulty was in choosing a focus. Two and a half years later, when most of my classmates already had jobs locked for the following year, I still had absolutely no clue what I wanted to do with my degree. I had excelled in my classes and attracted three job offers already, but had turned down all of them. Although I was interested in almost everything I had participated in, nothing made me feel that "oomph," that one hundred percent knowledge that *this* was what I was supposed to do. Two and a half years later, I was still looking.

"I see you looking for a cab, Crosby."

A pair of thick black glasses, bright white teeth, and a mop of curly black hair popped over the cubicle barrier. I smiled, careful to avoid my co-intern's eyes.

"I'm not looking for anything, Steve," I said. "Anyway, I'm not sure I'm going either."

"What?!"

Steve Kramer, a student at Boston College, looked around briefly to make sure none of our supervising associates were in the common room before skittering around to sit on my desk, disregarding the legal pad under his butt. The two temps who shared my cubicle glanced up with mild annoyance before leaning back to their work.

"Dude," Steve said as he grabbed the arms of my desk chair and rolled me to face him. "You gotta come. The trial is finally over. It's our last drunken hurrah as interns together." He didn't seem to notice when I immediately rolled back to my original position.

"I know," I said. "But it's already so late. Plus, the weather is turning to shit, and I really need to finish this brief tonight."

"Finishing a brief" was the legal equivalent of telling someone you needed to wash your hair or walk your dog. Unfortunately, for all the promise Steve showed as a cutthroat attorney, he never seemed to clue into basic social cues from women.

"Come on, Crosby," he cajoled, again pulling my chair close. "I'm not letting you go until you say yes. It's our only opportunity to celebrate the end of this insane internship. You don't even have to pay— Cherie knows the owner at Manny's and can get us comp'd pitchers."

It wasn't really the end yet—we still had a whole week. But considering the fact that classes were starting on Monday, it was more fitting to celebrate the end now instead of next Friday, when most of us would be more interested in getting ahead on our reading than tipping back shots.

Manny's was a well-known bar in Chinatown and just a short cab ride away from the office. I wasn't much of a drinker, which made me less than excited about going. Nor was I particularly interested in fending off the odious advances of Steve, who had been trying to talk me into a date since September. He was okay-looking, but, like most of the men I'd been out with, just didn't quite do it for me. Apparently, I seemed to have the same problem with men that I did with choosing a job.

I sighed.

"You know he's not going to leave you alone until you say yes."

I glanced over to a neighboring cubicle, where Eric, my classmate and neighboring intern, hadn't even looked up from his work to make the dry comment. I looked back at Steve, who waggled his prominent eyebrows. I sighed again.

"Fine!" I said and turned back to my desk. "I'm going, I'm going. Can I get back to work now?"

~

We arrived at the tail end of happy hour while the band was finishing their sound check. We weren't alone—Manny's attracted the twenty-something young professional crowd of Boston, most of whom consisted of lawyers, bankers, and grad students working around Beacon Hill. The men wore a standard after-work uniform of suit pants and striped, button-down shirts, matching jackets tossed over the backs of chairs and ties loosened as they tossed back cheap beer. The women were dressed much like myself, in pencil skirts or pantsuits, their blouses undone one extra button to make it clear this wasn't an interview. I kept my buttons where they were.

I filed into the small booth that had been claimed by my cohort and allowed Steve to hang my coat on the hooks next to us. Steve and Cherie jetted off to the bar and returned shortly with a tray full of tequila shots and a pitcher of PBR. Everyone eagerly took one of the shot glasses and the accompanying limes. I was the last to take one after Steve looked pointedly at me. With a quick eye roll, I raised my shot along with everyone else.

"This is the end," Steve intoned, mimicking the words of Jim Morrison. "My only friend, the end."

"Shut up and drink," jeered Cherie.

"Hey, hey, hey!" Steve protested, stopping everyone from drinking. "I bought the shots, I get to toast. Okay. It's been a pleasure working with you all, and I'd just like to say: may you finish the year without flunking out of law school in your last semester. May you all succeed and get filthy rich like I know you want to with these over-priced degrees. May you all make name partner within five years. Except not at Sterling, because that's going to be me."

We all yelled and threw balled-up napkins and cardboard coasters at him before gulping down the harsh liquor. It was the cheap stuff, of course, but it would no doubt get everyone trashed while liquor was half price. Steve began to dole out PBR-filled pint glasses.

"Thanks, but I'm good," I said, slipping out of the booth to his obvious disappointment. "Don't worry, I'm just going to get my own drink."

"Too good for the blue ribbon, huh?" Steve teased.

"Everyone's too good for that horse piss," I retorted with a grin before making my way over to the bar, where I ordered a whiskey with a splash of water.

"Not a PBR fan?"

I turned to find a good-looking guy next to me, leaning against the bar. Like the other men, he also wore a button-down and suit pants, with his sleeves rolled up his forearms to reveal an expensive and ostentatious watch. Flashing with a bright band and even a few small diamonds encrusting the edges, it was the kind of watch meant to tell people he had money. The top button of his shirt was undone, and his dark-blue tie was slightly askew. He was cute, in that young M.B.A. kind of way, with close-cut brown hair and a square, goatee-lined jaw. He also held a glass of brown liquor, which he raised.

"Not so much," I said as I slipped the bartender my card and nodded that she could cash me out.

"Trevor," he said, reaching out a hand.

"Skylar," I said as I accepted the firm handshake. That watch really was bright and shiny. I took a sip of my whiskey and closed my eyes momentarily with pleasure.

"What are you guys celebrating over there?" Trevor asked.

"The end of a trial," I replied. "We're all interns at Sterling Grove."

"Ah," Trevor said knowingly, although his lack of further response made it clear that he knew little more than the name of the firm. "I'm an analyst over at Chase."

He said it in a way that was obviously meant to impress me. While he probably didn't know much about my life, I was extremely familiar with his. One year on Wall Street had been more than enough to convince me I needed to do something for a living that wouldn't cost my soul and sacrifice others' in the process.

But despite his occupation, Trevor had a nice face. I was in no hurry to return to Steve's attention, and after talking with Trevor for two more drinks, I started thinking about other places we might go.

It had been a long time—too long for someone my age who had no attachments and no hang-ups about casual sex. But I would have been lying if I said that any of those encounters were more than barely satisfying. Most of them had simply scratched a strong, primal itch to be with another person, but also ended up with me scratching myself better, later, alone.

It didn't help that when I did get attached, it was with the worst people on the planet. Out of the two major relationships I'd had, the first, my high school sweetheart, was currently serving time for aggravated assault. Poor Robbie hadn't stood a chance, growing up with the remains of the Brooklyn mob living within a five-block radius of his house. The second...well, let's just say I avoided talking about him at all. Patrick's serial philandering had left a scar that was still fairly raw.

So, my classmates knew me as a loner. But that didn't mean I wanted it to be that way forever. Just because things hadn't worked out before didn't mean they couldn't in the future.

I looked at Trevor, who was jabbering about some kind of deal he had made that week. He stopped when he found me staring at him.

"Something wrong?" he asked. "You need another drink?"

I looked down at the remnants of my third glass of whiskey,

which was nearly empty. I had reached my self-imposed limit for the night, where I was tipsy but wouldn't be hungover the next morning.

I pushed the glass away.

"Let's dance," I said, and held out my hand so he could lead me to the back of the bar, where a bunch of people had started an impromptu dance floor next to the jukebox. As the lazy riffs of "Beast of Burden" came on, Trevor pulled me into his chest and swayed awkwardly and out of sync with the music while Steve, Eric, and Cherie all watched with interest. He smelled like bourbon and body spray, but I enjoyed at least the feel of his arms wrapped tightly around my waist and the muscles of his chest beneath my cheek.

"Hey," he said as the Stones launched into the chorus the second time. I looked up, and he touched his nose to mine.

All right, why not? Jagger asked if he was strong enough, and I closed my eyes as Trevor leaned in.

His tongue slipped into my mouth and touched mine before darting out again. He did this again. And then again. It was...not pleasant. Like being kissed by some kind of reptile. When I pulled away, he moved his mouth, rubbery and wet, to my neck before leaning back with obvious, drunken desire gleaming in his muddy brown eyes.

"You're really hot, you know that?" His words were slightly slurred. "I have a total thing for redheads, and you are at least a nine. Maybe even a ten by Boston standards."

"Um, thanks," I muttered. My long red hair, which was wavy, unruly, and roughly the color of an heirloom tomato, was almost always the subject of tired come-ons. I was proud of my natural color, but it was like these guys literally couldn't see anything but the top of my head.

"You want to get out of here? My place is just off Newbury." Like Chase, the street name was meant to impress—Newbury was a nice part of town, and expensive.

Five minutes ago, I might have said yes, but I had no intention of having sex with Captain Jabbing Tongue of the Good Ship Sexism that night. I gently untangled myself from Trevor's grip and was careful not to answer the question. "I'm going to stop in the ladies' room."

Trevor nodded happily. "I'll just go close out my tab, honey."

I ducked through the crowd back to the booth, where Cherie hooted, and Steve pretended not to notice me.

"I'm heading out," I told them as I grabbed my coat.

"Skylar's gonna get some!" Cherie crowed, clearly worse for wear. "I saw you making out on the dance floor. Girl got a hot date!"

I snorted. "Hardly. Trying to get rid of one, if you know what I mean. I'll see you guys on Monday. Tell Eric I said bye, wherever he went."

Cherie and Steve waved slurred goodbyes, although Steve's was a bit lackluster. I checked the bar, where Trevor was patiently waiting for a bartender to ring him up. Once he turned his back to sign his tab, I wove around the crowd and out the front door.

Outside I was met by the makings of a full-on nor'easter as a blast of snow and wind pummeled me in the face. At least ten other people were standing on the curb, trying without any luck to hail cabs driving by, all of them occupied.

"Shit," I muttered, checking to make sure Trevor hadn't come out yet. I buttoned my wool pea coat and wound my scarf around my neck, wishing I had foregone my pencil skirt for pants and my goose-down parka. It might have made me look like the Michelin Man, but at least I'd be warm. The nearest T-stop was at least ten blocks away, and I was going to have to walk. Damn.

"Skylar!"

As one particularly cold gust nearly knocked me over, a cab stopped in front of me, with Eric popping out the back window.

"Hey!" I greeted him as I stepped out to the car. "I thought you were already gone."

"You're never going to catch a cab right now. Need a lift? Caleb is dropping me at a friend's place a few blocks away before he takes this one back to Chestnut Hill." He nodded his head at the unfamiliar guy sitting in the front, who waved. "You could call for a car and wait at my friend's place if you want. That is, unless you wanted to go home with Douchebag in there."

I followed his glance to where Trevor was pushing open the pub door. I turned back in a hurry. "Shove over and let me in, will you?"

~

ALSO BY NICOLE FRENCH

Broken Arrow: A FREE Bad Idea prequel

Discover the REAL first time Layla and Nico meet for FREE in Broken Arrow, a Bad Idea novella.

They call me every name in the book, and every one is true.

Violent. Criminal. Bad news.

And if they're lucky, I'll take my anger out on a punching bag instead their faces. If they're lucky.

Then I meet her. Sophisticated. Successful.

More culture in her finger than I have in my entire body.

She says I have more to offer the world than my fists. She says I can pick my own direction instead of taking the one I'm given.

But tell me, beautiful, how do you do that, when you don't know where to go?

How do you find the right path when your compass is broken?

**Download Broken Arrow FREE here:
bit.ly/BrokenArrowGiveaway**

The Discreet Duet

I was broken. A mess.

So what should I want with this man? We had a connection, sure, but overall, he was nothing but trouble.

Will Baker was grouchy. Arrogant. A total loner. He had serious control issues, and was waving every red flag known to man..

And yet.

Since we met, it felt as if the universe itself was tilting on its axis, trying to knock me into him. I couldn't stay away from him, even if I tried.

We might have been too broken for anyone, but together, we seemed whole.

Once upon a time, I wanted the spotlight.

He gave up his life to escape it.

Now the question is...can we remain discreet?

Start the duet here: bit.ly/DiscreetBook

The Spitfire Series

I had a plan.

Finish law school. Start a job. Stay away from men like Brandon Sterling. Cocky, overbearing, and richer than the earth, he thinks the world belongs to him, and that includes me.

Yeah, no. Think again.

It doesn't matter that his blue eyes look straight into my soul, or that his touch melts my icy reserve. It doesn't even matter that past all that swagger, there's a beautiful, damaged man who has so much to offer beyond private planes and jewelry boxes.

But I had a plan: no falling in love.

I just have to convince myself.

Book I is available FREE: bit.ly/LYwide

AFTERWORD

Thank you for taking the time to read True North and the entire Bad Idea series. These books are different from my other stories, in part because they are so close to my heart. There are no billionaires in these stories—no private jets or mansions.

A great deal of research and work went into these books, including but not limited to the FDNY, Cuban immigration laws, and New York City housing issues. Every location written about in these books were places I have visited personally, with the exception of Santiago. Those scenes were written using feedback I received from generous readers and research I was able to do outside of my own imagination. It was exceedingly difficult to locate accurate descriptions of records offices in Cuba, but I did the best of my ability, and apologize if there are any major inaccuracies in the book. It is fiction after all.

A few words about Carmen's immigration struggles: Part of the point of the books is to highlight not only the difficulties that many illegal immigrants face upon coming to the United States, but also the lack of information many receive. The separation of children from their parents is all too common. In a 2018 article, the *New York*

Times reported that approximately 1 in 7 migrant children placed with sponsors have been lost, with a program potentially connected to lack of follow-through from the Department of Health and Human Services. As of this writing, more than two thousand migrant minors have been separated from their parents and confined to detentions centers around the country, including children under the age of five. Likewise, despite the fact that Cuban refugees benefited from Cuban Adjustment Act of 1966, many did not benefit from it due to a lack of documentation. It is not out of the realm of possibility that Carmen, insulated by language barriers and a lack of documentation, would have received conflicting information about her options and lived a life of unnecessary fear.

Similarly, I did not intend any of Layla's struggles with mental health to minimize or invalidate individuals who struggle with similar or related mental health travails. Her difficulty recovering from her traumas as well as the coping mechanisms she utilized were purely conventions of the story—not at all an indictment or prescription for anyone struggling with their own traumas.

If you or anyone you know is suffering from the effects of an abusive relationship, please consider contacting one of the many resources out there that can help people cope, escape, and recover from abuse. You are loved. They are loved. And you are all worth it.

xo,

Nic

RESOURCES

YWCA
   Casa de Esperanza: an organization to help the Latinx community end domestic violence.
   National Resource Center on Domestic Violence
   National Network to End Violence Against Immigrant Women
   Battered Women's Justice Project

ACKNOWLEDGMENTS

First and foremost, to my family. My husband, two teenagers, and son are constant sources of support and humor in this life, and I love them so very much. Their willingness and patience for when I spent hours and hours zoned out with my characters is just as much responsible for these stories as my own mind.

Secondly, to my editorial team, alpha readers, and beta readers: THANK YOU for all of your hard work to make this book happen. To Danielle and Patricia: your never-ending support and feedback made all the difference in this book, and on top of that, you've become friends I truly treasure. Thank you to Kymberly, my last-minute beta and Nico-addict, for reading through and checking for continuity. Additionally, I am so grateful to work with the best editor and proofreader combo around. Emily Hainsworth and Judy Zweifel, you are the absolute best, and your patience with my slippery deadlines was much appreciated.

Thirdly, to the beautiful author community, and in particular, a fantastic group that gives endless support to one another: Ava, Harloe, CL, Jessica, Meg, Jane, Liv, Kim, Brooke, and Paige.

#squadpod is the best. Additionally, thank you to Maya for your wit and humor and willingness to tell me when you hate my covers.

Fourthly, and most importantly, to my readers, particularly those of you who take the time to review my books, respond to my erratic mailing list, or play around in my reader groups. You make marketing and social media not just fun, but a blast. I would have gotten out of this game after the first book if it weren't for you. Thank you.

ABOUT THE AUTHOR

Nicole French is a lifelong dreamer, Springsteen fanatic, and complete and total bookworm. When not writing fiction or teaching composition classes, she is hanging out with her family, playing soccer with the rest of the thirty-plus crowd in Seattle, or going on dates with her husband. In her spare time, she likes to go running with her dog, Greta, or practice the piano, but never seems to do either one of these things as much as she should.

For more information about Nicole French and to keep informed about upcoming releases, please:

Visit her website at www.nicolefrenchromance.com/.

Follow on Pinterest www.pinterest.com/nfrenchauthor

Check out Nicole's Goodreads page: www.goodreads.com/authornicolefrench

Want to hook up with other Nicole French readers or interact with the author? Join Nicole's reader group, La Merde.

Made in the USA
Monee, IL
19 June 2022

98279553R00249